THE CAPTURED BRIDE

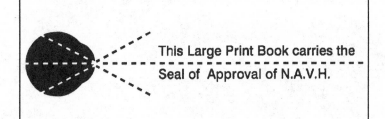

This Large Print Book carries the
Seal of Approval of N.A.V.H.

THE DAUGHTERS OF THE MAYFLOWER

THE CAPTURED BRIDE

MICHELLE GRIEP

THORNDIKE PRESS
A part of Gale, a Cengage Company

Farmington Hills, Mich • San Francisco • New York • Waterville, Maine
Meriden, Conn • Mason, Ohio • Chicago

GALE
A Cengage Company

LIBRARY OF CONGRESS CIP DATA ON FILE.
CATALOGUING IN PUBLICATION FOR THIS BOOK
IS AVAILABLE FROM THE LIBRARY OF CONGRESS

ISBN-13: 978-1-4328-5295-5 (hardcover)

Published in 2018 by arrangement with Barbour Publishing, Inc.

Printed in the United States of America
1 2 3 4 5 6 7 22 21 20 19 18

To my wilderness-loving daughter
and her redheaded mountain man,
Callie and Ryan Leichty.
And, as always,
to the Lover and Keeper of my soul,
Iesos.

ACKNOWLEDGMENTS

While writing is a solitary profession, a novel is never written alone. My hearty thanks go out to the critique partners who held my sweaty hands on this story: Yvonne Anderson, Laura Frantz, Mark Griep, Shannon McNear, Ane Mulligan, Chawna Schroeder, and MaryLu Tyndall. And also an honorable mention to Dani Snyder, my first-reader extraordinaire.

A huge thank-you to historical reenactors everywhere, but especially those who perform an awesome three-day event at Old Fort Niagara in upstate New York. If you ever get the chance to see the French and Indian War Encampment (usually held near the Fourth of July), it's totally worth the effort.

And as always, my gratitude to Barbour Publishing for taking a chance on a girl like me. Waving at you, Becky Germany.

Readers, you make this writing gig all

worthwhile. And guess what? I love to hear from you! Follow my adventures and share yours with me at www.michellegriep.com.

Daughters of the Mayflower

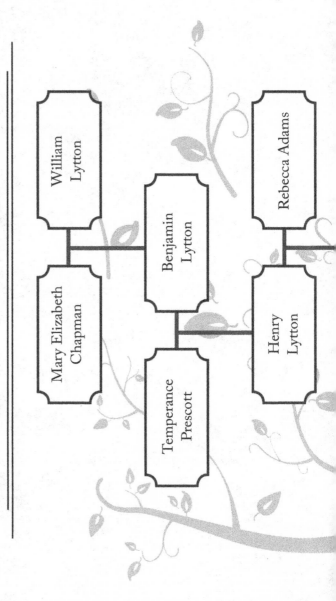

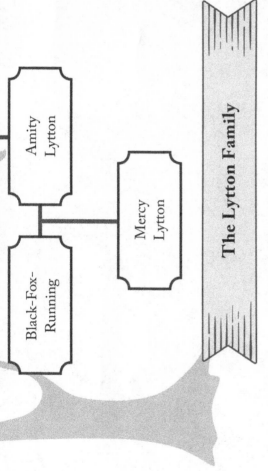

Black-Fox-
Running

Amity
Lytton

Mercy
Lytton

The Lytton Family

William Lytton married Mary Elizabeth Chapman (Plymouth 1621)
Parents of 13 children (including Benjamin)

Benjamin Lytton married Temperance Prescott (Massachusetts 1668)
Children included Henry

Henry Lytton married Rebecca Adams (New York 1712)
Children were Goodwill and Amity

Amity Lytton married Black-Fox-Running, a Mohawk warrior (New York 1737)
Only child was Mercy Lytton (Kahente)

MOHAWK LANGUAGE GLOSSARY

Aktsi:'a: Older sister
Ehressaronon: Wyandot
Iesos: Jesus
Kahente: Before her time
Kahnyen'kehàka: Mohawk nation
Kanien'keha: Native name for the Mohawk language
Kaia'tákerahs: Goat
Ó:nen ki› wáhi: Farewell for now
Ó:nen: Goodbye
Onontio: Big mountain
Rake'niha: My father
Sachem: Leader
Skennen: Peace
Skén:nen tsi satonríshen: Rest in peace
Tsi Nen:we Enkonnoronhkhwake: I love you forever

MOHAWK LULLABY

Ho, ho, Watanay.
Ho, ho, Watanay.
Ho, ho, Watanay.
Ki-yo-ki-na.
Ki-yo-ki-na.

Sleep, sleep, my little one.
Sleep, sleep, my little one.
Sleep, sleep, my little one.
Sleep now.
Sleep now.

FRENCH LANGUAGE GLOSSARY

Chiens Anglais: English dogs
Démissionner: Stand down
La fin: The end
Merci: Thank you
Regardez: Look
Rien, monsieur: Nothing, sir

CHAPTER 1

Fort Wilderness, upper New York, 1759
Five years into the French and Indian War
"It ain't right. *You* ain't right."

Mercy Lytton brushed off Captain Matthew Prinn's comment as easily as she rubbed off the dried mud marring her buckskin leggings. Too bad she couldn't so easily rid herself of the bone-deep weariness dogging her steps. Matthew had a point — somewhat. Going from a scouting campaign and on to the next mission without a few hours of sleep wasn't right.

She glanced at her self-appointed protector as they crossed the Fort Wilderness parade ground. " 'Tain't about right. 'Tis about duty."

Despite the blood under his nails and bruises on his jaw, Matthew scratched at three weeks' worth of whiskers on his face. "Seems to me by now your duty ought to be raisin' a troop of your own littles."

And there it was. Again.

She bit back one of the many curses embedded in her head from a life amongst warriors. A bitter smile twisted her lips, yet she said nothing. It was a losing argument — and she'd had her fill of loss.

So they walked in silence, save for the guffaws of a group of soldiers nearby, smoking pipes just outside a casement doorway. A late March breeze skimmed over the top of the palisade surrounding the outpost, and she shivered. She could forgo rest for a few more hours, but changing out of the damp trade shirt beneath her hunting frock was mandatory.

As they neared the brigadier general's door, a grim-faced Mohawk strode out and stopped in front of her, blocking her path.

"There is ice in that one's veins." Black-Fox-Running spoke in *Kanien'keha,* tipping his head back toward the general's quarters. Afternoon sun flashed like lightning in his dark eyes. "Return home, *Kahente.* We are done here."

Captain Prinn bypassed them both and disappeared inside the rugged log building. Ever the quick-witted strategist when it came to fighting, he clearly sensed a coming battle between her and her father.

Mercy widened her stance yet bowed her

head in deference. Searching for the right words, she studied the fine layer of gray dirt hardened on the toes of her moccasins. Appeasement was never a clever policy, but sometimes a necessary evil. "Your wisdom is unequaled, my father."

He grabbed her chin and lifted her face. His black gaze bored into hers. Even so, a hint of a curve lifted the edges of his lips. "Wise counsel or not, you will do as you will."

She stared at him but said nothing. A survival tactic — one her mother should have learned.

"The best *sachem* is not the one who persuades people to his point of view. He is the one in whose presence most people find truth." Releasing her, he squared his shoulders. "There is no truth left in the English father Bragg."

She sighed, long and low. He needn't have told her what she already knew. But this wasn't about General Bragg or Black-Fox-Running — and never had been. Reaching out, she placed her hand on her father's arm, where hard muscle still knotted beneath four decades of scars. "I respect your insight, *Rake'niha*. I will consider it."

His teeth bared with the closest semblance of a smile he ever gave. "That is the most I can expect from you, for you will land wherever the wind blows. *Ó:nen Kahente*."

"No!" Her breath caught. Why use a forever goodbye? She tightened her grip on her father's arm. "Only until we meet again."

Shrugging out of her grasp, he stalked past her, leaving behind his familiar scent of bear grease and strength. She watched him go, tears blurring her sight. While she hated yielding to the will of any man, for him she would almost bend.

Proud head lifted high, Black-Fox-Running called to a group of warriors, her brother amongst them, clustered in front of the pen with their horses. Without a word, they mounted. She turned from the sight, unwilling to watch them ride off, and focused on the task at hand. Better that than second-guess her decision.

She shoved open the brigadier general's door, and the peppery scent of sage greeted her. Across the small chamber, a few leftover leaves were scattered on the floor in front of the hearth. She bit her lip, fighting a sneeze. Did the man really think he duped anyone with this ruse? Even if she couldn't detect the smell of whiskey on his breath, his red nose betrayed his daily indulgence. He rose from his seat at her entrance.

She strode past a silent private on watch near the door and joined Captain Prinn, who stood in front of the commanding officer's desk. Matthew raised his brow at her — his silent way of inquiring after her conversation with Black-Fox-Running — but she ignored him and greeted the general instead.

"Pardon my appearance, sir. Captain Prinn and I only recently returned, and I had no time to make myself presentable."

"No pardon needed. It is I who am keeping you from the comfort of a hot meal and a good rest. God knows you deserve it." The general swept out his hand. "Please sit, the both of you."

General Bragg fairly crashed into his seat, knocking loose a long blond hair that had been ornamenting the red wool of his sleeve. Apparently the man had visited the supply shed with Molly the laundress as well as imbibing until he wobbled.

He coughed into one hand, clearing his throat with an excessive amount of rattling. "Now then, Captain Prinn has filled me in on the intelligence the two of you gained. It is my understanding you had quite the adventure keeping hidden from a Wyandot war party. Between Prinn's tactical strategies and your keen eye, I daresay we will win this war."

She shifted in her seat. Praise always prickled, for it usually meant she'd be asked for more than she was willing to give.

The general folded his hands on the desktop. No calluses thickened his skin. No ink stained his fingers. What did the man do all day besides chase skirts and drink?

"Normally I'd give you both some leave, but these are not normal days. There's been a recent development in your absence." Reaching for a stack of papers, the general lifted the topmost parchment.

Next to her, Matthew stretched out one long leg and leaned forward. "What would that be, General?"

"The Frogs are running scared, and that is good. Many are scuttling back over the border. A sortie of our men captured a group of them shorthanded, traveling with a load of French gold. We've got hold of one of them now . . . or I should say one of ours." He squinted at the parchment, then held it out to Matthew. "You recognize this name?"

Matthew's eyes scanned the paper before he handed it back. "No, sir. It means nothing to me. Congratulations on your fine catch, but what has any of this to do with us? Miss Lytton and I have done more than our fair share of *duty.*" Emphasizing the last word, he flashed her a look from the corner of his eye.

She flattened her lips to keep from smiling. The rascal. Using her own sentiment of duty.

"I needn't tell you our position here is tenuous, especially now with Black-Fox-Running pulling his aid. Fickle natives." Shoving back his chair, the general stood and planted his palms on the desk. "That gold's got to be moved into secure British lands. I want you and Miss Lytton to be part of that team. You will leave first thing come morning."

Matthew shook his head. "Why us? You have stronger, younger, more bloodthirsty men in the garrison. Why send a worn-out soldier like me and a young lady who spots trouble a mile away but can't fire a gun to save her life?"

"It is precisely for those reasons I chose you."

Mercy rubbed her eyes. Something wasn't right here. She lifted her face to the general. "Excuse me, sir, but what's to stop the French from simply taking back the gold as we move it, just as you took it from them?"

His wide mouth stretched ever wider, and a low chuckle rumbled in his chest. "That is the beauty of my plan. It won't be a shipment of gold."

Matthew cocked his head. "Come again?"

"We'll hide the crates in plain sight, under the guise of two wagonloads carrying naught but homestead belongings. The longer this war drags on, the more families are pulling up stakes and escaping back to civilization. You shall simply be yet more of those tired settlers who've had their fill of frontier life."

Matthew shifted in his chair, the scrape of his tomahawk handle against his seat as offsetting as the lowering of his voice. "You want us to move that gold overland instead of by river? Do you have any idea how long that will take?"

"A fortnight, if luck smiles on you."

A frown weighted Mercy's brow, and she glanced at Matthew. The hard lines on his face were unreadable. Scouting out danger from the safety of forest cover was one thing, but rolling along on a wagon in the open was quite another. Suddenly her words of duty tasted sour at the back of her throat.

She shot her gaze back to the general. "Captain Prinn and I hardly make up a family, sir."

"Indeed. And so I've enlisted a few others to add to your numbers. You shall have a recruit to play the part of your nephew.

Captain Prinn here" — he aimed his finger at Matthew — "will pose as the kindly father figure in your life, as he always does. And you, Miss Lytton, will no longer be a miss."

She tensed. If she ran out the door now and saddled a horse, she could catch up to her father in no time. She gripped the chair arms to keep from fleeing. "Pardon me, General, but what are you saying?"

"Why, my dear Miss Lytton." A grin spread on his face. "You will be wed by tomorrow."

CHAPTER 2

Mercy bolted out the general's door, heedless of the stares of milling soldiers. Without slowing her stride, she crossed the parade ground and raced to the sanctity of the women's tents. This being an outpost garrison, the men were afforded timbered shelters. The women got canvas, unless they were an officer's wife. There were only six ladies living in the tents — three who refused to leave their husbands, herself, and two who stayed simply because they had nowhere else to go.

Flinging aside the door flap, she ducked inside and closed the stained canvas behind her. Three empty cots were lined up before her like fallen soldiers. The farthest one called her weary bones to lie down and forget the world. Pah! As if she could. The general's words boiled her blood hotter with each pump of her heart.

"You will be wed by tomorrow."

"We'll see about that," she muttered, glad her tentmates were either out washing regimentals or nursing sick soldiers. "Men! Pigheaded, the lot of them."

Reaching up, she fumbled at her collar and pulled out the locket she never took off. She ran her thumb over the center of a ruby heart, surrounded by gold filigree, and slowed her breathing. Years ago, she'd worn the necklace out of rebellion. Now the heavy stone was a weight of penance and — oddly enough — comfort.

Oh Mother . . .

Wind riffled the canvas walls. She felt more alone now than she had in years.

With a sigh, she shrugged off a man's trade shirt that hung to her knees, untied her leggings and peeled them off, and lastly loosened the breechclout at her waist. She'd have to hang them up to dry before packing them away, but for now, she gave the heap a good kick, tired of straddling the line between male and female, native and white. Tired of everything, really.

Shivering, she knelt in front of her trunk and opened the lid. Pulling out a clean gown and undergarments, she frowned at the feminine attire as fiercely as she'd scowled at the hunting clothes. Why was she so different? Why could she not be like other women?

She blew out a sigh and slipped into a dry shift and front-lacing stays, knowing all the while there were no answers to be had. She'd been born different, and there was nothing to be done about that.

After retrieving a hairbrush, she closed the lid on her trunk and sank onto its top. For the moment, she set the brush in her lap, then began the arduous process of unpinning her long hair, her thoughts every bit as snarly. Why must everyone push her into marriage, as if she were some precious bauble that required protection? Little good it had done her mother. Brushing her hair with more force than necessary, she winced. In a man's world, survival came by acting and thinking like a man.

With deft fingers, she braided her hair into a long tail and was tying a leather lace at the end when footsteps pounded the ground outside her tent.

"Mercy, come on out." Matthew's voice leached through the weathered canvas. "We need to talk."

She dropped her hands to her lap. What was there to say? She'd given her answer. Not even a war party of Wyandots could make her change her mind.

"I know you're in there," he growled.

"And I won't go away."

Of course he wouldn't. She rolled her eyes. The man was as determined as a river swollen by winter melt. Tucking up a stray strand, she rose and opened the flap. "You're wasting your time. I will not entertain the general's suggestion."

"At least hear me out. Then make up your mind." He held up a blackened tin pot. "Besides, I've brought stew. Don't tell me you're not hungry."

Her stomach growled, and she frowned. Of all the inopportune times to remind him — and her — that she was human.

Matthew smirked.

She sighed. Ignoring him would sure be a lot easier with a belly full of hot food. "Very well. Give me a moment."

Darting back inside, she retrieved a shawl, then grabbed a horn spoon and wooden bowl.

Outside, Matthew already sat on a log next to a smoldering fire, dipping his spoon into his own bowl. She joined him. The rich scent of broth curling up to her nose nearly made her weep. And the first bite . . . aah. There wasn't much finer in the world than thick stew on a chill day — especially after going without for so long.

She shoveled in a mouthful before eyeing

Matthew sideways. "What'd you trade for this?"

"Rum."

"Your loss. Much as I'm obliged" — she paused for another big bite — "I won't be bought for a bowl of pottage."

" 'Course not." Afternoon sun glinted off the stew droplets collecting on Matthew's beard as he spoke. "You're worth far more than that."

The soup in her mouth soured, and she swallowed it like a bitter medicine. The man was forever prattling on about God's great love for her. "Don't start, Matthew. I can't bear a sermon right now."

"Fair enough." Lifting the bowl to his lips, Matthew tipped back his head and finished the rest of his meal. He swiped his mouth with his sleeve while setting down the dish, then angled to face her head-on. "Look, I don't like this any more than you do, but despite the danger of it, General Bragg's plan is solid. Like he said, with clear weather, it'll take but a fortnight to get the load over to Fort Edward."

"Fort Edward?" Her appetite suddenly stalled. The rangers were stationed out of that fort. Matthew's former cohort. Was this his way of saying goodbye?

She swallowed, the stew having lost its appeal. "I see."

His brows gathered together like a coming storm. "No, you don't. When it comes to that falcon eyesight of yours, you are unequaled. But in matters of the heart, you are blind."

"Matthew!" She spluttered and choked. After three years of scouting sorties with this man, surely he wasn't pledging troth to her. He was old enough to be her father!

"Certainly you are not hinting at . . ." She cleared her throat once more, unable to force out any more words.

For a moment his eyes narrowed, then shot wide. His shoulders shook as he chuckled. "No, girl. Nothing like that. Look at me, Mercy. Really look. What do you see?"

Lowering her bowl, she focused first on her breaths. In. Out. Slower. And slower. Sound was next. One by one, she closed off the hum of the camp — the whickering of a horse, coarse laughter from afar. The thud of men tromping about. Even the beat of her own pulse quieted until silence took on a life of its own. Only then could she see, and in the seeing, her heart broke.

Where whiskers were absent, lines etched a life map on Matthew Prinn's face. A chart of the years — decades — of toil and grief. Spent vigor peppered his beard and hair that were once raven. Even his eyes were washed out and gray now. In the three years she'd known him, he'd earned a new scar near his temple and a larger bump on his nose — all in the service of the king.

And her.

She set her bowl on the log beside her, no longer hungry. "What I see is a great man who faithfully serves the crown, relentlessly brings back intelligence, and keeps me safe in the process."

He shook his head. "That is what you want to see. The truth of it is I'm tired. This fight is winding down, and so am I." Pausing, he looked up at a sky as sullen as the furrows on his forehead. "I aim to go to Fort Edward, then keep on going east till I find me a nice patch of land and put down stakes."

"You're going to quit? Just like that?"

" 'Tis been a long time coming." His gaze found hers again. "You did not see it because you did not want to."

The accusation crept in like a rash, hot and uncomfortable. Of course she did not want to see it, because if she did, she'd have to look long and hard at her own life. She dropped her gaze and picked at the frayed hem of her shawl. He'd sacrificed time and again these past three years for her. Time now she returned the favor.

"I understand, Matthew. Truly."

A grunt resounded in his chest. "Good. Then we're agreed."

She jerked her face upward. "But that doesn't mean I will marry."

His teeth flashed white in his beard. "I did not say it did."

"But the general said —"

Matthew held up a hand. "If you'd have stayed long enough to hear the man out, you'd know we'll travel as a family unit in name only, not deed. Rufus and I —"

"Rufus *Bragg*?" She spit out the name like an unripe huckleberry.

"Aye. We will both have a cross to bear. He is to pose as my grandson, and he and I will man the rear wagon. You will ride the lead, scouting for trouble as always."

Picking up a stick, she stabbed at the coals in the fire, stirring them to life. "With my husband, no doubt."

"Like I said, in name only." His hand snaked out and stilled her frantic poking. "Why are you so skittish over this? I've never known you to back down from a request to serve. What of your high ideals of duty and honor?"

She pulled from his touch, wishing it could be as easy to shy from his question.

But she couldn't, for truth once spoken could not be unheard. "You're right," she mumbled. Slowly, she lifted her face to his. "But what shall I do without you?"

"Time you took stock of your own future, girl. Where is it to be? What is it to be? With whom is it to be spent?"

She jumped to her feet, grabbing up her bowl and spoon. She'd rather run barelegged through a patch of poison oak than consider the answers to those inquiries, for she wanted nothing more than to remain unfettered and free. "If we are to leave at daybreak, I need to pack and get some rest."

She whirled toward her tent, then turned back. "Tell me, Matthew, who is to be my, er . . ." The word stuck in her throat, and she forced it out past a clenched jaw. "Husband?"

He stood, gathering the tin pot and his bowl. "Fellow by the name of Dubois, more than likely."

"Dubois?" The French name festered like a raw boil, the food in her stomach churning. "Pah! I'm to be *married* to a Frenchman?"

"Oh, he is more than that."

Her hands shot to her hips. "What aren't you telling me, Matthew Prinn?"

"Dubois," he drawled, leveling a cocked eyebrow at her, "is a condemned traitor."

CHAPTER 3

Light crept in through the cracks between boards. Pale. Lethargic. Morning, but not quite. As if the sun hovered just below the horizon for the sole purpose of tormenting Elias Dubois, forcing him to live his last moments on this earth stuck between night and day. No matter. It felt like home, this in-between, the threat of death a familiar companion. But this time, more than his life would be on the line. Other men depended upon him if he did not make it back to Boston. And that single, bruising thought stuck in his craw, sharp as a wedged bone.

"You are a disappointment."

Lifting his hand, he shoved away his grandfather's words echoing from the grave and probed his swollen eye. The chains hanging from his wrist rattled like a skeleton — a reminder of what he'd soon become. A slow smile stretched his lips. At least he could see. Face the noose head-on and die with dignity. His smile bled into a frown. Was there anything dignified about the last beat of a heart?

"Dubois! You ready to die?" A voice, as chilling as the spring air, blasted against the storage shed door.

Elias pushed up from the crate he'd called a bed. "Now is as good a time as any." The lie flowed a little too easily, and he winced, regretting the falsehood . . . regretting his failure. Because of his error, a deadly French weapon would kill countless English and Colonials.

Unless he made it out of here — alive and with that weapon — the tide of the war could once again turn back to the French. Ah, but his grandfather surely must be rolling in his coffin to know that the fate of an entire war hinged on his prodigal grandson.

A key scraped against metal. A wooden bar lifted. The silhouette of a red-coated grim reaper darkened the door.

"Then let's be about it." Captain Scraling stepped aside, leaving enough room for Elias to pass yet not escape, for another soldier stood outside, five paces away from the door.

His smile nearly returned. Where would he run to inside a palisade with guards at the ready?

Stretching a wicked kink out of his neck, he strolled ahead as if the request meant nothing more than a call to a hearty breakfast. But once past the threshold, he stopped and studied the sky — gray as a corpse drained of life. He shot the captain a scowl. "You are early. The sun is not up yet."

Scraling shrugged. "I have many things to do today. You are the least of them. Follow the private, if you please." He tipped his head toward the Colonial regular.

Elias smirked. "And if I do not?"

The captain's fist shot out. Elias's head exploded. Reeling, he plummeted backward, unable to stop himself from crashing to the ground. Blast! Just when his eye had started to open.

The next strike drove the air from his lungs. Groaning, he rolled over and gasped for air. An impossibility though when Scraling grabbed the back of his collar and yanked him to his feet.

"Move it!" The captain shoved him between the shoulder blades.

He stumbled forward, catching himself before ramming into the man in front of him. And a good thing too for the private stood ready to pummel him as well.

"Lead on, Private," the captain ordered.

They marched across the parade ground.

Two wagons were being loaded near the front gate, not far from the rough-hewn gallows — a reminder to those arriving and departing that justice would be meted out, even here in the New York wilderness. Each step stole a breath from the few he yet owned, but he couldn't begrudge these men who prodded him onward. He was as guilty of the charges as Lucifer himself.

Birdsong trilled in the quiet of predawn, a pleasant accompaniment to the tramp of their feet. The shaking started then. First in his hands, working upward over arms and shoulders, diving in deep and spreading from gut to legs. It was always like this when the smell of death grew stronger — or was that his stench from being locked in a shed for two days without courtesy of a privy break?

He glanced skyward. *Is this it, Lord?*

A gentle morning breeze nudged the hanging rope. The movement was slight, barely noticeable, but enough to twist Elias's throat into a sodden knot. The hairs at the back of his neck stood out like wire. Was he truly ready to die? Was anyone?

Spare the lives of those men, God. The ones I failed. And forgive me for my lack.

Just ten paces more and —

The private made a sharp right, pivoting

away from the scaffold. Elias's step faltered. Was this some kind of trick? He looked back to the captain.

A fist smashed into his nose. Double blast! His head jerked aside, the force knocking him to his hands and knees. The ground spun. Blood dripped over his top lip. The captain taunted from behind, something about his manliness or lack thereof. Hard to tell. Sound buzzed like a beehive that had been whacked with a stick — but even louder was the anger inside him, pumping stronger with each heartbeat. His fury strained at the leash. Staggering to his feet, he bit back a curse and spit out the nasty taste in his mouth, then lifted his face to the sky.

"Forgive these men too, Lord, for I surely am not able to at this moment." He spoke in French, not only to prevent the satisfaction the captain would feel at his admission, but more importantly to irritate the Englishman.

"Move along!"

Head pounding, he tromped after the private, unable to work up any more curiosity as to why they bypassed the noose and neared the officers' quarters. Likely a last interrogation — and his last chance to talk his way out of this mess.

Please, God. More than my life depends upon this. Have mercy.

The private knocked and, after a gruff "Enter" grumbled from inside, shoved open the door.

Elias advanced, swiping the blood from his nose and breathing in sage and rotgut rum.

Brigadier General Bragg did not so much as look up from his desk. He merely flicked out his hand as if the lot of them were black-flies to be swatted. "Captain, Private, wait outside."

With a final scowl aimed at Elias, Captain Scraling stomped off. Clearly he was not happy for being told to wait like a dog — and the thought of his inconvenience made Elias smile, despite the way the movement stung.

The general pinched a document in his fingers and held it up, skewering him with a glower of his own. "This is a warrant for your death."

Elias frowned. Why show him the document before draining the life from his eyes? This was not standard procedure. He'd fold his arms and stare the man down were his hands not weighted by irons.

"And this" — Bragg paused and held up

a different parchment — "is a stay of execution."

A stay? What in all of God's great glory? A muscle jumped in his jaw, but he refused to gape, for surely the general expected such a response.

Though he'd regret it, the irony of the situation slowly unraveled inside him, and he chuckled. If only François could hear this. He laughed until the pounding of his skull could no longer be denied.

Bragg's brow darkened, as did the scarlet tip of his nose. "I fail to see the humor in this, Dubois."

"Are you seriously cutting a deal with a traitor?"

"I'd deal with the devil if I had to."

"Well, I suppose I am the closest thing you have to that." He angled his head. "What is your offer?"

Bragg leaned so far back in his chair, the wood creaked a grievance. "I have a shipment of gold needing safe delivery into British lands."

Elias advanced so quickly, Bragg reached for his pistol. Stopping short of lunging across the man's desk, Elias slammed his hands onto the wood, the chains adding to the startling effect. "Are you asking me to deliver the gold you stole from me?" The question echoed above the crackle of wood in the fire and the snort of the man in front of him.

"Yes."

Straightening, he lifted his face to the plank ceiling. "You never stop surprising me."

"We've only recently met."

He aimed his gaze back at Bragg like a loaded musket. "I was not talking to you."

The general shifted in his seat, laying his pistol in his lap. "My terms are these: You will be part of a four-person squad, traveling under the guise of a family moving back to civilization. Reach Fort Edward with the gold intact, and your execution will be pardoned, though the required jail time is nonnegotiable."

His stomach clenched — and not from lack of food. Something wasn't right about this. "Why me?"

"I don't think I need to tell you, soldier, that you will be crossing dangerous ground. The chances of making it alive to Fort Edward are slim. You're a condemned man anyway. Expendable. And if you don't make it . . ." He shrugged.

Interesting — but completely implausible. Elias grunted. "What is to stop me from killing my companions and running off?"

"They will be armed. You will not."

No one could survive in the wilderness without a gun or a knife. Elias shook his head. "Then I might as well die here."

"With good behavior, you shall walk free. Eventually." Bragg held up both papers, shaking them so that the documents rippled like living things. "So, what will it be? Life . . . or death?"

Elias shifted his gaze from one to the other. Was this an answer to his prayer? Or a fiendish jest?

Reaching out, he snatched the parchment sentencing him to the gallows. He could end this here and now. Stop the running. Finish the vagabond life that he'd come to hate. Just a quick jerk from a tight rope, then a blissfully peaceful eternity with the only Father he'd ever respected.

Bragg's jaw dropped.

Elias smiled from the satisfaction of it.

Then ripped the document to pieces.

CHAPTER 4

Morning stretched with a gray yawn across the sky, unwilling to fully awaken. Mercy frowned as patches of rainwater, frozen to brittle sheets by last night's chill, crackled beneath her feet. If the cloud cover tarried and the earth held firm, at least they would make good time today. The sooner this journey was over, the better.

Across the parade ground, a curious sight snagged her attention. Three men filed past the gallows, then veered away from it. The raggedy one in the middle strode the proudest, shoulders back, gait sure, despite the shackles weighing him down. The man was so filthy it was impossible to see the true color of his coat or breeches. Was this the traitor who would play the part of her husband? But no, clearly he was in no condition to travel anywhere except back to the stocks.

The prisoner turned to the captain behind

him, and a fist knocked him to the ground. Not an unusual sight given the nature of the fort, but what followed put a hitch in Mercy's step.

The man staggered up from the blow, turned aside and spit, and then, with as much grace as a buck, lifted his face to the sky. His sudden stillness reached across the distance and pulled her in. This far away she couldn't hear his words, but the sacredness of the moment stole her breath. Clearly he spoke to his God, and she got the distinct impression his God bent and listened with a keen ear. Growing up in a Mohawk camp, she was no stranger to the mystical ways of shamans, but this? Gooseflesh prickled down her arms, and she was unaccountably glad when the captain shoved the man forward into the brigadier general's quarters.

Shaking off the unsettling feeling, she shifted her hold on her bundle of belongings and upped her pace. The man was none of her concern. She had bigger wolves to slay this day, namely setting out on a journey with a husband she did not want — even if it were in name only. Maybe she could persuade Matthew to let her ride with him instead. As a rule, she did not like working with strangers, and she especially did not pine for it when the man had a name like Dubois.

Drawing near the two wagons at the front gate, she caught Matthew's eye and hailed him with a tip of her chin. After so many years learning each other's ways, words were a hindrance.

He helped a soldier shove a crate up a ramp into the wagon, then strode her way. "Stow your pack. And you wanna check those supplies?" He hitched his thumb, indicating a box on the ground up near the other wagon. "Prob'ly ain't much."

"We've been through lean." She glanced past Matthew's shoulder to where another soldier had taken his place in the loading. Both men strained their muscles against the next trunk. She recognized one private, but not the other. Neither was a bowlegged effigy. "Where's Rufus?"

"I imagine he'll show when the work's done."

"No doubt. Is that man over there my . . ." The word *husband* crawled back down her throat. Thinking it was one thing. Speaking it into being, an impossibility.

Matthew shook his head. "He ain't showed yet either."

Relief hit her as sweet as the brisk morning air. It would be short-lived, but she savored it nonetheless. Her bundle clutched to her chest, she bypassed the length of the canvas-covered wagon with four horses hitched to the front of it and neared the back of the other wagon. She hefted her pack over the back gate and tucked it snug beside six fat trunks that rode shoulder to shoulder, close as friends huddled near a fire — clearly more comfortable at the prospect of the ride than she.

She turned from the sight and rifled through the contents of the remaining crate on the ground. A blackened tin pot. Several packets of hardtack. Dried beans and some strips of meat so old and shriveled as to be beyond recognition. There was one jug of watered ale and several handfuls of root vegetables, all as wrinkled as tribal elders. This far from civilization and after a winter spare of game, they were the best victuals to be had.

She secured the lid, then heaved the crate into the wagon, grunting from the effort. For such mean supplies, the box weighed heavy. Footsteps thudded on the hardened dirt, and she turned.

Rufus Bragg wasn't much of a man, for he barely held on to sixteen years. So gawkily built was he, his bones put up a fair fight to support his garments. Were it not for the knobs of his joints, he'd have to tie the shirt to his skin to keep it from falling off. Mouse-colored hair hung over one small, dark eye. The other one blinked at her. He said nothing. Not only did he own no manners, it seemed he never intended to purchase any.

But beyond looks and manners, the mark of wickedness was the young man's worst fault. She'd once seen him torture a rabbit kit just for the enjoyment of it. Were he not the brigadier general's son, he'd have been cashiered long ago.

She glanced over at the other wagon, where the men loaded the last crate, then pursed her lips and speared Rufus with a scowl. "Right on time, as always."

His mouth parted in a toothy grin. "Ne'er too late and ne'er too early."

"Never around to lift a finger, more like it."

He shrugged, and she feared the sharpness of his shoulders might cut through his shirt and coat. "Cain't be blamed if the men don't wait for me."

She clenched her jaw. Matthew was right. They would both be bearing crosses. Sidestepping Rufus, she strode back to Matthew. "As you thought, there's not much by way of food. Have to hunt along the way. Could slow us down some."

Matthew rubbed his jaw, clean shaven but not for long. "Now yer eager to be rid of me?"

"That is not what I meant, and you know it. The sooner we reach Fort Edward, the sooner" — she lowered her voice as the man-boy swung around the back of the wagon — "we'll be rid of Rufus. We ready to go?"

"Soon as your man shows."

She gasped. "My man?" The familiarity he awarded a known traitor and a French one at that roiled the bellyful of chicory coffee she'd swigged for breakfast.

"Quit yer chafing. Gotta play the part, *Daughter.*" He rested a big hand on her shoulder. "If we don't swallow our roles now and trouble comes along, our lives are on the line."

"Fine. But I don't like it."

"You have made that quite clear." His hand fell away, and the rebuke in his gray eyes scorched like an August sun.

She dipped her head. "Very well. I will be the most obedient daughter ever to grace the wilds of upper New York."

"That don't worry me. I'm fretting over how you will manage to act the goodwife."

■ ■ ■

Elias shivered, naked and cold. Having just left the general's office, he'd expected to be outfitted for the upcoming trek — but not with an icy drenching. He gritted his teeth to keep from gasping when the next bucketful hit. Captain Scraling and the private laughed — then the private picked up yet another bucket and did it again. Elias shook his head like a dog. He should be thankful for the washing, but Lord have mercy, this was humiliating.

"Get yourself dressed. I ain't no lady's maid and those wagons are itchin' to leave."

The private lobbed a ball of clothing at him. He caught it just before the bundle landed on the wet ground.

Scraling leaned against the general's quarters, gun at the ready. Did the man truly think he'd need it? Only a fool would make a stripped-bare run for it in the company of soldiers long deprived of a good fight.

Elias shrugged on a shirt too small and breeches better fitted to a scarecrow. His own clothes had been ruined beyond repair, thanks to men such as these. He shoved his arms into the sleeves of a linen hunting frock, and forgave the tightness of the garments beneath, for this coat with its long sleeves and longer hem covered a multitude of sins. He grabbed up his own leather belt and secured it, then jammed his feet into his moccasins, both mercifully unscathed save for a few nicks.

Once again he fell into step between the private and the captain, who led him around the building. Scraling rapped on the general's door and Bragg emerged. Daylight wasn't kind to him. Though dawn hardly grabbed hold of the day and cloud cover did its best to vanquish even that weak light, broken veins showed clearly on the fleshy parts of the general's face.

"So, there was a man beneath that filth." The general nodded at Scraling and the private. "Thank you, men. That will be all. Dubois, follow me."

Elias kept time with Bragg's hike across the parade ground. The noose dangling from the gallows waved as they passed, and Elias tugged at his collar. While this wasn't his day to swing by the neck, that did not mean death wasn't crouched nearby.

Narrowing his eyes, he studied the figures ahead. A tall man, silver-fox hair shooting wild from beneath his hat, conversed with a woman, who stood not much shorter. If it weren't for a long braid of dark hair tailing down her back and a dun-colored gown flaring out at her hips, he almost might have mistaken her for a man, so wide was her stance, so confident the stretch of her shoulders. Two soldiers strode away from the rear wagon, revealing a lank-limbed, scruff-faced younger man.

"If the weather holds" — Bragg's voice interrupted his assessment — "it should take you a fortnight to reach Fort Edward, though given the rain we've had, the going could be treacherous. You are adept at handling a wagon, are you not?"

He bit back a smirk. The man had no idea. "Are the loads weighed even?"

"Captain Matthew Prinn, your . . . er, *father-in-law,* will have seen to that."

He grunted. "Then yes. I am no stranger to hauling goods."

"With a name like Dubois, I thought as much."

Elias let the slur slick off him like water from a beaver's tail. With a French surname, he'd heard it all before. Most English thought him either a voyageur, a criminal, or a scalp-taker — and they were right on all accounts. Or at least he had been in the past. But if Bragg knew what British blood also flowed in his veins, the man would bend a knee and plead for mercy.

The general stopped just paces behind the woman. "Miss Lytton, Captain Prinn, allow me to introduce the last member of your team, Mr. Elias Dubois. Keep an eye on your weapons, for under no circumstance is this man to be given one."

Anger scorched a blaze up his neck, erasing any memory of his earlier cold dousing. A man couldn't survive without a gun and a blade, especially not in the company of this sorry-looking lot. They would be lucky to make it to nightfall. His hands clenched at his sides, itching for the feel of a musket stock or knife hilt. "That is a mistake, General. Unarmed, I am of no use to anyone."

"As I said, you're expendable if need be. Godspeed." The general wheeled about.

So did the woman. Brown eyes bored into his, just about level with his own. This close, she was taller than he'd first credited. Dark of hair, darker of gaze, with cheekbones high and eyes large and wide enough to dive in and swim around. He might almost place her as a native — were it not for skin so fair, it glowed soft and white. He sucked in a breath. By all the blessed stars above, how had he ever thought her to be mannish?

"Ma'am." He dipped his head in greeting.

Her lips parted, full and surprisingly deep in color, yet she said nothing.

"Mr. Dubois." The man behind her stepped forward and offered a hand. "I'm Matthew Prinn."

"Elias, please. If we are to pose as a family, it would be best to be on a first-name basis." He clasped the fellow's hand and measured his character by grip alone. Strong. Unwavering. Calloused and hard. But not overpowering, revealing a kind of stalwart humility.

"I s'pose you're right." The man let go and nudged the woman with his elbow. "This here is Mercy."

Elias clamped his jaw. An apt name, for Lord have mercy, she captivated like no other woman, and to his shame, he'd known quite a few.

She lifted her chin. "Daylight's wasting. We should be on our way."

She whirled so fast, her long braid slapped his arm. Her skirts swished as she stalked toward the front wagon.

Elias's brows shot up. There was nothing skittish about this one.

Prinn's gray eyes followed the woman while his jaw worked. "Mercy can be a little . . . Let's just say she is a fiddle string wound tight and about to break. Might wanna ride quiet for a while. If she snaps, it will leave a mark. She'll get over it soon enough. Rufus! Hike yerself up to the seat. I will take first scout." He turned, leaving Elias standing alone at the rear, caught between the empty gallows and the fort gates swinging wide, gaping open to a wilderness filled with danger.

Elias cracked his neck one way then the other. Had he escaped one sure death only to face another? He lifted a prayer as he hiked toward the front wagon. More than one life depended on his survival — and with the worn man, young buck, and fiery woman, he'd just added three more to that count.

CHAPTER 5

Mercy studied Elias Dubois as he swung up onto the wagon seat beside her. She had never thought this day would come. She sitting next to a man purporting to be her husband — real or not. She gripped the wagon's side to keep from pinching her skin to check if this was some kind of nightmare. After years of watching her mother being subdued so thoroughly by her father, she had sworn not to put herself in the same position. Ever. Not even as a farce.

To Mr. Dubois's credit, the man said nothing, merely spit out a "Get-up" and slapped the reins, lurching the wagon into movement. It was a small act, one she did not want to admire, but clearly he owned some sense — both in coaxing the horses to tow such a heavy load and in allowing her time to settle in silence.

Beneath a felt hat, his dark hair hung wet to his shoulders, stark against his colorless linen collar. One eye was purpled nearly shut. His good eye stared straight ahead. A fresh cut drew a red line on his cheekbone, just above the scruff of his beard. He sat tall, but not much higher than her. A bump rode midway down his nose, the legacy of a fighter, but not nearly as pronounced as the crooked bend of Matthew's. His skin was tanned to burnt honey — a rarity this time of year, unless one lived outside regardless of the seasons.

Her gaze shifted down his arms. While one hand gripped the reins, the other rode on his thick leg. His knuckles were grazed raw. Fighter, indeed. How many men had those fists struck? She stared harder. Worn grooves marked the flesh between his fingers — ruts worn by rifle balls, a testimony of years spent caressing a gun.

Yet despite his rugged exterior and the fact that he rode toward God knew how many years of imprisonment, he guided the horses as if he were on a Sunday drive. A strange contentedness flowed from him, as if he'd lived and walked around in hunger and need, then strolled out the other side a more peaceful soul for the journey.

"Your assessment?" He spoke without pulling his gaze from the narrow trace they followed.

His voice carried a strange mix of accents. French. British. And oddly enough, a throaty twang she couldn't place at first — and when she did, she narrowed her eyes at him.

Native . . . but which people?

"You're capable enough," she admitted. "Leastwise I don't think I shall have to be saving your hide."

"So, you think it is a hide worth saving then?" He flashed her a smile, one that did strange things to her belly.

"You tell me."

His grin faded. A shameful loss, that. His blue gaze — the color of an October sky — held hers with as much intensity as she might employ.

"You are a bold one," he said simply.

"And is that the sum of your appraisal?" At the quirk of his brow, she continued, "Don't bother denying it. Even without looking, you have been measuring my strengths and weaknesses since we left the fort."

He threw back his head and laughed, a warm sound, heating her despite the chill of the spring morn. He smelled of smoke — gun smoke, wood smoke, and the heated charge in the air left behind when lightning struck a pine.

Laughter spent, he faced forward again. "You are as much a riddle as me — and I think we both know it."

"At least I'm not a traitor." She bit her lip. Too late. An arrow once shot could not be re-quivered. If Matthew heard her, an ear-burning scolding would light her on fire.

But Elias — for yes, she ought to think of him as such, despite her misgivings — merely continued guiding the horses along the trail. "Judging on hearsay is a danger," he said in an even tone.

Her jaw dropped. This man, the one she'd seen shackled and dropped to the ground, was denying the accusation? She hitched her thumb over her shoulder. "Isn't this load of gold what you were moving for the French?"

"It is."

"But you have English blood."

"Indeed." He glanced at her sideways. "Sharp eye."

"Seems to me your loyalties are a-tangle, Elias Dubois."

His shoulders shook. For one beaten half-dead and parrying an earful of a woman's blows, he was generous with his humor.

The chuckle in his throat faded. "I would say my allegiances are no more conflicted than yours."

She smirked, then grabbed the wagon's seat as they bumped over a large rock. There was no answer to his remark — for he couldn't be more right.

"All right, here is my assessment then, since you asked." He turned to her, allowing the horses to find their own speed. "What I know is that you are fair to chafing in that gown, and lest you decide you are done with it, I had best keep an eye on my breeches. Your words are more crumpets than cowpeas, proving somewhere along the way you were raised by a proper lady, a curiosity considering you now travel with a ranger. But there is one thing I am hog-tied to figure out."

Don't ask. Don't do it. That was what he wanted. But the need to know, ever her downfall, swelled like snowmelt on the Genesee River. "What's that?" she asked.

"If that lilt to your voice is Mohawk or Mohican."

Scowling, she faced forward once again, ignoring the man and his questions. He could wonder about her heritage all he liked — for she had no intention of sating his curiosity.

They rode in silence until it was her turn to swap with Matthew on scouting duty. Only once did they break their pace to water the horses and gnaw on a hardened crust of bread and a pouch of pemmican Matthew had seen fit to bring along. Matthew commented to her that he was surprised Elias was still in one piece. She'd shot back that she noticed Rufus was too, to which he'd answered the day wasn't over yet.

And she couldn't agree more. Would this day never end? With no sun to gauge by, she figured there were maybe two more hours of travel time until they hit the clearing to camp for the night — but when they turned a bend in the trail, she revised that opinion.

An enormous oak lay sideways in their path. Why hadn't Rufus run back to tell them? The man was worthless as a scout, though it shouldn't have surprised her. The only thing he excelled at was shirking his duties and complaining.

Elias set the brake and hopped down. So did she.

Eventually, Matthew joined them in front of the felled blockade. "That is a big one."

He wasn't jesting. Laid flat, the trunk stood as high as her knees. She frowned at the barrier, fighting the urge to kick the thing.

Elias turned to Matthew. "How many axes have we?"

"Two."

Her frown deepened. A fool's task, an idea brought on by too much brawn and not enough brain. "If we backtrack a half mile or so, I know a way around this. 'Tis an old *Kahnyen'kehàka* trail but ought to be wide enough."

Elias shook his head. "Too dangerous. We stick to the route."

What gall! Why did this man — this *traitor* — think he owned the last word? She whirled to Matthew. "If we turn around now, we can —"

"Go grab the axes, Mercy." Matthew cut her off.

"Matthew!" His name shot past her lips like a hiss. Was he really siding with a man he barely knew over her — and a branded turncoat at that? "You know I can walk this land blinded. I'm telling you my way will be faster."

"I don't doubt your knowledge, girl. But this time of year, after a winter of holing up, those trails are a-swarm with braves keening for a fight. I reckon you know that too. So like Elias says, we'll bust up this tree and continue on. Agreed?"

Her hands curled into fists. Unbelievable! Why did men always think they knew better? The time it would take to clear a path would put them behind schedule on the first day out. But the cut of Matthew's jaw and the blue steel in Elias's gaze fairly shouted they would not be moved.

"Fine," she strained out. "I will scout up ahead."

She stormed along the length of the trunk, spying out the best place to heft herself over. It was a grand and glorious lie she'd told, for she couldn't scout a thing — not with the red haze of rage coloring everything.

Night fell hard and fast in the forest. Elias worked quickly in the dark, spreading an old army blanket across the tops of the crates in the wagon. If anyone asked what he was doing, he could say he was preparing a place for Mercy to sleep — which he was. Now. But before darkness had eaten up the last of day's light, he'd rummaged to find the crate he'd notched and made sure the weapon he'd tucked safely at the bottom was still there.

"Dinner's ready."

Mercy's voice seeped through the canvas, competing with the low whirr of a few brave insects. Shrugging out of his coat, Elias added the extra layer to soften the bedding. It would make for a lumpy mattress, but if the sky's rumble held true, at least it'd be dry.

He climbed out of the wagon and headed back to the fire — the small flames of which were an allowance he and Matthew would abide for this night only. This close to the fort there likely weren't any scalp-takers on the prowl, not with soldiers frequently ranging this far out. But the farther they traveled into the backcountry, the more careful they would have to be.

Rufus and Matthew already sat cross-legged on the ground, holding out their bowls. Mercy stooped over a pot, stirring the meal. He took a spot opposite them all, the orange flames a barrier between him and the men, and held out his fingers to the warmth. It would be a cold one tonight, but late March was ever fickle in its temperament.

Mercy ladled out a watery broth with softened salt pork and root vegetables, the earthy aroma mouthwatering on the evening air. The stew hardly hit the bottom of Rufus's bowl before he moved to take a slurp of it — the beast.

"Hold off, Bragg." Elias skewered the young pup with a piercing gaze. Wilderness or not, a lady deserved respect, one of the few lessons from his mother that had ever taken root. "Wait for the lady to take the first bite."

Rufus spit out a curse. "Who died and put you in charge?"

"If you would act as a human instead of a beast, I would not have to tell you." Half a smirk twitched his lips. How many times had he heard that himself growing up? He could almost feel the swat of his grandfather's big hand across the seat of his breeches.

"You are a disappointment."

His smirk faded at the ghostly reminder.

Mercy scowled and sat next to Matthew, her own dinner in hand. "Such manners are for fine ladies at white linen tables. Neither are here."

Elias shrugged. The women he'd known back in Boston would've taken his words as a kindness. "A lady is a lady, no matter the setting."

"The man's just lookin' out for you, girl." Matthew nudged her with his elbow. "Take a bite so we can get on with it."

Silently, Mercy lifted the bowl to her lips, her gaze fixed on Elias the whole time. What went on behind those dark eyes of hers? She stared warily, as if he were a rattler about to strike.

The silence wore on until he could take

no more of Rufus's slurping. Setting down his bowl, Elias swiped his mouth. "We will need to leave come first light to make up for today's loss of time."

Mercy set down her bowl as well, breathing out guttural words too fast and low to identify.

Matthew frowned at her for a moment, then met Elias's gaze over the fire. "I'm surprised you're eager to reach the fort. Seems a man in your situation might want to drag his heels."

He stared the captain down. "I never shirk a duty, even when it is not to my liking."

A chuckle rumbled in Matthew's chest. "You sound an awful lot like someone I know."

But there was no humor in the shadows on Mercy's face. "You seem to have no qualms about which side those duties are for. Do you, Mr. Dubois?"

Her challenge crackled in the air like the pop of wood in the fire. He clenched his jaw. There was no easy way to answer that, leastwise none that wouldn't give away his true colors.

Matthew broke the standoff by setting down his bowl. "Rufus, you take first watch. Mercy, grab second. I will take —"

"I will take third," Elias offered. A smile

as thin as the stew twitched his lips. "But I will not be much of a guard without a weapon."

"By the looks of you, you're a scrapper. I have no doubt you can take down a man without a gun in your hands." Matthew stretched out on the ground vacated by Rufus, the younger man already having stalked off into the dark. "Besides, you got a voice, don't you?"

Elias grunted. His bellow wouldn't be much of a defense should someone decide to attack them in the blackest hours of the night.

Mercy gathered the bowls, wiping them out with nothing but moss and the hem of her apron. She lifted the pot from the fire with a large branch, letting it cool in the dirt. Elias was just about to ask her if she was finished when she plopped onto the ground and curled up next to the fire. Did she seriously think to sleep outside? What kind of woman did that without a mutter of complaint?

He stood and stretched out his hand to her.

She looked at his fingers, firelight making it impossible to read what went on inside that mind of hers. Regardless, she did not move.

So he lobbed his own challenge. "You are not afraid, are you?"

With a hiss, she grabbed his hand, allowing him to hoist her to her feet — but when her warm skin touched his, a jolt shot through him. Instantly he released her, shaken beyond reason. Of course he'd held women's hands before — and much more than that — but never, *ever,* had one left a mark on him like this.

And by the sound of it, she felt the same, for she sucked in a sharp breath.

He turned away, unwilling to ponder the strange sensation any further. Must have been the chill spring air getting to him in naught but a shirt. "Follow me."

Her feet tread silently behind him. Were it not for her musky sweet scent, he'd wonder if she followed at all. He led her to the wagon and nodded for her to climb up.

Her brow furrowed at him. "You need me to fetch something for you? Why not do it yourself?"

"Nothing of the sort. Just go on up."

She stood silent for a moment, only God knowing her thoughts. Then without another word, she hiked her skirts and climbed up.

He bit back a grin. She'd been surprising him all day, and the thought of surprising her right back warmed him as much as if he wore his hunting frock.

She ducked inside, and he hesitated. Should he wait here for her gratitude or go back to the —

A fury of dark hair and flashing eyes sprang down from the wagon seat, landing in front of him. If the woman could kill by glower alone, he'd already be bleeding out on the dirt.

"I may not be the kind of woman you're used to, Mr. Dubois, but I am *not* that kind." She whirled, the thick coil of her braid once again whipping his arm. Her feet pounded hard on the ground.

What in the name of God and country was she going on about? Couldn't she —

His breath hitched as her meaning sank teeth into his conscience. Did she think . . . ? He hadn't intended that at all.

He charged after her. "Thunder and turf! Rain is in the air. Most women would be happy to bed down in a dry space. I thought you would be pleased."

Her steps did not slow. "Stay away from me."

Instantly Matthew was in front of him, a deadly set to his jaw. "Is there a problem?"

"Yes!" Elias threw out his hands. "By the name of Mercy Lytton."

Matthew glanced over his shoulder to where Mercy whumped onto the ground, her back to both of them. Then he quirked a brow at Elias.

Elias stifled a growl. Somehow being locked in that stinking storage shed with shackles on his wrists seemed preferable to this drama. "All I did was make a dry spot for her to bed down. Alone. Nothing more. I swear it."

A slow smile spread on Matthew's face, then he tugged Elias's sleeve, leading him out of earshot of Mercy. Matthew's gray eyes, black now in the dark of night, peered into his.

"A word of advice. Mercy can't be prodded. She can be led, but only if she trusts the leader. You ain't earned that trust yet, and with what she knows of you, it might take a long time. A very long time. Same goes for me. While I appreciate your hard work today and that you have not tried to run off, just know that I've got my eye on you."

Elias blew out a breath, long and low, easing some of the tension but not all. Were the tables turned, he'd feel the same way. "Point taken."

"Good." Matthew turned to go but then doubled back. A peculiar glint in his gaze

— like that of a freshly sharpened blade —
cut through the darkness. "One more thing.
You ever try to touch that woman, and she
doesn't finish you off first, I will kill you."

CHAPTER 6

Rain tapped a tattoo against the canvas, trapping Mercy in the foggy world of awake-yet-not. Though the patter did its best to lull her back to sleep, she forced her eyes open. The soft light of a morning yet to come washed everything gray. For a moment she lay there, blinking, thankful she'd taken Elias up on his offer of dry bedding — though in the end it had been Matthew's words that had persuaded her. Yawning, she pushed up, the scent of Elias Dubois's coat still thick in her nose, peppery and smoky. A manly smell — one she did not wish to know so intimately. She snatched up his hunting frock and climbed out of the wagon.

Outside, water dripped everywhere. Heaven's tears, weeping life into the earth, made everything soggy. At least it wasn't snow. While not likely, a final strike of winter wasn't out of the realm of possibility.

Thick snores cleaved the predawn, tearing

out from inside the other wagon. It must be Rufus, for Matthew had taken the final night watch. Ahead, Elias stood with his back toward her, fingers busy checking harness buckles on the horses. The linen fabric of his shirt stretched tight across his broad shoulders.

She advanced toward him with his coat outstretched. He had to be miserable without it, though the gleam in his blue eyes as she approached did not hint at such. In fact, he looked all the more rugged and thriving without it. She pressed her lips tight to keep from an openmouthed stare. The man was an enigma. Once she'd gotten over the fact that he'd meant no ill intent by making her a cozy shelter, she truly had been thankful. Not even Matthew would've provided in such a personal way. Why had Elias Dubois?

Elias nodded, the hair unprotected by his hat wet and curling at the ends. "Good morning."

"Morning. I think you will be needing this today." She thrust the hunting frock into his hands.

He grunted then proceeded to shove his arms into the sleeves. "I trust you slept well."

"I trust you did not," she shot back, but she added a half smile to soften her banter.

Tying his belt, he said nothing, yet the smirk on his lips acknowledged her attempt at levity.

Though the rain was light, the dampness of it soaked into her bones, and she removed her shawl from her shoulders to resettle it over her head as a mantle. She should've thought to grab her hat. "Thank you, for the shelter last night, I mean. I . . ."

Her words stalled as his gaze locked onto hers. The same queer rush of heat fired inside her from heart to belly like when she'd gripped his hand the night before. It was a new feeling, unexpected — and completely uninvited. What kind of magic did the man wield?

She forced the rest of her words out in a rush. "I appreciate your sacrifice."

With his forefinger and thumb, he ran his fingers along the brim of his hat, flicking off the water dripping onto his face. Then he jutted his chin toward the wagon where the next loud snore ripped through the air. "I have suffered worse than Bragg's wood sawing."

She cocked a brow. "And his stench?"

For a single, breath-stealing moment — and quite against her better judgment — she shared a grin with Elias Dubois.

He turned and pointed at a mug sitting

on a rock, a flat biscuit atop it. "There is a cup of chicory and a square of hardtack, rain-softened by now. I figured you could eat on the road. We should head out."

Her smile flattened. Ought she be cross that the man had thought her incapable of keeping herself fed — or flattered that he'd set aside food for her? If she had to think this hard on every odd thing he did, she'd be addle-brained by the time they reached Fort Edward.

Pushing aside a pine bough, Matthew strode in from the cover of the woods and eyed them both. "We ready? Besides Rufus, that is. A nudge with a gun barrel will get him moving fast enough."

She flung the loose edge of her shawl over her shoulder, securing the fabric snug against her head for a venture into the woods. "I will be, after a moment. Go on ahead. Elias and I will catch up."

She pushed her way into the damp green of the New York wilds, breathing in the pungent odor of wet dirt and bloodroot crushed beneath her step. All the stress of the past few days seeped away the farther she ventured. This was home, this maze of trees and rock. A place where she was master, where the only one she had to be sure about was herself.

Surveying from trunk to trunk, she set a course for a private spot to answer morning's call. With a last look around, she squatted, unwilling to admit the convenience of a skirt for such a purpose. Breeches were nice for running, but cumbersome when it came to other necessities.

After a moment, she stood. She ought to rush back, but the pull of creation tempted too strongly. Closing her eyes, she gave in to the luxury of inhaling a few breaths of peace and moist moss. Soon this journey would be over, and she would return to . . . what? With Matthew wanting to settle, she'd be alone. No one would hire a woman to scout on her own. It was a shaky future, as uncertain as chaff caught by the wind. Where she'd land was —

Her eyes shot open. She froze, still as death, for her life might depend upon it. Senses heightened, she scanned the area. She should've thought to grab her gun, but the blue gaze and kindly manner of Elias Dubois had scrambled her normal thinking. How foolish.

Around her, rain tapped the same as always. Rivulets whooshed from rock to rock where the ground drank no more. The only movement was that of freshly sprouted leaves bending from the steady beat of droplets. At ground level, trillium quivered from the constant pelting. Nothing else moved.

Even so, she pulled out the knife she wore against her chest. Something wasn't right.

She sniffed, hoping to catch the scent of whatever it was that bristled the fine hairs at the base of her neck. She breathed in the same zesty aroma of a wet March morning — but this time something more muddied the air.

The rank tang of bear grease.

She whirled, knife raised.

And two eyes — darker than her own — stared into her soul.

Elias glanced over his shoulder from his perch on the wagon seat, studying the trees yet again. No buff-colored skirts broke the green monotony — and that rankled him. It had been too long since Mercy had hied herself into the woods to take care of her morning business. The grind and suck of Matthew's wagon wheels were nothing but a memory by now. Maybe that stew from last night hadn't set well in the woman's belly.

Or maybe she had met with trouble.

He swung down to the ground, heels sinking into the soft earth. Thunderation! What he wouldn't give for a gun to grip.

Following the route of flattened greenery, he worked his way into the woods. Every so often he spotted a small footprint pressed into the mud. Only one set of prints though. No other humans or animals. He thought about calling softly for her, so as not to startle her if she really were just doubled over with cramps or such. The ways of women were and always would be a mystery.

But he changed his mind as he scented a faint whiff of bear grease. Alert to the slightest sounds, he crept onward, bent low, one thought burning white hot: *Kill or be killed.*

Oh God, for Mercy's sake, let me find her before it is too late.

Twenty yards farther he stopped and molded his body against a black-trunked hemlock. Ten paces to his left, Mercy stared wide-eyed at a mountain of an Indian, her face stricken. One swipe of the man's massive hand could split her skull. Yet she stood still and straight, God bless her, neither wilting nor swooning.

Elias's blood ran colder than the rain trickling in between collar and skin. He'd have to move fast and quiet, a panther on the prowl.

Step by step, drawing on all his experience of shadow walking, he advanced, edging in behind the warrior. Two paces more and he'd snap the man's neck — a sorry sight for Mercy to have to witness, but better the man's life than hers.

Her eyes widened, as did her mouth. "No!"

Elias lunged. Too late. The man had turned. Elias's grip slid into a mere chokehold. Blast! The man's feet scrabbled for purchase on the slick ground as he clawed at Elias's arm.

Elias choked all the tighter — until his own feet slipped.

They whumped to mud and rock, tumbling in a death roll. Whoever landed on top would hold the advantage. If he died here, what would become of Mercy?

Lord, give me strength.

With a feral growl, he tore into the Indian, riding atop him. His fist crunched into the man's nose and sank into cartilage, splitting his knuckles.

"Enough!" Mercy screamed. "I know this man!"

The words stung, making no more sense than the drone of hornets, nor did the following guttural language she spewed. For a single startled moment, he pulled back, hand still clenched and ready to strike. Was this some kind of foul trick?

The big man shoved him off and stood. Turning aside, he spit out a mouthful of blood.

Elias rose on jittery legs, the drive to fight still flexing each of his muscles. Keeping one eye on the Indian, he spoke to Mercy. "Are you all right?"

"Of course I'm all right." She threw out her hands. "Onontio is my brother."

Brother? He eyed her warily. "You are not in danger?"

She frowned. "I am not some fair maiden in need of saving, especially not from that one." She tipped her chin at the big man.

Words flew between Mercy and her supposed brother, and Elias tried to read their body language, so foreign were the words. Of only two things he was certain — they definitely knew one another, and the man was a Mohawk.

As if reading Elias's mind, the brute turned a savage glower toward him.

Mercy laughed.

Elias shot his gaze to her. "What did he say?"

"He says for one so small, you hit like a fallen boulder."

"Small!" His hands clenched once again.

Mercy shrugged. "To Onontio everyone is small."

The man's eyes flashed back to hers. Despite her claim of kinship, there was nothing alike about them. He was night to her day, beast to her feline sleekness. More words passed between them until each held up a hand.

"*Ó:nen k› wáhi,* Onontio." Her farewell was plain enough to understand.

"Ó:nen k› wáhi, Kahente." The big man gave the slightest of nods, then stalked off into the woods.

Kahente? Was that her native name?

Mercy turned on her heel and strode back toward the wagon, not pausing a step as she called over her shoulder, "We should make haste."

Elias caught up to her and grabbed her arm, pulling her back. "Hold on. You cannot expect me to let this pass without first telling me what is going on."

A crescent dimple curved like a small frown on her chin. "Onontio" — she glanced at the man's retreating form — "is my half brother. He came to warn me — us — there are signs the Wyandot are on the move. The sooner we make Fort Edward, the better . . . unless you prefer to meet up with your French allies?"

Elias huffed out a low breath, spent and weary. He'd been at this duplicitous game far too long. He could more than hold his own with the Wyandot, but the woman in front of him and the ranger he was coming to respect wouldn't stand a chance. As for Rufus, well . . . better not to wish so horrific an end even to such a slackard.

He pulled back his hand and flexed his sore fingers. "You are right — it is best we move on."

Her brow raised with a flicker of skepticism, but she turned and trod through the wet woods on feet as silent as his.

He guarded her back the whole way, but each empty-handed step was a grim reminder that should a war party cross their path, he was no match unarmed. "I would be a lot more help to you and everyone if you would just give me a gun," he muttered.

"You could be a lot more dangerous too." She reached for the wagon seat and hefted herself up.

He snorted. "As dangerous as a Wyandot bent on a killing rage? You have no idea."

The woman blinked down at him. "And you do?"

He shook his head, fighting back memories of slaughter and carnage. He'd seen things, done things, no woman or man should ever have to witness, all for the call of duty. Sickened, he felt his gut twist. Save for God's grace, he'd still be such a monster.

Mercy bent down toward him. "I'm not afraid of Wyandots, Mr. Dubois. Nor am I afraid of you."

"Maybe you should be." He lowered his voice. "Because if killing any of you were what I was about, I would have done it by now."

He stomped to the other side of the wagon. If what her half brother had warned was true, they had best get a move on, for the Wyandots were ruthless killers.

A fact he knew far better than most, for he'd learned his skills from them.

Chapter 7

Five days of solid rain — and as many wet nights — yet still no sign of the danger On-ontio had warned about. Mercy tugged the brim of her old felt hat lower, glad she'd brought it along. Though they had not run into any Wyandot thus far, she'd rest easier once they made Fort Edward.

"Cursed weather," she mumbled.

On the wagon seat next to her, Elias angled his head, moisture collecting like tiny diamonds on the ends of his beard. "There is no shame riding inside, especially after scouting in the rain. Go dry off."

She shook her head. " 'Tisn't that. It's just such blessed slow going. We won't reach the fort in two weeks. We've traveled six days already and aren't near to a third of the way there."

"You tired of my company?" He flashed an easy grin.

Too easy. Must the man be as bountiful in

87

his humor as he was in good looks? And therein lay the problem — she *wasn't* tired of his presence, and in fact was beginning to develop an unhealthy appetite for it. She turned her face before he could read the truth warming her cheeks. Despite his claim of latent violence, Elias Dubois was far too good-natured.

"So tell me." His voice rumbled along with the wagon wheels. "What does it mean? Your name, that is."

The query tangled into snarls as thick as those she brushed from her hair each night. "You bow your head over meals and betimes steal off to bend your knee, and yet you ask me such a question? Clearly you know the meaning of mercy and believe in a God who grants it, elsewise you'd not go to so much trouble."

"Trouble?" His brows shot high. "Nay. 'Tis a privilege. An honor. Why is it you sound as if belief in such a God is a struggle?"

"I never said that." She tucked her chin, shrinking from the uncomfortable turn of conversation. It wasn't that she did not believe a merciful God existed, for truly, was not the first cry of a newborn babe or the way the mists rose on a summer morn proof enough? No, indeed. God was real, as close as the breath filling her lungs.

She just wasn't sure she could trust Him. Her mother's faith in a merciful God surely hadn't protected her. Absently, she reached up and fingered the locket through the fabric of her gown.

Elias clicked his tongue and slapped the reins, urging the horses through a slick of mud. "What I meant was your people's name — Kahente. I have been thinking on all the Mohawk words I know, which admittedly are few, and I cannot square it."

She clenched her jaw to keep from dropping her mouth. No sense letting the man know how often he surprised her, for that would only encourage him. "You speak Kanien'keha?"

"Just enough to get me killed." His white teeth flashed in the gloom of the day.

A smirk twisted her lips. That he knew any of the people's language warmed her heart in a strange way — though she'd not admit it aloud. "*Kahente* means 'before her time.'"

Rows of furrows marred his brow, but he did not prod her any further. Obviously the man's curiosity was as insatiable as her own, yet he shied away from forcing the matter.

She hid a smile, her esteem for him growing. "There's not much to it, really. I merely did not wait the nine moons to leave my mother's womb, but came at seven."

"A credible explanation." He flicked the reins, snapping the horses into a faster pace. "But I think whoever gave you that name had much more in mind."

How could he know what thoughts Black-Fox-Running had pieced together those many years ago? She studied Elias's profile as he drove, looking for some hint of what he meant. His strong-cut jaw did not so much as twitch, nor did he look at her. Was he baiting her for the sheer sport of it, or did he truly have another thought on the matter?

"What do you mean?"

"You speak your mind without pausing to listen to reason. You don't wait for danger to pass but run headlong after it. So in those respects, I would say you are before your time, for there's nothing patient about you." He slipped his gaze her way. "Kahente."

The anger that had been building from his stinging assessment melted away with the heat of his gaze. Her native name flowed so easily from his lips, she couldn't help but stare. His was a fine mouth. Wide and strong. Thick and full. What would it feel like to —

She jerked her face forward. So many

queer feelings churned inside her belly that she had to be some kind of sick. What was wrong with her? Maybe a visit to a healer ought to be her first order of business when they did make the fort. Likely she had tick fever or some other such ailment.

"Who gave you the name?" he asked.

She frowned. Maybe she should have taken his suggestion and crawled back beneath the canvas, for he was getting far too comfortable with conversation.

"My father." She pressed her mouth shut. That was all she'd offer, no matter what inquiries followed.

But no more questions came. The wagon rattled along on slickened weeds. Rain fell slow and steady.

And blending with it all came the bass murmur of Elias's voice. "So your mother must be white . . . which explains a lot."

She cocked her head. What did this stranger think he knew of her? "Such as?"

"Your ability to speak two languages. Your ease among the British and their acceptance of you. Your uncommon knowledge of this land." He faced her head-on. "Your beauty."

"Beauty?" She flung the word back at him as a surge of anger shot through her. She'd heard that before, usually followed by an unsolicited touch. Why was it that once a man discovered her mixed heritage, he suddenly thought her easy prey?

She narrowed her eyes. "Better men than you have mocked me, Elias Dubois, only to find themselves flat on the ground."

"Oh, I assure you, Miss Lytton, I meant every word."

She went back to scanning the road. Better that than natter nonsense with a man who had an answer for everything.

Far in the distance, shapes thickened on the road. Scooting to the edge of her seat, she grabbed the wagon's side for balance and peered ahead through the wet veil. One by one she shut down all other senses save for sight. The slog of the wheels faded. The creak of leather and jingling tack disappeared. The jarring ride on the hard seat vanished as she focused far down the trail, beyond what should be seen.

Breathe. Breathe.

And there . . . rocks. Lots of them. A pile of stones had slid onto the road, blocking the route.

"There's a problem ahead." Her own voice pulled her from the trance.

Elias frowned at her, then narrowed his eyes into the distance. "I see nothing."

"You will."

With his free hand, he rubbed his eyes,

then leaned forward and rescanned the trail. "No, nothing . . . or maybe . . ."

The wagon rolled along until the undeniable shape of a mound of jagged rocks came into view. It appeared to be a rockslide, the rubble having fallen from a steep bank on one side of the road. With so much rain, it was no wonder. But even so, she snatched up her gun and loaded the pan.

Elias pulled back on the reins and set the brake. He scanned the area as well, but breathed out in a whisper, "How did you see that?"

Was that awe or accusation roughening his voice? Not that she could answer, for she'd never come up with a suitable way to explain her keen sight even to herself. So she didn't bother. Her gift was as much a part of her as her hands or arms — and she never had to explain those away.

Hefting her leg over the side of the wagon, she scrambled down to the wet earth and probed the immediate area. On the other side, Elias did the same.

In time, Matthew's low, "Whoa," and the snort of his horses caught up. By now, both she and Elias had met and stopped at the edge of a four-foot-high pile of rocks, wide enough to lay five bodies head to toe across. She could feel the gaze of Elias's blue eyes hitting between her shoulder blades, but she did not turn, not even when he joined her side and asked her again how she'd seen the rockslide from so far back.

Matthew's footsteps tromped up to settle on the other side of her. A low whistle passed his lips. "This journey is cursed."

Rufus skittered up next to Elias, then bent and hefted one of the fallen rocks with his own curse. He lobbed the chunk of granite with another profanity.

In spite of the rain, Elias yanked off his hat and ran his fingers through his hair. "It appears Rufus has the right idea."

Mercy gawked at him. "We're to stand here and curse the rocks away?"

"No." He reset his hat and turned to her. "We will heft them out one by one."

Matthew hissed through his teeth. "There goes the rest of the day."

Mercy frowned. The thought of wasting more time pinched tighter than the stays digging into her ribs. If they backtracked to Megrith Crossing and headed west, they would meet up with a passage just wide enough to accommodate their wagons, a trail riding on higher ground — ground not littered with a ton of rock.

She peered at Elias from beneath her hat brim. Would he listen this time? "I know another way. 'Tis a little narrow, but it'll do." She swung about to face Matthew. "What say you?"

Matthew looked past her to Elias. Some kind of manly conversation took place, but hard to tell what with naught but a grunt and a half shrug from either of them.

Rufus hefted another rock. "Listen to the half-breed, she oughta know —"

Elias moved so fast, air rushed past Mercy's cheek. He grabbed Rufus by the collar and hoisted him up, letting his gawky body dangle like a shirt pegged on a line. Rufus's face purpled to an ugly shade of dark, his feet kicking and his hands clawing at Elias's arm.

"Her name is Mercy — and I will have none of the sort for you the next time you call her otherwise." Elias's tone was deadly flat. For a breathless eternity, he held Rufus aloft; then his fingers splayed.

Rufus dropped. Gasping and rasping, he staggered like a soldier on leave.

Mercy glanced at Matthew to gauge his reaction, for she wasn't sure what to make of it. He said nothing, but his lips twisted into a wry smile.

Bypassing Rufus, Elias strode toward the wagon and called over his shoulder, "Remount. This time we will try Mercy's way."

It took all of Elias's resolve not to gape at the woman next to him as he urged the horses back to plod through the same mud slick they had slogged across before. He often marveled at God's great wonders. The pounding rush of spray at the bottom of a waterfall. A spiderweb dazzling silver in dawn's breaking light. The sacrifice of a mother's heart. But Mercy Lytton took his astonishment to a whole new level. His eyesight was keen — enough to shoot a lead ball through the eye of a raven in full flight at five rods off. Yet he hadn't seen that rockslide until a fair sight after Mercy spied it, and he couldn't fathom how she did.

Nor did he like it.

"There." She lifted a slim finger and pointed. "Just past that stand of sugar maples."

He slowed the horses as they neared the spot. Green growth, thick and wild from the rain, tangled as high as the horses' shoulders, in some places near to touching their withers. Easing back on the reins, he quirked a brow at her. "That is a road?"

She jutted her chin, eyes dark and unreadable beneath the brim of her hat. "I did not say it would be easy."

And it wasn't. Turning at such a sharp angle from a trail not much wider than the wagons was a miracle. Coaxing the horses to pull at an even speed so as not to foul the wheels with grabber-vine was another. But it wasn't until the trail took off up a steep incline that the truth of her words sank in like claws.

She was right. There was nothing easy about this.

Sweat beaded on his brow as he yelled, "Hyah!" then whistled through his teeth, calling upon every trick he knew to keep the horses plodding upward. If they stopped now, the weight of the cargo could yank them backward — right into Matthew's oncoming wagon. Picking rock would've been less work than this. To her credit, Mercy remained silent, leaning forward as if to will the horses onward.

By the time the trail leveled, sweat ran as freely as the rain on his skin from the toil of it. Once he cleared enough space for Matthew's wagon to rest behind, he stopped to breathe.

Reaching back, he massaged a cramp in his shoulder, knotted into a rock-hard bulge from the strain. "Well, that was some ride."

"Yet you managed it."

"Aye. Barely." He lowered his fingers, a half smile curving his lips. "Next time remind me to ask if there are any mountains involved."

"Oh, well . . ." White teeth nibbled her bottom lip, far too beguiling for a bone-weary moment such as this. She lifted one hand and pulled out a locket from beneath her bodice, then clutched it like some kind of amulet. He'd seen her do it several times throughout their journey. Clearly the thing gave her some kind of assurance . . . but for what?

"That wasn't the hard part," she mumbled.

His smile faded. "What do you mean?"

"This ridgeline runs about a half mile beyond that next bend."

He blew out a sigh. "And I suppose the decline will be just as treacherous."

"Not so much." Her coil of hair unraveled lopsided beneath her hat, and she tugged the long braid free of the felt, shifting it to trail down her back. "The slope is gentler going down, and it empties onto the trail we were on, bypassing that rockslide."

He scratched his jaw, his fingers rasping against a week's worth of stubble. Trying to track the logic of Mercy's words was sometimes as twisted as the trails they journeyed.

"Then what is so hard about it?"

Footsteps tromped from behind, and Matthew's grizzled face appeared on Mercy's side of the wagon. He glowered up at her. "Blazing fires, girl! Don't tell me you just led us up to Traverse Ridge."

She stared straight ahead, as if the man were nothing more than a passing shadow. "We'd hardly be through a quarter of that rock pile if we'd stayed, and you know it."

"Traverse Ridge?" Elias repeated, hoping the voicing of it would shake loose some memory connected with the name.

A growl percolated in Matthew's chest. "Nothing to be done for it now. We sure as spit can't go back the way we came." His gray eyes burned into Elias's. "Take it slow, but keep moving, no matter what. Just keep moving."

He strode away before Elias could query him further. Mercy refused to meet his questioning gaze.

He gathered the reins and edged the horses forward. The trail was wide enough for the wagon before it dropped off to a maze of tree spires below. Surely Matthew did not think this was dangerous after what they had already ascended? Perhaps age had made him overcautious. Lord knew the older Grandfather got, the more he'd placed restrictions on him as a young boy. It seemed elders were ever skittish about taking risks.

But then the path curved, following the bend of the rise, and he sucked in a breath.

Ahead, the road continued straight and narrow, but at such an angle that all the weight of two tons of gold would be laid into the outer-edge wheels. If the load shifted or one of the spokes cracked from the pressure, there'd be no stopping a tumble down the steep drop of rock and trees. He scrubbed a hand over his face. He'd have to keep them in one piece for a whole half mile? A groan rumbled deep in his throat, mimicking Matthew's. No wonder the man had been so chary.

Holding a taut rein, Elias restrained the horses to a sluggish yet steady pace. Too fast and those wheels would snap like kindling. Mercy grabbed the side of the wagon to keep from falling out. At least the rain had let up some. A gift, that, but it did not make the wet ground any less slippery. If he lost this load now, more than just their lives would be at stake.

God, please.

Foot by foot, the wagon creaked along, so cattywampus that he and Mercy leaned hard to the left. The horses balked at the grade and weight of the wagon tongue pressing against their collars, but Elias held strong, never letting up on the steely tension of the reins.

Rocks plummeted, knocked loose from their passage. With the ground so saturated, no wonder that slide had let loose. The crash of granite chunks jarred like thunder as they collided with tree trunks, then rumbled off. An eerie sound. Like the breaking of bones — their bones if he gave in to his shaking forearms.

At last the road flattened. As much as he wanted to jump down and see how Matthew fared, there was no time, for the descent began as soon as the rear wheel evened out.

As Mercy claimed, the decline wasn't as extreme, but it made for perilous going nonetheless. By the time they finally met with the original road, his ribs ached from strained breathing.

Pulling far enough ahead for Matthew's wagon to clear the flattened trail, he halted the horses. Heart racing, he sank back against the canvas and closed his eyes, every muscle jittery.

"Well done." Mercy's words were quiet.

An offering, he supposed.

He glanced at her — and couldn't help

but smile. Any other woman would be pale-faced and wide-eyed after that trek. Mercy's cheeks glowed pink, her brown gaze bright, as if her existence hadn't just depended on the strip of leather in his hands that he'd gripped for dear life.

"You just might be the death of me, Mercy Lytton."

He swung down to solid ground before she could reply and stalked over to her side of the wagon. Bending, he studied one wheel, shaking it to see how the spokes fared, then did the same with the others, praying the whole while he'd not see a problem.

But God was good. The spokes held true.

He strode to where Matthew squatted near his own back wheel, Rufus at his side, swearing down brimstone and damnation on them all for putting him through such a dangerous ride.

Matthew looked up at Elias's approach, his face as dark as the thickening black sky. "This wagon's not as stout as yours. One more trail like that, and these spokes will give way."

CHAPTER 8

Mercy rolled one way, then the other, seeking comfort where none would be found — certainly not on a bunched-up blanket laid on damp dirt. With a huff, she flipped onto her back, lying flat and staring up at the darkened cave ceiling. Finding this cavern had been a boon in the downpour, and she was thankful. Still . . . she flipped to her stomach. Guilt stole all the peace out of that gratitude.

Though neither Matthew nor Elias had disparaged her for their perilous trek along Traverse Ridge, Rufus had — when out of earshot of the other men. But he needn't have wasted his breath. Ever since she'd learned of Matthew's weakened wheel, she'd been flaying herself mentally. Sleep wouldn't come to call when such an intrusive visitor occupied her mind.

With a huff, she scooted over to what remained of the fire. On the side nearest the cave opening, Matthew stretched out on the ground, hat over his face and chest rising at an even pace. Rufus was gone — out on watch. On the other side, Elias sat cross-legged, the smoldering mound of embers casting a glow on his face. He looked like a god forged from the flames. Only his eyes acknowledged her approach.

She sat opposite him, pulling her shawl tighter at her neck. Not much warmth radiated from the dying fire, so she grabbed a stick and poked it, coaxing a few licks of red to life. All the while the man's gaze asked questions she did not want to answer — so she avoided looking up.

"Can't sleep," she explained quietly.

"There is no rain."

She quirked her head, listening. The shushing drone outside had ceased, replaced by stray drips looking for a home.

Elias's lips curved. "There is no pattering to lull you to sleep."

Would that were the only reason. A sigh emptied the air from her lungs, and she went back to poking at the fire. "No, 'tisn't that. I want to apologize for taking us up that ridge today. I did not consider the weight of the cargo. I could have gotten us killed."

"Well." His soft voice curled around her

like smoke. "No real harm done. And we did make good time, better than if we had moved those rocks. That would have set us back a whole day."

A more than gracious response — but suspect. Ought not a criminal facing years in jail drag his heels instead of running into such a destiny?

Lifting her face, she studied the man. He sat so calmly still one would think him at peace with the universe. But how could that be, when he yet faced charges of sedition? And why had such an outwardly peaceful man decided to take up treachery to begin with? Was he a traitor of convenience, or did he do it for mere capital gain? Or perhaps his principles ran deeper and he was somehow proud to serve time for an action of conviction?

So many questions swirled in her head that she couldn't stop at least one of them from leaking out. "Why are you so bent on reaching the fort? You will be locked up, likely for years on end. There's no guarantee you will survive it."

Elias's blue eyes glimmered with some kind of knowledge, something she couldn't understand. He knew things of darkness and beyond, of blood and honor — which made her all the more curious.

She threw aside her poking stick. "Why did you trade loyalties in the middle of a fight? What made you turn?"

A muscle jumped in his neck, and he lowered his chin, hiding his face in the shadow of his hat. He was silent for so long, the drippings outside faded away.

She folded into her shawl, prepared to wait him out. She'd sat in more rugged conditions than this while holing up on a scouting mission.

Eventually, his low voice purled soft. "You are inquisitive tonight."

Obstinate man. Her lips pursed into a pout. If he thought to make her stray from her line of questioning, he'd be sorely disappointed. "And you're full of silence — a technique better used on army interrogators, not me. I have nowhere else to go and nothing else to do but wait for you to answer."

"Has anyone ever told you that you are a stubborn woman?" His tone changed, dark and cold as the cave. He leaned close to the fire, light riding the strong planes of his face.

She tensed at the formidable sight, both attracted and repelled, yet met him stare for stare. "Aye. I believe you have mentioned it a time or two."

He snorted. "What is it you really want to

know, Mercy Lytton?" His query dangled like a rope from a gibbet. "Think carefully, for I shall only answer one question tonight."

"Why did you defend me against Rufus earlier today?" The words barreled out before she could stop them, and she bit her lip. Where on earth had that come from?

"Of all the . . . ?" Rearing back, he shook his head. Astonishment smoothed out the road-weariness from his face, making him appear as a wonder-eyed boy. "You never stop surprising me."

She squirmed, warmth spreading up her neck and onto her cheeks like a rash.

But just as suddenly, his jaw tightened and a storm cloud gathered on his face. "Men like Rufus are too ignorant to see who you really are."

She swallowed, afraid to speak, afraid not to. "Who do you think I am?"

"A beautiful creation of God."

His words were pleasing to the ear, but it was the reverent way he stared at her that became embedded deep in her heart. He meant what he said, but more than that, he knew what he said was as true as if God had come down and spoken to him alone. A staggering thought, one that stole her breath.

"You really know Him, don't you?" she whispered.

He nodded. "I do — and you can too."

She stiffened, the turn of conversation feeling like stays yanked too tight. This was too intimate to even think of, let alone talk about with a man. "I think I shall retire now."

His teeth flashed a knowing grin. "See you come morning then."

She scooted back to her corner of the cave, more painfully awake now than when she'd first left it. Flinging herself down to her blanket, she faced away from Elias Dubois.

How could she both love and hate the way someone made her feel?

Elias watched Mercy edge away from the fire, her pale skirts light against the darkness of the cave. She was a ghost in the darkness, one who would surely haunt his thoughts for the rest of the night.

He stared into the embers long after she disappeared, listening to the rhythm of Matthew's breathing and the rising chorus of insects outside. Ah, but the woman was spirited, an even match to his own willfulness. A slow smile lifted his lips. And if he were right, if she truly were like him, she had no idea of the fire about to blaze down and refine her.

He glanced up at the jagged ceiling. "So . . . You are working on her, eh, God? She could use it." Huffing out a breath, he bowed his head. "And so could I. Lord, make us both pleasing in Your sight."

The tromp of Rufus's feet drew near outside and pulled him from his prayer. He met the young man just outside the cave opening on a slick of gravel and mud.

Rufus eyed him as he might a wolf that could spring. Good. The young upstart needed his anger tethered to a taut rein — and Elias was more than happy to be the one to hold it. Scrubbing a hand along his jaw, he masked a grin. Rufus Bragg reminded him entirely too much of himself at that age. Would to God someone had kept him in line — not that Grandfather hadn't tried.

He tipped his head at the young man. "No sign of anything?"

Rufus stopped just out of reach and widened his stance, likely a show of power — but it did not work. The young man's knobby-framed body would break like a November twig were Elias to charge him.

A sneer curled Rufus's upper lip. "Nothing to worry your pretty head over."

The mockery hung in the damp air, and Elias left it right there, hovering. "Listen, Rufus, this is going to be a long journey if we do not work together."

Faster than he thought possible, Rufus swung up the muzzle of his Brown Bess, aiming square at him. From this range, a hole through the chest would kill him on the spot.

"Yer right." Rufus cocked open the hammer, the click of metal loud in the woods. "I could just shoot you now to save us both the trouble."

"You could." He eyed the barrel, noting the steady hold. The boy knew how to handle a weapon, he'd give him that. "But who is going to drive that wagon? Mercy or you? The way I see it, neither of you could manage such a haul, not on your own."

With a flick of his chin, Rufus spit to the side. "You think you got all the answers, don't ya, Frenchie boy? What do you care if we manage to reach the fort or not?"

"I care not whatsoever." And he didn't. Mercy and the boy were right to question him, for he had no intention of letting that gold reach Fort Edward — leastwise not one crate in particular.

But what would the boy make of his answer? He stared into Rufus's eyes, survey-

110

ing his reaction. By the spare light of a sky now sprinkled with stars, it was still too dark to read with any accuracy what went on inside Rufus's head. Clearly the boy didn't see an unarmed man as a threat.

Elias threw back his shoulders, calling the boy's bluff. "Go on then, pull the trigger. You will be doing me a favor."

Once the challenge passed his lips, Elias sharpened his whole body into stillness, for his life teetered on the thin line of Rufus's integrity — if the boy had any. It would be a shameful way to go, breathing his last from the shot of an angst-filled boy-man. But at least he knew where he'd go, for he'd made his peace with God nigh on two years back. If only he could have settled things with Grandfather, a regret he'd take with him to the grave.

The boy stood fixed — the kind of rock-hard bearing only a seasoned killer would dare. Apparently Rufus had taken life before. Many, judging by his deadpan gaze.

Sweat beaded on Elias's brow. For the first time the thought crossed his mind that perhaps he had risked too much.

Metal clicked. The gun lowered. Elias let out a breath.

"You ain't worth my lead," Rufus hissed through his teeth, then turned and strode into the cave.

Once the boy was out of sight, Elias's shoulders sagged. His life had been spared. Again. Clearly it was God's will his delivery made it to Boston.

Nonetheless, it would be difficult with Rufus begging for a fight every blessed minute. A sigh deflated him, and he glanced at the sky. *How am I to do this, Lord, without bloodshed?*

CHAPTER 9

Bumping along in the wagon, Mercy lifted her face to the sun, strangely content after a night filled with dreams of a questioning blue-eyed man and a God who spoke to him face-to-face. She pulled off her hat and closed her eyes, soaking in the spring warmth. Tree silhouettes splotched black against the orange background, and she breathed in the freshness of the damp woods. By her reckoning, this was the finest first day of April since the year she'd surprised Black-Fox-Running with a basket full of wild garlic shoots. He'd praised her industry — but Mother had frowned. Her locket burned hot against her breast.

Mercy's eyes shot open. Better to face the present than live in a world of past hurts.

She gave in to the soothing sound of the wheels and the caress of a mild breeze, until loose hair tickled across her cheek. Working stray strands back into a braid that never stayed tight, she angled her head and listened. Something else pickabacked on that breeze. A shushing.

She peeked at Elias, only to find his gaze already studying her.

Despite the sunshine, his face darkened. "Did you not say the Nowadaga crossing was fair passable?"

"Usually."

His mouth drew into a grim line. "I have a feeling it is not going to be so fair this time around."

He faced forward, urging the horses toward the rushing sound. When the slope of the river came into sight, her own lips flattened.

Ahead, the Nowadaga overran its banks like a warrior gone mad with battle fever. The river was half again as wide as its usual spread.

Elias halted the horses with a low "Whoa." Behind them, Matthew did the same. Climbing down from the wagons, they all gathered on the bank — even Rufus. No one spoke. Not for a long time. Elias paced along the shore, blue eyes scanning from ripple to ripple. Mercy could only guess at his thoughts. Hers were a-tumble with danger, not for the depth of the water, but for the speed.

Eventually, Elias pulled his hat from his head and ran his fingers through his dark hair before slapping it back atop. "Daylight is wasting. We should get a move on."

Mercy reached for her locket. Surely he did not mean . . . "Don't tell me you're thinking of crossing this today?"

Elias looked down at her. "You have another back trail in mind?"

Swallowing the shame of yesterday, she averted her gaze. "No. The next ford is twenty miles off."

Matthew grunted. "I'm with Mercy. Crossing now ain't worth risking our load and our lives."

Rufus rolled out a string of curses —

Until Elias's dark glower ended the unraveling. "I've about had it with your vulgarities. Mind your tongue in front of a woman."

"She ain't no . . ." Whatever cutting remark Rufus had in mind ended when Elias took a step toward him.

"Nothing," Rufus mumbled and held up his hands. "I ain't saying nothin'."

Elias shifted his gaze to Mercy. "What do you know of this stretch of river? Any peculiarities?"

If she closed her eyes now, how many sweet memories would swell as strong as the rushing water? The glide of Onontio's canoe as she sat in the bow. The sting of December water on her fingers when dipping in a jar. The way autumn leaves bobbed. But that was farther up, near the headwaters, where the Kahnyen'kehàka camped.

She shrugged. "The Nowadaga is not usually deep. The current not strong. But I can't vouch for it while being this rain-heavy. I say we wait till it goes down some. A day. Two at most."

"No." The combined voices of Elias and Rufus thundered louder than the river.

Elias frowned at them all. "The longer we stay in one place, the higher our chances of ambush."

"Fair enough." Matthew rubbed his hand along the back of his neck. "And you, Rufus? Why you so breeches-afire to cross?"

Red spread over the young man's face like a bruise, his eyes narrowing. "Tired of yer company. Sooner we make the fort, sooner I'm done with you all."

Mercy held her breath. One of these times Elias or Matthew would be done with Rufus's yapping and bite down hard.

But Elias ignored him and instead faced Matthew. "Are you up for testing the depths with me?"

Matthew nodded. "Aye."

They strode back into the tree line, hunting for a straight limb long enough to plot the best possible route through the river. Mercy yanked her bonnet back on, tired of the string tugging at her neck, tired of strong-bent men, and more than tired of this journey.

Rufus turned aside and spit. "That man of yours is crazy."

She'd sigh, but Rufus Bragg wasn't worth that much effort. "He is not my man."

"Yeah? I seen the way you look at him."

Her hands curled into fists. Whether she looked at Elias cross-eyed or doe-blinking, Rufus Bragg had no call to be watching her in the first place. "If a fight's what you're after, Rufus, then go get yourself a prodding stick and tussle with the river."

He spewed out another foul curse. "Not me. Those fools will get themselves washed downriver."

"Those men have more courage than you will ever know."

"You don't know nothing 'bout me." A queer gleam in his dark eyes streaked like lightning. Then he turned on his heel and stalked to the wagon.

By now Elias and Matthew stood at the river's edge, ten paces apart. On Elias's mark, they stepped in, water passing over their feet. Pace by pace, they worked their way into the rushing river.

Midway through, water swirling thigh high, Matthew stumbled.

Mercy strangled a cry. To scream might set Elias off-balance — and he had his own step to care for. Yet even in the midst of fast-flowing water licking against his legs, he remained stalwart, exuding an unearthly kind of peace.

Thankfully, Matthew shored himself up with his big stick, and Mercy started breathing once again.

They waded to the far shore then back, landing dripping wet from the legs down in front of her.

"Well?" she asked.

Matthew eyed Elias.

Who eyed him right back. "I say we give it a go."

"Could be worse, I suppose." Matthew leaned hard on his stick. "We have a fair shot at it if the horses don't spook."

"Then we will make sure they do not. If you and I walk along with the lead animal, calm and steady, there will be less of a chance for them to go rogue. Mercy and Rufus can mind the reins."

Biting her tongue, Mercy turned on her

heel and tromped back to the wagon, following Rufus's earlier route before she said something she'd regret.

This was a bad idea.

Elias hid a smile. Mercy hadn't said a word against his and Matthew's plan, but she didn't have to. The braid swishing at her back and furious swirl of her skirts said it all. Did she really think her silence wasn't shouting loud her opposition?

Hefting his stick onto one shoulder, he hurried after her. "Mercy, hold up."

She did not stop until she reached the wagon, and when she turned, he was glad he'd held on to the piece of wood, so lethal did her eyes spark in the afternoon sun.

"Just listen." He softened his voice. Iron against iron would only make for more sparks — a fact he wished he'd learned earlier in life. "Either we stand together, or we die together. If I did not think we owned a good chance of making a safe crossing, I would not ask this of you."

She tucked her chin like a bull about to charge. "The power of that water is more than we can fight. I saw Matthew stumble, and he is as sturdy as one of the horses. You have no idea —"

"Do not think to question me when it

comes to the wiles of a river." Anger surged a rush of blood to his head, his pulse beating loud in his ears. He knew better than anyone the vicious clout of water gone wild.

Slowly at first, memories began to rise, then flash-flooded him all at once. Jacques, Henri, Arnaud . . . and François, his one true friend. His throat closed, and for a moment, no words would pass. All brawny men — and all lost to unforgiving currents, pulled under by greed, pride, and, in the case of his friend François, ignorance.

He sucked in a ragged breath. "I have seen men die — *friends* die — from lack of respect for water. Believe me when I say I would not take such a risk if I did not think it possible. Trust me, I know whereof I speak."

Red flamed on her cheeks. "Why should I?"

The question punched him in the gut. Exactly. Why should she entrust her life to a man she thought was a traitor?

Even so, he dared a step closer. "I respect your mistrust of me, but know this . . ." He stared deep into her eyes, as if by virtue of will alone he could impress upon her the truth of his words. "I will not let harm come to you. I vow it."

She looked away, her eyes hidden in

shadow, obliterating any chance he might have of reading what went on in her mind. Did she believe him — or did she think he merely said what was necessary to get her to go along with him?

Eventually the hard line of her shoulders sagged, and she reached for her locket.

He pressed the advantage. "All you have to do is hold steady on the reins. I will do the rest. Mercy . . . please."

"Why?" She threw the question like a tomahawk. "Why is this so important to you?"

He clamped his jaw. Men's lives depended on his timely arrival in Boston — possibly the fate of an entire fort — but he couldn't tell her that. So he said nothing. Just stared her down, admiring and hating the pluck in Mercy Lytton.

"Pah!" She threw out her hands. "I can see there's no moving you. Stubborn *kaia'tákerahs*."

He couldn't stop the smile tugging at his lips — nor the words that followed. "I do not know what you just said, but it sure sounds pretty coming from your lips."

She whirled and reached for the wagon seat. Scrambling upward, she put as much space between them as possible.

His grin widened, but it did not last long.

Though that battle was over, an even bigger skirmish was about to ensue.

Craning his neck, he searched for Matthew. The man stood next to his lead horse, with Rufus holding the reins of the other wagon.

"Ready?" Elias shouted.

Matthew nodded. "Aye."

With a last glance at Mercy, Elias strode to the front of their team and grabbed hold of the headstall on the lead horse. He held the prodding stick in his other hand, ready to encourage a skittish mount or simply to use it for balance once in the water. "Onward!"

The first rush of water over his feet wasn't nearly as cold this time, for his skin was already clammy up to the top of his thighs. Pace by pace, the river rose higher, from ankle, to shin, to knee. Only once did the horse buck its head, but Elias kept his grip firm, letting the animal know he'd brook no nonsense. If the leader spooked, the rest would follow suit.

Halfway across, Elias's foot hit a hollow. He canted to the side, the rush of water yanking him from the team. He flung out his arm to counterbalance, desperately seeking a hold for his stick. No good. The current grabbed that too, and his legs shot out from beneath him. His grip on the headstall kept him afloat, yet he was no longer leading the team. The river led him.

And it was winning.

"Elias!" Fear shredded Mercy's voice.

Sensing the dilemma, the lead horse faltered a step. If the team stopped now, the river would gain the upper hand . . . and once those crates hit the water and broke open, there'd be no gaining back the weapon he'd taken such pains to transport this far.

There was nothing to be done for it then. *God, please give Mercy strength.*

"Keep going!" he yelled at her.

Then he let go.

The current dragged him along. With strong strokes, he fought against the pull, straining to swing his feet around. Careening headfirst down an unknown stretch of swollen river was never a good idea. His lungs burned with the effort. Gritty water slapped him in the face, filling his mouth and nose. He worked his way toward the shore, scraping and banging against rocks.

At last, the flow lessened, and his feet purchased a solid base. He shot up, some twenty yards downriver of the wagons, coughing and spluttering.

And when he caught his breath, he let out a big whoop.

Mercy, God bless her, laid into the horses and drove them right up the side of the bank. The rear wheels cleared the river, hauling up the load of crates to safety.

"Thank You, Lord," he breathed as he waded toward shore.

Matthew's wagon was at the halfway point now — but thankfully the man must've seen where he'd taken his fall, for the ranger led his team a hair more upriver. Smart man. Rufus's thin arms jutted out in front of him, reins wrapped tight in his hands.

Elias stopped in shin-deep water, watching the progression. To distract any of them now could mean the loss of the second wagon.

Little by little, Matthew advanced. His moccasins hit the bank. The first pair of horses cleared the water. The second pair. Elias held his breath. So close.

The first set of wheels rolled out of the river, slanting the wagon so that all the weight rested on the back two wheels.

And a crack split the air.

CHAPTER 10

Mercy eased back on the reins, bringing the horses to a slow stop. They deserved a rest. So did she. Every muscle in her arms jittered from the harrowing crossing.

Dropping her hands to her lap, she leaned back against the canvas and closed her eyes, just as she'd done before they had crossed the Nowadaga. The sun beat warmer, the air smelled sweeter. Life seemed less burdensome. Why was it that her gratitude heightened only after a vexing experience? How much peace did she miss out on by appreciating a rainbow instead of valuing the rain beforehand? Should she not thank God for both?

The questions chafed. She'd not thought this much about God in a long time, not since she'd left behind her childhood. And Mother. Mercy flexed her fingers, working out the last of her tension and fighting the urge to reach for her locket. Elias was far too much like her mother in his spirituality — yet there was nothing soft about him. Nothing cowardly. Maybe — just maybe — faith did not have to mean weakness.

A scream of horses ended her contemplations, followed by men's shouts. She set the brake and bolted from the wagon.

Dread pumped her legs as she tore back the way she'd come. Some kind of argument waged between Rufus and Elias, accompanied by the drone of Matthew, speaking calmly to squealing horses.

Her steps slowed as she descended the slope of the riverbank into chaos. Matthew held tight to the lead horse's headstall. The others snorted and strained at their harnesses, trying to break free. And she didn't blame them. Behind lay a cockeyed wagon, rear barely dragged out of the water and digging hard into the soft ground. Rufus had bailed from his seat and stood on the mucky bank, cussing at a half-drowned Elias.

She stopped, gaze fixed on the dislocated spokes — sticking out of the wheel weakened when they had taken Traverse Ridge. The peace of moments before vanished, replaced by a sickening twist in her belly.

This was her fault.

"Mercy!" Elias's voice shook through her,

and she yanked up her head.

He stood soaked to the skin beside Rufus near the rear of the wagon. "Grab the horses. We need Matthew to help haul these crates from the river."

Without a word, she walked in a daze over to Matthew, the image of the spokes askew and the curve of defeat in Elias's shoulders strong in her mind.

All Matthew's shushings and "Easy now" murmurings had stilled most of the madness in the horses. Either that or the animals had figured out they no longer lugged a scrape-bottom, off-kilter wagon up a hill. But whichever, Matthew didn't let go until she wrapped her fingers around the leather band on the lead horse's head.

She peered into Matthew's gray eyes. "Are you all right? No one's hurt, are they?"

He shook his head. "No, girl. Thank the good Lord. Keep a firm grip — on this horse and yourself. They take off running, you let go, you hear?"

Swallowing against the tightness in her throat, she nodded. If she'd never suggested that ridge shortcut, if she'd just kept her mouth shut, they wouldn't be in this sorry situation.

Most of the crates had been strewn along the bank when the horses charged off in a frenzy. One crate remained on the wagon bed. Only three of the ten had landed in the water, so it didn't take long for the men to lug them up to the muddy shore. Pots and pans, gold bars, and some opened packets of trade silver sparkled in the shallows, contents they would need to collect before nightfall. The rest of the flotsam was likely already a mile downstream, pulled by the current.

Stroking the velvety nose of the horse to soothe the beast and herself, she waited until the men caught their breath. "Now what?"

Matthew pulled off his hat and flicked the sweat from his brow with the back of his hand. "We'll have to unload the other wagon and bring it back down to collect as much of this mess as we can."

Elias nodded. "After we unload that, we will come back for the broken wagon."

Turning aside, Rufus spit on the ground, then jabbed his finger her way. "This is your doin'. We get a passel of Indians breathin' down our neck, you remember that."

In two strides, Elias planted himself between Rufus and her. "Leave off. This is your only warning."

But it was too late. Rufus's accusation heaped another coal onto the fire of her own guilt, the shame of which would burn for a very long time.

Matthew jammed his hat back atop his head. "You're doing a fine job with the horses, Mercy, so just stay here. We'll be back with an empty wagon to collect the rest."

The men stomped off, but Rufus's indictment stayed. He was right. If Onontio's warning held true and a band of Wyandot came along, they would be easy to find and too small in number to fight back. But what was to be done for it now? How could she possibly make the situation better?

Slowly, she released her hold of the bridle, cooing all the while. She inched from the horse, testing the skittishness of the leader, but by now they had all discovered the green shoots breaking up the ground in patches. The pull and chomp of well-earned provender played an accompaniment to the steady rhythm of the rushing water.

From this angle, she viewed more clearly the devastation where the land sloped into the river. Contents from the crates littered a wide swath of mud — and what contents they were! She'd already seen the household goods that had been stored in the top half of each crate, but she'd not imagined so much gold, so many packages of trade silver.

She couldn't begin to guess at the value. No wonder Elias and Matthew were so bent on getting this load to Fort Edward. If anyone discovered them with this much treasure, their throats would be slit before they could holler.

A shiver shimmied across her shoulders, and she forced her gaze to move on. Nearby, a fallen wooden box wasn't too damaged, though it was mostly empty. If she dragged it down to the water's edge, she could at least begin collecting what had spilled.

Treading on light feet so as not to scare the horses, she picked her way down the bank. Near the toe of her moccasin, a gold bar lay half-embedded in the muck. She bent to retrieve it — and was surprised at the weight. It took two hands to pry it out and heave it into the crate. The linen-wrapped packages of trade silver weren't any lighter or easier to free from the suction of wet earth. Eventually though, she rinsed each item off and filled the box. Now to drag it up a ways.

Planting herself uphill, she grabbed the edge with two hands and pulled. The thing didn't budge. If anything, the bottom edge dug deeper into the muck.

But she wouldn't be thwarted. Sucking in a huge breath, she grasped the crate's side yet again, and this time she lifted before she pulled. The wood moved, but not much, so she grunted and strained for all she was worth — which by now wasn't much.

The momentum did not mix well with the slick ground. The box lifted but her feet slipped. The crate crashed. Pain exploded in her left foot, shooting agony up her leg. One hundred fifty pounds of heavy metal smashed her toes against a rock, trapping her.

She let out a wail that wouldn't be stopped.

Elias trotted back to the river, leaving Matthew and Rufus to turn around the empty wagon. That broken wheel would set them back days . . . days he didn't have to spare. Hopefully Matthew was a better wheelsmith than him, for he had no experience. He was about to turn back and ask him when a cry keened from the river, loud as a scream from a red fox.

Mercy!

He sprinted, wishing to God he held a tomahawk in his grip. Even so, weapon or not, if anyone harmed her, he'd kill. Fury colored the world blood red as he scanned for movement.

Past the horses, by the end of the broken

131

wagon, Mercy hunched on the riverbank, holding her leg. A crate hid the bottom half of her skirt from view.

Taking the bank half-sliding, he skidded to a stop next to the box — fully loaded. He crouched and lifted the crate. She lurched back. As soon as she was free, he dropped the box and scooped her up. Even with her wet skirts, she weighed hardly more than a feather tick. Cradling her against his chest, he hauled her up to level ground, then set her down.

Her eyes pinched shut, trapping her in a world of private pain. No tears cut tracks down her cheeks, nor did she cry out anymore. Still, the single scream she'd let out earlier would haunt him in nightmares to come.

"This is going to hurt, and I regret it, but it has got to be done." He hunkered down near her foot and, as gently as possible, lifted her mucky leg so that her shoe rested in his lap. Ignoring propriety, he pushed up her gown to gain a better look. Stockings, torn and dirty, covered a shapely leg, thankfully not bent or crushed. She must have taken the full brunt of the weight on her foot.

She didn't make a sound as he unlaced her moccasin. She didn't swoon or flinch.

She just sat, grasping handfuls of her skirt into white-knuckled fists, eyes still closed but face resolute.

He tugged on the heel of her shoe and slid it off. When it caught on the end of her toes, she sucked in a breath — he did too. Blood soaked a stain into her gray stockings. That fabric had to come off. Now.

"Mercy, this is going be hard, but I need you to take off your hose."

Her eyes blinked open, either from shock or anger, he couldn't say. Without a word, she released her handfuls of skirt and reached for her bodice. A blade appeared, shiny and sharp in the late afternoon sun.

His brows rose. No wonder she hadn't feared traveling with him or any other man. Between her knife and Matthew's overseeing, the woman was thoroughly protected.

She bent forward and sliced a line through the fabric around her ankle. Breathing hard, she leaned back and tucked her knife away.

"Go on." Her voice shook. "Do what needs to be done."

He gritted his teeth. Would to God he could take the pain for her. Bit by bit, he peeled the fabric down from her ankle. No swelling there. No odd angles or broken skin. The weight must've hit farther on.

He pulled the thin wool past the arch of

her foot, steady, using a constant force, and faltered only once — when the stocking stuck to the bloodied pulp of her last two toes.

His chest tightened. That had to hurt.

Horses' hooves plodded behind him. The grind of wheels. Matthew's voice. "What happened?"

Before Elias could answer, he heard the sound of Matthew's moccasins hitting the ground. "So help me, Dubois, if you hurt that girl —"

"Enough!" Mercy cried. "Your infighting is making me sick."

"Easy," Elias whispered to her as he would a skittish mare. Then he glanced over his shoulder. "I need some water here. Mercy crushed her toes."

Matthew loped off.

Elias turned back to the woman. Thankfully, now that her foot was free, color seeped back into her cheeks. A light wind teased a runaway lock of dark hair across one of those cheeks, and the urge to brush it back tingled in his hand. He curled his fingers tight, annoyed by the base response at such a moment.

"What were you doing?" His voice was flat, even to his own ears.

Her big brown eyes stared into his. "I

thought to gather some of the spilled contents."

He frowned. "Gathering is one thing, but trying to move a full crate on your own? What were you thinking?"

Her eyes narrowed. So did her tone. "Clearly I wasn't."

"Well," he sighed. "It could have been worse. One — maybe two — toes look to be broken, but thank God it is not your ankle." He allowed a small smile. "You should be kicking Rufus's hind end in no time."

Matthew returned and handed him a canteen. "We'll start loading. Join us as you're able. But you" — he shifted a cancerous gaze to Mercy — "stay put."

She frowned at Matthew's retreating back. Though she said nothing, Elias got the distinct impression that any other man who'd just told her what to do would be wearing that knife of hers through the back.

He uncorked the metal flask. "How long have you two been together?"

"Three years," she murmured.

"Three? Have you been tangled in this war for that long?"

She nodded, loosening more hair in the process.

Setting down the cork, he shifted her foot so that the water would run off into the grass instead of his lap. Best to busy her tongue to keep her mind from the pain he was about to inflict. "Why did Bragg even consider taking on a woman?"

He poured a stream over her toes with one hand, the other supporting and rubbing off bits of mud with his thumb.

"I'm good at what I do." Her voice strained and her nostrils flared, but she kept talking. "My sight is a gift. And no one expects a woman scout. A messenger, yes, but never a scout."

He grunted. No argument with that, for he'd never run across such.

Dousing her foot afresh, he bent and studied her toes. Now that the blood was gone, the damage was easier to assess. The little toe, as suspected, was likely broken, already swollen to nearly twice its size. She'd lose the nail for sure. The toe next to it pulsed an angry shade of deep red, but it wasn't as puffed up. More like a deep bruise. She'd live to fight another day — and soon.

He set down the canteen and faced her. "War does not last forever, thank God. What will you do when the fighting is done?"

Her brown eyes glazed over, but this time he guessed it wasn't from pain. Gently, he resettled her foot on his lap and dried off what he could with the hem of his hunting frock.

"I suppose I shall cross that creek when I come to it," she said at last.

His gaze shot to hers. "There is no man waiting for you on the other side?"

Her lips curved, sunlight painting them a rosy hue. "I've been told I am a handful . . . not to mention stubborn. Even were I to want a man, not many are up for the job."

While spoken in jest, her words sank low in his gut, and a strange urge rose to meet such a challenge. He cleared his throat, then shrugged off his hunting frock and balled up the fabric. He set the lump on the ground and eased her foot to rest atop it. "Let this dry off while I help load those crates. I will bind that toe when I am finished."

Her chin jutted out. "I am fully capable of binding my own foot."

Proud woman, as stubborn as she was beautiful. He scowled. "Just promise me that when I am down there loading" — he hitched a thumb over his shoulder — "I won't turn around and see you next to me, lugging up a crate."

A small smile flickered on her face. "You have my word."

It was a small victory, her giving him her

word — so why did it make his heart thump hard against his ribs?

Rising, he turned toward the task at hand. Would that fixing the broken wheel would prove as easy a conquest.

CHAPTER 11

Sun beat down surprisingly hot for an early April day. The afternoon warmth on Elias's back joined the heat from the heaping pile of glowing coals in front of him, and sweat trickled down between his shoulder blades. After two days of whittling spokes that never seemed to fit, the need to be on the move burned hotter than the sun and embers combined. Despite the threat of roaming Indians, they'd had no choice but to build a fire. Moisture dripped down his temple, and he shoved the dampness away with the back of his hand. Heat blistered off in waves from the coals, hinting the temperature was just about right — hopefully.

Throwing down his stick, he reached for the flat steel tire, then worked it flush into the fire so that all sides heated evenly. This would work. It had to. He glanced up at a cornflower-blue sky and lifted a prayer as the metal heated.

Please, God. A little help here.

Behind him, Matthew readied the wheel. Once the flat-tire heated through, they would have to work fast, especially since they labored without tongs or pincers. One wrong move and the metal would set cockeyed, or one of them could suffer a wickedly bad burn.

He faced Matthew. "Are you ready to give this a go?"

Matthew hoisted the wooden wheel, the new, crudely carved spokes fixed between axle and rim. He gave it a last once-over with his hawkish eyes, then set the thing down in the sandy spot they had created. "Aye."

Grabbing two stout sticks, Elias jiggered the flat-tire loose. He rushed the charred metal ring over to Matthew, and the two of them set to whacking the band over the felloes. Long before they could pound it on the wheel straight, it cooled and shrank, setting lopsided.

Frustration churned the blackened fish he'd eaten at noontide. If that metal rim weren't righted now, there'd be no prying it off without rebreaking the wheel, and they would have to start all over. *If* they could even get it off. He dropped one stick, hefted the other in two hands, and brought the end down with all his might. The stick hit the edge of the metal — and slid. The force of it lifted the opposite side of the wheel, shooting it into the air. He and Matthew dodged backward. Though the metal was too cool to fit as it should, it would still pack a flesh-searing burn.

The wheel juddered back onto the sand. The metal tire sat mostly on but partly off. If they attached that to the wagon, the first turn would crush it.

"You are a disappointment."

Elias yanked off his hat and slapped it against his thigh. "Blast!"

A laugh rumbled in Matthew's chest, as if nothing more than a game of stickball had been lost. Retreating to a nearby log, the ranger sank onto it. "You're a man of many talents — but wheelwrighting ain't one of 'em." He swept his hand toward the crooked wheel.

Elias blew out a long breath. No sense taking offense at the truth. Cramming his hat atop his head, he joined the man on the log. "You're right. I am surely no wheelwright."

Matthew's smile faded. "Then what are you?"

Elias tensed, the turn of conversation as troubling as the ruined wheel. "What do you mean?"

141

Sweat trickled down the older man's brow in rivulets. "Well . . ." He paused and pulled out a dirty kerchief, rubbing off the offense. "It seems to me you took to that water like an old friend. Dubois is your surname. And you're accused of consorting with the French. If I don't miss my mark, you have voyageur blood in you."

Elias stared him down, saying nothing. Clearly the man had been giving him some thought, and by the sounds of it, quite a bit. That was a danger. Nothing good ever came of too close a scrutiny.

But then Matthew elbowed him, an easygoing smile returning to his face as he tucked his cloth away. "There's no shame in it. I've yet to meet a harder working lot, and you have more than proved your mettle this past week — excepting the wheel, that is."

Matthew's good-natured teasing loosened the tight muscles in Elias's shoulders. The man was a honey-dipped hound on the hunt, he'd give him that. Yet for the most part, it was a pleasant way Matthew had about him, seeking information with amiable conversation instead of at knifepoint.

Unlike his own father.

Elias frowned. Normally he didn't think about the man, but Matthew's speculation had unearthed an ugly patch of dirt. He kicked at a rock with his heel as he spoke. "My father runs pelts up north of Kippising — or did, depending on if he yet lives. I traveled with him for a time. It was . . . an experience."

His throat closed, shut down by too many memories. Those years had been harder to bear than the tears in his mother's eyes when Bernart Dubois had left her alone with a young boy clutching her skirts.

As if sensing the turmoil, Matthew's grizzled face softened. So did his voice. "Why'd you leave?"

The question pierced straight through his chest, and he sucked in a breath. The man could have no idea of the wounds he prodded.

"It was my father's dream, not mine," he muttered. "The life of a wanderer is not for me."

"Yet here you are."

He shot to his feet. The stink of smoke and sweat clung to him, the odor of travel and toil — things he'd sworn to change.

Yet here you are. Matthew's words taunted him, especially with the end of his wandering within reach. It had seemed simple at the outset. One last trek to Boston and his drifting days would be done — if only that blasted wheel didn't lie in a broken heap.

He faced Matthew. The man wasn't the only one who had questions rattling around like rocks in a can. "And here you are. Judging by the way you send Mercy to scout for enemy tracks before we leave and your chafing at keeping to known paths, I would say you are a ranger, for those are two primary rules of rangering, are they not?"

Matthew angled his head, sunlight sparking humor in his gray eyes. "It appears you have been studying me as well."

Elias held the man's gaze. "You are pretty far afield for a ranger — and a lone wolf at that. Not a common sight. Mercy tells me you met up with her three years back."

All humor fled from the man's face. "She saved my life."

He couldn't stop the lift of his brows, picturing the lithe-limbed Mercy snatching the barrel-chested man in front of him from the jaws of death. "How did she manage that?"

"I did not mean it in that sense, though there is more strength in that girl than in most men I've known." For a moment, Matthew grew silent, his eyes glazing over with a faraway look. Deep ruts lined the parts of his face not sporting bristly scruff. How many years had this man seen?

Matthew scratched at the week-old growth on his chin. "I strayed out here, abuzz with a bellyful of anger. Sometimes those you fight alongside of aren't there for the cause, but for themselves. Meeting up with Mercy, well . . . would to God the rangers had more men like her."

The captain lapsed into silence for so long Elias wondered if he'd finish his tale or not.

At last, Matthew pushed up from the log, meeting him head-on. "Mercy reminded me that a few bad men are just that — few. That there's still a lot of good in this world. It was her zeal what breathed new life into these old bones. When that girl puts her heart into something, there's no holding her back."

He needn't close his eyes to imagine her, so branded in his mind her face had become. The way her long braid swung down to full hips. The determined gleam in her brown eyes. How she'd fit so light yet strong in his arms. "She is a rarity," he murmured.

As if by speaking so, the woman herself appeared from out of the tree line, at a sprint despite the hindrance of skirts and limp favoring her sore foot. Something urged her to such a pace — likely something bad.

A battle charge ran along each of his muscles, and he took a step toward her. So did Matthew.

"Someone's coming," she warned.

Sucking in air, Mercy caught her breath. Judging by the way Matthew's hand hovered over his tomahawk and by the icy blue streak in Elias's gaze, she'd better get her words out before they tore off on a killing spree.

"Two wagons," she huffed. "Three men, one leading on a mount, coming from the east." She shoved back the hair from her eyes, lungs finally filling. "There're two women, three littles. One's a babe in arms."

Matthew looked past her, where the route cut a path through the greenery. "How far out?"

"Two miles or so."

Elias narrowed his eyes at her. "You cannot see that far, not with the bend of the road and the scrub in the way."

A familiar rage flared in her belly. She had yet to meet a man who trusted her ability when it exceeded his own. Still, after twenty-five summers, ought she not have learned to master such anger? Black-Fox-Running told her so often, but that did nothing to change her on the inside.

She lifted her chin. "That is what scouts are for, Mr. Dubois. You told me and Rufus to keep a sharp eye while you had a fire going."

He folded his arms, looking down the length of his nose. "I also told you to mind your foot."

She rolled her eyes. The man harped on her more than Matthew. "My foot's near to better."

"You are still limping."

"Not as much."

Matthew stepped between them. "No time for bickering. We'll have company soon. I say we help 'em on their way across the river as fast as possible. We can't have so large a party staying the night with us. That many people attract too much attention — something we can't afford."

Elias nodded. "Agreed."

Matthew turned back to the wheel on the ground. Though his big shape blocked part of her view, from her angle she could see things weren't right. The metal rim choked the wooden frame, jutting off where it ought to lay flat. Her gaze strayed to Elias, his broad back toward her now as he crouched beside Matthew, conferring. No wonder he was so ornery. The wheel was no more fixed than when she'd set out hours earlier.

Beyond them, orange coals yet glowed. She might as well make the most of them. There'd been no sign of any Wyandots, and if any were about, they would have attacked by now. A pot of stew would lighten everyone's mood, especially since they had eaten nothing hot in over a week.

After rummaging in the provisions box, she procured some root vegetables. Chopping up the few turnips and potatoes didn't take long, so she cut up some salted venison as well. She tossed it all into a pot of water, and while that heated, she hunted the nearby growth for wild ginger shoots to add a tang. By the time the water boiled and the scent of pottage wafted strong, Rufus wandered in from his scouting.

Just as a man on a horse rode into camp, coming from the east.

Elias and Matthew advanced toward him, Rufus tagging their heels. Mercy hung back, staying near the fire. Holding the reins with one hand was the sandy-haired man she'd seen with the wagons. She'd detected he seemed to coddle one arm, but this close up, she saw why. His arm lay limp in his lap, bound with linen strips soaked through with a yellowy-orange discharge. Brown stained the edges of that mess. That kind of injury needed an open-air salve with a light pack of dried cottonwood batting at night, not a strangle of cloth — and filthy cloth at that.

He dipped his head in greeting toward the men. A single, garish peacock feather tucked into his hatband bobbed with the movement. "Good afternoon, gentlemen."

Her brows shot skyward. *Gentlemen?*

" 'Tis a right fair one." Matthew tipped his head up at the man. Judging by his stance, all loose-legged and thumbs hitched into the front opening of his hunting frock, he didn't see the newcomer as a threat.

But when the man's gaze strayed past Matthew, beyond Elias, and lighted on her, she clenched the stir stick in her hand until her arm ached. Too much interest glimmered in his green eyes. Far too much curiosity. She knew that look, for she parried it often.

Elias sidestepped, blocking the man's view. "Are you looking to ford the Nowadaga?"

"I am. I have two wagons to guide across."

"Yer a guide?" Rufus turned aside and spit, then wiped a smear off his chin.

Even from yards away, Mercy saw the stranger's upper lip curl. For once she was in agreement with Rufus. This man was no guide, leastwise not an experienced one.

Ignoring the question, he slid down from his mount, taking care not to jostle his sore arm overmuch. "My name's Logan. Garret Logan, guide to the Shaw party." He offered his good hand to Matthew.

Matthew shook it. "Matthew Prinn."

Logan moved on to Elias. For a moment, Elias stood rock still, not taking the man up on his greeting. Did he sense something not right about this guide as well?

Finally, he gripped the man's hand. "Elias Dubois."

Rufus shot out his hand — the one he'd used to swipe away the spit. "I'm Rufus. This here's my grandpappy." He elbowed Matthew with far too much gusto.

Logan barely touched Rufus's fingers before pulling back and stationing himself in front of Matthew once again. He aimed a finger at the wagon with the broken wheel. "Met with hardship, have you?"

Though the man spoke to Matthew, Elias cocked his head toward Logan's arm. "Looks like you met with some of your own."

A smile lightened the man's face, teeth white in a mat of a sandy-colored beard — far too trimmed and smoothed for trekking through the wilderness. Perhaps if he'd paid closer attention to his surroundings instead of his grooming, he wouldn't have suffered such an injury in the first place. "I acquired a knife wound, I'm afraid, and it is festering more than I'd like."

By now the other two wagons had rumbled into the clearing, filling the space near to full. Two men, two women, and two children piled out. As they drew near, Mercy studied the men first. Both were tall and big-boned, giving the impression of competency, but each wore a sunburned nose, as if neither had the intelligence to don a hat during the heat of day. Strength without common sense was worse than dangerous. It was deadly. Shaggy haired, with shaggier beards, they were the opposite of Mr. Logan with their fine coating of dirt and travel grime. They sported similar noses and the same color eyes, the hue of a blue trade shirt washed one too many times in murky water. Were they brothers then?

Tagging one man's heels were two young boys. Mercy set down her spoon and folded her arms, shoring herself up for trouble. She'd once seen raccoon cubs destroy an entire season's worth of dried berries by sneaking into an impossibly small crack in a storage hut. These two boys were capable of far more than that, with their torn breeches, untucked shirts, and freckles scattered across their cheeks like a handful of pebbles tossed into a pond.

"Jonas! James!" A spring day of a woman caught up to them, surprisingly light of step despite her protruding belly large with promise. What on earth was a woman this close to birthing doing out here? Sunlight glinted off her spectacles as she bent to haul each boy back with a tug on his shoulders.

Joining the group last was another woman, holding a bundle of swaddling close to her chest. Her skirt hem was caked with filth, a queer contradiction to the pristine white baby wraps in her arms. While the two men introduced themselves, Mercy stepped around the fire to gain a closer look at the woman. Something wasn't right about her . . . but what?

"Wife, come over and meet the Shaws." Elias stretched out his hand toward her, an inviting smile curving his lips.

She bristled. Must he carry out this charade with such easy cheer? Unfolding her arms, she smoothed her skirts and joined his side. When he wrapped his arm around her waist and pulled her close, she clenched her hands, fighting the urge to yank out her bodice knife and end such a liberty here and now.

"This is my wife, Mercy. Mercy, meet the

Shaws. Amos and his wife, Mary."

"Pleased to meet you." The older man tipped his hat, and the dark-haired woman next to him offered a tremulous smile, pulling her gaze from the babe in her arms only for a moment. Her face was like the moon, pale and round, one that could change in the night. A strange light shone in her eyes, hinting of madness, not a rabid savagery but the kind that caught a person off-guard with its stealth, like it might reach out at any time and snatch a bit of Mercy's own sanity.

Elias's fingers dug into her waist, reminding her to respond.

"Pleased to meet you, Mr. and Mrs. Shaw."

The other man and his wife stepped forward, both dipping their heads. "I'm Nathan Shaw and this here is my wife, Emmeline. 'Tis surely good to see some fellow travelers. We have not run across any since Fort Edward, and I know my wife and my brother's could use some womanly conversation."

Mercy sucked in a breath. Surely they did not plan on staying that long. Elias's forearm tensed against her back, and next to him, Matthew cleared his throat. Only Rufus seemed to ignore the suggestion of the Shaws remaining long enough to strike up companionship, for he ambled off with a whistle.

"Well," Matthew's voice rumbled, "we'll be happy to help you ford the river if you like. There's still enough light left to cross with time to spare for you to make camp on the other side."

"Very generous, but it seems you folks could use our help first. What do you think, Mr. Logan?" Nathan Shaw looked to where the man had taken up a silent residence at their flank. "Mightn't we stay here a day or two to help these folks with their wheel?"

The man opened his mouth, but Elias interrupted. "No need. We would not want to hold you up."

Nathan stepped nearer, turning his face away from his wife, and lowered his voice. "The truth is, the women and little ones could use a break. We've been pushing them hard. Too hard. We can spare a day or two, and that's a fact."

"No! You cannot stay here." The words tumbled out of Mercy's mouth before she could stop them. All eyes turned her way.

Elias chuckled, but compared to his usual good humor, this laugh sounded strangled. "You will have to pardon my wife. It seems she is a bit hard up for conversation as well.

If you will excuse us, I shall have a word with her now."

He hustled her aside before anyone could question her and did not stop until they rounded their wagon and were out of hearing range.

The forced smile on his face fled, and a stranger stared out at her through his blue eyes. "Do not raise suspicion like that. A single misspoken word can ruin an entire mission. I have seen it happen."

She looked away, preferring to study the stained canvas of the wagon cover instead of the accusation in his gaze. He was right, and that shamed her more than her loose tongue. "I apologize," she mumbled, then she shot her gaze back to his. "But those people can't stay here, not with us. You know they can't."

He pressed his fingertips to his brow and rubbed. Was she giving him a headache, or were the Shaws?

"Listen," he said. "I do not like this situation any more than you do. But whether they move on or stay, we have to play the part, *Wife.*"

He tossed the word like a knife to be caught. Should she grab the challenge with an open hand and work with him? Or not? Yet was it not her duty to carry out the assignment given her?

"Very well." The agreement she spit out tasted bitter, but even more sour was the smile she forced after it.

The sooner the Shaws crossed that river, the better.

CHAPTER 12

Daylight died a long and anguishing death. The time for the Shaw boys to bed down wouldn't be soon enough for Mercy's liking. Their whoops and chatter violated the peace even down at the riverbank. A nest of rattlesnakes wouldn't make as much noise or wriggle about so.

She threw another handful of wet sand into the stew pot and scrubbed the bottom, breathing in the damp evening air. Across the river, dusk smeared shadows together into a blend of ashy charcoal. The sky was on the verge of rolling over from indigo to onyx, and peeper frogs piped a chorus despite her presence. This time of day was holy, a reverent peace settling everything down for the coming night — or it would be without the Shaws' ruckus.

Dipping the pot into the water, she rinsed out the sand. The tin inside practically gleamed, she'd been at it so long. Never easy around women, she'd kept her distance from Mary and Emmeline. They were probably fine people if she'd give them a chance — which she wouldn't. Too risky. She had ever preferred the plain speaking of men. Women most often attacked sideways and upside down with their catty remarks whenever they felt threatened. She purposed to give the Shaw women no cause for such spite.

Heavy footfalls crunched at the top of the bank. She'd heard the approach long ago, but an irrational hope that whoever it was would go away kept her from turning, for it surely wasn't Matthew or Elias. They trod with ghost feet.

Garret Logan slid-walked down the slope, then stopped next to her. The tip of the peacock feather in his hatband riffled with a slight breeze. "Good evening, Mrs. Dubois. I hope I did not startle you."

Rising, she stretched her mouth into a small smile. "It takes more than footsteps to startle me, Mr. Logan."

His green gaze swept over her like an ill wind, and she shivered.

"Yes, I suppose it does."

Clutching her pot, she whirled to climb the bank, letting his first volley sail over her head. No sense asking what he meant. The hardened gleam in his eyes indicated he'd already summed her up to less than nothing — the usual reaction of men who couldn't look past her height and independent ways.

She'd just gained level ground when a grunt of pain back at the river's edge slowed her steps. The suppressed moan that followed stopped her feet. The third cry turned her around. Even a suffering wolf merited either a quick slit to the throat or some healing help to end its suffering.

Below, Logan kneeled near the water, his arm — now unbound — dipped in the river. The tight hunch of his shoulders screamed louder than his groans.

She blew out a sigh, unable to stop the softening of her resolve against the man, and retraced her steps. "I will leave out an onion from our stores, Mr. Logan. Mash it up and put the paste on that wound of yours for the night. Come morning, wash your arm again, then leave it air-breathing. The festering will stop, and it will heal."

He stood and faced her, arm dripping at his side. Darkness hid his face but not the revulsion in his voice. "An old Indian trick? I will not partake in such savagery."

This was the gratitude he showed for her compassion? She clenched the pot handle tighter. If she stood any closer, she'd swing it at his head. " 'Tis a common enough cure out here in the wild, known to whites and reds — and you'd know it too if you were a true guide. Tell me, Mr. Logan." She dared a step closer. "How much are you fleecing the Shaws for, and what kind of trouble are you running from?"

His head jerked back. A direct hit. "It is women like you, Mrs. Dubois, too independent, too free with your mind, who are a stain on the fabric of this land."

A slow smile tugged her lips. If Elias heard this conversation, Mr. Logan would have more than a festering arm to heal from.

"I am the land, sir — a land that will chew you up and spit you out. You won't make it to Fort Wilderness in one piece. Neither will the Shaws. Their blood is on your head." She turned to hike the bank and called over her shoulder, "I will set your onion out if you want it."

Though each step carried her farther from the hateful man, she upped her pace anyway, even if it did shoot pain from her crushed toe clear up to her shin. By the time she reached camp, she'd blown off most of her anger — but not all, apparently, for as she neared the wagon, Elias stepped out of the shadows and grabbed the pot from her.

His blue gaze held her as firmly. "What

160

has you so riled?"

She swung her braid to trail down her back, loosening her shoulders and her ire. "Just needed a brisk walk."

"I could use one myself." He glanced over to where a fire blazed, lighting the faces of the Shaw men and one of the women — Mary, with her babe yet clutched in her arms. Did the woman never set the little one down?

Elias shifted his gaze back to her. "I have put out that fire twice now, but every time I turn my back, those men are hell-bent to kindle it again. I am surprised they made it this far from Fort Edward without being set upon."

Elias's low voice soothed in a way that wrapped around her shoulders — or mayhap not his voice, but the land-wise knowledge that was so much a part of him. She respected that. And more.

"I will see to this pot." He strode off on soundless feet — so unlike the earlier stamp and crunch of Mr. Logan's steps.

She followed. Better to get that onion out now and hole up in the wagon for the night until it was her shift to keep watch. "Where're Matthew and Rufus?"

"On first watch. We need two pickets at a time with this much noise and smoke." He winked down at her.

When they reached the wagon, Elias crouched and set the pot underneath, upside down, to keep it dry and clean. She stood on tiptoe over the back gate and rummaged in the provisions box.

"Need something?"

She stiffened at his nearness, his scent of horse and smoke far too alluring. Likely it simply reminded her of Onontio — though she'd never felt quite this tingly with her brother standing next to her.

"An onion," she answered.

He cocked his head. "Is your toe not healing properly?"

"The skin's mending fine." She grabbed the onion and faced Elias. "I told Mr. Logan I'd leave one out. That arm of his will do him in if he doesn't treat it soon."

Elias's jaw hardened. "When did you talk to him?"

"Down by the river."

The call of a whippoorwill worried the night air, mingling with Elias's grunt. "That man is trouble. Keep your distance."

This time his command didn't rankle nearly so much. Were she to hold his words in her hand and examine them by sunlight, they might almost sparkle with endearment. Flit! What was she thinking?

She set down the onion on a nearby rock, then straightened at the approach of swishing skirts and thudding boots. She and Elias turned at the same time.

Amos Shaw and his wife, Mary, drew near, his arm holding her close about the shoulders. "My wife here is weary-worn. We came to say good night before you two cozy up for the evening."

The innuendo stole her breath. Of course they expected her to sleep with the big man next to her. A reasonable enough assumption, but one that lit a fire in her belly.

Elias shook his head. "I am about to go put that fire out, then I shall take the next watch. Get yourselves to bed, and we will see you come morning."

Mary's amber eyes landed on Mercy, a frown dimpling her chin. Something wasn't right about the woman. She was like a beautiful china cup, turned so you couldn't quite see the ugly chip in the porcelain. What was it?

The babe in her arms lay deathly still and quiet. Another mournful *whip-poor-will* haunted the air — and then Mercy knew.

She pressed her lips tight to keep from gasping. In all the hours the Shaws had been here, that baby hadn't made one squawk — not a cry, a peep, or a movement. Nor had the woman set the bundle down. That was no baby. It was a swaddled mass of grief not even her husband could pry from her arms.

Mary's lower lip folded into a pout, and she looked at Elias. "Do not trouble yourself about the fire, sir. It is near to go out. Your wife is sorely in need of you." She lifted her face to her husband. "Mrs. Dubois doesn't have a little one yet, Amos. Surely we can spare them a night?"

A night? Mercy's pulse took up a war beat, and she inched away from Elias. His big hand caught hers before she could make a run for it.

Amos kissed his wife on the brow. "That is my girl." He beamed at them. "Mary is right. There's no need for you to take any watches tonight with us here, Mr. Dubois. There's plenty enough men to cover for you. How long has it been since you two have had some time to yourselves?"

Mercy's gasp collided with Elias's. Her gaze snapped to him. His dark eyes burned into hers, wide open.

Amos chuckled. "That is what I thought. Go on now. We'll relieve your men when they come in."

Elias let go of her hand. "No, I —"

"Go on now. I mean it." Amos shooed him

164

off with his free arm. "The missus and I won't move a step till you settle."

"Not a single step," Mary repeated.

Beside her, Elias blew out a low breath and mumbled, "Much obliged." Then he pivoted and stalked off.

Leaving her alone. Blinking. Feet itching to tear off into the woods. But that was not what a wife would do, was it?

Grabbing handfuls of her skirt, she padded to where Elias waited at the front of the wagon.

His face was more shadowed than the twilight. "After you." He swept out a hand.

Surely he couldn't be serious. Yet there he stood, unmoving, a determined clench to his jaw.

Swallowing, she climbed into the seat, then worked her way through the opening of the canvas, more aware than she ought to be of the man following her.

Once inside, she immediately turned. Better to face a danger than be attacked from behind. If he thought to act upon that which the Shaws had hinted at, she'd gut him before he could holler for help.

But his blue eyes merely burned into hers, some kind of pleading bending his brow. "Mercy, I —"

His voice weighed heavy with an emotion

she did not want to guess, for her own feelings surged in a dangerous swirl.

She backed over the crates and pulled out her knife, brandishing the blade for a quick strike if need be. "Keep your distance, Mr. Dubois."

The heat of a summer day warmed Elias's back. Small puffs tickled the hair at the nape of his neck, as feverish as an August breeze. His spirit quieted, so peaceful and calm the moment. It was a dream. He knew it. But he held on to the sweet sensations with all his strength. This kind of tranquility hadn't bathed him in years. Decades, were he honest. He rolled over, sinking deeper into such serenity.

Until a faint coo shot his eyes open.

A breath away, in the soft light of early dawn, an angel slept deep and even. Mercy's familiar scent of pine and woman instantly awoke his every nerve. Her dark lashes curved shut above high cheekbones. Her lips were parted, barely, issuing the warmth he'd felt on his neck — which now brushed against his mouth like a kiss. How sweet would that taste?

He should leave. Now. Crawl right out the canvas opening and let the cold air slap him in the face. He should. He swallowed. All

166

the *should* in the world never had kept him from reaching for trouble. Only the grace of God had stayed his hand.

Give me strength now, Lord.

Slowly, his gaze moved from the sleeping eyes, to the full lips, to the hollow at the base of her bare neck where a gold chain hung heavy, weighted by a ruby heart. Her long hair, free of her braid, draped over her shoulder, spilling across her waist and highlighting the swell of her hips. A charge ran through him. If he moved, slightly, he could pull that body against his and —

He bolted up, not caring if his rash movements woke the sleeping beauty. He needed air, and lots of it. He dove out the canvas opening and scrambled to the ground.

Straight into the barrel of a musket. His hands shot up in reflex.

"There a problem, Mr. Dubois?" Matthew's voice, barely above a whisper, shouted a threat as cold and hard as the muzzle shoved into his chest. The man's eyes were hidden in the thin light of a morning just waking and the thick shadow of his hat brim, pulled low. Had he been out here all night?

Elias lowered his hands and lifted his chin. "Nothing to concern you."

Matthew looked past him, gun still trained

on his heart. "You all right, Mercy?"

He didn't need to turn around to know a brown-eyed woman stared out from the canvas hole.

"I am fine."

Her words were sleep-laced and breathy, rekindling his desire.

Slowly, the gun lowered, and Matthew nodded at him. "Get yourself out on watch. A walk will do you good."

Bypassing the older man, Elias stalked off, glad for the task. Matthew couldn't have been more right. He did need a walk — a *very* long one.

By the time he returned, sun painted the camp brilliant. One Shaw woman sat on a log, fussing with the wrappings of her baby. Her sister-in-law hauled one of her boys with a firm grasp on his ear toward the wagon she shared with her husband. The other boy scampered too close to the fire. Matthew and the two Shaw men worked with the broken wheel. And Rufus, as usual, was nowhere to be seen.

Mercy stood on the far side of the clearing, red-faced and aiming a finger at Logan much the same as the muzzle he'd faced earlier this morn. What the devil?

He strode over to the pair, catching the tail end of Mercy's heated words.

168

"Stray near those belongings or me again, and your scalp will be swinging from my apron ties." Elias's brows shot skyward.

Logan's face paled to an ugly shade of gruel. Without a rebuttal, he pivoted and trotted off like a hound from a cornered badger. Even the ridiculous feather in his hat seemed to droop.

Elias stifled a chuckle. "Remind me not to cross you."

She faced him and her hand flew to her mouth, her eyes wide. So she hadn't thought before shooting her word arrows.

This time he couldn't stop a laugh. "What did Logan do this time?"

Her hand fell, and red crept up her neck. "He was poking around our load. Said he was looking for a whetstone to sharpen his knife. A whetstone! You'd think we'd brought the whole of a fort's provisions with us. Why, I —" She cocked her head. "Why are you looking at me like that?"

Sunshine warmed her skin to a burnt-honey glow, highlighting every curve he'd appreciated earlier in the dark. The fire of her words reminded him all too much of the heat she'd radiated next to him in the wagon. His grin widened. If he answered her question, his scalp would be swinging from her apron strings right next to Logan's.

He wheeled about and retraced his steps back to where the men worked. Matthew and Amos Shaw pounded away on the iron tire ring. Nathan Shaw sat on a rock, whittling a new spoke.

Squinting against the sun, Nathan peered up at him. "Looks like you married a feisty one." His lips parted in a sloppy grin. " 'Tis worth it, though, especially once the young-uns come along. Love's always worth the trouble, eh?"

Was it? He had no experience. Nothing to measure Nathan's words against. He cast a glance over his shoulder. A brown braid swished wide down Mercy's back as she darted toward the fire to yank away the Shaw boy.

Yet as he watched her pull the lad from danger, he had a niggling feeling that Nathan might be right. For the love of this woman, any amount of trouble might be worth the effort.

CHAPTER 13

Moisture trickled down Mercy's back as she darted toward the fire. She'd been chasing after fools all morning. First little James Shaw, unattended down by the river. Then Garret Logan, poking around their belongings as if he owned them. Now James's twin brother, Jonas, played an insane game of pitching rocks onto the fire, shooting up sparks and scattering the coals the men would need for the wheel. If one of those burning embers flew out and hit the five-year-old, the child could be branded or blinded. She upped her pace, unsure which provoked her more — the mischievous boy or Mary Shaw, who sat on a log nearby, ignoring all but the bundle of empty swaddling in her arms.

Jonas hefted another rock, raising it high. Mercy sprang, grabbing the boy's arm before he could swing.

"Enough!" She tugged him around, his

brown eyes widening from the surprise attack. "Fire is not a plaything. You could get hurt — ow!"

Pain bit into her shin, and the rascal wrenched from her grasp. Jonas Shaw scampered off laughing while she sported the beginning of a bruise from where he'd kicked her. She clenched her fists, breathing out a string of oaths in Mohawk. The scamp reminded her far too much of Onontio when he was a boy.

The fuss broke the trance of Mary Shaw, who peered up from her perch on the log. "You shall make a fine mother, Mrs. Dubois."

She froze, breath hitching in her chest. What was she to say to that?

"Oh, don't fret." The woman smiled, clutching her blankets tighter to her chest. "I see the way your husband looks at you. It'll happen soon enough."

Despite the warmth of the day, a shiver ran across her shoulders. Mary Shaw was crazy, plain and simple. And she ought to know, for as a young girl she had frequently been in the presence of insanity. How many times had she sat cross-legged with a heart full of doubt, listening to the tribe's milky-eyed oracle spin crazy tales of fire monsters or talking trees?

Unbidden, her gaze strayed to where the men worked. Elias's broad back all but blocked her view of whoever it was he was talking to. His felt hat rode proud atop his tousled hair, the ends of which curled against his shoulders. A waft of breeze carried his scent, so well did she know it by now, for she'd breathed it in all night when he'd lain beside her, separated by only a blanket and her knife. Her mouth dried to dust at the memory, shame rising up. She'd meant to stay awake the night through, on guard against any untoward advances. But the peace of his steady breathing and the comfort of a warm body at her back fighting the chill of evening air had embraced her in a way she'd never known.

Without warning, Elias turned, his blue eyes seeking hers, pulling her close in ways that pulsed warmth to her cheeks. She gasped at the tangible connection. How had he known she was looking at him?

She spun back to Mary, then wished she hadn't, for the woman's gaze was every bit as canny as Elias's.

A smile beamed on the woman's face. "The only thing better than the love of a good man is bearing his little one."

Mercy turned and fled, following the earlier route of Jonas when he'd escaped her. She needed air, solitude, a lung-clearing scream, something. Anything but the strange allure of a traitor and the babble of an addlepated woman. She rounded the corner of the Shaws' wagon, intent on beating a path to the river, when Emmeline Shaw appeared, a wriggling boy in her grasp.

"Pardon me, Mrs. Dubois, but I saw what my son did to you, and Jonas here has something to say." She nudged the boy forward, planting him between herself and Mercy. "Go on, Jonas."

The boy kicked at the dirt with one toe. "Saw-ree-missus-do-bwa," he mumbled.

His mother thumped him on the head. "Jonas Shaw, you apologize proper, right this minute, or I will have your father take care of this."

His chin shot up, the threat flaring his little nostrils. "I apologize, Mrs. Dubois."

She pressed her lips together, making him squirm a bit, then offered the boy a smile for doing the right thing. "Apology accepted. Now, stay away from the fire, you hear?"

Jonas nodded then darted off before his mother could yank him back.

Emmeline's gaze followed the lad, a frown creasing her brow. "Those boys are like to be the death of — oh!"

A groan stole the rest of the woman's words. Emmeline Shaw bent, hand on her swollen belly, gasping.

Mercy shot into action, wrapping her arm around the woman's shoulders and leading her to a crate near the wagon. She guided Emmeline to sit, wishing she could drop onto a seat as well. Every time a woman in the village went into the birthing hut, Mercy ran the other way. Some women relished the process of bringing a new life into the world. Not her.

"Mrs. Shaw, tell me true." She crouched and peered into the woman's face, moisture dotting both their brows. "Is that baby coming?"

Emmeline sucked in a big breath, then straightened, color returning to her cheeks. "No, not yet, I think. Leastwise I hope not. It is too soon."

Though the woman appeared to be recovering, unease tightened Mercy's chest. If that babe came now, Mrs. Shaw would be likely to lose it — and possibly meet the same fate as her sister-in-law, clutching a heap of empty swaddlings and crooning lullabies to a nonexistent child. Blast that Mr. Logan for leading this family out at such a time — unless there was some reason she didn't know about.

She smoothed back a hank of blond hair from Emmeline's face, sneaking a feel of the woman's forehead in the process. Cool to the touch. That was good. She sank back onto her heels and smiled at Emmeline. "Tell me, Mrs. Shaw, why did you leave Fort Edward? Why did you not stay until the baby came?"

"Mr. Logan said we needed to reach the lake before the heat of summer."

"The heat of summer?" She cocked her head. "I never heard of such a thing. Usually guides are more concerned about winter snows."

Mrs. Shaw rubbed her belly, arching her back but not groaning. "Mr. Logan says heat is the bane of all travelers."

Maybe for that big skin of hot air, but a larger problem would be the war being waged on whites and reds alike — and these people were headed in the direction of land that was in the heart of it all. She frowned. "What lake are you talking about?"

"Lake Ontario."

She stood and smoothed her skirt with her hands, schooling her face to hide the horror the woman's words birthed. How could the Shaws have missed hearing about a war that'd been raging for near to five years now? "Surely you know, Mrs. Shaw, that there's already a post — a French post — at Fort Niagara, on the westernmost shore of Lake Ontario."

"Exactly." The woman nodded, eyes flashing bright. "We'll be the first to set up an English post in that territory. My husband and his brother say there's a lot of money in fur nowadays — more so than they could make in a lifetime had we remained in New York. We've scrimped and saved for a year now, selling all to purchase a load of trade goods. That is the beauty of it."

"That is the danger of it!"

"But Mr. Logan says this is the only way to gain an edge over the traders on the Mohawk River. We'll have first access to the finest furs before they travel from the Great Lakes on down to New York."

Mercy's hands curled into fists at her sides. Sure, they would have first access, but only if they lived long enough to establish a foothold in the trading industry — and with Logan leading them out beyond Fort Wilderness, that wasn't likely.

Splaying her fingers, she swung her long braid back behind her shoulder. "How did you say you met up with Mr. Logan?"

"Mr. Logan placed a post in the *Evening Gazette and Universal Advertiser*. Did you know he is one of the top ten guides listed in the paper? We were fortunate he took us on."

Ill fortune, more likely. She cleared her throat to keep from snorting. "Well, there's nothing to be done for it now, I suppose."

"How's that?"

"Look, Mrs. Shaw, you have not yet begun to face danger. Once you pass Fort Wilderness, you will be on your own with no one between you and peril but Mr. Logan. Mightn't your husband consider turning south, or better yet turning back? At least hiring a different guide at Fort Edward?"

"Turn back?" The lady worried her bottom lip with her teeth as if the words tasted bitter. "I don't understand."

Blood. Gore. Death and sorrow. It was a blessing Emmeline did not understand what was ahead of her — and far be it from her to tell the woman. "I'm thinking your Mr. Logan isn't as experienced as he claims."

For a moment, the woman's brows pulled in to a tight knot, then slowly loosened. "I appreciate your concern, Mrs. Dubois, and I sorrow over whatever misfortunes made you and your family head back east. But regardless of Mr. Logan, I trust my husband. Nathan's looking out for us as surely as Mr. Dubois looks out for you."

A sigh drained the rest of her fight, and

she rose to her feet. The woman's trust in her husband was commendable — but completely naive. From what she'd seen of the Shaw men, they didn't have half the wilderness sense of Elias. Or Matthew.

She spun and stomped off, annoyed that Elias came to mind sooner than her old friend.

An early evening breeze blew away the chatter near the fire. Where he stood, yards away, Elias drank in the moment of relative quiet, save for the squawk of a jay on a nearby branch. He crouched in front of the newly constructed wheel, examining the workmanship for a last time before joining the others. Running a finger along every seam, he tested the strength of each new spoke, then squinted to blur the outline and gauge the shape. The thing appeared to be the picture of sturdiness, a testament to the value of many hands lightening the work. Not that the Shaws were expert wheel-wrights, but they labored as a team — unlike Rufus and Logan.

"I've brought you something."

Startled, he shot to his feet, reaching for a gun he did not have, a reaction honed from years of experience — yet one unnecessary in this instance. He turned to face Mercy, who smirked at his obvious surprise.

He grinned in return. "Even with a toe on the mend, you move on panther paws."

"I wouldn't be a good scout if I banged around like the Shaws. Here" — she held out a mug — "I figured it a wifely thing to bring you some of this."

The rich scent of coffee hit his nose, as stunning as her words, and he took the cup from her. "Thunder and turf! Where did you find this?" He slugged back a mouthful of the brew, ignoring the burn and relishing the flavor.

"The Shaws have many unnecessary things. Mr. Logan's ideas of provisions are peculiar at best." She leaned against the oak trunk, scaring the jay off its perch. Her gaze landed on the wheel at his feet. "Matthew says you will be able to give that a go tomorrow."

"He is right." He savored another mouthful, appreciating both the coffee and the ranger. "Matthew is a good man. I see why you took up with him."

She nodded, still staring at the wheel. "I will miss him, for certain."

She'd miss the man? He grunted. What was Matthew — or she — planning? "Who is doing the leaving, you or him?"

"He is, when we reach the fort." She

180

scowled up at him. "He says he will be turning in his ranger uniform and is bent on becoming a farmer."

The tone of her voice, the curve of her shoulders, the way the first shadows of night darkened her face all spoke of her displeasure. He lowered his cup, intrigued. Most women would think such a pursuit admirable.

He advanced a step toward her, pulled by such an anomaly. "You think he is making a mistake?"

Defiance glinted in her brown eyes. "I know he is. Plowing dirt's not the same as running footloose atop it, free to come and go at will."

He blew out a long breath, feeling the bone-crushing weariness of years on the run. What would she say if he told her Matthew's plans were exactly what he'd be about once he returned to Boston? "Running gets old, Mercy. Everyone realizes that at some point."

"What about you?" She cocked her head, much as the jay had earlier. "After you get out of jail, that is. I expect you will run far and wide, not tie yourself to a patch of ground."

Laughter rumbled in his chest. She would've been right even a year ago, but not now. His chuckle turned to ashes in his mouth. *Oh François.* Had his friend not been washed down the Petawawa River, he'd also planned on leaving behind the voyageur life and putting down roots. Would the knife in his heart ever get pulled out?

He gulped back the rest of the coffee, grounds and all, then swiped the back of his hand across his mouth and handed her the cup. "The truth is, Matthew's plan is the same as mine. I intend to settle on a little place down in Connecticut, near Hartford. Build a house, have some children."

She snorted. This close, he saw her nose bunch much the same as a rabbit's — altogether too charming.

"You might want to find a wife first, Mr. Dubois."

"I already have one. You."

Color rose on her cheeks, and he grinned. Teasing this woman was far too gratifying.

"Your sense of humor is as ridiculous as Mr. Logan's peacock feather," she shot back.

He studied her for a moment, questions sprouting up like a freshly seeded field. Was she never lonely, roaming the woods, always on the move? Did she not long for a home other than the trees overhead or a night in a cave? What kind of woman didn't yearn to dandle a babe on her knee?

He dared a step closer. "Do you never think of settling down?"

She shook her head. "Matthew does that enough for me."

"I find it hard to believe no man has ever struck a fancy for you." Why had no one pursued this rare woman?

A small smile lifted her lips. "More like I've never taken a fancy to any man."

She peered at him, a peculiar gleam deepening the brown of her eyes. The same charge he'd felt when first holding her hand sizzled in the air between them.

He edged nearer, almost breath to breath. Slowly, he brushed his knuckle from her brow to her cheek, then lower to rub against the softness below her jaw. She didn't lean into his touch, but neither did she veer back or run. She didn't move at all, save for the rapid rise and fall of her chest.

"What is it you want out of life, Mercy Lytton?" he whispered — then froze with a sudden realization.

Everything in him craved for her to say, *"You."*

Her lips parted. He leaned closer — any closer and she'd be in his arms.

"Peace," she murmured.

His hand lowered, and a grin rose. He was

a fool. One didn't expect something as ethereal as star-shine to hunger for a man — especially one such as him.

"Well." He retreated a step. "Seems we are in agreement then, just going about it in different ways."

"I —"

A scream ripped through the air, cutting off whatever she'd intended to say. A keening scream, shot through with fear and pain. Much pain.

CHAPTER 14

Mercy dashed after Elias, his long legs outdistancing hers — but not by much. They halted just about even at Nathan and Emmeline Shaw's wagon. Nathan stood at the front of it, gripping the kickboard, face drained of color and visibly shaking. Jonas and James held on to Nathan's legs, for once silent. Rufus and Mr. Logan were out on watch, so the footsteps pounding behind her had to belong to Matthew and Amos Shaw.

Another scream ripped out from behind the wagon, lifting the hairs at the nape of Mercy's neck.

Letting go of the kickboard, Mr. Shaw took a step toward her, dragging his boys along with him. "You got to help her, Mrs. Dubois."

She clutched her hands in front of her to keep from grabbing Elias's arm for support, feeling as unsteady as Mr. Shaw looked.

"I —" Her throat closed. How to explain she could gut an elk, elbow deep in blood and gore, but the thought of seeing a baby birthed turned her stomach inside out?

"Mercy." Elias's voice was hardly more than a whisper, but it was a command none-theless.

She lifted her face to him. His blue gaze blazed strong and confident. What she wouldn't give for some of his strength right about now.

"You can do this, you hear me?" His words flowed with the power of a mighty river. "Go on."

Sucking in a breath for courage, she forced one foot in front of the other, then stopped cold when the next wail of agony rent the evening air.

Lord, give me strength.

The wailing ceased, and she pressed on.

"Emmeline?" Her voice trembled as much as she did.

Emmeline Shaw stood hunched over, shored up against the wagon, one arm cradling her big belly — with a bloody puddle at her feet. For now, the woman was quiet, but that wouldn't last long.

Mercy escaped back to the front of the wagon, gasping for air. This was beyond her. A normal birthing, maybe she could attend, but this? No. Most emphatically not. She scanned the gathering at the front of the wagon, looking for a blond woman clutching a heap of swaddling. Four pairs of worried eyes stared back — the same four she'd left. "Where's Mary? Emmeline needs her help."

Amos Shaw shook his head, avoiding eye contact with his brother Nathan. "My wife, well, she can't. She . . ." He retreated a step, tugging his hat brim lower. "No."

Nathan advanced, his face paler than a winter moon. "Can I . . .?"

Her stomach sank. The man would be less help than her. She closed her eyes, wishing that when she opened them, this would all be nothing more than a nightmare. But another scream pried her eyelids open. There was nothing for it. Either she did this, or the blood of Emmeline Shaw and her baby would haunt her for the rest of her life.

"Tell us what to do." Elias's strong voice was a lifeline.

Swallowing back the acidic taste rising past her throat, she skewered Emmeline's husband with a stare she hoped looked imposing. "Boil some water. Keep it hot and bubbly all the while, and make sure to keep your boys with you."

Without a word, he pivoted and ushered his young ones toward the campfire.

"Mr. Shaw." Her voice yanked up Amos Shaw's chin. "Bring me whatever clean cloths you and your wife can find. Have them to me as soon as you're able. Can you do that?"

He nodded, then turned tail and ran.

Next, she sought Matthew's face, all the while fumbling in her bodice for her knife. "Here, sharpen this." She tossed him her blade.

He caught it with ease and strode off.

Elias stood alone, his eyes twin blue fires in the gathering shadows. "What about me?"

"Get me some kind of light —"

Another scream howled, ragged with desperation.

Mercy clenched her teeth, wishing to God she could trade places with him. "And pray. Just . . . pray."

She spun and ran back to Emmeline before she could launch herself into Elias's arms and bury her face in his shirt.

Behind the wagon, Emmeline arched and panted, one hand planted into the small of her back. The crazed sheen in her eyes looked far too much like her sister-in-law's. As Mercy neared the woman, Emmeline grabbed her by the arms. "Am I going to lose my baby?"

Mercy pinched her lips shut. By the looks of it, yes, the woman would — but she forced a small smile. "Of course not. We shall —"

Emmeline's head dropped and her grip tightened, her fingers digging deep into Mercy's flesh. A raspy groan tore from the woman's throat. This was going fast. Way too fast.

Mercy rubbed little circles on her back, wishing she could think of something better to do. "Shh, shh."

Surprisingly, Emmeline calmed. Not much, but enough to give Mercy an idea. Slowly, quietly, she sang — not a birthing song, for she knew none, but a lullaby. The woman wouldn't know the difference anyway.

"Ho, ho, Watanay.
Ho, ho, Watanay.
Ho, ho, Watanay.
Ki-yo-ki-na.
Ki-yo-ki-na."

By the time her voice stilled, so had Emmeline. "Thank you," the woman whispered.

She wrapped an arm around Emmeline's

shoulder and gave a little squeeze. "Come on. Let's try to walk a bit, shall we? I don't know much about birthing, but I know it is good to walk."

Between singing, mopping Emmeline's brow, and shifting the woman from walking to leaning against her, the hour wore on. Nothing seemed to work, not for long. Night fell hard, yet despite the cool evening air, Emmeline sweated and writhed as if the heat of a July afternoon bore down on her. Between her groans and moans, she called for her mother.

And Mercy did not blame her. She'd not missed her own mother so keenly since the day she'd walked away from her grave three years back. In between Emmeline's pains, Mercy fingered her locket. Her mother would have known what to do in this situation. She always knew when it came to matters of women. How to soothe. Ways to comfort. Methods of easing the hurt. For the first time in her life, she wished she'd listened to her mother rather than despising her soft ways.

Emmeline stilled suddenly. So did she. Was this it? Would the woman die in front of her? Blast that Mr. Logan for hauling the Shaws out to the wilderness.

"God, please," Mercy breathed out. "I'm

not much for prayer, but save this woman and her child despite my lack."

During one of their treks around the wagon, Elias had set a lantern on the ground next to a pile of quilts at the back, giving them a privacy of sorts. In the soft glow of lamplight, Emmeline Shaw's gaze shot to hers and her mouth opened into a big O, but no sound came out. Suddenly the woman grabbed the back of the wagon and lowered into a squat, all air huffing out of her lungs.

Mercy's heart stopped — until a wriggling mass landed on the blankets.

Emmeline sank back, breathing hard. Mercy grabbed a clean cloth and scooped up the babe, wiping the newborn's nose and mouth.

A lusty cry broke out. This time the squall of a little one.

Mercy's arms shook as she rubbed the wetness off Emmeline's new daughter. She wrapped the girl tight in another cloth, then handed her to her mother.

"Ohh." Emmeline's one word — and not even a word at that — rang sweetly in the thick night air. It was a victory cry. A benediction. An all-is-well-with-the-world kind of coo.

For the first time in hours, the tension in

Mercy's shoulders unknotted. The woman wasn't quite out of danger yet, but hopefully the worst of it was over. Giving Emmeline a moment to breathe, Mercy stood and stretched. It would be best to put everyone's mind at ease. But as she took a step forward, the lantern's glow highlighted a white face in the darkness.

Mary Shaw stood at the edge of the reach of light, glowering. Her arms empty at her sides. The swaddling blankets lay in the dirt.

Elias's head bobbed to his chest, then immediately snapped up. He couldn't afford to doze off, not when those Shaw boys could awaken at any time and sneak off in the darkness. Rubbing a hand over his face, he leaned his head back against the tree trunk, then blinked over to where the boys lay sleeping on the ground. His frock coat, thrown over the top of them, didn't move a whit. Good. The rascals were still a-slumber in the quiet.

Wait a minute . . . *quiet?*

He jumped to his feet, instantly alert. Leaves shushed overhead. Night insects clicked. Across the clearing, the fire yet crackled — unattended. And not one groan or moan droned on the air.

Elias padded past the boys on silent feet,

then lengthened his steps into a long-legged stride. Amos Shaw, arm slung around his weeping wife's shoulders, led her off to their wagon. Mercy stood in conversation with Nathan Shaw in front of the other wagon, but not for long. The man scrambled to the back side of the canvas, where Elias had earlier laid out blankets and a lantern.

Upping his pace, Elias clenched his teeth. By the looks of it, a whole lot of grief had broken wide open, and Mercy had been the one to have to deliver the awful news. It was his fault, the way she rested her hand against the wagon's side and propped herself up. Her long braid drooped. So did her shoulders. She'd not wanted to attend the birth in the first place — and he'd been the one to suggest it.

He drew up in front of her, the urge to pull her into his arms so strong, he flexed his fingers. "How is Mrs. Shaw?"

A weak smile curved her lips. Ah, but this woman was brave.

"Emmeline and her daughter are fine for the moment. But Mary Shaw —"

"Whoa." He shot up a hand. "The woman *and* the babe are doing fine?"

She nodded. Loosened hair — her hat dispensed of hours ago — fell onto her brow, and she pulled it back. "They are."

He chuckled. "Thank God. And thank you. You are a wonder, you know that?"

"Nature's a wonder, not me." She reached for her locket, this time already worked loose from her bodice. How many times had she clutched that thing for strength during Emmeline's arduous labor?

She peered up at him. "Would that I could do something for Mary Shaw. I fear she has lost whatever sense she had left."

The mournful wail of a screech owl sounded from the woods, adding a haunting quality to Mercy's words. Life could be harsh sometimes, downright throat-slitting harsh . . . and well did he know it.

So did Mercy, judging by the bow of her head.

He reached for her, wishing to soothe away all that she'd endured this night — then pulled back before his fingers touched her hair. He had no right to do so, no claim on this woman, so why the persistent desire to touch her? A strange fire burned in his belly, and he retreated a step.

"How do you fare?" His voice cracked at the edges.

She didn't seem to notice. She merely angled her face and stared off into the night. "You know that feeling after a breakneck run, when you're bone-weary but the excitement of it is still jittering through your body?"

He nodded. "I do."

Her gaze slid to his, and she smiled, so brilliant it shamed the starlight. "That is how I feel."

He couldn't help but grin back. "You did a good thing."

"Well, I'm not finished yet. There's more to be done." She turned to leave.

But he stayed her with a hand to her shoulder. "You want I should haul that boiling water over?"

Her brow scrunched and she cocked her head; then as suddenly, the look disappeared and she laughed. "No, it is not needed."

Her words chased circles in his head, never landing in a coherent line.

"Then why did you have Mr. Shaw tend that water this whole time?"

She shrugged, taking her braid along for a ride on her slim shoulders. "He needed something to do other than worry himself over his wife and babe. Besides, we can use it to launder the soiled quilts."

He sucked in a breath. The woman was cunning, but not like most women. He'd had his fill of the conniving sort, always trying to gain what they wanted at the expense of others. But the brown-eyed beauty blinking up at him was nothing of the kind. Though he was her sham husband in a faux marriage, he suddenly understood some of what Nathan Shaw must've felt this night at the thought of losing the one he loved most.

"Tell me true, Mercy, if we had not been here — if *you* had not been here — would Mrs. Shaw and her baby have made it?"

She said nothing, just stared at him. But she didn't have to. The owl answered for her, chanting its woeful dirge.

Rage prickled hot up his spine. "Blast that Logan!" He wheeled about.

"Elias? Where are you going?"

"To have a word with the man," he called over his shoulder.

"Why don't you sleep on it? Save it for morning."

He left her and her questions behind. Too much pent-up anger simmered to a boiling point. Rufus's slights and grievances were nothing in comparison to Logan's. That fool led these honest people to their deaths. He tromped down the trail to the riverbank, where Logan should've been on watch, should've heard him coming — or at the very least seen him.

But the man sat with his back against a rock, eyes closed, head tilted and mouth open. Snores issued on the inhales.

Elias nudged the man's leg with the toe of his moccasin, hoping the restraint of not kicking the fool in the gut would please God — for it surely did not satisfy him. "Get up, Logan."

The man's head bobbed forward. "What? Who's —"

"I said get up." Bending, he grabbed a handful of the man's coat and yanked him to his feet. "That Shaw woman nearly died because of you tonight, and you sleep?"

Fully awake now, Logan glowered and batted at his arm. "Unhand me!"

He clenched the fabric all the tighter, wishing he'd grabbed higher and squeezed the man's neck instead. "I ought to string you up myself."

The man's face blanched in the darkness. "Put me down!"

"Fine." Using all his muscle, he whumped the fellow to the ground, flat on his back.

Logan gasped for air.

Elias widened his stance and stood over him, like the Grim Reaper come to call. "When you get these people to Fort Wilderness — *if* you can manage that — then you find them another guide. You are done. You hear me?"

"You cannot dictate" — he wheezed — "what I . . . or the Shaws do."

"True. I cannot." He folded his arms. "But if I hear you led these people out beyond the fort, what I can do is hunt you down. And that is a promise."

"As will I." Matthew's voice shot straight and true over his shoulder.

Elias stifled a smirk. No doubt Mercy had told the ranger about his murderous retreat.

Rolling to the side, Logan staggered to his feet. Without a word, he retrieved his hat where it lay on the ground, then scurried off toward camp like the rodent he was.

Matthew blew out a long breath and faced him, an odd gleam in his gray eyes. "Mercy warned me you were about to put the fear of God into that man. As much as I appreciate it, you know I can't allow you to hunt anyone down. Don't make me shackle you up just when I'm beginning to like you. I expect better than that from a man of your caliber."

He bit back a smile. Lord, but he admired this man. Maybe — *perhaps* — if Grandfather had used such encouraging words more often, he might not have strayed so far in rebellion. Who knew? But one thing he would bet on. Matthew Prinn would make the finest grandfather a boy could have. He clapped the man on the back. "I will take Logan's watch. You go on back."

Turning, he strode off along the riverbank, keeping to the weeds. Matthew and Mercy were good people. The best. And the longer he stayed with them, the harder it would be to leave them.

But even harder would be convincing his Wyandot contacts not to harm them.

CHAPTER 15

The squawk of crows jerked Mercy awake — but not fully. It took her a few blinks to attach meaning to the overhead branches and back side of a wagon. She pushed up with a yawn, thankful the long night of midwifery was finally over. She'd rather outrun a Seneca with a war club than attend to another birthing on her own, for Emmeline had bled thick and heavy after the delivery. Truly, it was a wonder Mrs. Shaw's heart yet beat after the loss of so much blood.

Mercy glanced down at the woman sleeping next to her. Emmeline and her new babe nestled together beneath a faded quilt, both breathing evenly. The woman looked hollow-cheeked and pale, but the babe, while impossibly tiny, held good color and slept soundly. Having made it through the night, the child stood a fighting chance of survival — as good as any of them could hope for in the middle of a war-torn wilderness.

She tucked the blanket snug where it had fallen away at Emmeline's back, then dared to run a light finger over the little one's cheek. Silky. Warm. With each stroke, a foreign yearning welled stronger. What would it be like to nuzzle a downy-headed babe of her own? To hold in her arms a child created in love, with a tuft of dark hair and eyes the color of an endless sky, blue as —

She drew back, stunned by the rogue desire. Lack of sleep and the strain of the journey were getting to her.

Taking care not to jostle Emmeline or the babe, she crawled out from beneath the shared blanket and arched a kink out of her back. Sun slanted lines of shadows from a stand of nearby hemlock, and she rubbed her eyes — then berated herself. She was no better than Rufus. Morning was already half spent and here she stood sleepy-lidded. A fine cup of the Shaws' coffee would be just the thing, if Mary were of a mind to share — or if she were of a mind at all. The woman might not yet have a grip on her senses.

Rounding to the front of the wagon, she neared the campsite and scanned the area. Elias, Matthew, Rufus, and Nathan Shaw huddled near the broken wagon, the repaired wheel at the ready to put back on. The Shaw twins each grasped a shovel and were furiously digging a hole — or trying to. Breaking ground next to a broad-trunked maple was near impossible. A small smile twitched her lips. Had that been Elias's idea to keep them out of mischief? Had he given that worthless guide Logan some busywork to do as well? For that man was conspicuously absent.

But so were Amos and Mary. Turning on her heel, Mercy headed to their wagon. If Mr. Shaw was with his wife, perhaps a request for coffee would be a possibility.

Rounding the back of the wagon, she slowed her steps. A low voice — one frayed to ragged threads — filtered out from the canvas.

"I can't take this anymore, Mary. I can't lose you too, not like our boys. Please, Wife, come back to me. Come on back. Don't do this to us."

The raw grief etched deep in Amos's words seared Mercy's ears. Would that she could brew a tea, blend a salve, do something for the man's wife. Broken bones, torn flesh, those things could be mended, but how did one heal a mind so ravaged by sorrow?

Mercy turned away from Amos Shaw's murmurings. Such intimacies should be left in private. Better she dip her feet in the river than interrupt such a moment for a trifling cup of coffee. Cold water would work just as well to fully waken her.

She retreated and strode across the campsite, bypassing the men shoring up the wagon. Elias and Matthew strained all their muscles into wielding logs they used as levers while Rufus and Nathan shoved a makeshift stand beneath the back edge of the wagon. She paused, heart swelling in a strange way at how well Matthew and Elias worked together. With the combined effort, bit by bit, the wagon rose. By tomorrow, they ought to be back on their trek to the fort.

Turning from the sight, she padded the rest of the way to the river with a soft step, a habit from years of walking invisibly. If her mother had learned to do the same, she would not have suffered such derision. *Oh Mother.* She sighed as she sank to the ground and unlaced her moccasins, shoving down the bitterness that still dogged her years after her mother's death. Would she never be free of wishing things had been different? Be released from the anger her mother's faith still bubbled inside her?

"Trust, Daughter. Trust in a God who is big enough to make the universe, yet kind enough to dry each of your tears."

She frowned. Would that God had never given cause for tears to be created in the first place.

Before she left the safety of the spring growth, she scanned the banks for any sign of danger. Black water flowed undisturbed, upriver and down. No canoes. No unexpected rustle of brush on either side. All appeared to be — No, wait.

One by one she shut down her senses, focusing on a pinpoint of blue that ought not be flashing against the muck left behind from receding waters.

She shoved her feet back into her shoes and gathered her skirts, trekking down twenty yards or so to the sight. Bending, she plucked a peacock feather from the mud. Why would Mr. Logan's treasured ornament be here? He was a proud enough man to take great care of his belongings. This was no accident.

Her gaze dissected the immediate area. Five paces farther, hoofprints marred the mud — headed toward the water. She hiked her skirts high, impropriety a thing she'd long ago learned to discard at a moment's notice, and waded into the Nowadaga.

Thankfully the rain-gorged river had decided to calm into a proper stream, and she crossed without a tumble.

On the other side, curved gouges in the soft dirt led out of the water, heading straight into the trees. Never once in the days they had spent together had Mr. Logan ridden off in such a fashion. Why now?

Standing tall, she shaded her eyes against the sun and squinted into the woods. A thrashed path beat a trail as far as she could see. Clearly the man had ridden off toward Fort Wilderness, but — She pursed her lips. That he'd made it so obvious did not sit well in her empty belly.

She let go of her clenched skirts and worked her way south along the riverbank, scouring for any sign of disturbed ground. After a mile or so, the growl of her stomach urged her to turn around and break her fast, ignore the silly man who'd ridden into danger, and —

She stopped, gaze snagged on a depression in the muck from where a rock had sat. A stone that size wouldn't just up and march off like a soldier. Something had kicked it into the water. Shifting her gaze, she stared inland. Bent weeds, not much, but spaced wide enough to accommodate the leap of a horse. Her brow tightened.

Why had Mr. Logan taken so much effort to show he'd ridden into the water, away from camp, then doubled back and hidden his return? Was he even now stretched out and snoring on his bedroll, having completed whatever harebrained errand he'd been about?

Pivoting, she tromped back to the crossing, angry with herself for having fallen prey to Mr. Logan's antics and even angrier with him for having put them all in danger by running off into the forest. She'd give him an earful and then grab an oatcake for breakfast.

She stalked back to camp, not caring if she had to wake the man for being such a dolt, but when she got to the spot where he'd set up his own lean-to, the ground beneath it was barren. No bedroll. No pack of belongings.

And no Mr. Logan.

Elias grabbed a canteen and sank onto the ground. Back propped against a hemlock, he stretched out his legs and swigged back a long drink before he joined Matthew and Rufus in loading the crates. Getting the wheel on took more grit than he'd reckoned. Still, God was good. How long would it have taken without the strong back of

Nathan Shaw to help them?

As if he'd conjured the man, Nathan strode over and sat cross-legged next to him, handing over a strip of jerky. " 'Tisn't much, but you wouldn't want me to cook a meal."

"Thank you." He bit into the meat and tore off a chunk.

So did Nathan. As the man chewed, his gaze followed the movement of his boys, directly across from them beyond the trail. Their shovels forgotten, James and Jonas had dropped to their knees and were scraping up dirt using some rocks.

Nathan shook his head and faced him. "It is a sad shame you don't have little ones yet. The way you keep my boys in line, you will make a fine father. I've learned a trick or two from you."

The jerky stuck in his throat. Him, a father? And a fine one at that? He swallowed hard at the ridiculous notion. He knew nothing of little ones or their ways. No, his knowledge of human nature — be it younglings or elders — had been forged in the flames of experience. It took a scheming mind to know the function of another's, may God forgive him.

"No tricks involved." He swigged back a drink and swiped his mouth. "You cannot stop someone bent on mischief, but ofttimes you can redirect it."

Nathan cocked his head. "How so?"

"I told your James and Jonas a story I heard once, of an Indian cache of arrowheads buried at the base of a tree just like that one." He nodded his head toward the boys. "And they have been at it ever since."

Nathan chuckled. "My wife and I are beholden to you."

"There is no debt." Tearing off another bite of jerky, he shrugged. "You helped us make repairs. It seems we are even."

"Far from it. Emmeline is more valuable than a broken wheel. If Mrs. Dubois hadn't helped her, my boys and me might be digging something worse than an aimless hole right about now. Your wife is a fine woman, stepping in to help the way she did."

A memory of her pale face surfaced, the sheen of dread blinking at him from wide eyes, just before Mercy took on the delivery of the Shaw baby. She'd been terrified, but she'd done so anyway — and without complaint. Indeed, she was a fine woman, in more ways than one. He grunted in agreement.

"But you're not really married, are you?"

The question flew like an arrow in the dark, sticking him through the throat without warning of an attack. He forced his expression to remain as stoic as a Wyandot sachem while scrambling for a response that wasn't an outright lie. "What makes you say that?"

Nathan's gaze bored into his. "There's a tension between the two of you, a wanting and not having. Like a couple courting and being denied."

His gut clenched, and he was hard pressed to decide if it was from the fact that the man had been studying them far too keenly, or because there was some small measure of truth to his observation.

Regardless, he corked his canteen and stood. "My thanks for the jerky, but we'd best get on to loading our cargo."

Nathan shot to his feet, staying him with a hand on his sleeve. "No offense. 'Tain't none of my business."

He pulled away. "None taken."

They both turned at the sound of swishing skirts. Mercy drew close, pink of cheek and huffing. "Hate to tell you this, Mr. Shaw, but your guide is gone."

Logan gone? Though slipshod, at least the man was a guide, of sorts. How were the Shaws to manage with a newborn babe, a mother not yet recovered, and a woman who even now suffered so cruelly she'd not let go of her husband?

He stepped closer to Mercy, studying her face. Maybe she meant something different, though what, he couldn't imagine. "Gone where?"

"It appears Mr. Logan beat a clear path toward Fort Wilderness, but a mile downriver, he doubled back. I did not follow it any farther, thinking he'd likely come back here. But all his belongings are gone."

"Worse than that." Matthew's voice turned them all around. "He has taken some of our belongings along with him."

CHAPTER 16

The sunny day turned blood red. So much anger shook through her, Mercy retreated from Matthew and Rufus lest she strike them for Logan's thievery. She should've known the man was up to something when she'd caught him poking around their cargo yesterday morn. Across the way, the Shaw boys hollered at each other, and her own scream begged to join theirs.

Next to her, Elias turned to Mr. Shaw. "Go get Amos. This needs to be sorted out."

Sorted? She choked. The situation needed more than a peace talk. As soon as Nathan Shaw was out of hearing range, she growled out, "I should've knifed that man when I had the chance."

Matthew frowned at her. "Violence only begets violence. You know that as well as I."

"Not if I grounded him first. I should have —"

"There is no time for should-haves," Elias

interrupted. "What did Logan take?"

"Gold. Near to half a crate." Rufus shot out a broad fire of expletives. "I'm with Mercy. We grab our guns and hunt him down for the skunk he is."

Rufus wheeled about, and for a half second Mercy considered joining him.

Matthew yanked him back by his collar. "Tracking in a rage makes for mistakes. Elias and I will set out. Logan can't have gone far."

Rufus sneered. "Dubois ain't even got a gun."

"Do you really think I need a musket to bring in Garret Logan?" His voice was a panther's growl.

"You managed to get hauled in while totin' one."

"Enough!" Matthew cuffed the young man on the back of the head. "Rufus, go run a scouting check on the area. Elias, come with me."

Matthew turned. Elias stalked after him.

And so did Mercy. "I'm coming along. You know I can see farther than the two of you combined."

Elias just kept on striding to where the horses were hobbled.

But Matthew stopped, his gray eyes kind yet firm. "I need you here, girl. Those Shaw men have to be talked out of going any farther into the backcountry, and you're just the one to do it."

Frustration roiled in her empty belly. "Why me?"

"Because you're the best one to remind them of their wives."

"But —" She clamped her mouth shut.

Matthew had set his jaw. Once he did that, there was no point in going any further, not even with a stick in hand.

She whirled, stifling a huff, and marched ramrod straight over to where the Shaw brothers rounded their wagons. Both had aged years in the space of three days.

She stopped in front of them. "My father and husband" — she paused, swallowing back the sour taste of the lie — "have gone off to bring back Mr. Logan."

Nathan Shaw nodded, his shoulders bent as if he alone bore the weight of the world. "We're much obliged, Mrs. Dubois. Seems we've brought more trouble upon you folks than any of us reckoned."

"Don't fret on our account. Life is trouble, and there's no stopping it. It is in the darkest skies we see the brightest stars."

Amos Shaw tugged at the soiled kerchief around his neck, his Adam's apple bobbing. "Wise words."

"Then I hope you will listen to what I have to say next. Come, let us sit." She bypassed the men and settled near the ashes of the spent fire. Even though no flames flared, the familiar position of working through issues at a fire pit was too ingrained to even think of sitting elsewhere.

She waited for the brothers to sink onto the ground across from her before she began. "You have already been cautioned on the dangers of continuing to Fort Wilderness and beyond."

"We have." The brothers exchanged a glance, then Nathan Shaw faced her. "Yet we're not to be moved. There's no going back east for us, with or without Mr. Logan's guidance."

She bit her lip. Willful men! How to upend minds plowed so deep into a rut? There could be no better outcome than the sharp end of a tomahawk if they journeyed west. But what about south? An idea began to unfurl, lifting her chin with the possibility of it. "I have an alternative."

Neither man spoke a word, but both their heads cocked.

"There is a closer fort you might want to consider. While I can't promise the route will be any safer, I can say for certain 'tis a lot shorter."

Nathan Shaw rubbed his jaw. "We ain't heard tell of no other garrisons out this way."

Of course not. There weren't any. But this was the next best thing — and the only idea she had left in her quiver. She forced a small smile. "It is more of a fortified house than a garrison."

"Speak plain, Mrs. Dubois. No need to fancy up your idea. I give you my word I shall consider it." He glanced at the other man. "Amos?"

His brother nodded. "Me too."

"All right." She leaned forward. At least they had given her a fair shot, which, despite Matthew's confidence, was more than she'd expected. "Not far past where the Now-adaga drains into the Mohawk River, there's a trading post set up by a man named Johannes Klock."

"But we —"

She held up her hand. "I know you aim to set up your own post, and you will. But for now, it might be best if you sheltered with a family who can teach you how to interact with the people of these lands. It takes more than slapping up four walls and hanging an 'open' shingle on your door. You need patience, understanding, and a fair amount of cunning. The Klocks know this."

215

Amos Shaw blew out a big breath.

Nathan shook his head. " 'Tain't what we had in mind."

She speared the man with a pointed stare. Sometimes a direct hit, while cutting to the bone, did the most good. "Neither was a babe come early with a mother still too weak to lift her head." She snapped her gaze to Amos. "Or a wife broken by grief."

Amos Shaw reared back as if she'd slapped his face. Nathan's lips folded into a grim line.

She held her breath. Had she pushed them too far?

For a long while, no one said anything. Only the chatter of the boys across the way — for they had given up their bickering — carried on the morning breeze, mixing with birdsong and the soft squall of a newborn.

Nathan ducked his chin. "Give us a few moments alone, Mrs. Dubois."

"Of course." She stood. "I will go check on Emmeline."

"Wait."

She turned back at the sound of Amos Shaw's quiet voice.

"Could you — *would* you mind checking on my wife too?"

She nodded, then swung around and grabbed up a mug of water on her way to

Mary Shaw's wagon. Dread dogged each step. What would she find? Would the woman light into her for bringing a babe not her own into the world? Would there be tears? Screams? The swipe of claws or worse . . . gaping silence and hollow stares?

"Mrs. Shaw?" she called out as she neared the wagon.

No response.

"Mary?" Reaching for the seat, she hauled herself upward. Still no answer.

Sucking in a breath for courage, she grasped the canvas covering the opening. "I'm coming in."

Growing up amongst warriors, she'd seen things that had turned her blood to the chill of a winter night, but as she crawled into the Shaws' wagon and gazed upon Mary, she shivered.

Mary Shaw curled into a ball, naked as the day she graced the world. Wicked red scratches covered her arms and legs, everywhere her nails could've possibly ripped away skin. Most were dried scarlet, yet some still oozed. Her eyes followed Mercy's entrance, fiery and cavernous, but did she even see her?

"Just me, Mary. 'Tis Mercy." Another shiver shimmied across her shoulders, and she forced her arm to hold steady as she held out the mug. "I brought you some water."

Mary didn't move. Didn't blink. Didn't anything.

How to deal with this? A cornered badger could take down prey three times its size — and Mercy suddenly knew exactly how that prey felt. Keeping her movements fluid and steady, she set the cup down, then dared to inch closer.

"Mary? You all right?"

She reached out a tentative hand and rested her fingers on the woman's bare back. Sometimes a gentle touch calmed more than a soothing voice. Slowly, she rubbed a circle on skin prickled with gooseflesh, avoiding the scratched areas. Mary did not move, so she edged closer and rubbed some more.

What seemed like hours passed, and in that eternity, the sun slanted higher where it worked its way up the canvas back opening. Mary's shoulders sagged looser. The woman's grip around her knees loosened. Her eyes never closed, but the glassy sheen eased to normal. Perhaps this was working.

Quietly, for anything loud might shatter the tentative peace, Mercy hummed the same lullaby she'd sung to Emmeline the night before.

And a tiny sob gurgled in Mary's throat.

"Oh dear one." The words, her own mother's, slipped past Mercy's lips unbidden. "I don't know how many babes you have lost, and I don't need to, but what I do know is this kind of grief isn't made to fit inside your body. You must allow your heart to break so that the sorrow runs out. My mother used to tell me there's more love in Christ for us than there can ever be brokenness. Only in turning to Him can you be healed on the inside."

Her hand paused, stilled by a sudden insight. Was that how her mother had survived the loss of her family? Her captivity amongst the Wyandot — and later the Mohawks? Was it her mother's continual turning to Christ that had given her such joy, her reason for not fighting against her captors?

Perhaps the weakness in her mother that she'd reviled all these years had really been strength — God's strength. Why had she never thought of that before? Shame withered her spirit, curling it up every bit as much as the woman shrunken before her.

"*Iesos*," she whispered. "Take this scorn from me, the pain from this woman, and heal the broken parts in both of us."

Mary stiffened. She did too.

For the warmth of a thousand suns suddenly filled the wagon.

Elias walked on silent feet in the water, his moccasins leaving no mark where the Nowadaga ran smooth along the bank. Matthew followed, gun in hand. It rankled to have his own fingers hanging loose at his sides, but there was nothing to be done for the injustice.

The sun beat warm and the river nipped cold as it leaked into the seams of his shoes. He frowned. Had he known he'd be so waylaid from his original course to Boston, he'd have taken extra care last time he greased the leather.

Five paces later, he stopped and crouched, studying grass barely bent, a slight indentation where a rock had once sat, and a river that flowed unrelenting. Not much to go on.

Lord, but Mercy had a keen eye.

Satisfied, he straightened and nodded toward the opposite bank. Matthew shadowed his steps, neither of them splashing nor hardly rippling the water. The ranger knew how to track as silently as any brave — he'd give him that.

On the other side, they paused and scanned the rocks. Sand and shrub ran sparse up to the wood line, making it harder to distinguish disturbed ground. He shook his head, annoyed this foray was eating time he didn't have.

"I never should have threatened Logan last night." A sigh trailed the end of his words. "This is on me. He is running scared."

"He is running stupid to think he can get away." Matthew pointed five yards farther south, where the bank dropped off from the trees. Beside a row of tree trunks, a depression flattened the middle of a patch of wild ginger — not big, but enough to give away the tread of a horse.

Elias smirked. "Well, I never did credit Logan with much sense."

Climbing the bank, he grunted, pleased. The man had made no effort to hide his trail. Maybe this wouldn't take so much time after all.

"Truth be told" — Matthew pulled up alongside him — "I did not credit you with much sense at first either."

He glanced sideways at Matthew, as off-center as the statement. Why such a confession? "Sounds like you changed your mind."

"In most respects."

"And others?" Turning his head, he gazed at the man full-on.

Matthew shrugged. "It depends."

His step faltered. The ground rose and dipped, the uneven remains of a long winter's freeze — but the terrain had nothing to do with his sudden imbalance. A foreign longing troubled his step — a desire for Matthew Prinn's good opinion. "What would that depend on?"

"How much space you give Mercy."

Space? What was he to make of that? He paused, searching for a hint in the lines on Matthew's face. "I do not follow."

One brow rose. Was that mistrust or astonishment?

"Don't tell me you have missed noticing the girl's smitten with you."

He snorted. Unbelievable. Perhaps he'd credited Matthew with too much sense. He veered away from the man and his preposterous idea, following the angle of a hoof gouge pointed northwest. "Mercy would as soon knife me as she would Logan."

"No, you're wrong. I've seen how she looks at you. I've never known her to give any man a passing glance, but you? You she studies. Memorizes. I wager there's a battle raging fierce inside her that she can't begin to understand."

Heat as from a dying sun scorched through him, and he sucked in a breath.

Was such a notion true?

He shot forward, prodded by a realization he dared not reach out and hold hands with. "You are sorely mistaken, Prinn. Mercy is of a sharp mind. She would not go wobble-kneed for the likes of me."

"I would have sworn she'd not go wobble-kneed for anyone — ever — knowing her history."

"Which is?" Elias turned back around, facing the man.

" 'Tain't really mine to tell, but —" Matthew rubbed his chin. "I s'pose 'tis common enough knowledge. Mercy's mother was a white woman, taken captive by the Wyandots."

He grunted. That explained her animosity toward the French, being they were practically one and the same. Still, something didn't sit right. He squinted at Matthew. "But Mercy is part Mohawk, is she not?"

"Aye." The man nodded. "Her Mohawk father stole her mother as part of a raid on the Wyandots' camp, taking her for one of his wives. Her mother never quite picked up the people's ways though, choosing instead to cling to her Christian faith, which of course the other women scorned. Mercy included. Troubles her to this day, whether she owns up to it or not. And I will not see her troubled further by the likes of you."

He held up his hands. "I have not touched the woman."

Matthew's gray eyes bored into his. "Good. Keep it that way. I will not see her heart pierced through, not by you. Not by anyone."

The thought of Mercy weeping over any man curled his hands into fists. "On that we are agreed."

Turning, he shrugged away from Matthew's intense gaze. Better they give the entire conversation concerning Mercy a good distance.

Matthew fell into pace beside him, and for a long while, they stalked quietly. Logan's trail was simple enough to follow. The fool had no idea how easily he could've been pursued by those bent on killing.

" 'Tain't none of my business, but I am a mite curious." Matthew shoved aside a swath of dogwood branches, allowing them both to pass. "Why did you switch sides?"

He blew out a long breath, disgusted more by the answer than the question. He'd known going into this he'd lose face with his countrymen. And in truth, before he'd met up with Matthew and Mercy, that had never bothered him. His brow tightened into a knot, for it surely did trouble him now. What would Matthew think if he shared his story of intrigue and espionage? Would the man believe him — or brand him a liar, bent on talking his way out of prison?

His shoulders sank. As much as he valued Matthew's esteem, he couldn't reveal his mission.

"It is . . . complicated," he finally said.

Matthew chuckled. "Good."

He jerked his face toward the man. "What?"

"That was no easy answer." Matthew clouted him on the back. "Enemy or not, I respect a man acting on conviction."

He pressed his lips flat, stifling an open-mouthed stare. How much of a different man — a *better* man — would he be if he'd had this man for a father? No wonder Mercy fretted over parting ways with this ranger.

Ahead, sticks snapped. Tender young plants swished. Something moved. Fast.

Toward them.

He dropped. Matthew flattened against the trunk of a fat maple. Neither of them breathed. Matthew cocked his hammer full open.

A horse emerged. A black-tailed bay. Riderless — but laden with saddle and bulging bags.

Elias shot up and dashed after the horse, easing it with a low, "Here boy, good boy," on his advance. The animal slowed, and he snagged a loose rein, then led the mount back to Matthew.

Matthew pulled out a handful of dried berries and offered them over with a flat palm. "So, where's your master, eh, fella?"

With the horse occupied, Elias tied off the lead on a nearby branch. "I wager he is not far, being on foot — which begs the question, why? Logan would not willingly let a treasure roam far from his grasp."

"Aye." Matthew nodded.

They both plunged farther into the woods, then stopped short a quarter mile later, just before the ground gave way to a ravine with a sheer rock face. Were this a creek, the cut of it would make for a spectacular waterfall.

Elias peered over the brink. Below, a dark shape lay unmoving, head jutted at an unnatural angle.

Garret Logan.

CHAPTER 17

Twilight padded in from the wood's edge, silent, thick, and gray, like a great wolf on the hunt. A chill came with it, teasing curls of steam from the bowls in Mercy's hands. She handed them over to Amos Shaw.

"Thank you." He nodded.

She rubbed her hands along her apron, wiping off the moisture from a few drips. "You might want to save that thanks until you take a bite. I'm not much for cooking. How does your wife fare?"

"Better since this morning. I don't know what you said, but it got her dressed, and she is willing to eat." He held up the bowls. "No matter the taste."

"I am glad for it." And she was, truly, but in her belly a remnant of disappointment yet churned. After the strange sensation she'd experienced in Mary Shaw's wagon that morn, she'd felt certain the woman couldn't help but be as changed as she. As lightened of spirit. As freed. But Mary Shaw had yet to emerge from the confines of her wagon.

Still, the easier step of Amos Shaw and the lift of his shoulders as he retreated squelched that disappointment. He was pleased with his wife's progress. That would have to be enough.

Grabbing her own bowl, she turned to find a spot to sit. Nathan and his boys took up one log. Elias sat on another — with enough room to spare. She sank next to him and, for one blessed moment, relished taking the weight off her foot. Her toe was healed — mostly thanks to comfrey soaks every chance she could manage one — but it still felt good to ease up on it now and then. She sighed before digging into her pottage.

"You sound as weary as I feel." He flashed her a smile before tipping his bowl and draining the rest of his stew.

She cocked a brow. "I did not think you ever tired."

Swiping his mouth, he set down his bowl and faced her. "Retrieving Logan's body out of that ravine was harder than either Matthew or I expected. He must have been riding at a good clip to have been thrown with such a force. Then there was digging a grave, reloading our cargo, mm-hmm . . ." He closed his eyes. "Sleep will come easy tonight."

"Tell us a story, Mr. Dubois?" Food flew out of Jonas's mouth, right along with his question.

"Yeah!" His brother bounced beside him, soup spilling over the bowl's rim and darkening his breeches in a wide splotch on his leg. "Tell us another one."

"Now, boys," Nathan interrupted, "let the man eat his supper in peace."

"Aww!" Their combined voices keened into a fine whine.

Mercy gritted her teeth, spoon hovering above her bowl. What those boys needed was a firm hand for such insolence. Mr. Shaw merely shoveled in another bite of his soup, ignoring the rascals and their complaints.

"Well . . ." Elias hunkered forward, resting his forearms on his thighs. From her angle, he was all shoulders and back, muscle and strength.

"Since I am finished with my supper, as long as you boys promise to finish your meal and pack right off to bed when I am done, I will tell you a story."

"Deal!" they said in unison.

"All right. There is a tale told by some

229

northwoods trappers near Montreal, way up in New France. It goes like this."

The boys stilled. So did Mercy. Elias had a way of mesmerizing like none other — grasping her attention and pinning it down — and she wasn't sure how to feel about that.

Elias lifted his hat and ran his hand through his hair, shoving it back beneath the band, out of his eyes. "There was a woman who lived in those northern woods, a beautiful woman, so comely no one could figure out why Mademoiselle Delphine lived by herself in the wilds. Some say she was a witch, but surely you boys do not believe in witches, do you?"

Two sets of wide eyes stared back at him from the other log. No, three. Half a smile tugged her lips. Apparently Nathan Shaw loved a good story as well.

"I suppose that is neither here nor there though." Elias sniffed. "The fact is that Mademoiselle always carried with her a set of keys. Some say she used them to lock up lads who were naughty, but I do not think you boys have anything to fret about. Montreal is far off, and you two are not of a mind for mischief tonight, are you?"

A duo of undertakers couldn't have shaken their heads more solemnly.

"Good." Elias slapped his hands on his legs, making them all jump. "Now where was I? Ah, yes, the keys. Early one morning, as Mademoiselle leaned against the rail of her pigpen, she spied a pig she'd never before seen. This swine was larger than the rest, grunting and rooting louder than any. When she slopped the trough, he crowded out the others, letting none but himself fill his belly. Seeing this, she grabbed her key ring and struck the big pig on the nose. Soon as she broke skin and the blood flowed, the pig disappeared — and a tall, handsome man stood in his place."

The boys stared, drop-jawed.

Mercy frowned, disgusted. Filling children's heads with happily-ever-afters only set them up for disappointment later in life. She knew that better than most. None of the stories her mother ever told her had come true.

She speared Elias with a stare. "And I suppose they shared a lifetime of bliss with scores of little ones at their feet, hmm?"

He winked at the boys, then smiled at her, his blue eyes twinkling. "No. The handsome young man tipped his hat, said, *'Merci,'* and walked away just like that." He lifted his hand and snapped his fingers, sharp on the evening air. *"La fin."*

She blinked, stunned. Must he always keep her so off-kilter? Snatching up his empty bowl, along with hers, she stood.

"All right, boys." Nathan Shaw stood as well. "You have had your story and filled your bellies. Off to bed."

"Aww!" Jonas wailed.

Next to him, James glowered. "Just one more?"

"Your father is right, lads." Rubbing a muscle at the back of his neck, Elias rose. "We break camp just before dawn. You shall be crossing that river as the sun blinks over the horizon, so get yourself some sleep."

Like two pups, the boys scrambled up from the log and rambled off, chattering all the way. Poor Emmeline. Hopefully she and the babe would rest easy once the boys quieted, for no one could sleep with their ruckus. But perhaps she ought to check on the woman before night fell hard and they all settled down.

Before she could turn aside, Nathan approached her and Elias. "Once again, much obliged for the way you bear with my boys." Then he faced her. "And I thought I'd let you know, Mrs. Dubois. Amos and I talked a piece. We'll be heading down to the Klocks'. My thanks to you for the suggestion."

Relief filled her as much as the stew. When neither man had spoken of her idea all day, she'd thought for sure they were bent on going their own way. Not that the journey would be any easier, but at least it would prove a mite safer and cover a lot less distance.

"No thanks needed, Mr. Shaw. If we do not work together, we die together." She pressed her lips shut, surprised at how easily Elias's words had slipped past them in the first place. It was as if part of the man had moved in and taken up residence inside her head.

Nathan Shaw tugged the brim of his hat then ambled off.

Elias stared at her. "So are you willing now to work with a traitor?"

"I did not say that." She collected all the dirty bowls, ignoring any response the man might make. Let him think what he would, for he often did the same to her. After giving the dishes a good scrubbing, she stowed them in a crate, along with a covered tin of leftovers for when Matthew and Rufus came in from watch.

With a yawn, she trekked toward the sound of a mewling babe's cry inside the Shaws' wagon. But as she rounded the front of it, she paused. Amongst the beginnings

233

of a night chorus rife with scritches and rustlings and croaks, something more high-pitched whistled at the edges. She cocked her head.

A warbler trilled. Her pulse beat a rush of war drums in her ears. Warblers sang in sunlight, and twilight already darkened into dusk.

She dashed back to her wagon, retrieving her gun. Overkill for a small bird — but not for a man imitating such. After priming the barrel, she strode off on silent feet into the woods.

Shadows thickened. The loamy smell of earth, damp now in the evening air, filled her nostrils. She inhaled as she wielded her way past brush, praying to God she'd not smell the tang of bear grease or the musky scent of warriors, ready for battle.

Darkness grew. Night animals stirred. No more warbler trills. Had she been mistaken?

Pausing near a tree trunk, she studied the ground she'd already covered, checking to make certain no one had doubled back to sneak up behind her. Satisfied, she turned and strained to see ahead through the maze of trees and shadows.

Far off, a doe ambled by with a tentative step, nosing the air. Closer, leftover autumn leaves rustled as an opossum passed. She stood still for so long, the chirrups of tree frogs struck up a song around her.

Slowly, the tension in her shoulders slackened. No man-shapes emerged from the growing darkness.

But a hand clamped over her mouth.

Elias pressed his fingers against Mercy's lips, gentle yet firm, fighting the urge to throttle the woman. When he'd seen her grab her gun and slip off into the trees, his gut had twisted into a thick knot. Why must she run headlong into danger? She truly would be the death of him.

Beneath his hold, she stood rigid, neither weak-kneed nor quailing. Not a whimper. Not a sound. What kind of woman did that?

"Shh," he breathed into her ear.

He released her — then wished he hadn't. A musket barrel pressed cold against his chest, and he froze.

"Don't move," she hissed and widened her stance. "What are you doing here?"

Meeting her challenge, he stared right back. "Warblers do not sing at night."

Without pulling her eyes from him, she lowered her gun. "You heard it too." Her whisper was more a statement than a question.

He nodded, hiding a grin. Ah, but she was

a picture, framed by the darkening woods. Her skin glowed soft in the last remnants of light as she stood at the ready, stance poised for a fight or a swift-legged escape. The musket in her hands was as much a part of her as the long braid tossed over her shoulder. She'd knotted up her skirts, and her slim legs, hard with muscle, peeked out bare and stockingless from her knees down. Upon his soul, he'd never seen such a singular beauty.

A rogue desire to pull her into his arms coursed through his veins, but she'd only half-set her hammer, not fully closed it. Judging by the gleam in her eye, she'd as soon blast a hole in his chest than yield to his embrace.

The buzzing squawk of a woodcock cut into his thoughts — thankfully. This was no time for moon-eyeing a doe, not even a comely one such as Mercy.

"See anything?" he whispered.

She shook her head.

"Me either. Come on." On silent feet, he stepped past her and led the way farther into the woodland. It was a risk, bringing her along, but keeping her near seemed the lesser of whatever evil lurked in the growing darkness.

Ten paces apart, with her on his left, they

stole from tree to tree, her tread as light as his. A marvel, that, for he'd never known anyone to move as a shadow other than himself. They scouted side by side for near a half mile, until night fell too hard to see beyond a few paces.

Mercy closed the distance between them, signaling with a tip of her head they ought to turn back. "Whatever it was, we lost it."

Defeat always tasted bitter, and he swallowed. "I do not like it, the not knowing."

"Nor I." Her dark eyes lifted to his.

"But you are right." A sigh deflated him. "There is too much darkness now. Maybe Matthew or Rufus got a lead. Whatever gave that call, it is not this way."

They stalked back toward camp, his mind buzzing with dangerous possibilities. He'd wager his lifeblood that he'd heard that warbler trill twice. Were they not leaving in the morning, he'd give this stretch of wood another good scouring come daylight.

"Could have been a hermit thrush," Mercy murmured beside him. "Makes sense. Still . . ."

A half smile twitched his lips. Apparently her thoughts swam the same direction as his.

She shifted her gun to her other shoulder. "Maybe I heard wrongly."

"Do not doubt yourself. It *was* high in pitch." The words came out gruff, a reprimand to himself as much as to her. They couldn't have both imagined the same sound, could they? Then again, how many unexplained screeches and growls had shivered down his backbone during murky nights while traveling with his father?

"Though I suppose" — he softened his tone — "I have heard stranger things."

She slanted him a glance. "You sound as if you clasp hands with doubt yourself."

"Not quite. Not yet. Let's sweep back along the other side of those boulders." He veered north, taking care not to trip over a downed maple. Mercy trailed him, close enough that the chill air curling over his shoulder carried her sweet, musky scent.

Twenty yards out from camp, they rounded the last of the rocky stretch. Leaving the light-colored lichen plastered against the boulders was a shame, for it proved a guideline for his steps, keeping his feet close to the line of rocks. The rest of the way would be dark-stepping on black ground, as black as the circles —

Circles?

He dropped into a crouch. Mercy gained his side and squatted next to him. Her sharp intake of air could only mean she understood exactly what he saw carved into the lichen at the base of the last boulder. The cut of the two spheres was fresh, connected by a line through the middle — a native sign denoting two days.

He lifted his eyes to the black woods and stared hard into darkness now so thick there was no telling if whoever left this sign remained behind a tree or not. Or worse, if there were more than one.

He shifted his gaze to Mercy. The same question creased her brow.

What would happen in two days?

CHAPTER 18

Night faded like a bruise, the predawn darkness lightening in increments from black to indigo, painting the world in deep blue. Mercy passed the cluster of men discussing the surest way to cross the river on her way to the front wagon — Emmeline and Nathan's, poised to venture across the Nowadaga. James and Jonas huddled on the driver's seat, likely scheming some kind of trouble despite the early hour. She hauled herself up and nodded them a greeting, though neither responded.

"Emmeline?" she called as she crawled through the canvas opening. "I came to say goodbye."

Inside, the new mother and her babe reclined atop crates heaped with blankets. Emmeline held out her hand. "I was hoping you would. I shall miss you."

"And I, you." The truth of her words hit a soft spot in her heart, and she sucked in a breath. She *had* enjoyed this woman's company.

Drawing near, she smiled and clasped the woman's cold fingers. "You keep that little one fed and warm, and she'll grow up just fine."

"Thank you. I will." Emmeline squeezed her hand. "I'm sure it won't be long till you hold a babe in your arms."

Her smile faded. Emmeline was wrong. Her arms would not cradle a wee one anytime soon, but maybe someday . . . Her lips flattened. What a ridiculous notion.

Leaning closer, she kissed the babe on her downy cheek then let go of Emmeline's grasp. "Godspeed to you all."

"I shall never forget you, Mercy Dubois."

As always, the false name went down sideways, and she swallowed. "Neither shall I forget you, Emmeline."

Working her way around in the confined space, she wriggled back out the front canvas hole and faced James and Jonas. "You boys behave yourself. You have a mother and sister to look after, you hear?"

Jonas frowned at her. "Mr. Elias already told us that."

She hid a smile. As much as she hated to credit a traitor, Elias would make a fine father one day. "Then mind what he said, and mind your father as well. Go on inside now."

The boys scrambled past her, bickering over who got to peek out the back canvas hole. She climbed down, emotions swirling. In the few days she'd spent with Emmeline, she'd grown to like the woman. Given more time, they might've been great allies.

Matthew, Rufus, Elias, and the Shaw men still stood near the horses, though as she passed by, she noted the conversation had moved on to final route advice. None lifted their eyes to her. Just as well. When had a man ever taken a woman's word on directions?

Eight paces past them, she stopped even with the front of Amos Shaw's wagon. Mary sat atop, bundled in a gray woolen shawl and long-brimmed bonnet. She stared, as usual, but this time not unseeing. Had the real Mary Shaw left behind the netherworld of bleak sorrow and ventured back into her own body?

Mercy smiled up at her. Indeed, the woman's eyes shone clear, and a faint flicker of a smile curved the edges of her lips.

Lifting her hand, Mercy spoke a blessing, wishing with everything in her that it would come true. "*Skennen*, Mrs. Shaw. Skennen."

The deep blue light left over from night

faded as the morning sun rose. Time for their own departure soon enough. With a nod to the woman, she set off up the road to camp, where their wagons sat at the ready, aimed east instead of west. It wouldn't hurt to scout ahead a bit, now that the coming sun lessened the shadows. She'd grab her gun, poke around, then swing back to rejoin the others as they returned from helping the Shaws cross the river.

Holding on to the wagon's side, she hefted herself up to the seat — then froze. Goose-flesh prickled hundreds of bumps along her arms. A scalp lock with a turkey feather yet attached to the bloody skin was draped on the bench.

She snapped into action, grabbing her gun from inside and hitting the ground with silent feet. A trail of moccasin prints led to the wood line, and she lifted her gaze. Shutting out the morning chill, the shush of wind, the trill of birds, she narrowed her eyes and stared, hard. A man stepped out from behind a sycamore trunk, armed with bow, arrows, tomahawk, and war club.

A mountain of a man.

She shouldered her gun and broke into a run. "Onontio!"

But her steps faltered as she drew near her brother. Beneath the red and black colors of war painted on his face, a gash split his flesh from temple to chin. One eye was purpled shut. Blood darkened his breechclout, spreading from thigh to knee on his deerskin leggings. By the looks of it, that scalp lock on the wagon seat had been bought at a great price.

"You're hurt!" she cried.

He lifted his chin, smelling of sweat and battle. "I live."

Proud man. Proud, stupid man. What had he gotten himself into? A frown weighted her brow. "What happened?"

"I came for you with a dark tale when a snake crossed my way." Murder glimmered in his eyes. "The Wyandot snake is no more."

"Only one?"

He nodded.

"Not a scout then." Shoving loose hair out of her eyes, she thought hard. A lone man. An enemy. Why would a single warrior venture so close to their camp when — Of course. The circles carved into the lichen. She stared up at her brother. "A messenger. What do the people hear? What do you know of what might happen in two days?"

"I know nothing." Onontio's face hardened to granite. "And our people are no more."

The words skittered about in the air like a swarm of gnats, ones she'd like to swipe away. "What are you saying?" she whispered.

"After warning you, I returned home." The cut of his jaw slanted grim. "To death and ash."

"But Father?" She shook her head, a useless act to ban the black thoughts that would not be stopped. "Surely not Rake'niha!"

She grabbed his arm, hoping, wishing, needing to know that what she suspected surely wasn't true. Couldn't be true. Not Black-Fox-Running. Never him.

Onontio nodded swift and sharp, the movement cutting like a razor-edged blade — slicing her heart in two.

No, this couldn't be happening. Grief slammed against her chest, seeking a crevice to breach, but she would not let it in. One tear, half a whimper, and she'd be undone.

She lifted her chin. "Who did this? Why?"

For a moment, Onontio's nostrils flared. Whatever went on in his mind could not be good. "After severing ties with Bragg, Rake'niha allied with Johnson, promising our men to fight against the blue coats' Fort Niagara. Before the traveling sun, a raiding party of *Ehressaronon* swept down from the north. None in our village survived."

Despite her hold on him, she swayed, and

his other arm shot out, balancing her. The world turned watery. She blinked, fighting against tears, swallowing back thick pain. She'd always known there'd be graves coming. Darkness coming. Heartbreak. But not now. Not yet. Suddenly she knew how Mary Shaw felt.

After a few deep breaths, though everything in her screamed to plow into him and weep against his chest, she pulled away. She had to be strong, leastwise in front of her brother, for he shared the same hollow ache that carved a gouge in her breast.

She blinked up at him. "What will you do?"

"I will hunt them down." Blood marred his words, dripping from the slash on his cheek to his lips.

Another piece of her heart broke off. He didn't stand a chance. "You are but one man, my brother."

He flung back his shoulders, swiping away the blood from his mouth. "That is of no account."

"I can't lose you too!" Her ragged voice ruined the sanctity of the early morn, staining the birth of the new day with the portent of death.

He reached out, his big thumb running rough over her cheek, leaving behind the dampness of his own lifeblood. "Our paths were meant to split, *aktsi:'a.* You have walked between two worlds, but no more. You must choose life. Prinn is a good long knife. Go with him."

Her shoulders sagged. There was no way she could tell him Matthew had plans of his own to leave her. Her brother had enough to bear without the thought of what would become of her.

"*Ó:nen* Kahente." He pulled back his hand. *"Tsi Nen:we Enkonnoronhkhwake."*

"Tsi Nen:we —" Her throat closed. Looking at her brother for what might be the last time on this side of heaven, she choked. He looked so much like a younger Black-Fox-Running, it was like speaking to her father. A sob welled up, begging for release. She'd never get another chance to tell her father she loved him forever. And in truth, this just might be her last shared endearment with Onontio.

She sucked in a breath and forced out a clear voice. "Tsi Nen:we Enkonnoronhkhwake, Onontio. Ó:nen."

Their gazes locked in a last goodbye; then he turned and stalked into the woods. As he walked away, a shiver blew through her soul like a cold moan. She stared, long and hard, until even her keenest eyesight could no longer distinguish his strong, broad shoulders. Would she ever see him again?

Loss stretched out bony arms and pulled her to its bosom, crushing her in a chokehold of an embrace. Despite her resolve to stay strong, to be brave, she dropped to the ground.

And wept.

Water squished between heel and sole in Elias's left moccasin. He'd have to ask Matthew tonight for some extra grease to stop up that leaky seam. But for now, he'd yank off the shoe and let it dry while he drove.

Morning light blazed a halo above the rear of the wagon as he approached. It hadn't taken long to help the Shaws cross the river, especially now that the waters ran low and slow. But it had still taken time — time they didn't have. Time *he* didn't have. If all went well and he stole off just before they veered north toward Fort Edward, he'd still have a hard go of it to reach Boston. Four days of tough riding. Possibly five. The enormity of the undertaking crashed down on him like a rockslide. So many things could go wrong. For a moment, he gave in to hanging his head with the weight of responsibility —

And saw fresh tracks leading away from the wagon.

He dropped to a crouch, his gaze following the indents of two sets of footprints. The first sank deeper into the ground. A big man, then, shod in moccasins much like the ones he wore.

He narrowed his eyes and studied the other set, but it didn't take long before his breath hitched. The length was short, with a sharp solid curve digging heavy on the right side. Mercy's step. Nearly on top of the other set of prints. Apparently she'd followed someone into the woods, but with no sign of struggle.

Rising, he stared into the maze of brilliant greens and browns. Wherever she went, she'd gone willingly.

He pivoted and faced the wagon behind his, lifting his palm toward Rufus. "Hold on."

Rufus turned aside and spit off the side of the wagon, then spit out a curse as well. "We ain't got time to be waiting!"

Elias frowned. He knew that better than anyone. Strange though to see Rufus ruffled up about anything other than the next meal.

"This will not take long." He strode off, glad to leave behind the sour-faced complainer. It was a wonder the young man had lasted this long as a regular without a cashiering.

The trail was easy enough to follow, with no trace of care being taken to cover the tracks. Ahead, twenty yards into the forest, a small shape took on form, bent low to the ground. At twelve yards, he distinguished a dark stripe splitting that shape — a long, dark braid — and he upped his pace. He stopped only steps away from where Mercy curled over in a patch of flattened trillium. Alone. Was she sick?

"Mercy?" he murmured so as not to startle her. "What ails you?"

She jerked upright, the cloth across her shoulders stretched taut. She said nothing, nor did she face him.

"Are you ill?" he tried again.

"I . . . I am fine. Give me a moment."

The hesitation, the stutter, the slight tremble shimmying down her backbone all twisted a knife in his chest. Something was wrong. Very wrong.

In two strides he bent and gripped her shoulders, pulling her to her feet. Before he could turn her around, she wrenched from his grasp and scuttled away, picking up her gun where she'd dropped it.

He froze, fully prepared for her to swing the barrel straight for his chest, but she did not. She just stood there, cradling her gun, breathing hard — and that kindled a fear in him more terrible than staring down a cold, gray muzzle.

"Mercy, look at me. I would see your face."

"Go." Her voice shook, throaty and unsteady. "I will take first scout."

"Matthew is already on it." Using all his skills at shadow walking, he approached her on silent feet, stopping inches behind her. "Now, turn around."

She whirled, eyes red, wet stains yet shiny on her smooth cheeks. "Go away!"

The tension in his jaw loosened. This she-devil he could work with. "Your brother brought news?"

She sucked in a sharp breath, her dark gaze narrowing. "What would you know of that?"

"I followed two sets of prints from the wagon to the wood's edge. Yours and those deep and long enough to belong to a big man, just like your brother. I did not figure you would go willingly with anyone else."

She sighed, mournful as a dove. The nod of her head looked as if it took all her strength — and more. Sweet mercy! What awful news had the man brought her?

He looked past her, expecting the painted shapes of warriors to spring out at any moment. "Are we in danger?"

"Life is danger." The emptiness in her tone chilled the sun's warmth. No one should sound so hollow.

He cut his gaze back to her. "What happened?"

Her lower lip quivered. A single fat tear fell, riding the curve of her cheek. "Our father —" Her voice broke.

So did his usual reserve. The woman was naught but a sorrow-filled waif, gripping a gun too big and a grief too great. He opened his arms, offering, hoping, and surprisingly willing to take on her pain instead of running the other way. He hardly knew himself anymore.

And that was a very good thing.

Mercy blinked, loosing a fresh burst of tears — then dropped her gun and plowed into him. He staggered from the force of her assault, her weeping, her ragged cries. Wrapping his arms around her, he held on through the storm.

"My father is gone," she wailed into his chest. "My village . . . and now my brother. There is nothing for me to go home to."

Her pain lanced through his heart, making it hard to distinguish from his own.

"I hardly know the meaning of the word *home*," he mumbled against the top of her head, more to himself than to her. He knew the horrid feeling all too well, the sudden ripping away of the ground he'd always stood on. The plummeting sensation of not knowing where to land, how to land. If he'd land. All the emotions of losing his mother as a young lad, the regret of not making peace with his grandfather before he died, barreled back, unexpectedly vivid.

He clung to Mercy every bit as much as she pressed into him.

Eventually her breathing evened, and she stilled. It wouldn't be long before she pulled away, but for now, he cherished the trusting way she leaned against him, drawing from his strength. Would that they might stand here forever, him bearing her up, her warming his arms. A perfect fit. Like none he'd ever known.

"Dubois! Where are you?"

Rufus's voice hit him from behind, shattering the moment. Mercy jerked away and retrieved her gun, the loss of her from his arms near to unbearable.

He blew out a sigh, letting go of the gift. He'd learned long ago that nothing beautiful lasted, save for eternity. "Did your brother know anything of that sign we found last night?"

"No. He killed the man before he could talk." She glanced at him as she passed by.

"But he was a Wyandot."

Once again he gazed at the endless stretch of trees. Wyandot. Had that message been for him? Because if it was, then he really had trouble. Good thing they would put plenty of time and space between this place and themselves by the time two days were spent.

If the new wagon wheel proved road-worthy.

CHAPTER 19

Mercy ran, the gun at her back bouncing a rhythm against her spine. The strap dug into her chest, but that did not slow her. Driving herself hard and fast, she ignored the fatigue in her quivering muscles. She could outpace Matthew, who'd been tracking her for hours now, but it was impossible to outrun a demon — especially the one that gnawed to get out from the inside. Still, a trifle such as impossibility had never stopped her before.

And she wasn't about to show any more weakness.

So she pumped her legs faster and leapt over a downed maple, barely catching herself with a wild swing of her arms, then pressed onward. If the world had an end, she'd find it and fling herself off the edge, putting a stop to all the ragged emotions burning inside.

But as the afternoon dragged on, the futility of her race caught up to her. Lungs heaving, she slowed, body spent and near to ruin. Any farther and she'd collapse. Not a bad idea, but it wouldn't be fair to Matthew. She'd given him enough of a challenge.

She bent and planted her hands on scraped knees, gasping for air. It did no good. All the running. The distance. In spite of secluding herself yesterday and the better part of today, the ache was still there, raw and unrelenting. The same grief raged. The same humiliation churned. Nothing had changed save for the new rips in her hiked-up skirts and fresh gashes on her legs.

She sank onto a rocky ledge, letting her feet dangle. Below, the woods encircled a small glade where spring flowers sent up green shoots. Come the corn-planting moon, this patch of dirt and sun would yield a beautiful swath of purple and white, fresh and innocent. And for some odd reason, the thought of such magnificence was too much to bear.

With her remaining strength, she snatched up a rock and threw it, squashing a small patch of plants far below. A churlish thing, but unstoppable. She'd never been so out of control in her life.

And that scared her more than anything.

Behind her, ferns rustled, crushed beneath

a heavy step. Labored breathing whooshed along with a slight breeze tickling the overhead maple leaves. The tangy odor of sweat wafted up to her nose as Matthew flopped down beside her. She ought to lower her skirts and cover her bare legs, but honestly, she just didn't care. Besides, it was only Matthew.

Yet when he opened his mouth, a stranger rebuked her. "I gave you plenty of space yesterday and most of today, but this stops here and now. You're officially off duty until my say-so."

The command was steel cold and just as hard. She jerked her face toward him. "You can't do that."

"You know I can." His gunmetal eyes sparked a challenge — one she'd best not meet. She'd seen only one man ever survive it, barely.

Tucking her chin, she sighed. "What I mean is you *can't* do that. How could you? I can't sit on a wagon seat all day, not with this burning inside me."

"Oh girl." He shook his head, the familiar Matthew peeking out through his softening gaze. "I know you're hurting, but it is time to quit running."

She peered up at him, drawn by the tenderness in his tone. More white whiskers than she remembered peppered his bristly beard. Weathered lines cut into his cheeks below a purple bruise that spread from his eye. She squinted, studying his face more closely. A cut marred his jaw and a scrape made a red stripe on his forehead. Were those wounds purchased at the expense of chasing her?

She slumped. He was right, as usual. All her running hadn't eased her pain but instead had given him some.

"Elias told me about your father. Unh-unh." He wagged a finger. "Don't get all puffed up about him telling me your business. I forced his hand. He said it was yours to tell, but after a tussle, he broke."

Her eyebrows shot skyward. "You wrestled with Elias?"

"Flit! I ain't in the grave yet." He rubbed his jaw, the rasp of it soothing in an odd sort of way. "But I admit he packs a powerful right hook. Truth is, I think he took pity and lightened up."

Unbidden, the feel of Elias's embrace wrapped around her once again, and just like all the other times she'd relived that moment, she was powerless to stop it. He'd stood there open-armed, inviting her in but at her own pace. Even now if she inhaled, she'd likely still breathe his scent of smoke and danger. Ah, but there in his arms, for the briefest of time, she'd experienced a release like none other when she'd wept into his shirt. He'd stood there, taking her sorrow, shoring her up like a great beam. Waiting her out until she settled. No one had ever done that. Not her father, her brother . . . not even Matthew. Elias was like none other. And if she dared to admit it, if he ever opened his arms again, she'd run into them headlong and unflinching.

She hung her head. What kind of daughter thought of another man when mourning her father? A weak one, that was what. She was weak as the woman she'd scorned for such softness all these years. With a sigh, she reached for her necklace.

Matthew's big hand patted her leg. "Grief never comes easy, girl. It never comes calling at an opportune time. I grieve for your loss."

She stared at the skin on the back of his hand, all leather and snaked with blue veins. "You're all I have left."

"Someday a man will steal your heart, maybe already has, and I won't be but a memory."

"No." She snapped her gaze to his. "No one will ever take your place."

He chuckled. "Well, I expect we'll always

remember our times together."

The faintest of smiles whispered over her lips. "Does that mean I can be back on duty?"

He reared back and looked down his nose. "You are a wonder, Mercy Lytton. A full-out, stubborn-headed —"

His words cut off like a snuffed candle, and they both sat rock still, listening.

Mercy drew up her legs and flattened to her belly. Beside her, Matthew lay flat as well. Below, at the edge of the glade, a flash of blue and white marched in. Twenty. No, twenty-four. A full squad.

Of French soldiers.

Tree line. Road. Tree line. Road. Elias pinged his gaze from ruts and rocks to the dark green of forest on either side, looking, hoping, praying for some sign of Mercy or Matthew. It'd been too long. Far too long. The twinge in his gut said so, as did the lengthening shadows heralding day's end.

"Hold up!" Rufus's holler bellowed louder than the turn of the wheels — which all held solid, even the one they had recrafted.

He pulled on the reins, slowing the horses to a stop, and waited for Rufus to jog up alongside him.

The young man swiped back a swath of

stringy hair, then reset his hat and peered up at him. "It'll be dark soon. I say we stop for the night."

Elias pulled his gaze from the young man and scanned the area. Thick trees closed in on both sides — too thick to wedge a horse's rump through, let alone an entire wagon. Surely even Rufus knew they couldn't stop mid-road and spread out bedrolls in an occupied stretch of wilderness. He grunted. "Not here."

"Din't mean here, you half-witted —"

The deadly scowl he aimed at Rufus ended whatever tirade the man-boy thought to spew.

"What I meant was —" Sniffing, Rufus ran his sleeve beneath his nose. "We turn off past three-oak boulder, just a spell farther, and there's a nice patch o' land hidden by a ridge. That is where we camp."

Elias chewed on the information like an overly spiced piece of meat, the kind that had been smothered in strong flavor to hide rancidity. Something rotten was hidden in Rufus's words, for the young man was never that accommodating.

He narrowed his eyes. "Now how would you know that?"

One of the more colorful profanities flew out of Rufus's mouth. "That old man and

Mercy aren't the only ones what know this countryside. I been to Fort Edward before."

Reaching back, Elias kneaded out a knot in his shoulder while he thought on Rufus's proposal. Judging by the slant of light, they had maybe an hour, hour and a half of day remaining. Since yesterday morning, they had put a good distance between themselves and the Nowadaga crossing, so whatever ill omen that sign had portended, they were far enough afield to miss it. Hopefully. And Lord knew Mercy could use a good sleep. Valid reasons, all.

So why the sudden prickles on his scalp? He lowered his hand. Other than the queer feeling, there was no other basis on which to turn down Rufus's suggestion.

Against his better judgment, he nodded. "All right."

Rufus scuttled back to his wagon, and Elias slapped the reins with a "Giddap." The horses kicked into a trot, and he went back to his tree line–road–tree line–road routine. Still no sign of a dun-colored skirt or a barrel-chested old ranger.

Just past a moss-covered boulder at the base of three oaks, the woods thinned on the south side as Rufus had predicted. Teasing the right rein with steady pressure, he turned the horses off the road and onto uneven ground. His teeth chattered as the wagon bumped over virgin growth, felled tree limbs, and rocks. Near to a half mile in, he wondered if the narrow path would ever open up — and when it finally did, if he were a swearing man, he'd have put Rufus to shame.

He drove the wagon into a grassy clearing, flat and wide, protected on three sides by a ridgeline of rocks, a perfect enclosure for a campsite — and for an ambush. He should've known better than to trust Rufus's suggestion.

Pulling hard to the left, he turned the wagon around so that once Rufus caught up, they were side-by-side and face-to-face. "This is your idea of a 'nice patch o' land'?"

"Unless you wanna camp on the road." He paused to pick at his teeth. "Next glade I know of is five miles off. Be dark by then."

"If you knew that, then why not say something back when we had a chance to pull off earlier?" The low-grade anger that had been simmering all day started to boil, shooting heat up his neck.

Rufus's bony shoulders merely jerked skyward in a sharp shrug.

Closing his eyes, Elias counted to twenty. First in English, then in French. It was either that or leap over and throttle the dunderhead.

Disgusted, he blew out a sigh and jumped off the seat, then resurveyed the area. He had to admit the flatland was suitable for bedding down, and they would be sheltered from the road. It could work — if three kept watch while one slept.

He frowned. It would be a long night.

"Well?" Rufus prodded.

"All right." He turned back to the man. "See to the horses. I will take a look around."

He tromped over to where grass met rock and climbed to the top of the ridge. For a while he scouted along the western edge, poking around for Indian sign. The most interesting things he uncovered were some bear scat and a rabbit warren. So he swung back around and worked his way eastward. More bear tracks, some wolf paw indentations, and then suddenly the crack of a twig.

He cocked his head, every sense heightened. No more cracks. No rustle of underbrush. Just that single, isolated snap.

That was no animal.

He dropped belly down in a thick patch of wild senna and held his breath.

A minute passed, then more, until his lungs burned — and the step of a foot crushed a swath of leftover leaves.

He lifted his gaze to see a pair of brown-legged breeches cross ten paces in front of him. Sucking in a breath, he rose.

In front of him, Matthew spun, musket leveled. Then his eyes widened, and he lowered his gun. "Might wanna think twice before you do that again. I can't be blamed if I put a hole in you for jumping out like that."

Though he was no longer a target, his pulse pumped loud in his head. Why was Mercy not with Matthew? "Where is Mercy?"

Matthew's gaze shifted just past his left shoulder.

Elias turned. Mercy stood, quiet as a shadow, staring at him with hollow eyes and even hollower cheeks. When was the last time she'd eaten? Torn skirts hung askew from her hips. Her braid was undone and wild to her waist, and a cut marred her jaw.

He took a step toward her. "What happened? Are you hurt?"

"I am well, but we may not be for long. There's a French squad, twenty-four men, five miles off."

The news rippled through him like a pebble thrown into a pond. French? Could he use this to his advantage? Possibly, but not without the capture of Matthew and

Mercy. Or Rufus. He frowned. French captives were notoriously mistreated, especially women. The thought of Mercy enduring such brutality twisted his stomach. No, better to stick with his plan.

"Don't even think it, Dubois." Matthew's threat blasted him from behind.

Shaking his head, he turned to the man. "You have nothing to worry about from me."

Mercy's soft steps drew up alongside him. "You know these people. Why is there a squad here? We are not near a fort."

"If it is only one squad, they are more than likely men who have been replaced, on their way to Montreal for reassignment. I doubt they are looking for trouble. There were no Wyandot with them? No Seneca? Ottawa or Shawnee?"

Matthew shook his head. "None. All white."

"Like I said then, men on their way home. My guess is they will soon cut northward."

Matthew grunted.

Mercy shifted her stance, resettling the gun on her back. "Then we continue with our ruse of settlers returning east?"

The set of Matthew's jaw did not bode well — nor did the black gleam in his gray eyes. "I've got a few changes."

Elias stiffened. "Such as?"

"If any of those French soldiers recognize you, or take sport and rummage through one of our crates, this mission is over. We are captives. Or dead."

Elias threw out his arms. "Bragg's men already killed the men who knew me."

"You sayin' there ain't more?"

Blast, but the man was cagey!

"I cannot say that for certain, but Bragg knew that, even when he put me on this team. His orders were to travel as a family, keep my head low. That is what I aim to do."

Mercy advanced toward Matthew, peering at him all the way. "He is right, but what's your plan, Matthew?"

His gray gaze shifted to Mercy. "We hide the gold, tie up Elias, and move out in the morning. After the squad passes us, we double back and retrieve our belongings, then go on as usual."

Elias's breath hitched. If anyone unpacked that gold but him, they would discover his secret. He strode over to the duo and glowered at Matthew. "Are you mad? It will take too long to bury all that gold and repack the crates."

A muscle on the side of Matthew's neck jumped, and he deadlocked Elias with a stare, daring him to break away first.

But Elias held — a trait he'd learned from the best. His father.

"Bah!" Matthew spit out then stalked past them both. "Get a move on. That gold ain't gonna bury itself."

For a moment, Mercy looked at him with cavernous eyes, then turned aside and followed Matthew on silent feet.

Thunder and turf! The two were a pigheaded pair. He stalked after them. He'd have to make sure he was the one unloading the marked crate, or their lives could be in danger.

As he worked his way down the ridge, other possibilities surfaced. While he did not relish being tied up, this could be the perfect time to slip away once the wagons rolled off — providing Matthew didn't tie too awful a knot. He'd have to leave the gold behind. A loss, that. But if he could manage to hide the leather packet of metal tips between hunting frock and shirt, at least he had a fair shot of making it to Boston in time to help the men of Fort Stanwix.

He landed on the flatland, heels digging hard in the soft ground. Should he leave? Or stay? Both were risky.

Stifling a groan, he trudged toward the wagons. Lord, but he was tired of risk.

CHAPTER 20

Fighting a yawn, Mercy traipsed through shin-high wildweed, tired enough to drop in her tracks. Why was she doing this? Roaming free and outsmarting the enemy had always given her a thrill, but now, as she trudged after Matthew with the prospect of a long night of backbreaking work, still aching from the loss of her father and possibly her brother, she had a hard time remembering that excitement. Perhaps Matthew was right. Maybe it was time to leave behind this vagabond life.

She slapped her way through a swarm of biting midges, shoving the rogue notion away as well. Exhaustion sure had a way of dulling her mind. For it had to be fatigue, this nettling idea of wanting to settle. To pack her griefs and troubles into a lockbox and stow the thing under a bed in a solid-framed house. She kicked at a rock, sending it skittering through the grass. Fatigue. She would accept no other reason.

Ahead, Rufus yanked off his hat and slapped his knee, shouting an oath. Apparently he wasn't excited about burying the gold either. As she drew nearer to where he stood talking to Matthew at the side of his wagon, the last of day's light painted his reddening face a deep shade of rage.

"I will have no part of this! I will see you court-martialed for disregarding my father's orders." He stomped off, leaving a trail of obscenities in his wake.

"I hate to say it, but this time I am siding with Rufus." Elias's low tone came out of nowhere.

Startled, she jerked her face aside and stared up at blue eyes pinned on her. How had he caught up to her without rustling the weeds?

"Matthew's doing what he thinks best for us all," she murmured. "I trust him implicitly."

Elias shook his head. "God alone is worthy of that kind of trust."

A grimace crept across her lips. The man sounded far too much like her mother.

Matthew advanced toward them, a shovel in each hand. He threw one to Elias, who caught it without effort.

"The ground is softened where water runs

down off that rise." Matthew jutted the tip of his shovel to where the three of them had recently descended. "We dig there. Mercy, hitch those horses and drive the first wagon over, if you please."

They parted ways, Matthew and Elias swooshing off through the grass. She stopped by her wagon to grab a bite of jerky, then braided her loose hair before she crossed to where the horses yanked up tender greens. The munch and crunch was a soothing sound, and for a moment she stood mesmerized, her heart swelling with compassion. The poor beasts had no idea their dinner was about to be ruined. Was that how it was for God, looking down on them?

"Poor fella." She patted the lead horse on the neck and grabbed his rope. "Just when you thought you were done for the day, hmm?"

Night fell with a heavy hand by the time she positioned Matthew's wagon next to the beginnings of a long, shallow ditch. Her task was to take out the heaps of household goods while Elias and Matthew pitched shovelful after shovelful of dirt. Together they unpacked the gold and trade silver, nestling all in the earth, like so many cold bodies into a shallow grave. Once the crate was emptied, she reloaded the goods, pounded the top back on, and moved on to the next.

The night was more than half spent by the time they finished one load and she drove over the wagon she and Elias usually occupied. The ground wasn't nearly as soft as Matthew had expected. Hours later, the cloud cover cleared, brilliant stars dotted the heavens, and the temperature dropped, bringing a chill that, despite her hard work, made her shiver from head to toe.

About halfway through the load, Elias planted his shovel and hefted himself out of the ditch. "Mercy is spent. She needs some rest. I will take on her part of the job."

Despite her exhaustion, her eyes shot wide open. Where had that come from? She'd not lagged, despite her screaming muscles. She'd neither tripped nor bellyached nor gone off into the brush to take care of necessities.

She dropped the bags of trade silver into the hole, freeing her hands to prop them on her hips. The man's command crawled under her skin like a mess of biting ants. He spoke of her as if she were naught but a child. "Thank you for your concern, *Husband.*" It was a snippety thing to say, but it wouldn't be stopped. "Yet I will rest when

272

we are all done."

Matthew leaned against his shovel handle and blew out a long breath. "The man's more than right, girl. You need some rest. We all do."

She shook her head. "I'm not sleeping while you two are working."

Elias advanced, his voice warm in the cold air. "You have more than proved yourself. I think I speak for us both in that I or Matthew would not think any less of you."

"*I* would think less of me!"

Matthew straightened. "Then we bury the rest of it whole. We're running out of time as it is. We'll dig deeper and toss in the last of the crates without separating the contents."

Elias shook his head, a disgusted rush of air passing his teeth. But he set back to work, as did Matthew.

By the time they buried the remaining crates and reloaded the wagon with the much lighter contents, Rufus ambled in. Late as usual.

"We ready to leave?"

Two shovels dropped. So did Mercy's jaw. "In this dark?"

Rufus hitched his thumbs in his breeches, the dark silhouette making him more of a scarecrow than ever. "I figure if we near

273

those soldiers soon as they set out at sunrise, we can follow 'em back at a distance, then cut in here and retrieve our load soon as they pass. By day's end, we'll cover a fair amount of miles instead of none."

Matthew's chest rumbled, but whether out of agreement or wanting to throttle the young man, Mercy couldn't tell.

"First we cover this ground with rock and brush, then we will see how close it is to daybreak." Matthew heaved his shovel into the wagon, the scrape of it competing with Rufus's curse.

"Why waste time with that?"

Mercy arched her back. Indeed. Every bone in her body cried out to set herself down on that wagon seat and nod off for a spell. She turned to Matthew. "Do we have to —"

"The faster we cover up this dirt, the faster we get on the road."

They all set to work, and glory be, Rufus did too. By the time they finished and the first hint of gray edged in from the east, a thick layer of rock and briars hid the disturbed ground. Anyone chancing upon it wouldn't be the wiser, especially since they also made sure to beat down the grass in other areas as well, turning the whole glade into a confusing twist of wagon tracks and flattened weeds.

She forced one foot in front of the other, drawn by the call of the wagon seat, longing to sink down. The wood would surely feel like a velvet cushion.

"Mercy, grab your gun and fetch some rope."

Behind her, Matthew's words hit hard between her shoulder blades, and she tripped over her own foot. She knew this was coming. Knew it had to be done. And she wouldn't argue against it.

But as she grabbed the rope from where it hung inside the wagon, she squeezed the hemp as tightly as the squeeze of her heart, wishing Elias wasn't a traitor.

That instead, he was the honorable man she wanted — nay, *needed* — him to be.

Elias smirked as he trudged along the ridgeline. Here he was, marching between two guns again. Mercy in the lead and Matthew behind. This time, though, he strode toward freedom — provided he could work his way out of the bindings that cut into his wrists at his back and retrieve the hidden weapon before they returned.

The coming dawn etched a gray outline on the shaggy tree branches, dissipating the ominous shadows. He'd hoped for thick cloud cover awash with a hard rain, but soon enough, sunshine would poke holes in the dark woods. It would be difficult to cover his tracks, especially from the keen eye of Mercy — and then it hit him. His step faltered. He'd be running *away* from her, putting a forever kind of distance between him and the only woman he'd ever thought twice about.

"Over there, that stand of hemlocks." Behind him, Matthew's voice prompted Mercy to veer westward.

They stopped at a trio of trunks. Nearby, a spruce sapling — tall and thick enough to provide cover — obscured the base of one of the trees.

Matthew tipped his head toward him. "Hunker down between the spruce and that tree." He slid his gaze to Mercy, his gun never lowering from Elias. "Mercy, train your barrel on him while I tie him up. Open hammer."

A scowl ferocious enough to make a grown man back off darkened her face. "You really think — ?"

"You know the treachery of man more than anyone."

"No need." Elias crouch-walked his way past the scratchy limbs, working his body into the space between the trees. "I will not fight against you." He dropped to the ground, back against the trunk.

Even so, the click of Mercy's hammer violated the innocence of the morning. Matthew set his gun near her feet and then grabbed the rope.

The whole while the man secured him to the tree, Elias stared up through the breach in the spruce branches to memorize the shape of Mercy. The curve of her pert chin. The hollow at the bottom of her throat. The way her braid swung over her shoulder and rode the swell of her breast, tailing off at the spread of her hips. Even in a torn skirt and with dirt smudged along her jaw, the woman was a dangerous beauty. She belonged here, in these woods, a daughter of earth and light. What would it be like to really be her husband instead of the farce they had been playacting? How passionate? How all consuming? For he had no doubt this woman would give her all to the man she loved.

He lifted his gaze higher, meeting her eye for eye, wanting — *needing* — one last look. She cocked her head. Questions swam in those brown depths, almost as if she knew he was saying goodbye.

Pain dug into his chest as Matthew whaled on the rope, and he grunted.

Mercy scowled. "You're hurting him!"

"Just snugging it tight. Won't be for long. We'll be back before noon. Besides, he is the one who will get a good piece of shuteye while we face the dragon."

Matthew's footsteps circled the tree, then he crouched next to him, smelling of hard work and weariness. "I'm just doing what's got to be done, but I think you know that, aye?"

He nodded. "I would be doing the same, were I in your shoes."

"Good. Then I hope you understand this." In one swift movement, Matthew yanked off his neckcloth and shoved it in his mouth, like a bit in a horse, and tied it tight behind his head.

"Matthew! You're taking this too far." Mercy's voice scraped fierce against the cheerful drone of early morning bird chatter. "He has never once given us a lick of trouble."

Her defense of him was a sweet balm against the way the cloth cut into the corners of his mouth.

The ranger rose and retrieved his gun. "Can't take any chances of him calling out when those French pass. Now, turn around and start walking."

He couldn't see her, not with the way

Matthew's hulking figure stood between him and her. But it wasn't hard to imagine the flare of her nostrils as she strained out, "Why?"

"Do it." Matthew's voice was flat, commanding. Deadly.

He bit down hard on the cloth in his mouth. What did the ranger have in mind? For the first time, he wondered if he'd been foolish to allow himself to be bound. Had he misjudged Matthew Prinn's character?

Mercy stamped off. Not her quiet-stepped pace, nor her silent scouting tread. Each thud of her feet shouted her anger.

Matthew turned back to him, gun in hand. "I am mighty grieved about this, Dubois."

He lifted his gun higher.

Elias strained against the ropes, wild to break free — and even wilder to spit out the gag, for a terrible understanding broke as clear as the rising sun. It had been two days since he and Mercy had read the Indian sign carved into the moss on the rock. Whatever that message portended would happen today, and they hadn't covered much ground since then. Danger lurked nearby, and he'd be a fish in a barrel should that portent come to pass. He growled like a cornered bear.

And the butt of Matthew's gun stock cracked against his skull.

Then blackness.

Pure, blessed blackness. One he could lie in wide-armed and float upon for days and days. Maybe he should. So tired. He was so, so tired. Yes, he could live here in this silent dark, nestled in nothingness . . . were it not for the niggling drive to swim out of it. He had somewhere to be, didn't he? Someone to save? An important errand?

Nay, none of that mattered anymore.

Not one thing mattered.

He awoke to a blackfly buzzing on his nose. Pain hammered a beat in his skull, centering just above his left ear. Burning, throbbing, anguishing. So sharp it shot down through his jaws and choked him.

Rays of sun slipped in through the spruce boughs, and he closed his eyes. Too bright. But *how* bright?

He forced his eyes back open, squinting along the length of a beam, judging the angle. Couldn't be much past dawn. If Matthew had meant that wallop to the head to keep him out until their return, he should've taken into account the thickness of his skull and grit in his spirit, for his senses barreled back with surprising clarity. He had to move.

And he had to move now.

Biting down hard on the cloth in his mouth, he wriggled to work the ropes on his wrists against the bark of the tree. Pain bounced around in his head like a shot let loose from a musket, so sharply the world spun. But more than that agony was against him. So was time.

Warmth trickled down onto his fingers as he rubbed away rope fibers and flesh. He worked a steady beat, insanely matching his movements to the throbbing — and then he stopped. Rock still. Listening with his whole body. Had he heard something?

There, between the scampering of squirrel paws and caw of a crow, footsteps rustled the underbrush. Soft. Steady. Stealthy. Moving in from the north. Drawing closer.

Nearer.

The stink of bear grease and man sweat closed in, breaths away. He held his. If a warrior found him here, his throat would be slashed before he could blink.

God, please. Hide me beneath Your wings.

Ten, maybe twelve, warriors slipped past him, stealing toward the ridgeline. Red and black painted their faces. A war party then. Each man's hair was shaved to the scalp on the sides of his head, the rest bristling down his back beneath a stiff roach headdress, the identifying factor for which the French named this tribe Wyandot.

Silently, they fanned out, spanning the rocky cleft above the glade, leastwise near as he could tell from his vantage point. Then stopped. Words passed, quiet as the breeze, too low for him to identify anything other than, "We wait."

Blast! His head pounded. His hands were yet bound. And a war party blocked his way to retrieve the French weapon. What in the world were they waiting for?

The pain in his head shot down to his heart with a sudden, awful awareness. These savages were hunkering down until Matthew, Rufus, and Mercy returned. How they knew the wagons would come back was beyond his reckoning and would have to be pondered at a later time.

For now, his sole focus was to work his way free without alerting any of the killers.

CHAPTER 21

Blue coats surrounded them, muskets at the ready. Mercy sat rigid on the wagon seat while Matthew and the sergeant communicated in a mix of broken French and English. Really, she couldn't blame the enemy squad for such caution — but she did anyway. Were the French not down this far into New York Colony, neither would their native allies have ventured this far south.

And her father might still be alive.

"Put your guns down and take a look." Frustration pinched Matthew's voice, especially when the French soldier stared at him blankly, and he jerked his thumb over his shoulder. *"Regardez!"*

The sergeant narrowed his eyes. Great heavens . . . had Matthew just insulted the man? Maybe they should've brought Elias along to translate. At the thought of him, she ran her thumb over her own wrist. She still hadn't quite squared Matthew's crack to Elias's skull — and had let him know about it all the way here. Had Elias awakened with a monstrous headache, if he yet woke at all? Was the flesh of his wrists rubbed raw from the tight ropes?

With a sharp nod from the sergeant, four soldiers broke rank and marched to the back of the wagon. By the sounds of more feet thudding on the ground behind them, four others had gone around to the back of Rufus's wagon as well. Soon the creak of lids being pried off and the clink-clunking of pots and goods being rummaged through worked their way up to the wagon seat.

Some of the coiled tension in Mercy's nerves unwound, and she was glad now they had worked all night to bury the gold. Those men would find nothing and so have no reason to hold them. They would be on their way in no time.

But when the soldiers returned to their formation with a *"Rien, monsieur,"* the sergeant's glower deepened.

Until Matthew reached into his pocket and pulled out a sovereign.

Mercy's jaw dropped as the gold coin arced in a ray of sunlight and landed in the sergeant's dirty glove.

"Démissionner!" the sergeant shouted.

At once, muskets lowered and swung to a resting position on each soldier's shoulder.

"Goodbye, *chiens anglais*." The sergeant's thick accent dismissed their party, and the entire squad stood aside.

Matthew slapped the reins, and the horses snapped into action.

Once they were out of earshot, Mercy eyed him sideways. "Where'd you get that gold coin? Wait a minute . . . you gave them one of their own, did you not?"

He chuckled.

So did she. Ah, but she'd miss this man.

Her smile faded. In just under a fortnight, they would reach Fort Edward and part ways. What was she to do with her life then? Everything had been so clear before Elias and his load of gold had showed up, but now? She tipped back her head and closed her eyes, giving in to exhaustion with a long sigh.

"You're not going to start harping on me about Elias again, are you?" Matthew's voice rumbled along with the wheels. " 'Cause I'm done jawin' about that."

"No, 'tisn't that." She opened her eyes and faced him. "What is it that made you become a ranger?"

He shoved a finger in his ear and jiggled it. "What kind of question is that?"

She frowned. It was an odd question, to be sure. But maybe — just maybe — if she understood what drove this honorable man to do what he did with his life, it would give her some guidance for what she ought to do. "I want to know."

"Well . . ." He scratched the side of his jaw, whiskers rasping with the movement. "I suppose I wanted to change the world. Right the wrongs, heal the hurts of this land. I aimed to stake my claim of honor by doing big things with my life." A strange smile curled his lips, as if he chewed on a crabapple. "I've come to learn, though, 'tis the small things that really make a change."

"Like what?"

"Like you."

Unease closed in on her. Was he calling her small, or telling her she was in need of change? "What's that mean?"

He slowed the wagon as they neared a space wide enough to turn around, then faced her. "I have come to believe 'tis more important in this life to make one person feel loved than to go around killing and grasping for power."

Such peaceful words were incongruent coming from the war-worn face of a ranger. She searched his gray eyes, yet nothing but sincerity stared back. "You going soft on me, Matthew?"

"Loving someone isn't a show of softness, but of strength, for there is no stronger bond."

She swallowed, shoving down the ember of emotion burning in her throat. How many times had this man thrown himself into harm's way for her? Unbidden, words her mother had planted deep into her heart as a little girl surfaced. "Greater love hath no man than this, that a man lay down his life for his friends," she murmured.

Matthew's jaw dropped. "What's this? Mercy Lytton spouting the Bible?"

A rising smile would not be denied. "Despite raising me in a Mohawk camp, my mother made sure I wasn't raised a heathen."

"Time we get a move on!" Rufus's voice needled them both from his wagon behind.

"Hate to say it, but he is right." Matthew slapped the reins, lurching the wagon into motion. "Close your eyes now while you can. We'll soon have a load of gold to repack."

Leaning her head back against the canvas, she pulled down the brim of her old felt hat, shading her eyes, then nodded off to the quiet jingle of harness and rhythmic vibrations of the wagon seat. She did not awaken until the timbre of the wheels changed from a somewhat graded road to wilder terrain. Tall hemlocks, pines, and oaks closed in on them as Matthew guided the wagon back onto the narrow path leading to the glade.

Blackbirds chattered as they rolled into the clearing. A rabbit bounded off to safety, splitting a trail in the tall grass. The pile of rocks and brush where they'd hidden the gold remained as they had left it. She scanned the ridgeline, glancing from tree to tree. Nothing was different. A man would be hard pressed to find a more peaceful patch of woods.

Even so, the small hairs on the back of her neck prickled.

Something wasn't right.

Matthew stopped the wagon but did not set the brake, nor did he look at her. "You see anything?" His whisper was deadly soft.

"You feel it too," she whispered back, more a statement than a question. Scanning the area, she began to shut down all other senses — when Matthew angled his body in front of hers.

And she heard the *thwunk* of an arrow piercing him through the neck.

The world blurred, a whirl of green and

brown streaked with light. Gasping for air, Elias slowed from his mad sprint to a stop and shored up against a tree trunk, waiting out the dizziness that muddled his vision. The burning of his bloody wrists was nothing compared to the throbbing in his skull. Running full out after a blow to the head was never a good idea, a lesson he knew well. Yet here he was, tearing through the woods like a wolf bent on a fox, wishing for all the world he could put himself between Mercy and the war party instead of skirting the woods behind the killers. His heart branded him a coward, but running off and then doubling back down to the road was the best — the only — way to prevent an attack.

If he could reach the wagon before they swung off the road.

He slowed his breathing. In. Out. Deep. Slow. And the crazy swirl began to sharpen into straight lines. A stand of maples. Squirrels darting. Gnats swarming. All took on shape, and he glanced over his shoulder, hoping, praying he'd not spy a war-painted Indian on his trail. It would grieve him to put an end to a lost one, but better a native than Mercy.

Nothing moved. Apparently the killers had been too intent on the glade in front of them to pay attention to what dangers might've lurked behind — a mistake he'd made only once in his life. And he had the scars to prove it. Time to press on.

He shoved off and broke into a jog. Slow and steady might serve better than breakneck. But with each step, it took everything in him to keep from bursting ahead at full speed. No doubt those wagons were on the move back toward the glade, and if he did not stop them . . . Time slapped him cold, an enemy too ethereal to fight back against.

God, grant that I reach them in time.

Deeming his progress far enough, whether in truth or just because, he swung south, working his way to the road. Hopefully. Hard to tell for certain, when he'd never actually traversed these backwoods before. Yet based on the scant snippets of descriptions Mercy and Rufus had shared, this was the route. It had to be.

Oh God, please make it so.

An eternity later, the woods thinned. He pumped his legs harder, lungs screaming, pain blinding, and nearly overran the road. Staggering to a stop, he doubled over, hands on his thighs, and caught his breath.

Then lost it.

Multiple sets of wagon tracks marred the ground, which meant they had passed this

way twice. Heading away from the glade —
and heading toward it.

This time he broke into a dead run.

CHAPTER 22

The ridgeline exploded with warriors. Ten. Twelve? No time to count. Heartsick and burning with white-hot rage, Mercy shoved off Matthew's deadweight where he'd toppled sideways against her. She'd have to grieve later — if she lived that long.

As she bent to grab her gun, a rush of air grazed past her cheek. The thwack of an arrow pierced the canvas behind her. Having grabbed her gun, she snatched up Matthew's, his fingers forever frozen in a desperate reach, then dove inside the wagon.

An arrow hissed behind her. Pain seared the top of her right shoulder. The tip ripped through fabric and flesh then stuck deep into a crate behind her. She hunkered down, working her body into a crevice where the cargo had shifted. A poor cover. A deadly one. But all she had for now.

"Rufus?" she hollered. "Rufus!"

No answer. Just the lethal sound of rocks

cascading from the rushing tread of moccasins. Men breathing heavy on the hunt.

They were coming.

They were coming for her.

Ignoring the sharp burn in her shoulder, she primed the pan of Matthew's gun and balanced the weapon on the crate next to her. Then she primed hers and clicked the hammer wide. Which way to aim? Front? Back? Clammy sweat dotted her brow. It was futile, this need of hers to fight, but she owed it to Matthew to take out at least a few of his killers.

Oh Matthew. She could yet hear his voice, grumbling with emotion. *" 'Tis more important in this life to make one person feel loved than to go around killing."*

Her grip on the gun slackened. He wouldn't want her to kill for him. But she couldn't sit here defenseless either. Perhaps if she could lure the warriors to the front of the wagon, she might have a chance to slip out the puckered hole in the rear and make a run for it. But what to use for a distraction?

Scrambling for an idea, she scanned the wagon's contents. A wool blanket. Some rope. A shovel and a bucket. Maybe she could — too late.

A war hatchet sliced into the back canvas.

She turned and fired. A groaning gurgle followed.

So did the thud of feet climbing up to the front seat.

She threw down her gun and seized Matthew's, hands shaking so much half the gunpowder jiggled out of the pan. *Hold, hold.* It wouldn't do to spend her last shot on nothing but air.

The front canvas rippled. The whites of shiny eyes set deep in a band of black paint peered in and locked onto her.

Mercy pulled the trigger.

A flash. A fizzle. A misfire.

A slow grin slashed across the face of the warrior, and he advanced.

She scrambled back — and an arm snared her from behind, pulling her against a sweaty chest. Her gun fell, and she clawed at the thick arm holding her. A knife flashed, poised to split the flesh of her neck.

"Hunh-ha!" the man in front of her shouted.

The one holding her growled, a low roar that reverberated in her own chest.

But the knife slid away, and she was yanked out the back of the wagon, a captive of a nameless warrior whose face she couldn't see. Another man lay flat on his back, eyes unseeing and a hole in his neck, just like Matthew. Had she done that?

Her stomach spasmed, and unstoppable tremors shook through her. She'd never killed a man before — and never would again. The startling violation of snatching what was only God's to take slammed into her. She jerked her head aside and retched.

The man holding her let go, yanking the hat from her head as he did so. She dropped to her hands and knees and heaved until there was nothing left — then heaved some more.

The black-striped warrior hefted her up by her arm. Sunlight flashed off the ring in his nose and larger silver wheels on his ears as he bound her hands in front of her. She put up no struggle. What was the point? She'd already given her best fight.

And lost.

A thong cut tight into her wrists. Then a wider lash looped over her head and settled around her neck, connecting her to the black-painted man via a short lead. All the while, he studied her with narrowed eyes, some kind of recognition flashing deep within. But what? She'd never seen him before.

Had she?

With a sharp tug on the leather, he indicated she was to follow. He led her past the wagon, around natives hauling out crates and busting them open, and beyond the front seat where Matthew yet lay.

If only she could join him.

Running toward danger was nothing new. It was a way of life. For once, Elias was thankful for his years of rebellion. Any sane man would be putting distance between himself and a band of warriors — especially being unarmed. But he pressed ahead at top speed, straining for a glimpse of two wagons bumping along the road.

He did not slow until he reached the turnoff leading into the glade — and then he didn't just slow. He stopped. So did his heart. Flattened weeds marked ruts through the vegetation. Deep, defined, and sickeningly fresh.

And a gunshot cracked a wicked report.

He was too late.

Or was he? He couldn't credit Rufus with much sense, but Matthew and Mercy? Between the two of them, perhaps they had seen the danger and bailed. Hied themselves off into the woods and taken cover. It was a frail chance, wispy as spider webbing, but he wrapped his hands around it and refused to let go. If only belief alone would make it so.

Drawing upon every shadow-walking skill he'd honed, he backed away from the furrows and eased into the spring growth. Though full bloom was months off, enough greenery lent him concealment. Thank God it wasn't winter.

He darted from tree trunk, to scrub fir, to dogwood shrub, head still throbbing, wrists still raw. A whiff of musk and sweat carried on the air, as did the clank of metal upon metal. Not much farther then.

With one eye on the ground to keep from a misstep, he edged as close as he dared to the clearing and crouched in a patch of toad lilies. Ahead, two wagons sat one in front of the other, barely past the tree line, but no sign of Mercy or Matthew. For the first time since the Indians had arrived, the heavy weight stealing his breath began to lift. Mayhap they had sensed the threat and escaped.

But when a tall native rounded the corner of the last wagon, strutting like a rooster, all air and hope whooshed out of his lungs. Mercy's hat perched atop his shaved head. The old felt that she loved. The one she'd worn when he'd last seen her.

And blood splattered the man's face.

Oh God, please don't let that be Mercy's.

He clenched his jaw to keep from roaring

and started counting heads — tallying up just how many he could take down on his own with nothing but fists and rage. Two men threw out crates from inside the last wagon, where four others pried off the tops and emptied the contents. The devil wearing Mercy's hat joined in. That made seven.

He jerked his gaze to the first wagon, where tatters of the canvas flapped in the breeze at the rear. One warrior lay unmoving on the ground, forgotten — for now — amongst a heap of open and abandoned crates. Near the second wagon, a pair of men had unbridled the horses and were leading them toward the rise.

Eight, nine, ten. Blast! Four or five men he might be able to ward off — and that was a huge stretch — but ten? He hadn't felt this helpless since holding François's blue-lipped body in his arms as he'd pulled him from the river . . . yet another time he'd been too late to be of any real use.

Shoving away the memory, he duckwalked closer and huddled behind a wildwood shrub. The leaves blocked his line of sight, but the shortened distance made it easier to distinguish their quiet words.

"White dogs! There is no treasure here."

"English lips cannot help but lie. Their hearts are thick with deceit."

"We are the fools, making a pact with pale-faced devils."

"All is not loss, my brother. Even now Nadowa leads Black-Fox-Running's daughter to camp. Let us return and see his glory walk."

Some of the tension in his jaw slackened. It must be Mercy they spoke of, for he could believe nothing other than she was yet alive — maybe not for long — but breathing at least as long as it would take for the warrior named Nadowa to haul her into camp. For the first time in hours, a ghostly smile haunted his lips. He'd hate to be the man trying to drag her anywhere against her will.

He waited out the pillaging warriors, listening for the clanking of housewares to cease. Eventually, after a final barrage of hateful epithets against the whites, he heard the sound of moccasins padding off. A few rocks clacked down the ridgeline, knocked loose by careless feet. Then the forest returned to nothing but birdsong and squirrels rustling about. Every muscle in him yearned to burst into a sprint and follow their trail, specifically Mercy and Nadowa's. But prudence rooted him until he was certain no one had turned back or laid in wait for God knew what purpose.

Creeping out from behind the shrub, he

paused and studied the glade. The wagons stood stripped naked save for the canvas coverings, one of them flapping in the breeze. Up on the ridge, no sign of movement. It was still a risk to expose himself to the clearing, but was not all of life a perilous gamble?

He skulked to the rear wagon, sitting in the late morning sun like a pile of bleached bones and just as devoid of life. No blood. No sign of struggle. He passed it by and moved on to the next.

The slashed canvas rippled. A dark patch of bloody grass cried up from the earth where the fallen warrior had lain. Judging by the flattened trail leading off from it, the war party had hauled their fellow fighter away with them. Weaving through a maze of upturned crates, he worked his way to the front . . . where he nearly dropped to his knees.

Stretched out like a slit-throated buck, the mighty ranger, Matthew Prinn, lay draped over the driver's seat, an arrow pierced through his gullet. Elias staggered. That could've been him. He'd not been happy about Matthew tying his bonds so tight and cracking him in the head, but the man's actions had saved his life.

Stunned, he lifted his face to the impossibly blue sky. "Oh God, bless that man and thank You. Once again You have provided in ways I do not deserve."

His gaze snapped back to Matthew. Black-flies flitted near the wound, his glassy eyes, his gaping mouth. Elias swallowed back a burning ember of sorrow and remorse. As gruff as the ranger had been, he'd be sorely missed. The weeks they'd shared had gone a long way toward healing some of the raw wounds left from his grandfather's death.

"Receive this man into Your arms, Lord," he whispered.

He waved away the flies, wishing he had told Matthew everything, his true mission, and maybe even enlisted Matthew's help. But too late now. Blowing out a long breath and then filling his lungs, he stared at the dead man's chest. Matthew would never have such a pleasure again.

Nor did Elias have the pleasure of loitering.

He broke into a jog, dashed around to the other side of the wagon, and scrambled up to the seat, expecting to see Rufus's corpse inside. An empty wagon bed stared back. Pivoting, he shaded his eyes, careful not to jostle Matthew's repose. He scanned the glade from edge to edge. No more bodies sullied the grass. Apparently they had hauled off Rufus as well.

He lowered his hand, then bent to pull Matthew inside the wagon. Heaving the stiff body proved a challenge, and he regretted the way the ranger landed inside with a thud. It wasn't much of a grave, but it was the best he could do for now. At least the man's body wouldn't be out in the open. He ran his fingers along Matthew's shirt and down his legs, hoping to find a knife. Nothing. The Indians must've thought of that as well.

Sitting back on his haunches, Elias quickly rifled through his options. Truly, there were only two. Dig up that crate with the French weapon and hightail it out of here for Boston, saving countless lives in the process — or light out after the woman he loved.

He gasped. *Love?* Was that what this burning need firing along every nerve meant?

A groan rumbled in his throat. How could he risk the lives of an entire fort to go chasing after one woman?

How could he not?

Quickly calculating distance, time, and need, he came up with three days. He'd give it three days to find her, then turn around — even if he didn't locate her.

Mind set, he scrambled out through the

canvas hole. Though it grieved him to leave Matthew's body, he jumped down to the ground. Time was something he could no longer afford to spend, even on respectful purchases. He trotted off toward the ridgeline and began scouting for telltale signs of passage, one question niggling all the while.

Who were the pale-faced devils who had bargained with the Indians for the treasure?

CHAPTER 23

Two days. One nightmare. An ugly, black, never-ending nightmare. Mercy trudged after the Wyandot brute, the back of her neck raw from the leather thong. If she didn't keep step, the bite of it would gouge a deeper stripe into her flesh — and the skin was already chafed to a pulp from her unrelenting belligerence. Not that it had done her any good. With the big man leading and ten others spread out behind, she did not have a chance. No woman could best eleven warriors. She frowned. The thought should've comforted her in some small measure. *Should've.* But it didn't.

So with each tread, she stored her anger. Her grief. All the frustration of a world turned upside down and shaken into something she didn't recognize anymore. When the time was right, she'd open the door to those foul emotions and run away with them, never to return. But for now, she forced one foot in front of the other. There was nothing else to do.

Yet.

Behind her, footsteps crushed the forest's undergrowth, soft but fast. The man holding her tether stopped and turned. For a blessed moment, the pressure at the base of her neck eased.

Another man sped past her, stopping close to her captor. While they talked, she tried to listen to their tones of voice, hints of emotion, anything that could give her a clue about what they might be discussing, for she didn't know the language. But sweet heavens, it was hard to hear over the rush of rage pumping in her ears — the scoundrel who'd advanced wore her hat atop his head. *Hers!*

She gritted her teeth. She'd have that hat back or die in the trying, for why not? She was a corpse walking anyway. As soon as these men reached their camp, she had no doubt she'd be used in some kind of ritual — the killing kind.

The bigger warrior unwrapped her tether from where he kept it bound to his wrist, then passed it off to the man in her hat. She tensed. This was new. Until now, she'd remained with her original captor. Why would he turn back from the way they had already trekked?

Dark eyes slid to hers from beneath her familiar felt brim, a cold gleam in the man's gaze. Were he not in possession of what belonged to her, she might have given in to fear, but as it was, fury simmered hot in her belly. She'd use this to her advantage. But how?

Slowly, the man pulled the lead taut, then in increments yanked tighter, until the slicing pain at the base of her neck could not be denied. She had no choice but to take a stilted step forward. Again the slow pull, the incremental yanks, the awful buildup of pain until she took another step. Closer and closer, his dark eyes undressing her as he reeled her in, the rope pooling at his feet with each successive tug.

Pooling?

She flicked her gaze to his hands, then away, so he'd not notice her fixation. But one glance was enough. The fool had not wrapped the tether around his wrist like the bigger man, but held it with his fingers, so that the end of it rested on the ground. She flattened her lips lest she smile. This, she could use.

Maintaining the same amount of resistance, she allowed him to draw her nearer, until the rotted-meat stench of his breath filled her nostrils.

She reared back her head, then jerked it down. The front of her skull cracked into the man's nose, breaking it with a sickening crunch. In that split instant of shock and acute pain, she whipped around and tore into the woods.

The world blurred by. She was wind, blowing past trees, gusting over rocks. A mad, desperate race, for the man would give chase. Her gaze shot wild, searching for a hiding place. Anywhere. Anything. A rotted stump or a hidden cleft of a ravine.

Footsteps kicked up a frenzy behind her. If she didn't find something soon, he'd spot her and —

She whumped to the ground, face first, jerked by a misstep on the rope dangling from her wrists. Sticks and gravel bit into her chin. Lungs heaving, she pushed up, frantic to retrieve the knife in her bodice. Fingers met the bone hilt. The blade slid out.

And an iron grip yanked her upward from behind, spinning her around. The knife flew from her grasp.

Blood flowed red from the man's nose to his neck. White teeth flashed in a macabre grin. He swung back his arm and backhanded her full across the mouth.

Her head jerked. She reeled. A coppery taste repulsed her — the warm tang of blood draining from her split lip. She turned aside to spit.

The next strike knocked her flat, turning the world black.

She lived in that darkness for a very long time, but not long enough to make the pain go away. Hours later, when her eyes did open, it wasn't much different. Her head throbbed. The wound on her shoulder still ached deep to the marrow of her bones. So much hurt that she couldn't see straight — could she?

She blinked, trying to focus. Some kind of wall was inches from her face. Deerskin? Birch bark? Did it even matter?

The low drone of voices hummed somewhere overhead. A grating sound, bass and throaty. Her best guess was she'd been hauled into the enemy's camp and deposited in some kind of hut, likely guarded.

Unbidden tears slipped from her eyes. There was no getting out of this. Not this time. No Elias or Matthew to help. Had she ever really thanked them for their care? For the times when Matthew had protected her with a backup shot while scouting? For all his fatherly advice and grudging affection?

Or Elias? The tender touch he'd used in

binding up her foot. His thoughtfulness in lending his coat for her warmth — even to his detriment. The way he stood up to Rufus or Logan, defending her honor. She'd never once showed him the kindness of gratitude, had she?

A sob convulsed her, and she curled into a ball. Regret was a living, breathing demon. Not only had she never shown them gratitude, but she'd never had the chance to say goodbye. And now it was too late. She'd lost them. She'd lost everything. Her loved ones, her dignity, her hope. What a failure. She was nothing but a weak woman.

Just like her mother.

Tears flowed freely, choking her, bathing her. Would that she could shove back time, return to her girlhood, and redo how she'd treated the woman who'd birthed her and loved her to her dying day. She reached to clutch the locket.

"I'd be kinder, Mother," she whispered. "Less spiteful. More loving."

"Don't cry, lady."

She froze.

"Your mother must know you love her."

She rolled over — and stared into blue eyes.

Elias thanked God for three things. Nay,

four. That he yet breathed. That he tracked a large number of Indians, for trailing any less would have been nigh impossible in this wilderness. And though at first horrified, he was thankful for the small, bone-handled knife lying in the dirt. He knew the blade well, for he'd faced it an eternity ago in the dark of night.

Crouching, he grasped the weapon in a loose-fingered grip, almost reverently. When had it last warmed against Mercy's skin? The flattened growth around him suggested a struggle, but as he narrowed his eyes and studied the length of the blade, the rest of his fear blew away on a waft of late morning breeze. No remnants of blood darkened the steel. Despite the few droplets he'd spied defiling the trillium, he had no reason to believe a slaughter had happened here.

He stood and secured the treasure between belt and waist, most of all thankful he'd not yielded to the strong discouragement urging him to turn around and quit this chase.

With renewed confidence, he strode onward. Having already measured the pace of the warriors, he looked for signs of passage every yard or so. A low-growing branch broken by a careless step. A kicked rock leaving behind a depression not yet eaten up by forest growth. And as he gained on them, now and then he was prized with a slight indentation from the back edge of a moccasin heel.

Smoke, at first a faint whiff, strengthened in scent. So did the pungent odor of man. Calling upon his shadow-walking skills, Elias crept on silent feet, at one point slipping through the outward ring of scouts protecting the camp he neared.

He stopped at the edge of a small clearing, sided on the north by a fast-flowing stream. Squatting behind a leafed-out shrub, he took measure of the site. Two makeshift shelters of skins and bark nestled next to a larger lodge. Off to one side sat a smaller hut, guarded by a folded-armed warrior. Near one of the shelters, two men worked on weapon repair or arrowhead construction. Directly in front of him, three stood in discussion, blocking his view of the front of the larger lodge, but near as he could tell, no women or children lived here. It all indicated that this was a temporary encampment, a staging place for summer forays. He tucked away the information, adding to the intelligence he'd hand over once he reached Boston.

One of the men broke away from the group in front of him — and strode straight for him.

Elias froze, not daring to so much as breathe.

But the man shouldered his bow and passed by, likely off to replace one of the scouts.

Taking care not to snap a twig, Elias eased back, blending with dirt and trees, and waited.

Steps, while quietly chosen, drew nearer. When they passed, he sprang.

Elias grabbed the man from behind, the biting edge of Mercy's knife nicking into the warrior's throat.

"Whose camp is this, my brother?" He whispered the Wyandot words into the man's ear, then lessened his grip just enough to let the man speak.

"Uwętatsih-anue."

Red Bear, here? Immediately Elias released him, smiling wide. "Good. I would speak with Red Bear. Lead on."

For a moment, the man stared at him as if he were mad. And he just might be, so giddy with the blessing of having an ally in this place. If Mercy weren't here, at least his former contact would have plenty of information, especially once a pipe circulated from hand to hand.

Even so, he kept the knife in his grip as he

followed the man out of the trees and into the clearing. The warriors working on weapons looked up at his entrance, wary curiosity shining in their dark eyes and murmurs passing between them. The two men who'd earlier blocked his view fell in behind him, no doubt with hands covering the tomahawks strapped to their sides. While the brave he followed led him toward the largest lodge, Elias's gaze lingered on the smallest shelter. If Mercy were here, still alive, that was where she'd be.

They stopped in front of a low-burning fire, more ash than flame, smoldering in front of the council lodge. On the other side of the fire, a man rose, impossibly broad of chest and decorated with three golden gorgets, the ornaments denoting him as the tribe's sachem. A single turkey feather adorned his scalp lock, the black hair streaked with unnatural red glints in the late morning sun. He flicked a glance at Elias, neither acknowledging nor disowning their friendship, then trained his gaze on the native with the bloody nick-line across his neck.

Next to Elias, the man who'd led him here stepped forward. "This man would speak with you, Uwętatsih-anue."

Red Bear grunted. "Where did you find him?"

"He found me."

"Then this day you have been spared by Shadow Walker." Red Bear jerked his head once, dismissing the man.

Without a word, the warrior strode away.

Finally, Red Bear's gaze sought his, and a glimmer of amusement sparked in the dark depths. "I did not think the English would hold you for long, Shadow Walker."

Elias grinned. "As always, great sachem, you speak truth."

Pleasure twitched the man's lips, not quite a reciprocal grin, but a hint of a smile nonetheless. "You come at a good time. We celebrate tonight when the rest of the men return."

It took all his willpower to school his expression into nothing but mild interest. Usually a celebration meant a victory — often one that involved captives. Were both Rufus and Mercy here?

"That is good," he lied. "Yet I am not long for this camp. I seek only information and will be on my way."

"Then come." Red Bear drifted a hand toward the council lodge behind him. "Let us smoke. We will trade what our heads and hearts have gathered."

Red Bear turned and entered the lodge. Elias followed, as did the two men behind him.

Crossing from brilliant light into shadows, he blinked, then sucked in a breath. Red Bear sat next to a warrior already cross-legged on the ground — one who wore Mercy's hat perched at an angle atop his black hair. A sharp-edged anger sliced through him, and his fingers twitched to snatch the hat away and demand to know where Mercy was. But any show of emotion could cause Red Bear to question him, or worse, to demand that he leave.

So he sat adjacent to Red Bear, keeping an angle to view the door. He'd seen one too many men take a tomahawk to the back for want of staying vigilant.

Without looking any man in the eyes, he held out his hands to the small fire. "Tell me of this celebration. Has there been a recent victory?"

"No." The man with the hat huffed. "And yes."

Red Bear lifted the ceremonial pipe from its stand, pausing before he lit it. "It was not the victory we expected," he explained.

"Often those are the most rewarding, Great One."

Nodding, Red Bear lifted the pipe, paying

homage to earth and air and fire. Elias waited for the ceremony to begin, not speaking and hardly breathing. Every part of him itched to tear out of here and search the few shelters for sight of a dark-haired, wide-eyed woman, but any impatience on his part would be frowned upon.

Eventually, Red Bear wafted pipe smoke to his nose with one cupped hand, then passed it off to the man in the hat before he spoke. "Long have the Fight-Hard-with-Knives been a burr hooked into our skin. But we have been awarded a vengeance coup. Nadowa believes he has captured the daughter of their dead leader, Black-Fox-Running. I cannot say if she is or not, for my path never crossed with the woman. Only with her father."

The fragrant scent of sweet tobacco began to fill the lodge, far more soothing than Red Bear's words. Could that woman be Mercy? She spoke fluent Mohawk. She bore native features. But was she truly a daughter of a sachem?

"And if she is not?" he asked.

Red Bear shrugged. "We will sacrifice her anyway in exchange for not receiving our promised goods."

The pipe passed to him, and he sucked in a draught of smoke, held it, then blew it out, letting the tobacco work its wiles with his tense nerves. Whoever the woman was, she needed to be removed before nightfall.

Cupping his hand, he wafted smoke to his face, then passed the pipe back to Red Bear. "I may be able to help you identify this woman. Bring her here."

The sachem's brow creased. "You know Black-Fox-Running's daughter?"

"Perhaps."

And if he did, then God help them both.

CHAPTER 24

Wrists yet bound, Mercy shoved her hands onto the ground and pushed up to sit. Pale blue eyes watched her every move. In front of her, a girl — not long before the bloom of maidenhood — sat with her back against a strip-barked wall, knees drawn up in front of her. By Mercy's best calculation, she could be no more than ten or eleven summers, but stillness radiated out from her, like that of a sage old woman. The girl's blond hair tangled past her shoulders, draped over a wrinkled and dirty gown, yet she bore no scrapes or bruises. Apparently their captives were treating her well — which meant the girl would be either adopted or given in trade.

"Who are you?" Mercy asked.

"Deliverance, but call me Livvy, like my mother did." The girl's voice cracked, and she sniffed. Pain creased her brow, and Mercy knew better than to ask. Lord knew what the girl had suffered before landing here.

Livvy's brow dipped lower, concern thickening her young voice. "They did not treat you very nicely, did they, ma'am?"

"No, they did not." The throbbing in her skull and festering ache on her shoulder screamed in agreement. And judging by the way her hands were still bound, she could expect more cruelty to follow.

Even so, she forced a small smile. "I am Mercy, and you are very kind. How long have you been here, Livvy?"

The girl's comely shoulders lifted in a shrug. "Long enough that the days and nights are not so cold anymore." Sunlight slanted through a gap in the wall, illuminating crystalline seas, brilliant and without shores, in Livvy's eyes. "I am certain my papa will arrive soon."

Mercy frowned. That wasn't a likely outcome, especially since the girl had already been here for a month or maybe two. Still, loath to snuff out the girl's hope, Mercy lightened her tone. "How do you know this?"

"Well, besides what God has promised me, there is a man here who speaks some English. He told me I am to be traded."

Mercy shifted on the damp dirt, unsure

what disturbed her most — that the girl expected to be traded back to her father, or that she apparently knew God as well as Elias and Matthew had. A fresh wave of sorrow nearly drowned her, and she sucked in a shaky breath. Oh, how she missed those men.

"So," she drawled, desperate to put her mind on something other than loss, "God speaks to you, does He?"

"Of course." Livvy unfolded her legs and angled her head. "Do you not hear Him?"

A bitter laugh begged release. She swallowed it down. Must everyone around her perceive the Almighty's voice while the only whisper in her ears was that of doubt? How could she be so blessed with keen eyesight yet lack so woefully in hearing? What was wrong with her? This turn of conversation was no better than dwelling on the gaping loss of Matthew and Elias.

She hung her head. "No." Misery seeped out with the word. "I do not."

Livvy pushed off from the wall and scooted next to her, wrapping her arm about Mercy's shoulders like an old soul comforting a child. "Don't be sad, Miss Mercy. I can tell you what God says. He says to trust. Always. Trust and believe, for He is your only hope."

The urge to shrug off the girl's hold and scamper to the far end of the hut was so strong she trembled. The words were those of her mother, Matthew, and Elias blended into the unwavering voice of a young girl. Could God have been speaking to her all these years, and she'd just not heard it?

"It can't be that simple," she whispered, more to herself than anyone.

"It is." Livvy squeezed her shoulder.

They both turned when the door flap opened.

A warrior entered, just barely, so small was the space. Crouching, he held a bowl in one hand and a water skin in the other. The savory scent of roasted meat filled the hut like a sweet dream. Mercy's stomach cramped as he handed the food to Livvy. To her, he gave nothing but a dark glower.

"Thank you, Ekentee." Livvy nodded at the man, then held out her bowl to Mercy. "Would you like —"

"No!" The man's voice cut sharp, and the girl flinched. "No food for that one, Livee."

"But she is hurt!"

Dark eyes shot to her, piercing as an arrow. "She is dead."

He reached out and grabbed Mercy's arm, yanking her toward the door. Was this it?

Were hot coals even now readied to burn the life from her in front of the men who'd killed Matthew and Rufus? And then what? What waited on the other side of a horrendous death?

She dragged her feet. The man yanked harder. A sour taste filled her mouth. She wasn't ready to die. Not now. Not like this. A hot, ragged sob welled in her throat.

God, please, I will trust You. I will! I am nothing. You are all. Oh, that You would save me.

The ragged prayer, desperate and terrible in intensity, raged inside her as the warrior dragged her out the door.

"Where are you taking her?" Livvy's question was muffled into oblivion by the dropping of the door flap.

Mercy blinked, blinded in the brilliance of daylight. The man jerked her to her feet, and she staggered. No men gathered about. No fire blazed either. But if they weren't going to burn the life from her, then . . . *Oh God.* Did they have something worse planned?

Grabbing hold of the rope at her wrists, the man tugged her toward the largest shelter. The tension cut a fresh stripe into her raw flesh.

She stumbled after him. "If I am to be killed, why do we go to the council lodge?"

The man didn't so much as look over his shoulder. His big strides just kept eating up the ground. But he did answer. "Shadow Walker would see you. His eyes will read your manner of death."

Her shoulders sagged. Whoever this Shadow Walker was, if he recognized her as Black-Fox-Running's daughter, then the torture would be horrendous indeed.

A blue haze hovered just above the circle of the five men seated cross-legged around the council fire. Elias blew out one more mouthful of smoke, adding to the ghostly cloud, then passed the pipe to Red Bear. Did the man notice the slight tremor in his fingers?

He forced his mouth to remain pressed shut, a monumental task when everything in him wished to rage against these killers and then tear out and grab Mercy. But rushing anything — the conversation, the smoking, the vengeance kindling inside — could get both him and Mercy killed.

Red Bear's dark eyes shifted to his. For a while he said nothing, just stared, the etched lines in his weathered face neither lifting nor falling. The man wearing Mercy's hat darted his gaze between them both, a purple swell to his nose, mid-bridge. He'd taken a strike recently, a hard one. The other two warriors merely sat like old women content to perch on a front porch and while away the long day — yet there was nothing frail or feeble about the size of their biceps or the breadth of their chests.

"Know you a General Hunter?" The sachem's question floated as ethereally as the suspended smoke.

Mentally, Elias matched the name from face to face in a collection of British officers he stored in his memory for just such a purpose. None corresponded. "No. Why?"

"We have held his daughter long, hoping to earn Six Fingers back in a trade. Still no word."

Elias hid a frown. If that trade happened, a vicious warrior would once again be on the loose.

The pipe passed into Red Bear's hands. Taking a last draw, the sachem held the smoke in his mouth, then set the pipe on the two rocks in front of him. Straightening, he blew out a white cloud, wafting the smoke back to his nostrils with repeated sweeps of his hands.

Beside the occasional pop and crackle of the fire, quiet enveloped them. It was always like this, the interminable breaches in conversation, the placid pace of information exchange, so unlike the clipped and hurried debriefings of the British.

Red Bear lifted his chin, and Elias leaned closer. "The girl will bring a good price elsewhere, or maybe make peace with Dark Thunder."

Elias tensed. Dark Thunder was as notorious as Six Fingers. A brute of a man. A disease amongst humans. The protective side of Elias would have grabbed a tomahawk and raced out to rescue the girl, no matter who she was. But the prudent side of him held every muscle in check. He counted ten slow breaths in and ten out before he spoke again. "Where did you take this girl?"

Only Red Bear's eyes moved, his gaze slipping as gracefully as the passing of a pipe to the man seated at Elias's right hand.

Next to him, the warrior answered Red Bear's silent command. "The girl was taken en route to Fort Bedford. A small party, two women, the girl, and four soldiers. Hunter is a stupid man to let his women traverse these woods."

Two more women? He chewed on that thought like a gristly piece of meat, not able to spit it out but not wanting to swallow it either. This time he counted twenty breaths. "You hold one girl but not the women?"

"They were of weak blood," the man next

to him rumbled, disdain darkening his tone.

Elias's brow twitched as he held his expression in check. The girl must be something special, indeed, to have escaped the blade of the warrior who clearly harbored a sizable abhorrence toward white females.

Outside the lodge, footsteps neared, one set strong and determined, the other with a drag-slide cadence. Drawing in a deep breath of the sweet, leftover tobacco scent, he forced his face to remain blank — which took every bit of his will when Mercy was pulled stoop-shouldered into the shelter like a dog on a leash.

Her captor released his hold of her bound hands, then thrust her forward with a shove between the shoulder blades. Elias bit down hard, tongue caught between his back teeth, and savored the slow leak of blood in his mouth. Any outward show of hostility would be a death warrant — and he'd had his fill of those.

Mercy, God bless her, lifted her nose in the air, refusing to look at any of them. Purple bruised one of her eyes. A cut marred her cheek, and her bottom lip swelled at one end. Her gown was torn, and on her left shoulder, the fabric was matted with dried blood. More blood stained her bodice and sullied her neck, but near as he could tell, not hers. She looked nearly as awful as he had that first day she'd lain eyes on him — but this was entirely different. Not only was she a woman, but the one he'd lay down his life for . . . and just might have to in the end.

For the briefest of moments, her gaze slipped, and she glanced around the circle of men, then froze on him before resetting her proud stance. It hadn't been for long, but in that eternity, the awful questions in her eyes branded him a traitor all over again. But worse was the disappointment haunting those brown pools. Roiling, gut-wrenching disappointment shone deep and dark. The frail bridge of trust they had constructed during the past weeks collapsed to a thousand jagged-edged pieces — and he gasped from the loss, desperate for air.

Red Bear swept his hand toward her. "This is the woman Nadowa believes to be Kahente. You know her?"

A burning ember stuck in his throat. What he said from now on would mean either life or death for Mercy. He swallowed. "Yes."

Red Bear leaned forward, not much, but the movement signaled intense interest. "So this is the daughter of Black-Fox-Running?"

Was Mercy the daughter of a chieftain?

He could believe it simply by the way valor straightened her shoulders and courage shone in her eyes.

But thank the sweet Lord she'd never told him her true lineage, for he could honestly say, "I can tell you exactly who she is. . . . she is my wife."

Red Bear leaned back, clearly disappointed.

CHAPTER 25

"Shadow Walker has taken a wife?" The question traveled on a ring of whispers, repeated by each man seated at the fire. Disbelief hung heavy in the smoke-thickened air.

Elias slipped a glance toward Mercy, who yet stood willow straight, brown eyes unblinking. Thank God she did not understand the Wyandot language, for if she did, she'd no doubt pounce like a wildcat and scratch his face off for claiming her as his wife. It may not have been the only way to protect her — but it was the best he could think of at the moment. If he'd merely denied her kinship to Black-Fox-Running, at best she'd still have been sold. At worst, they would continue with their plans to burn her come evening.

He turned his face to Red Bear. "We were wed back at Fort Wilderness."

"He is a traitor!" Across from him, the

sinewy native wearing Mercy's hat yanked out his tomahawk, until a halting shift of Red Bear's eyes forced the

man to lay it on his lap.

Even so, murder darkened the voice of the sachem, lowering it to a growl. "How is it enemy gates open to you?"

Panic spread like a swarm of biting ants over his body. What to say? This whole situation was a tinderbox. The wrong words would spark an explosion.

Give me wisdom, Lord, for I am at a loss. Spare us, leastwise Mercy.

While his mind scrambled to hunt down a plausible answer, he sat motionless, this time thankful for the tradition of unhurried speech. Time stretched like a taut bowstring about to snap. If he remained silent much longer, Red Bear would see him tortured next to Mercy.

God, please . . .

And then it came to him, a gentle sigh of a thought. He tucked his chin, a bull about to charge. He didn't have to answer, not if he parried with another question.

"Tell me, Red Bear, how is it your men knew the wagons' whereabouts?" He narrowed his eyes. "You and I both know that was no chance meeting."

Red Bear's eyes widened to dark caverns.

"*You?* You are the one behind this?"

Elias clenched his jaw. Behind what? Was there a spy inside the fort feeding information to the French and their allies?

Once again, he scrambled for an answer. If he said yes, they would pry for more information. And if no, then he was back to being a traitor in their eyes. What to do?

He met the sachem's stare and said nothing.

Each pop of the fire was a gunshot. The breath of every man a dragon's. So much tension filled the lodge that even Mercy shifted her stance.

A quiver wavered on Red Bear's lips, and Elias watched the movement with a wary eye. Would a shout issue forth and a knife slit his throat?

But then the man's lips parted, his teeth bared — and a great laugh ripped out of the sachem, so hearty that the feather decorating his forelock shook and moisture leaked from the corners of his eyes. All joined in, even the villain in Mercy's hat. The warrior next to Elias jabbed him with a playful nudge of his elbow.

In the merriment, Elias once again slipped a covert glance at Mercy. She stared straight ahead, face unreadable, a stubborn set to her jaw. And he didn't blame her. Not one bit. Oh, what torturous thoughts she must be thinking.

He turned back to the sachem. Through it all, he remained stoic. Emotion shown too soon was like a ripple on a pond; he could never know on which banks the gesture may land him.

Finally, Red Bear's laughter faded. "Once again, your mysterious ways serve you well, Shadow Walker. But tell me, my brother" — the sachem's smile vanished, the lines of his face sharpening into a fierce snarl — "if this woman is your wife, why does she not look upon you?"

His chest seized. She truly would be the death of him. She'd shown no sign, not one acknowledgment that she even knew him. A proper wife would've flung herself into his arms by now. He breathed in a measured rhythm, fighting for yet another answer.

"She is overcome," he said at length.

"That one knows no fear!" The man with the hat half-rose from his seat. "Two-Pace's blood cries out from the ground because of her."

Elias's brow twitched from want of raising his eyebrows. She took down one of their warriors? Lord, have mercy indeed.

Ignoring the hotheaded warrior, Elias kept his gaze on Red Bear and tried another trail.

"I did not say it was fear that overcomes her. The truth is, great sachem, that the woman is angry with me. We exchanged hot words, and I left her behind. Likely, she thinks I abandoned her."

Elias held his breath. Would the man believe such a tale?

Lifting his face, Red Bear studied Mercy as he might scour a fort's walls for the best place to breach. She stood the assault without a flinch — and the admiration in Elias's heart grew tenfold. What other woman could withstand such a hard-edged stare and not swoon?

A small chuckle rumbled in Red Bear's throat. "Who can know the mind of a woman?"

Elias planted his hands on the fur-lined floor and pushed up before the man could probe any further. "You have given the information I came seeking, great sachem, namely my wife's whereabouts. I will take her and leave in peace. May the sun rise, the rains fall, and the moon shine from a cloudless sky until we meet again."

The sachem lifted his hand, but not in a return blessing. It was a command. A warning. "Take the woman out."

Elias dropped back to the ground, a spectacular feat, since everything in him strained to run after her.

Black gazes darted between the men. Silence crept back in like an unwelcome guest. Everyone, it seemed, held their breath.

"You are free to go, Shadow Walker." Red Bear swept his hand toward the open door. "Yet the woman stays. She is not mine to give."

"But she *is* mine!" Elias pressed his lips flat. Too late.

The warrior in Mercy's hat slid his hand to his tomahawk, his fingers curling like a threat around the handle. Red Bear shook his head at him. The man did not loosen his hold, but neither did he raise it. Would the sachem let such defiance stand?

Red Bear merely angled his head back at Elias. "Nadowa brought the woman in. It is your word against his."

"I tell you true, Red Bear." He swallowed, desperately trying to temper his tone. Making the same mistake twice could send that tomahawk sailing across the fire and into his skull. "The woman belongs to me."

Mercy's hat sank lower on the warrior's brow, shadowing a gaze already black as a new moon night. "You should not have lost her in the first place."

A mighty roar welled in his throat, but he

clamped down on it and all the outrage begging to let loose. If he let one word slip, too many would charge out along with it. Though it galled hotter than a branding iron to offer no defense, he couldn't very well admit he'd been bound and knocked out, for that would make him weak in their eyes — and strength was what he needed now.

He threw back his shoulders and faced Red Bear, charging ahead before he changed his mind. "Then I challenge Nadowa."

Audible gasps swept around the lodge like an unholy wind.

Red Bear gave a sharp nod. "So be it."

A smile slashed across the face of the man in the hat. "Shadow Walker is not as wise as the legends say. This day you will die, for Nadowa is unbeaten."

Mercy tromped after the warrior leading her, heedless of the way each stamp of her feet juddered clear up to her skull. Plenty of slack hung in the lead between her and the man. And why not? She'd rather hole up with Livvy and wait to die than spend one more breath in the presence of Elias Dubois, the scoundrel. The betrayer. Had he planned the whole ambush? Was he the reason Matthew and Rufus were dead?

She kicked a rock, and it skittered into the

ankle of the man leading her. The warrior pierced her with a scowl over his shoulder, as black as her raging thoughts. Not only had Elias spoken the enemy language like a native, he'd sat as a tribal member, completely at home with the band of killers. With her own nostrils she'd breathed in the smoky-sweet scent of a passed pipe, a lingering indictment that justified her charge. The man was a traitor. A filthy, lying-tongued conspirator.

But why did that accusation crawl in and unearth such bitter ground in her heart? She'd known all along Elias would be imprisoned as a defector upon reaching Fort Edward. Charges like that wouldn't just disappear, no matter what she desired.

Her step faltered. *Oh no. A hundred times no.* That was exactly what she'd hoped for. His freedom. His loyalty. His love. She scowled. When had she become such a moon-eyed ridiculous woman?

She dug her feet in harder. No more. Not one second more would she yield to base emotions. Ramping up her pace, she drew near the warrior and nudged him in the back. "You. A word."

The man swung around, black eyes smoldering, arm raised to strike.

She flinched but held her ground.

In an astonishing move, the warrior's rock-hard bicep relaxed, and he lowered his hand. "I spare you for the sake of Shadow Walker, but do not push me."

All those times Elias had snuck up on her suddenly made sense as she connected the Indian name to the man. But no matter. Whatever he was called, he clearly wielded some kind of power. What had he possibly said that might stay the hand of the warrior in front of her?

She lifted her chin, a poor attempt at dignity with the blood and bruises on her face, but she'd not cower. "Tell me what is to come."

Hatred glimmered in his eyes, yet his mouth leveled to a straight line. Nothing but the caw of some ravens and sounds of the camp answered her request. If the man had no intention of answering her, why did he not turn away? Yank on her leash? Backhand her as roughly as the brute who'd stolen her hat?

Finally, he sniffed, as if she were the stench of all that rotted in the world. "This night's challenge determines your fate, woman."

"A challenge." She drew out the word, mind awhir. "Who fights?"

"Nadowa." The warrior looked down his

nose at her and narrowed his eyes. "And your husband."

"But I have no —" *Husband?* She shut her mouth. What on earth had Elias told them?

A deep voice cut in behind her — Elias's — speaking guttural words she couldn't understand. The warrior holding her tether dropped the lead and retreated to the small shelter holding Livvy. Widening his stance, the Indian stood in front of the door and folded his arms, face entirely unreadable.

"Are you well?"

Elias's question turned her around, and she stared up into blue eyes. Furrows lined his brow as if he were concerned. Hah! Why the show? She barely contained a snort. "Does it matter?"

"Of course it does. Why do you think I came?" He grabbed her by the arms and leaned in close, staring deep. "What has gotten into you?"

"Truth, *Shadow Walker.*" She shot the name like the firing of a musket.

He winced. Good. May he feel the pain for such duplicity as sharply as the arrow through Matthew's neck.

"Mercy, I —" His voice was thick and torn at the edges. A small triumph, that. Perhaps he had a seed of humanity left somewhere inside him.

He cleared his throat. "I admit there is much you do not know, but trust me, my silence on matters is necessary."

"Trust you?" She gaped, hating his demand, hating even more the way his smell of smoke and danger tingled along every nerve. "That is a very pretty sentiment coming from your lips."

"There is no time to explain, but I vow that I shall get you out of here. I promise."

For a single, horrifying moment, she believed the passion sparking in his gaze. And more, she wanted him to make everything right. To not be a traitor. To just be a man — one she could love.

Sickened, she jerked up her bound hands and shoved him in the chest. "I don't need your help."

Her voice thundered down on him — and the entire camp. Without turning his head, Elias slipped his gaze side to side, then landed back on her.

"Forgive me, Mercy," he whispered.

"For what? For making me believe you cared — ?"

His mouth crushed against hers, stopping her words. Warm. Firm. Neither devouring nor gentle in intensity. It was the kind of kiss that broke her wide open and held her up all in the same embrace, and she leaned into it, her own body a traitor of the worst degree. She was a desert, and he the only water she'd ever wanted to drink.

A low drone of laughter slapped her back to reality. What was she doing? She jerked away, pulse beating out of control, and wiped her mouth on her sleeve.

"What was that for?" she hissed.

"Your life." Once again he grabbed her arms and pulled her close, and before she could wrench from his hold, he bent and spoke for her ears alone. "These people think you are my wife. Play the part well or we both die."

CHAPTER 26

"You scared, Miss Mercy?"

Was she? She should be. Sitting in the dark of a guarded hut. A harsh language in harsher voices leaching in like a disease from outside the bark walls. And soon she'd belong to either a broad-faced Wyandot or a sweet-talking traitor. But wonder of all wonders, the peace that had crawled into her soul earlier in the day when she'd cried out to God had unpacked and set up house in her soul.

She reached for Livvy's hand with both of hers, still bound, and squeezed the girl's fingers. "No, I am not frightened, leastwise not overmuch."

Livvy squeezed back. "I surely do wish they would have cut that rope from your hands."

"No doubt they soon —"

She jerked her face toward the removal of the framed bark door. Torchlight outside painted a black silhouette of a man . . . and outlined the shape of a floppy felt hat atop his head. She released Livvy's fingers and clenched her hands together so that her knuckles cracked. Surely this thief hadn't been part of the bargain, had he?

She launched toward him. He flinched. And a smile ghosted her lips. Did he yet feel the pain of her earlier head butt?

Grabbing hold of her arm, he dug his fingers into her flesh and yanked her into the night. He hauled her to a ring of men assembled in a loose circle near a large fire. Spectral light flicked over their bodies, painting a nightmarish scene of fiendish ghouls. Two parted, making room for her and her captor. The thrill of a fight brightened the eyes of every man there.

Directly across the flattened patch of ground stood the sachem. Golden gorgets hung from his neck, reflecting flickers of firelight. He stood like a god, arm raised, ready to call into action a battle to the death.

At center, two bare-chested men faced off, ten paces apart, but only one of them commanded her attention. Elias stood with his chin high and shoulders relaxed, at attention but not. A strange mix of nonchalance and wolf about to spring. Though she'd thought on it the better part of the day, she still had no answer as to why he was about to risk his life for her. He could have run free, escaping the locked cell that awaited him at Fort Edward. Why had he bothered coming after her? That question, and a host of others, crowded uninvited and unanswered inside her head, making it ache all the way to her jaws.

Without warning, the sachem dropped his arm.

And the big man charged.

Elias feinted right, then immediately swung back and struck. His first punch glanced off the big man's chin. Mercy did not know much about hand-to-hand battle, but if that was the best Elias could offer, he'd be dead within —

His second fist flew like a musket shot, catching her and the big man off guard. Elias's blow sank deep into the man's stomach, punching him back and doubling him over. Before he regained balance, Elias was on him, knuckles flying, blood splattering, driving him back.

Mercy gasped. She'd always sensed an underlying danger about Elias Dubois. Now she understood why. He struck so hard and fast, he beat the man toward her side of the circle.

Three paces from her, the big man teetered off balance, tipping her way. She retreated, only to be stopped by the chest of the man behind her. But at the last moment, Elias's attacker used his momentum to reach down and swipe up a handful of dirt on his upswing.

"Elias! Duck!"

Too late. The man whipped around and flung the dirt in Elias's eyes. He staggered back, blinded, and furiously rubbed away the grit.

Next to her, a warrior rumbled something low, then held out a hunting knife. Elias's attacker grabbed it and charged.

"No!" she shouted. "Elias, he has a —"

A hand covered her mouth, jamming her head backward against muscle and bone. If Elias's blood was spilled here and now, she'd belong to a killer with no honor.

Elias blinked, the whites of his eyes stark against the dirt on his face. He crouched low, hands out, with nothing to parry but the flesh of his bare arms.

The man advanced, slashing the knife downward. Elias twisted and reached for the man's knife arm with both hands — but the move left his belly open. The big man kneed him in the gut, and as Elias loosed his hold, the man sliced the blade in an arc.

A red line split open on Elias's chest, and

she could do nothing but watch as his lifeblood began to ooze out and run down to his breeches in long drips. Elias reeled, and her heart broke. Traitor or not, she did not want him to die.

The men around her howled their approval, and the big man advanced.

Mercy blinked away tears. Elias didn't stand a chance, not against a man a head taller and hornet mad, gripping a deadly stinger.

With each thrust of the knife, Elias backed away, until he crashed into the line of warriors behind him. The men shoved him forward.

A slow smile spread like a stain across the big man's face, the kind of grin only a nightmare such as this could produce. A slow chant began quietly then gained in strength as each warrior in the circle joined in.

Elias's attacker took another swipe, this time kicking his leg forward to tangle with Elias's and knock him off balance.

But on the downswing, Elias spun around to the man's back, seized the arm without a knife, and elbowed the beast at the base of the neck. The big man dropped to one knee — and Elias made a grab for the weapon.

This time the blade came away in his

hand. With a mighty roar, Elias slashed a gaping cut across the top of the big man's thigh, then jabbed a kick to his chest.

The man landed on his back, air whumping out of his lungs.

Elias pounced, pinning one of the man's arms with his knee, his free hand pinioning the other arm, and raised the blade high.

The chanting stopped. So did time.

Mercy froze. The muscles of the man holding her tensed. What was Elias waiting for?

Then he struck hard, hitting the warrior in the head with the hilt of the knife. Lightning fast, he raised the blade again and stabbed it into the ground next to the man's ear.

Panting, Elias stood. He flicked blood and sweat from his face and staggered a moment, then faced the sachem. Deadly silence filled the night. Mercy held her breath.

Elias's ragged voice cut the air in words she couldn't understand. The sachem glowered. Warriors to her left and right all grumbled and growled. What on earth had Elias said?

With a wild glance, she looked for the native who spoke English and spied him two men away from her. She wrenched her head free from the brute's hand on her mouth and called out, "What does he say?"

"He tells Red Bear he gives back Nadowa and asks for you in return."

Her blood drained to her feet, and the world started to spin. This was not to be borne, leaving a warrior down but not dead. Surely Elias knew the rules when he'd asked for the challenge. The rules demanded blood.

But if not Nadowa's or Elias's, then whose?

Fire burned a swath across Elias's chest. Thank God the slice wasn't deep, or he'd be the one stretched out on the dirt. Every muscle quivered. Every bone screamed. He wore each of his twenty-seven years like chains too heavy to lift. But if that was what it took to free Mercy, then so be it.

He met and matched Red Bear's stare. How generous was the sachem feeling? For it was no small thing that he'd left the knife blade sunk into the ground next to Nadowa's ear instead of in the warrior's chest.

Firelight glinted in Red Bear's eyes, fearsome as the flames of hell. "There is no honor in this. You shame Nadowa by letting him live. If I let the woman go while there is still breath in his body, it shames us all."

Armed with nothing but an arsenal of

words, Elias loaded and shot, praying for a direct hit. "Yet the blood price has been paid, Great One. I wear Nadowa's. He wears mine." He lifted his hands, knuckles split, the splatter of the warrior's blood mingled with his own. "And if you let my wife and me go free, I offer a payment that will benefit all, granting you far more victory and glory than the taking of your finest warrior's life."

A rush of whispers blew behind him, some laced with interest, others scoffing, and a few rumbling with restrained rage.

Red Bear folded his arms, chin held high. "Speak."

"I offer you the very riches your men were looking for when they found my wife."

The sachem's eyes widened. Indians weren't usually greedy for gold, but not so with Red Bear. This shrewd old rascal knew when an opportunity wafted beneath his nose. "How do you know this?"

"Why do you think your men found nothing in those wagons they ransacked? I was the one who hid the cargo out of necessity. I will lead you there come morning."

A slow smile curved the sides of Red Bear's mouth. "Shadow Walker is a man of many surprises. The trade is good. The woman is yours. Come and let us feast."

"Your offer, Great One, is well met." He stepped closer, speaking for only the sachem's ears. "But I have been without my woman for a long time. Grant us shelter alone for the night."

The implication drew a chuckle from the older man.

God, forgive me, Elias prayed silently, for the insinuation and the lie. But had not Abraham done the same when he alluded to his wife as his sister in order to save both their lives? Granted, this was the reverse and he was no Abraham, but even so, far more lives than his or Mercy's depended upon this. *Please, God.*

Red Bear tipped his chin toward the farthest hut. "It is yours."

Elias pivoted and walked tall, hiding a wince with every step. He crossed back to where two men helped Nadowa to stand. The warrior's head lolled, still groggy from the bite of the knife hilt. Some men might gloat over such a triumph, but he found no pleasure in seeing a beaten man. Ah, but he was weary to death of fighting and blood. He crouched and worked the knife free from the dirt.

Mercy stood unattended now, like a lost little girl abandoned at the side of a road. He strode toward her, her luminous eyes watching his approach. Warriors filtered past him, drawn by the fire and the savory tang of roasted venison.

On the way, he stopped and lurched sideways, snatching Mercy's hat off the head of the man who'd stolen it. The man whirled, murder glinting off the silver of his drawn blade.

Again? He'd not yet bandaged the slash on his chest. Even so, he hunkered into a fighting stance, hat in one hand, knife in the other.

Red Bear's voice thundered in the dark. "Shadow Walker reclaims his wife's hat and will pay for it come sunrise. Let it go, Standing Fist."

Working his lips, the man spat at Elias's feet, then stalked off to the fire.

Elias breathed in relief and blew out a prayer. *Thank You, God.* Then he turned and closed the distance between him and Mercy. Reaching out, he placed her hat atop hair so loosened and wild, it spread down to her waist like a mantle. Despite the affront of her capture, the cut on her cheek and the bruise near her eye, the woman was a beauty.

But best of all, and wonder of wonders, the disappointment in her eyes had vanished, replaced by a sheen of awe.

"Hold out your hands," he said gently.

She lifted her wrists. The leather thong cut into her skin, and for a moment he regretted not having killed Nadowa for such a violation.

"I don't know how you managed all that, but" — a gasp cut off her words as he worked the knife between her wrists — "I thank you . . . Shadow Walker."

He flashed a grin as her bindings fell to the ground. "I would say it was my pleasure, but in all honesty, I can think of far more pleasurable things than grappling with an angry Wyandot."

"Seems they are not angry anymore." Mercy rubbed the tender skin at the base of her sleeves. "What did you say to turn away the sachem's wrath?"

"Come, and I will tell you." He led her past the warriors already tearing great bites of venison from two does brought in earlier. Lewd comments followed him all the way to the makeshift longhouse, most about his manliness, some about her curves. All about what they expected would be going on once he was alone with Mercy. Sweet heavens, but he was glad she did not understand the language. It was humiliating enough that he did.

So he forced his mind onto a different trail

and glanced at Mercy. "I have not seen Rufus or heard word of him spoken. Was he taken along with you?"

"No." She shook her head. "I assumed he was killed, like Matthew."

He grunted. "There was no evidence. His body was not there. These warriors would have had no reason to haul him off and kill him elsewhere."

"You think he is still alive?"

"Hard to say. But Lord knows the man was ever good at hiding."

He shoved aside the door flap to the shelter and allowed Mercy to pass. Once he stepped inside, his body yearned to stretch out on one of the furs lining the pallets on either side of the wall. Instead, he strode over to where he'd left his few belongings and reached for his shirt — then gasped. Pain seared like a branding iron.

Mercy's light step caught up behind him, her soft voice a soothing balm. "Let me bandage that chest of yours."

Despite the cold sweat dotting his brow, heat ignited a fire in his belly at the thought of her warm fingers tending to his bare skin. "I can manage," he ground out.

"Not easily."

He blew out a breath. It would take him longer to bind up his wound on his own.

And time was scarce.

He turned. "Fine. But I will be tending to that wound on your shoulder as soon as you are finished. Ah-ah!" He wagged his finger at the pert angle of her chin. "Do not tell me that injury is not festering something fierce."

Furrows marred her brow as she frowned, yet she snapped into action. Low light from an untended fire at the center of the shelter grew as she lobbed wood onto it from a pile dumped near the door. He sank onto the hardened dirt next to the flames, shivers creeping over the bare skin of his back. He always felt this way after a fight, all jittery and sharp-edged.

Mercy lugged over a skin of water, set it at his side, then said, "Close your eyes."

What the devil did she have in mind? "Why?"

"I believe you asked me to trust you once. I expect the same courtesy."

How was he to argue with that? He closed his eyes.

A bit of rustling ensued, then the distinct sound of ripping fabric. A smile twitched his lips. Of course. She aimed to bandage him up good with the cloth of her petticoat.

"I am finished."

His eyes barely opened when cold water

doused him from overhead, shocking and nipping all at once. "Sweet mercy! A little warning would be nice."

"What did you think? That I would bind up a dirty wound?" She clicked her tongue like a mother. "Arms up, please."

He complied, and while she worked to wrap the torn strips of fabric tight against his torn skin, he wondered at her complete ease with the interior of a warrior longhouse and a half-naked man to tend to. But then again, perhaps she truly had grown up in a home such as this.

"Why did you not tell me Black-Fox-Running was your father?" he pondered aloud.

"My past is of no account."

He grabbed her hand as it crossed to the front of his chest and pulled her close. "Everything about you is of account, least-wise to me. Surely you know that by now."

She stared, long and hard, and for some odd reason, tears glistened watery and bright in the firelight. What on earth was she thinking?

She pulled away without a word and went back to wrapping the binding around his chest. The woman was a mystery. A glorious, beautiful mystery.

"And your mother? Let me guess —" He

grunted as she yanked the cloth tight at his back. "Was she the daughter of some high-ranking official?"

"Nay, my mother was nothing special save for her claim of her forefathers being the first to settle at Plimouth." Mercy's words kept time to the deft movement of her fingers. "Even so, I am of late coming to view her strength and courage as rivaling that of my father."

She retrieved his shirt and held it out. "As long as you don't go challenging any more warriors, that should hold."

"No more challenging." He grabbed the shirt and eased it over his head, then stood. "But we do have some traveling. We leave as soon as I tend to that shoulder of yours."

"Turn your back, and I will tend it myself."

"But —"

His rebuttal died a fast death from her murderous scowl. Perhaps it was better for her to tend to such a flesh-baring task. He crossed back to where his hunting frock, his belt, his newly acquired knife, and Mercy's blade lay on a fur.

"Why do we leave in the dark of night? It is not safe." The sound of fabric rustled, followed by water trickling off skin — and he nearly turned around when she sucked in an audible breath.

So, he had been right. That wound of hers did hurt something fierce. Blast the man who'd hurt her!

"Elias?"

He jammed his arms into the sleeves of his hunting frock more forcefully than necessary. "We need to make it back to the gold before Red Bear's pack of warriors."

She sucked in another gasp, then blew out a long breath. The sound of her pain twisted his gut.

"Why would they return to naught but empty wagons? They couldn't know . . ." This time the air rushing into her mouth was a threat. "You told them!"

He buckled his belt and snugged the hunting knife at his waist, glad to finally have a weapon, especially with the venom in Mercy's voice. "I promised them the gold. And I am no traitor, if that is what you are thinking. It was the price for your freedom."

"Why did you not simply kill that man?"

At the sound of her next sharp intake, he wondered that very thing. The man should've paid for his rough handling of Mercy. And he would one day, unless God's grace saved him from the same darkness he himself used to wallow in.

His finger traced the hilt of the knife at

his side. "It is God's place to take a life, not mine."

More water trickled, followed by a long silence. Finally, she murmured, "You are a complicated man, Elias Dubois. Oh, and you can turn around now."

"You are quite the tangle yourself." He snatched up her knife and strode back to her. A worn piece of petticoat peeked out from the rip on her shoulder, her wound as freshly bound as his. She'd endured it all with but a few gasps. What kind of woman did that?

The kind of woman I want.

He planted his feet wide to keep from staggering. The realization hit him harder than the beating he'd just taken. He wanted this woman so much the yearning ached, warm and pulsing, in his soul.

"Mercy, I —" He what? He pressed his lips shut. This was mad. Heaven help him, now was definitely *not* the time for love. It wouldn't be fair to her for him to spout feelings he couldn't back up with action. Lord knew if they would even make it out of this mess alive.

He shoved down the words he wanted to say and instead held out her knife in an open palm. "I found your knife."

Her gaze shot from the blade to him,

admiration shining vividly in her brown eyes — a look he'd never tire of if he lived to be an old, old man.

"You never stop surprising me, Shadow Walker." This time his name was a purr instead of an indictment.

And he liked it.

She reached for the knife, her slim fingers brushing against his skin, leaving a trail of wildfire.

Oh, hang it all. He wrapped his hand around hers and pulled her to him. His heart beat a drum against his chest, eclipsing the pain of battle.

She came willingly and lifted her face to his. "It was no small thing what you did for me, but you have yet to tell me why." Her gaze bored deep into his. "Why did you not just run away to freedom?"

CHAPTER 27

Mercy held her breath, hoping for . . . what? That Elias would speak words of love here in the middle of a Wyandot war camp? Was that what she wanted? Though she did her best to ignore the obvious answer, a charge of warmth shot through her from head to toe.

She did. More than anything. She wanted to belong to the scruff-faced man staring at her with impossibly blue eyes and a mouth she'd tasted sweet and strong.

And that scared her more than a raging war party of warriors.

"Running off was never a choice for me, Mercy. I knew what they would do with you." A storm of anger and restraint clenched his jaw. Then, just like that, the squall passed. The sharp lines on his brow bowed into a grief so great, the weight of it pressed down on her.

He swallowed, his throat bobbing, and his

voice came out husky despite the action. "I could not let that happen. Not to you."

The intensity in his gaze reached out, pulling her closer. Without thinking, she rose to her toes and brushed her lips lightly against his bruised cheek, the rasp of his whiskers a powerful reminder of his manliness. A tremor shook through him, through her, through the heavens themselves.

"There is much honor in you, Elias Dubois," she whispered against his skin. "More than I credited."

For a moment, he leaned into her touch, sharing his warmth and strength; then he pulled back, releasing his hold of her. "We need to leave. Find what food you can. I will see to finding some weapons."

He turned and strode to rummage through some Indian's belongings . . . and the loss of his touch was staggering.

But of course he was right. If they were to retrieve the gold with any hope of keeping ahead of a pack of angry warriors, every minute now counted a hundredfold. She joined him in ransacking warriors' belongings for strips of jerky or handfuls of pemmican. Not much was on hand, but she found enough that they would have something to eat along the way.

Wood snapping turned her around. Behind her Elias broke arrows, shaft after shaft . . . which gave her an idea. She reached for a nearby bow and, yanking out her knife, slit the string in two. They fell into a destructive cadence, him snapping, her slicing.

"What is your plan?" she asked while they worked, hoping to somehow ask for Livvy to be incorporated into whatever scheme he had in mind. She couldn't leave the girl behind, especially when the warriors discovered their duplicity. Livvy would bear the brunt of their anger, maybe even suffer a revenge killing. A shiver snaked across her shoulders. She wouldn't wish that death on anyone.

Elias finished the last of the arrows, then faced her. "We get the girl, then the horses—"

"You know of Livvy?" Her brows shot to her hat brim, and it was a fight to keep from gaping. Did the man read minds as well as walk invisible? Her admiration for him grew, blocking out all her reasons as to why she shouldn't trust him.

"Red Bear mentioned another captive besides you." He flashed a smile. "But I'm not promising it will be an easy endeavor. Are you ready for this?"

She slit the last bowstring and dropped

the useless bow, then slung a pouch of food over her shoulder. "I am now."

He led her to the back door and nudged the flap aside. Leaning out, he glanced left to right, then turned to her. "Stay low. We will work our way to the girl, and I shall keep watch while you cut a small flap in the back of the hut, taking out any who chance your way. Keep the girl quiet and make for the woods. I will double back for the horses and meet up with you."

Reaching out, he brushed back a rogue coil of hair hanging in her eyes, his fingers lingering against the skin of her brow. Then he disappeared out the door.

She followed, crouching low, trying hard to mimic his moves. It was a risky thing, this escape. Deadly. Her step nearly faltered with the impossibility of what they were about to undertake . . . but had not God kept her safe thus far? A foreign yet welcome surge of faith urged her onward.

Elias moved ahead, stationing himself at the edge of the trees, twenty paces or so from the rear of the hut. The distance was a gaping flatland, making anyone who crossed it a target to be shot. But it gave Elias a wide enough view to spot trouble should any arise.

Dropping to all fours, Mercy crept

through weeds and shin-high grasses. She stopped inches away from the bark wall and listened hard. A song chanted on the night air. A few whoops. Some laughter and a holler. It seemed all entertained themselves at the fire — hopefully.

She pulled out her knife and started cutting. Ripping, really. The noise of the blade tearing into dried linden bark scratched a dead giveaway of her location. What Livvy could be thinking was anyone's guess.

Eventually she tore enough off to yank away a big square of bark. "Livvy?" she whispered.

Wide eyes peeked out of the darkness. Livvy opened her mouth, and Mercy shot her fingers to the girl's lips, then beckoned with the same finger for the girl to crawl out.

Livvy's shoulders wedged in the small space — too small for her to fit through. Mercy motioned for the girl to retreat, then stabbed her knife in again, sawing a larger hole. Her blade stuck once, and in that moment of silence, a terrifying sound crept closer from the front of the hut.

Footsteps.

She froze. What to do? She'd never make it to the safety of Elias's side before being seen.

Shallow breaths. Shallow. Anything more and the wound on Elias's chest stabbed sharply. It was difficult to maintain the rhythm though, as he squinted in the dark, concentrating hard on why Mercy might've stopped working.

He scanned the area — and his breath stopped completely. A black man-shape strode away from the fire, ghoulish light outlining his broad shoulders and determined step. And each step brought the beast closer to where Mercy lay low at the back of the holding hut. If she ripped off one more piece of that bark, he'd hear.

For the hundredth time this never-ending night, Elias prayed. *Lord, have mercy.*

Then he slipped the knife from his side and crept forward.

And while You're at it, forgive me, Lord, for what I am about to do.

A hacking cough filled the night air, adding to the ambient noise from warriors who'd swigged too much rotgut. What on earth? The cough issued from inside the hut . . . didn't it?

Elias paused and cocked his head. The coughing barked louder.

The man stopped, his head angling too.

Mercy yanked off another piece of the shelter with the next spate of hacking. The black hole gaped larger, and she dove in.

"Quiet!" The girl couldn't possibly know what the man said, but the threat of his tone was enough.

And as soon as the bark chunks appeared from inside the hut and blocked — mostly — the hole in the back, the coughing stopped.

Elias's lips curved. The girl just might be an asset instead of a hindrance.

But the small smile vanished as the man stalked ahead and rounded the side of the hut. Had he heard something other than the coughing?

The man planted his feet directly in front of the hole. He didn't crouch to study it though, but faced the woods instead of the hut.

Even so, Elias dropped to his belly, fighting a gasp from the pain, and skulked ahead, inch by inch. Would he have enough time to drop the man before he could yell an alarm?

A new sound stopped him once again. Liquid hitting grass, sprinkling in a stream. Elias loosened his fingers from the death grip on his knife hilt, waited until the man finished relieving himself, then tucked the blade away. Apparently far too much drink was flowing this night.

As soon as the man's footsteps faded, Elias crawled back to the safety of the trees, with Mercy and the girl not far behind. When they caught up, he jerked his head for Mercy to follow, her face pale in the darkness. Would that he could gather her in his arms and hold her until her trembling stopped. But no time. Would there ever be enough time?

He glanced at the girl, head even with Mercy's shoulder, blond hair a beacon. Surely he must look as frightening as one of the Wyandot warriors here in the dark, but she made no noise, not even a whimper. Brave girl.

Wheeling about, he led them from shadow to shadow, flinching every time the girl cracked a stick beneath her step. Not often, but enough that should another native venture aside to relieve himself, their movement would be detected . . . unless by now everyone's senses were skewed. One could hope.

And he did.

A quarter mile later, he spied an upturned hemlock, roots and dirt ripped up to form a chest-high wall. With a sweep of his arm, he ushered Mercy and the girl to shelter behind it.

He crouched in front of Mercy, whispering low. "I need one of your petticoats."

The whites of two pairs of eyes shone bright in the dark.

"What?" Mercy breathed.

But now was not the time to explain. "You heard me." He held out his hand.

Turning her back to him, she shimmied a bit and worked loose her under petticoat, then handed over the ragged bit of fabric. The girl shrank back, eyeing them both.

He winked at Mercy. "I owe you one."

Then he ripped the cloth into long strips and set off to locate the horses. It wasn't hard. The smell of horseflesh drew him and any other predator. Hopefully not many men guarded the animals.

He slowed as he came upon a small clearing on the north side of camp. Setting down the pile of bindings, he pulled his knife and melded against the shadows, traveling the perimeter. Only four horses dotted the area. What had happened to the other four? Not that he minded, as it made his task easier, but it made no sense they had left behind the others. Something about this wasn't right — but with Mercy and Livvy waiting on him, he'd have to puzzle over the mystery later.

Near as he could tell, only one brave kept watch — or should have been. The man hunkered down, his back against a heap of bridles and a piece of meat in both hands. His teeth ripped and his lips smacked.

Elias glanced heavenward, grateful once again that a God so big deigned to answer the prayers of a man like him.

He retrieved the bindings, then crept behind the man while he was still busy eating. A quick crack to his head knocked him sideways. As Elias bound and gagged him, he couldn't help but wonder how many more skulls he'd be required to smack this night.

Weary beyond measure, he rose and began loosing horses. He slapped two on the rump, driving them out in different directions into the night. The other two he bridled and led in a circuitous route back to Mercy and the girl. With any luck, the scouts would be confused, especially with the other two horses running who knew where.

Mercy emerged from the cleft of the overturned tree, the girl trailing. He handed her the reins of the larger horse.

She stared into the darkness behind him.

"Where are the rest of the horses?"

"We only need two. The girl rides with you. Mount up."

A frown darkened her pale skin. "But we'll never haul the gold with only two horses."

"We are not taking all of it."

"But you said —"

"There is no time. We ride hard. Now." Using the tree as a stepping block, he mounted. Horseflesh warmed his backside. Riding bareback would leave an ache in a few more muscles than he expected.

"Fine," Mercy huffed, then narrowed her eyes up at him. "But you will tell me all when we stop."

He yanked the horse around, leaving space for Mercy and the girl to mount as he had. Would that he could yank an easy answer out for her as well, for the harshness of her whisper screamed determination. How much should he tell her? How much could he? Thankfully he had a hard ride ahead to mull this over, for of only two things was he certain.

Mercy would not be put off.

He couldn't continue keeping the truth from her.

This was exactly why, in all his training, the one thing his commander in Boston had drilled on most frequently was the warning never to drop his guard around a woman. Now he understood why.

CHAPTER 28

After endless hours of riding, Mercy was spent. In the hollow of a ravine, beneath an overhanging slab of moss-covered rock, she sank onto a patch of ferns barely unfurled. The peppery-sweet scent conjured memories of happier times, of romps through the woods with her brother and of lazy missions scouting for nothing but a place to camp for the night with Matthew. Times when the threat of tomahawks or arrows wasn't just a wild ride behind her.

At her side, Livvy had already curled into a ball on the ground, asleep. It took everything in Mercy's power not to fling herself down and do the same. An all-night ride picking their way through darkness, the morning of speed and distance, and now an afternoon sky draped with clouds like a thick blanket all beckoned her to stretch out. But she pulled up her knees and wrapped her arms about them, refusing to bed down — not until Elias returned from seeing to the horses.

The *tchuk-tchuk* of a blackbird's call drifted down from the treetops, haunting, simple . . . grievous. A sound that tightened her throat and caused her eyes to burn. *Oh Matthew.* She blinked back tears. *Tchuk-tchuk* had been her friend's trademark call, announcing his approach or alerting her to danger. She'd never hear it again from his mouth. The image of Matthew's crumpled body fallen over the wagon seat flashed like a nightmare, and a single fat drip ran hot down her cheek. She'd not even gotten to say goodbye, just like her father. Just like her mother.

She drew in a shaky breath. Was all of life to be like this? Losing those she loved without a farewell? Was Onontio out there somewhere, even now lying cold and stiff?

Footsteps drew near, and she scrubbed away the dampness on her face with the back of her hand.

Opposite Livvy, Elias lowered beside her. "You should sleep. We will not be here long."

His low voice, strong and sure and very much alive, was a balm to her melancholy. Bundling up her sorrow and packing it away into a corner of her heart, she speared him with a sideways glance. "Long enough for me to get an answer."

He snorted. "If nothing else, you are persistent."

Without another word, he eased flat and slung his forearm over his eyes, blocking out the gruel-thin daylight — and her.

She smirked. Did he seriously think she'd be put off so easily? She leaned over and lifted his arm. "Well?"

Only one of his eyes popped open. "Sleep."

"You promised, Elias." She let his arm drop and leaned back on her elbows. "Unless you're the type of man who doesn't keep his word."

She hid a smile at the sigh that ripped out of him. It had been an unfair jab — but it worked, as she'd suspected.

Turning, he crooked his arm and propped his chin on the heel of his hand. "What is it you want to know?"

She narrowed her eyes to keep from rolling them. He knew exactly what she wanted to know. A question for a question was a ploy she'd used herself earlier in the day when Livvy kept asking when they'd stop.

"Tell me what you're really after, Elias Dubois."

"That should be apparent." The blue in his eyes burned brilliant, full of promises and intrigue, altogether dangerous . . . and far too alluring. "I am on the same mission as you."

"Are you?" She flicked away a bug hovering in front of her face and studied him, from the lines of his unshaven jaw to the curve of his cheekbones, landing on the slight lift to one of his brows. How was she ever to know when he spoke truth? "I wonder."

"You know as well as I we can no longer expect to get that load of gold to Fort Edward. Even had we taken four horses and tried to hitch up one wagon, we never would have made it. As it is, we will barely keep abreast of those men, even covering our trail and doubling back. The way I see it, by scattering the horses, we bought us some time as they try to figure out which way we went."

"You don't think they will go straight for the gold like we are?"

"They do not know where the gold is, now do they?"

She pulled her gaze from him and stared straight ahead, the green of the ravine blurring into a smear. He was right of course, and that rankled. Matthew had always been right too, but something was different in the way Elias answered her, always turning things back into a question. Like something tethered the words behind his lips from flying free.

"Then why go back at all?" She spoke as much to herself as to him, trying to work out the logic of why they should bother returning to the cache of gold, especially now that they had Livvy to see to. She swung her gaze back to Elias. "Maybe we should make for Fort Edward and come back with a squad of soldiers."

"If I go to Fort Edward, I will not be coming back."

If? Her eyes widened. "You don't intend to go?"

She drew in a breath, the truth hooking into her like a stickle-burr. She was the only one stopping him from escaping — and after the way she'd seen him fight, she was naught but a gnat to be swatted aside. Not that she blamed him. She might do the same were she faced with years locked in a damp, dark cell. But not paying the debt for a crime he didn't deny wasn't honorable . . . was it? How could she ever reconcile this man's acts of integrity against such a defilement of justice?

He pushed up to sit, a groan rumbling in his throat. That slash on his chest had to hurt something fierce, for the sting on her shoulder from the arrow yet raged when she moved too quickly.

Shifting, he leaned over her. "Regardless of what I intend, know this . . . I will see you and Livvy to safety. I vow it."

Safety? With a pack of angry natives likely even now on their trail? She shook her head. "But we'll never be safe from Red Bear, not after what you did."

"That is a burden not meant for you." He tapped her lightly on the nose. "Sleep now, for we will not rest long."

She frowned. She'd been the cause of that burden, had she not? This man with the purple near his eye and cut on his cheekbone had fought for her to his own detriment.

"I don't understand you," she murmured.

A grin broke white and wide in his dark beard, sinking deep and wrapping around her like a warm embrace. "Would you have it any other way?"

Without waiting for an answer, he eased himself back to the ground, arm once again slung across his eyes. In no time, his breathing evened, chest rising and falling in a deep cadence, sound asleep.

She lay down as well, but her eyes blinked long and hard, his question riding along with the continued *tchuk-tchuk*s of the blackbird. Would she want a man she could predict? One who wasn't full of surprises?

She forced her eyes shut, desperate to escape the answer to that and an even more hideous question that crouched, waiting to pounce at some point in the near future.

What were his intentions?

Elias squatted, studying the base of a tall maple. Morning dew hung like a string of beads along the almost invisible line of a spiderweb. This thick in the woods and with an overcast sky, it was hard to tell exactly where the sun rose, but spiders generally chose the south side of a tree to build their homes because it was the warmest. And a ways back he'd spied a woodpecker hole halfway up a dying hemlock, which was more than likely east. Mind made up, he straightened and grabbed hold of his horse. If they veered just a hair to the left, they ought to hit the ravine by early afternoon.

Using a rock as a mounting block, he swung up onto the animal. Two days and a hard ride without aid of even a blanket as a cushion ached in his backside and legs — but not nearly as nettling as the throbbing of his conscience. The torment of not having told Mercy the full truth yesterday competed with the necessity of his orders to keep silent. Both plagued him every time he looked in her eyes.

He nudged the horse with his heels and trotted back to where he'd left Mercy, refusing to meet her gaze. With a silent jerk of his head, he indicated for her and the girl to follow.

Hours later, the trees thinned somewhat. Ground growth thickened. The heaviness weighting his shoulders lightened a bit as they neared the drop before the glade. Once he retrieved that weapon, he'd see Mercy and Livvy to the shelter of the nearest town — Schoharie, if he calculated correctly — then ride like the wind for Boston. A good plan. A solid one.

As long as Red Bear and his men held off.

He guided his mount down the route at the side of the rock face, and with his first full glance at the clearing, he kicked the horse into a run.

No! God, no!

The broken crates lay in the open air like so many bones. But only one wagon sat at the center of the glade. Weeds lay flattened in two ruts where the wheels of the other one had turned in an arc and headed back out to the road.

And the dirt where they had buried the gold yawned open like an empty grave.

He yanked the horse to a stop and slid to

the ground, trying hard to ignore the searing pain of the slice on his chest. How could this be?

Stomping the length of the trench, he scoured the area for clues. Here a shovel cut. There a heel imprint — several, actually. All precisely where they had toiled to hide the gold — and nowhere else.

A skirt rustled close. Mercy's voice followed, pinched and strangled. "Matthew's body is . . ." She sucked in a shaky breath. "It is still there. What happened here?"

He shook his head, wishing with everything in him his suspicions were dead wrong. "You tell me."

She padded along the roughed-up dirt, her keen eye touching on the same signs he'd detected. Then she whirled, torn skirts swirling about her legs, her slim fingers curling into fists. Red patches of rage darkened her cheeks. "Besides us, only Rufus knew we hid the gold here."

"Are you surprised?"

"Blast!" The word shot from her mouth like a cannonball.

He coughed into his hand to keep from smiling.

"You all right, ma'am?" Livvy asked from behind.

Mercy bit her lip, then hollered to the girl,

"I'm fine." Her gaze drifted back to Elias. "I apologize."

He worked his jaw, stifling a chuckle. "No need to apologize. I feel the same. I should have known something was off, seeing as only four horses were taken and Rufus was not held captive along with you."

Mercy shrugged. "Like I said earlier, I assumed he'd been killed along with Matthew."

"Well, there is naught to be done for it now." He pulled off his hat and ran his hand through his hair, a vain attempt to straighten out his thoughts as well. No wonder Rufus not only suggested this clearing, but insisted on their reaching it . . . and put up a fuss at their burying the gold. Likely he'd worked it out with Red Bear to kill off whoever accompanied him, then split the riches with him. A sour taste filled his mouth, and he swallowed. Sweet suffering cats but he'd been wrong about the whelp! He should have known there'd been far more depth to Rufus's deviousness. But where was the man now? And with whom?

He jammed his hat back onto his head and faced Mercy. "Mount up. The trail ought to be easy enough to follow, especially if they turned onto any side trails."

"They?"

"You really think Rufus could do this alone?"

Mercy kicked at the dirt, and though she did not say it, he had no doubt a few more angry words exploded in her head. In the dreary light of a cloudy afternoon and with anger simmering inside, she radiated a fierce beauty.

"Elias." Her brown eyes sought his. "We can't go up against Rufus and who knows how many others with nothing but two knives and a young girl."

A storm was coming. He felt it deep in his bones. One that would blow clear away the secrecy of his mission. He should have run far and fast that first time he'd gripped her hand and the charge had run through him, for he could deny her no more.

"You are right." He spoke slowly, biding time. But for what? The longer they stayed here, the closer Red Bear's men drew. He pierced her with a stare. "And that is why you and Livvy will stay hidden while I get what I came for."

"No."

The word floated somewhere overhead, like a tuft of cottonwood blown by the breeze. *No?* She'd dig in her heels just like that, without nary a by-your-leave?

She folded her arms and tipped her chin,

a rock-hard gleam in her eye. "I'm not going one more step with you until you tell me what you're after and why."

And there it was. The fork in the road. The one where he either held tight to his course of silence alone or ran toward her and told all . . . . unless he appealed to her sense of fear and avoided the whole thing altogether.

He threw out his hands. It was either that or grab her close and kiss the defiance from her face. "We do not have time for this. I will tell you later —"

"Livvy, get yourself down," she called to the girl and whumped to the ground herself. "We rest here."

"Mercy, please." He gritted his teeth. "You know the longer we stay here, the closer those warriors get."

She peered up at him. "Then you had better talk fast."

Thunder and turf! The woman was as inflexible as a steel-edged tomahawk.

"Stubborn woman." He dropped down beside her and pressed the heel of his hand against his brow, fighting off a killer of a headache. He'd been in tight spaces before, faced death and torture, but never had he felt the need to expose who he was, what he was about, until now.

"What I am about to tell you goes against my orders and endangers your life. You cannot breathe a word of this, not even on pain of death." He measured the words out slowly, methodically, all the while looking for an opportunity to turn the subject on to a side route. "No one would believe you anyway."

How well he knew that. He scrubbed a hand at the base of his neck, right where a rope would bite.

"If you're thinking to scare me, it is not working."

Aye, he should have known better. He lowered his hand, and a smile tugged his lips. "You really will be the death of me, Mercy Lytton."

He sucked in a big breath and let it all leak out. There'd be no turning back now, not unless he jumped up and rode off, leaving the temptation behind. Leaving Mercy behind — and that was not an option.

He turned to her and grabbed one of her hands. A totally irrational move, but needful. A warm reminder she was skin and breath and worth the risk of everything he had to give.

"Elias?" Creases marred her fine brow . . . creases put there by him and his deceit.

He rubbed his thumb along the back of

her hand, watching the movement for a while, admiring the way her fine skin yielded to his touch — anything to distract, to keep him from thinking on what he was about to say.

"The truth is," he murmured, "I am not a traitor, leastwise not to the English."

She shook her head. "Then who are you? *What* are you?"

A disappointment. A hellion. A failure.

He shoved back his grandfather's words and looked her straight in the eyes. "I am a spy, sent to infiltrate the French under the guise of a turncoat."

CHAPTER 29

"A spy for the English. Not the French. Not a turncoat. Just a guise." Mercy nattered with an unhinged jaw, knowing all the while it wasn't helping. She could no more understand the words coming from her own mouth than she could from Elias's.

She stared deep into his blue eyes, trying — needing — to sift truth from deception. He didn't blink. He didn't flinch. He stared back, gaze clear and candid as if he looked upon the face of God.

Stunning, truly. All her life she'd prided herself on reading people. Sorting them out like a basket of berries, good in one pile, bad in the other. Had she been wrong about this man just as she had been wrong about her mother all these years? How had she, the one of keen sight, been so blind? And how had he been so cunning as to let her — and everyone else — believe such a thing?

She yanked back her hand from his hold.

"You were nearly hanged! Why would you do that? Why did you not tell General Bragg?"

A shadow crossed his face, though not a cloud dotted the sky. He pulled his gaze from her and reached for a pebble, tossing the thing back and forth, palm to palm. "As I said, no one would believe me. The truth of my mission is known only to a major in Boston, and in order to make my role believable, even he would deny me."

Toss. Toss. The stone dropped lazily from one hand to the other, as restless as the information she tried to line up in a neat row. He could be lying, but why invent such a fanciful story?

"Miss Mercy?" Livvy drew close, blond hair as wild and loose as Mercy's own.

She'd have to braid that, as soon as she finished combing through Elias's tale. Mercy smiled at the girl; at least she hoped it came off as a grin instead of a grimace. "I need a moment with Mr. Dubois. Here" — she shrugged off the food pouch strapped over her shoulder — "get yourself something to eat and close your eyes for a few minutes."

The girl reached for the bag, all the while studying Elias. The longer she stared, the more a dimple carved deep into her chin as she pursed her lips. The girl was not dim-witted. She must sense some kind of squabble hanging on the air.

Yet she said no more. She nodded, then retreated back near the horses and sat on the ground with the bag.

Mercy turned to Elias, unsure what to think anymore. Was he a spy? Wasn't he? If he were not a traitor — *if* . . . Her heart beat hard against her ribs as she traced the way the sun wrapped a glowing mantle across his shoulders. If he were a man of honor, then she was in even more danger, for there'd be nothing to douse the affection that had been kindling since the first touch of his hand.

She clenched her teeth, trapping a scream of confliction.

The rock slipped from his fingers, and he snatched it up again. "You do not have to believe me, Mercy. Sometimes . . ." He peered down at her. "Well, sometimes I can barely believe it myself."

She huffed out a sigh, wanting, not wanting. The few crumbs of information he'd served hardly sufficed, and in fact merely whetted her appetite for more. "What are you here for exactly? What is your mission?"

"Originally it was to find out which fort the French next intended to siege, which I did." He tossed the pebble in rhythm with his words. "I was even on my way back to Boston, but as I overnighted at Fort Le Boeuf, the whole thing turned into something more . . . deadly."

The tossing stopped. The rock plummeted. Elias's hands hung still between his knees.

Fear snuck up like a snake, slipping a shiver down her back. She'd seen him face an Indian with a knife, a river bent on pulling him under, not to mention a time or two when she'd swung at him with all her fury. But in all those times, she'd never seen the unvarnished terror now twitching his jaw.

"What did you discover?" she whispered.

He blew out a long breath, and when he spoke, his low voice threatened like an approaching tempest. "I am not sure, which is why I am in such a hurry to get back what I hid in one of those crates. The only thing I know for certain is that I have never seen any weapon quite so deadly."

He shot to his feet, brushing the dirt from his hands along his thighs.

She bit her lip, watching him as he stood there. Could be a ploy. He could be a consummate actor. But the solemn bow of his head, the restless energy rippling out from him, even the way he didn't plead or demand she believe him, all testified to the probable viability of his story.

Still she wasn't satisfied. She stood as well. "If I'm going with you — *if* — I need to know what it is we'll be transporting, especially with Livvy in tow."

He glanced at her from the corners of his eyes. "So . . . you believe me?"

"I did not say that, and stop changing the subject."

His mouth curved up at one side, then just as suddenly the half smile faded. He folded his arms and faced her, planting his feet wide. "All right. There's a battalion of French even now on their way to Fort Stanwix, but it is no regular threat. They intend to deploy a new weapon, one that will kill every man in that fort before a surrender can be arranged."

Every man? Prickles ran along her arms. "What is this weapon?"

"A grenade, of sorts. The likes of which I have never seen. The outside shell is glass, which of course inflicts a nasty spray of skin-piercing shards. But worse are the contents. Small bits of metal, sharpened, jagged, and coated in a substance beyond my understanding. Some kind of poison, I guess. These bits are loaded into the glass

389

grenades, launched over the walls by a new kind of mortar, and when they explode, whoever chances a single scratch by one of those pieces of metal dies shortly thereafter in agony."

"How do you know this?" Her voice sounded strange, even to her own ears. Then again, this whole conversation was morbidly odd. Were the sun not warming her shoulders and a breeze cooling her cheek, she'd question if she were awake.

"I witnessed the test fires" — a fearsome glower etched lines on Elias's face — "as they practiced on English prisoners, mostly men, some women and . . ." His Adam's apple bobbed, and he barely choked out his last word. "Children."

She gulped, suddenly needful of air. This was no playacting. The truth, the horror, the righteous rage emanating from Elias knocked her back a step.

His eyes narrowed to daggers. "If I bring in that weapon and our men can figure out what the poison is, perhaps an antidote can be created. If not, well . . . I know where the poison and the mortars are stored. We take out the supply, and the threat is leveled, leastwise for now."

He'd carried this weight all this time, come for her even when he knew each minute spent chasing after her was one taken from his mission. And he'd not even blinked with the prospect of adding a young girl into his care, despite the strain he already bore. The truth of who Elias Dubois really was punched her square in the belly, and she pressed her hands to her stomach.

"Livvy," she called out, her voice shaky but audible. "Prepare to ride."

Elias cocked his head at her, one brow lifted.

And surprisingly, she managed a small smile. "We've a wagon to catch up to." But then all mirth fled. That wasn't all to be done. Her eyes burned, and she blinked back tears. "But first we have a body to bury."

As much as she understood the urgency of Elias's mission, duty to Matthew came first.

Hours later, after a thorough check for signs of anything that breathed, Elias slid from his horse and emerged from the woods. Ahead, the road forked, one branch bearing south in a sharp turn. He needn't check, really, for Rufus no doubt continued on the northeast trail, toward Fort Edward, but all his training had taught him to be thorough. *Training?* Hah. A smirk twisted his lips. Why follow such minute protocol now when he'd already forsaken the number one tenet?

He followed the road to where it split. None of this would be happening if he'd never hidden the weapon in a crate of gold to begin with. He should've taken the risk of carrying the thing on his body. But hindsight . . . well, hindsight ever had a way of making the present look like a farce.

Slowing his pace, he scanned the ground, looking for signs of wagon wheels. Who helped Rufus was still a mystery, unless the Shaws had turned back and stumbled across him. Of only one thing was Elias certain — that all along Rufus had intended to bring that gold into the fort by himself. He not only would take all the credit for surviving an Indian attack single-handedly, but would receive a fat pay increase and gain another rank for having saved the load. The young scoundrel had been willing to see them all die just for his profit.

Shoving down a rising anger, Elias crouched and studied the dirt where the road divided. What the . . . ? He ran a finger along the weeds flattened in the curve of a rut. No doubt about it then.

"Which way?"

Mercy's quiet voice wrapped around him from behind. He stood and faced her, taking a moment to brand this image of her on his memory. She belonged here, framed by green wilds, one with God's creation. He'd never seen a lioness other than as a child in one of his grandfather's books, but this woman embodied all the traits of the queen of hunters. The way her chin tipped proud, that thick mane of hair riding her shoulders, the confident look in her eye. And now that she knew his secret, the power to crush him with a single swipe.

He scrubbed his face with his hand, wiping away that thought, then hitched a thumb over his shoulder. "Rufus turned off here, going south."

Her floppy old hat dipped low on her brow. "Hmm," she murmured. "A windfall for us."

"How's that?"

"Going south leads us deeper into my people's lands. We can make good time by staying on the road. Red Bear would be a fool to follow."

A bitter taste filled his mouth. "Red Bear is no fool. If he sees our tracks on this road, he will strike hard and fast."

"Yet we don't know for certain he has followed us this far. All our precautions are slowing us, and night will soon close in. I say we gain as much ground as we can by lighting out on the southward fork."

He grunted, then bypassed her as he chewed on her idea. It made sense, but something about it squeezed his chest like an ill-fitting waistcoat. He stalked back to the safety of the tree line, where Livvy sat astride Mercy's mount and his own horse nibbled on some grass shoots.

He peered up at the girl. "Livvy, how about you climb down and ride with me for a while?"

Mercy gained his side. "What have you in mind?"

"You are the one with the falcon eyes, and Matthew always said your scouting skills were second only to his." Grabbing hold of his horse, he swung up onto the animal's back.

Mercy frowned up at him. "Is that flattery, Mr. Dubois?"

"It is the truth. Scout back a mile or so and see if anyone follows." He reached down, offering Livvy a hand up. "We will continue south until you catch back up. If you see no signs, then we shall stick to the road. Agreed?"

Mercy nodded, and the girl wrapped her thin arms around his waist. As he nudged his horse into motion, a sliver of unease poked his conscience for sending a woman

— one he cared about very much — into the woods spying for trouble . . . until he reminded himself that that was what lionesses did. She was in her element, and that rankled deep. Would she ever consent to settling down in one place with a man such as him?

"Mr. Dubois?" Livvy's voice chirped from behind. Though the girl was nearly as tall as his shoulder and standing on the edge of womanhood, she was, after all, still a girl.

"You can call me Elias, Livvy."

"Mr. Elias?"

He smiled. Whoever had raised her had done a fine job of instilling manners. How different would his life have been had he listened to his mother and grandfather's lessons at such a young age?

Guiding the horse onto the side of the southward road, he murmured, "Aye?"

"When do you think I shall see my papa again?" Desperation haunted the girl's question.

"Hopefully soon. Miss Mercy and I are doing everything we can to get you to him safely, for he surely must be missing you."

"It must be awful for him managing without me."

Were it not for the compassion riding ragged in her voice, he might almost think her prideful. But over the past two days, seeing her compliance to Mercy, her willingness to please and encourage, he slapped that rogue idea away.

"You are quite the little lady, Miss Livvy." He dipped beneath a low-hanging branch, breathing in horseflesh and leather.

Livvy followed suit, leaning against his back. "I am all Papa has, since Mother . . ."

He tugged at his collar, loosening the knot at his throat. It shouldn't surprise him, the way suffering had a way of grabbing every human by the neck and shaking, ofttimes hard. But it never failed to shock when one so young must endure such tragedies.

Bless this girl, Lord. Hold her in Your hand.

He glanced down to where her hands rode loosely at his sides. How much did her papa ache to have this girl, this flesh-and-blood reminder of a love lost, returned to him? "I imagine your papa must love you something fierce."

"He does."

The conviction in her young voice stabbed him between the shoulder blades. What would it have felt like to have had a father like that? A frown carved deep into his brow. What was this? Self-pity? Had he not laid all that on the altar that stormy night two years ago in a Boston church?

"Just like your papa — oh! Mr. Du— Elias . . . I did not think to ask if your papa is still living?"

Was he? His knuckles whitened on the reins. "Truthfully, Livvy, I would not know."

"That is so sad."

He stifled a snort. Sad? Maybe. But even sadder that both his father and his grandfather had cast him out. "It is a sorry truth, Livvy, but not everyone has a loving father."

Livvy's hands patted his sides, motherly beyond her years. Then again, being held captive in a Wyandot war camp likely had added a score of years she'd never asked for.

"I bet your papa was a strong man, a brave one," she murmured. "Just like you."

"Aye, he was strong. You must be, to be a voyageur." His mind slid back to that first time as a young man, barely older than Livvy, when he'd traveled to Montreal to meet Bernart Dubois. The man was muscle and steel standing there on the banks of the St. Lawrence River . . . reeking of rum and rage.

"My father could haul three packs at a time and once paddled from Montreal to Grand Portage in six weeks flat — a trip that usually takes eight. Indeed, he was a strong man." He spoke as much to Livvy as himself, a good reminder that not all about his earthly father was wicked.

Behind him, Livvy shifted. "And brave?"

He chuckled, low and bitter, and shame stabbed him for the base response. But it couldn't be helped. How brave was it for a man to drink himself into oblivion? To leave behind the woman who loved him more than life, taking her honor, crushing her heart? To lash out at his own son?

Absently, he lifted a hand and rubbed the scar near his ear. "No, Livvy. There was nothing brave about him."

They rode in silence a ways. Just as well, for the girl's questions dredged up ghosts that haunted in ways he hadn't expected.

But a troubling noise behind them jerked him from such painful speculations. Far off, twigs cracked. Weeds swished. Someone was coming.

Fast.

He yanked the horse into the woods, barely clearing the side of the road when he caught sight of Mercy barreling down it.

She reined her snorting horse to a stop in front of them. "We've got to move. Now!"

CHAPTER 30

Death ran headlong somewhere behind them, wielding tomahawks and war clubs — but not many bows and arrows. Mercy couldn't help but smile at Elias's foresight in breaking those weapons before they'd escaped. Without any need to hide her tracks, she urged her horse as fast as possible, weaving through trees, dodging fallen trunks, leading Elias and Livvy southwest.

And by the sounds of it, Elias followed right behind. He hadn't asked one question. He'd just kicked his horse into a run behind hers, giving her the lead. Would she be willing to follow him so blindly? She still wasn't completely convinced all he'd told her was true, though everything in her wanted to. It took time to stop a river of thought and snake it back around the other way.

She cut off onto an old deer trace, taking the turn too sharply, and banged her leg against a tree. The pain barely registered. A bruise was nothing compared to the bloody torment that would be inflicted if those warriors caught up to them. And they weren't far behind. She'd scouted barely a mile back before sighting four braves running point. The horses gave her and Elias a distinct advantage . . . for now. Horses couldn't run forever though. If they could just make it past the Three Sisters, they would be safe — hopefully. One never knew with men driven mad by revenge.

Ducking low, she gave in to the feel of the horse, the heat of it, the speed, praying all the while that Livvy held tight to Elias with the crazed pace. Praying God would spare them as He had at the war camp. Praying this idea of hers wasn't in vain, for it was the only one she had.

A mile later, the trail began a descent. Gradual at first. Somewhat winding. Then sharper, steeper, forcing her to slow her mount. But it wouldn't be long now.

She glanced over her shoulder. Elias's blue gaze met hers, too far back to decipher the questions in his eyes. Livvy's arms squeezed his waist. Good. Mercy faced forward, pressing onward, straining to see the Three Sisters.

Minutes later, at the first hint of a break

in the trees, she shut down all her senses save for sight and . . . there they were. A glimpse of gray water, just beyond a massive boulder with a huge tree growing from the base of it. River, rock, and red oak. Hope, threadbare and flimsy, wrapped around her like a worn shawl at the sight.

Once the slope lessened, she dug in her heels and raced down to the banks, then splashed across the river. Water soaked her ragged skirt hem, splashing up as far as her arms, shocking and shivery cold, but a small price to pay . . . if this worked.

At the other side, she urged the horse up the rocky embankment. When the ground leveled, she turned right, following close to the edge of the water. Twenty yards or so more, and she slowed her mount to inspect a patch of barberries growing close to the bank. It would be prickly, the thorns a nettlesome bother, but the branches leafed out enough to provide excellent cover. This *would* work. It had to.

Turning at a sharp angle, she guided the horse into the woods, traveling a safe space — hopefully — to leave Livvy with the animals. She slid to the ground, her backside happy to have ended that wild ride.

Elias trotted up beside her, a grim line to his jaw. "Why are you stopping?"

"We need to know if those men are going to continue to pursue or if they turn around."

"Turn around?" His nostrils flared. "Why the devil would they do that?"

"Come. I will show you." She patted her mount and snagged the lead, holding the end out in one hand. "Livvy, you stay here with the horses. Can you do that?"

"Yes, ma'am."

Livvy loosened her death grip on Elias's waist and made to swing down — but Elias shot out his arm, staying the girl.

He narrowed his eyes at Mercy, a fierce storm churning in those blue waters. "Our lives are on the line here. You are certain about this?"

She tipped her chin. "As certain as I can be."

A slight frown puckered his brow, but he released his hold on Livvy and instead offered his grip to aid her down. Then he swung off and grabbed his own horse's lead, handing it over to the girl.

Mercy spun and retraced her route back to the barberries, Elias's steps close behind. Bracing herself for the tugs, pulls, and scratches of small thorns, she fisted her hands and elbowed her way in, protecting her face.

"No one in their right mind hides in a patch of barberries," Elias huffed behind her.

"Which is why those men won't give this bramble a second glance."

A branch slapped against her neck, stinging pain cutting into the tender place just behind her earlobe. Maybe Elias was right — maybe she was so travel worn that her thinking was skewed.

Eventually, she worked her way in to see the opposite bank, and if she turned just so, the Three Sisters came into view. Elias crashed to a stop beside her, exhaling an "Oomph."

Ignoring his complaint, she lifted a finger and pointed. "See that red oak over there? The one growing out of a rock?"

"I noticed it as we passed. Why?"

"There's a hatchet buried five paces west of it."

He pulled his gaze from the water and turned to her, one brow lifting in question. "Between the Wyandot and the Mohawks?"

She nodded. "Ten winters ago, long before this war broke out, Black-Fox-Running and Red Bear held a peace summit. This river marks the boundary that neither is to cross. They buried the war hatchet at the base of that oak as a reminder. Those warriors would be fools to cross over and bring down the wrath of my people against theirs . . . and you said Red Bear is no fool."

A smile broke, broad and brilliant. "Have I ever told you what an amazing woman you are?"

The warmth in his voice beguiled for a moment, until she remembered what he most often called her. "No, you're usually too busy harping on how stubborn I am."

"Well, I have since come to change my mind." He reached out to pick off a skinny branch barbed into one of her sleeves. "You are going to need a new gown after all this."

She pointed to a tear near his collar. "And you shall need a new shirt."

Quick as a flash of ground lightning, he caught her hand and pressed a kiss to the palm, his gaze never leaving hers.

And God help her, she never wanted it to.

"Mercy . . ." Her name was a whisper, a shiver, a need — one that plucked the same chord somewhere deep inside her chest.

Warmth traveled low in her belly, and suddenly it didn't matter anymore that thorns cut and men killed. That she'd sworn never to hand over her independence to anyone, least of all a blue-eyed soldier with a French name and a mind-boggling story.

She leaned close, drawn by desire, breathing in his scent of lathered horse and heated body. When her lips met his, soft, seeking, a tremor shook through him.

"Mercy." This time her name was a moan.

Heedless of scratches, she reached up and entwined her fingers in his hair, pulling him close.

A groan rumbled in his throat, and his mouth closed in on hers, ablaze with the same hunger that burned inside her. It dazzled, this fire, scorching her in places she'd never known could simmer to such an intensity.

But with the next breath, they broke apart, the moment doused by the splash of men's feet running full into the river.

Heart pounding hard enough for the warriors to hear, Elias froze. If this were his day to die, so be it, but Lord have mercy on the woman warming his side and on Livvy. Short of a miracle, they didn't stand a chance against the ten men tearing into the water. Red painted half their faces, black the other . . . blood and death. And who knew how many more men were still to emerge from the woods?

Fingering the knife at his side, he turned to Mercy and whispered, "Go. Take Livvy and ride."

Her jaw clenched. "Either we stand to-gether or we die together."

She flung the very words he'd told her like a well-aimed tomahawk. Now? She had to choose now to heed what he'd said?

He hardened his voice. "I am not asking. Do it."

"But —"

"Now!" He growled, keeping his tone just below the sound of kicked-up water. "Think of the girl."

A defiant gleam burned in her gaze. Even so, she slowly, carefully parted the lowest branches and crawled out.

Before she disappeared, he turned his attention back to the river.

Two men took the lead, paces now from the embankment, twenty-five yards down from his cover. And only a short sprint away from Mercy and Livvy.

God, please, see to their safety.

He pulled out the hunting knife, gripping it in a moist palm. If he shot up now and sprinted down the river, away from Mercy, they would gain at least some small measure of time to escape. Keeping an eye on the front runners, he crouch-walked backward to clear the hindrance of the briars.

"Cease!"

He stopped. So did the warriors. Red

Bear's command halted the very sparrows in the trees from singing.

The old warrior strode from the woods to the water's edge, near the red oak with its roots gnarled around the rock. "We go no farther."

Paces from Elias's side of the river, two warriors stood midstride. One turned, a bristle-haired man wearing a stiff roach headdress, and shouted back, "What of our honor?"

Red Bear folded his arms and stared the man down. "It is for our honor we turn back."

"Nay!" The rebel's voice and fist shook in the air.

Elias shifted for a better view of the uncommon sight. To defy a sachem was asking for more than trouble.

"We will take no life that side of the river." Red Bear didn't budge, in stance or deed. "Especially if the woman is Kahente."

"Your thinking is not clear, Red Bear."

A collective gasp rippled along with the river's flowing waters. No one dared move, let alone breathe. Only the slight breeze ventured to wave the turkey feather hanging from Red Bear's scalp lock and ruffle the hem of his long trade shirt.

Slowly, the sachem's face lifted, an imperial pose. The kind that brooked no argument. "Were your thoughts even a vapor when I, Red Bear, stood on this very bank, seeing with my own eyes the war ax laid into the ground?"

The rebel said nothing. He didn't have to. The baring of his teeth in a wicked snarl said it all.

Red Bear tucked his black-painted chin, the whites of his eyes stark against the scarlet smear of vermillion he wore as a mask. "Are you man enough to dig it up?"

Water churned from the rebel's strong stride as he waded toward the sachem. He stalked past the other men yet standing in the river, all still as a nightmare and likely as incredulous as Elias. Would the fool be brazen enough to raise a fist against the leader of his people?

Elias's brow lowered, weighted with guilt. How many times had he done the same to God? Lifted a clenched hand? Defied the One whom he ought to obey without question?

Oh God, forgive me for such arrogance.

Peace settled over him like a mantle. Would that the warrior now standing in front of Red Bear received such a grace.

The two stared eye-to-eye, ruler and ruled, man versus man. Would Red Bear abide such an atrocity if the hotheaded warrior dug up the war ax? And if he did . . . Sweat dotted Elias's brow. If the sachem stood by and allowed the man to break the peace, the blood spilled would be on Elias's hands for having allowed Mercy to lead them to this place.

A blood-chilling cry raged from the warrior's mouth. Then he retreated past Red Bear and strode into the woods behind him.

The breath Elias had been holding rushed out of his lungs. The other men in the water began striding toward the retreating Red Bear —

Save one.

A bare-chested man broke rank, kicking up water as he raced toward Elias's side of the shore. His feet hit the bank, scrambling on the rocks to make purchase.

The same man who'd stolen Mercy's hat.

Keeping low, Elias clambered out of the barberries. Surprise was his best weapon, for if the man had a chance to cry out a warning, there'd likely be no containing the rebel who'd stood up to the sachem . . . or maybe not even Red Bear.

He ran in a crouch, knife gripped tight and ready to slash. As soon as he gained sight of the man, now several yards in from the riverbank and looking for tracks, Elias pushed air past his teeth in a loud "whist!"

The warrior's head jerked his way. A smile sliced across his face, white teeth sharpened to fangs. The man's eyes narrowed to slits — then he hefted a tomahawk and reared back on the ball of one foot.

CHAPTER 31

Mercy guided the horse through woods she could traverse blind — a blessing and a curse, that. She knew the best hiding places should she and Livvy need to take cover, but she also knew the way so well that it gave her mind free rein to wander off to dark corners. If those Indians snubbed the decade-long peace between her people and theirs, tore right across that river, and discovered Elias, well . . . He'd proven his strength time and again, but not even he could withstand so many men set on killing. Would he end up being just one more person she couldn't say goodbye to?

Behind her, the thud of hooves trotted close, and Livvy drew up alongside her. It was strange to see the girl riding alone, a sharp reminder that Elias had yet to catch up to them. The girl's blond hair frizzled in a tangle. Dirt smudged across her brow, coating everything, really. Her gown hung ripped off one shoulder, her skirts tattered at the hem. The girl had lived a lifetime over the past several months, yet a certain innocence remained in her wide blue eyes.

"Miss Mercy?" she whispered.

Mercy nodded, silent. While it was unlikely anyone would hear should she speak aloud, the scout in her held her tongue on a short leash.

"God's watching over us, ma'am."

The words shivered down her back as if God Himself told her His gaze was upon her. Was this girl flesh and blood? Or was she an angel sent for encouragement? Either way, human or not, Livvy was a godsend. The girl dropped back to follow as before, but Mercy pressed on with a strange peace, and all the while she prayed that God was watching over Elias too.

Veering off on a connecting deer trace, she turned her thoughts as well, trying to forget the danger he was in, forget the passion in his kiss . . . and especially forget that every step of her horse drew her nearer to her village.

The one destroyed weeks ago.

Sorrow pressed down, as weighty as the sullen skies overhead. Part of her wanted to gallop toward home. The other part wanted to wheel about and ride fast and far. There

412

was no escaping the implications of either one. And the more ground her horse ate up, the stronger the urge to slip down and weep hot tears onto the sacred earth of her ancestors.

A little farther on, she pulled on her reins, halting the mare for nothing more than a gut feeling. Birds still sang in the late afternoon air, clouds yet blanketed the sky, muffling light and sound. A squirrel scampered in front of her, and her mount swished her tail. Nothing out of the ordinary.

But even so, she turned her horse about and, with a sweep of her hand, directed Livvy to get behind her.

Elias forced his gaze to remain on the warrior's eyes instead of the tomahawk — one of the few things he'd actually learned from his father. Timing was more than everything now. It was his life. Drop too soon, and the man would rush him, hacking into him before he could rise. Too late, and his skull would be split from the flying ax.

So he waited. Studying. Calculating. Anticipating that one heartbeat when an almost imperceptible narrowing of the warrior's eyes would give away his throw. *God, have mercy.* It was a terrible thing to stare death in the face with nothing to rely upon except a twitch.

And the warrior knew it. His sharp teeth gleamed white against his black-painted face, his lips pulled into a macabre smile. Then his eyes widened.

Widened?

The man's jaw dropped as if the joint came unhinged — and an arrowhead pierced through the middle of his chest, shot from behind.

Elias flattened to the ground, expecting a rain of more deadly projectiles. Had Red Bear changed his mind and even now he and his warriors were breaching the river?

But not one whizz of fletching cut through the air. No thwunks of arrows hit tree trunks or dirt. No splashes or war cries or anything. He lifted his head, listening hard.

The sparrows started singing.

He rose on shaky legs and hunkered back to the barberries. Picking his way inside the prickly shrubs, he went only deep enough to spy the other side of the river.

Not one warrior remained.

He watched for a long time, staring and hoping, afraid to thank God and afraid not to. The last of his battle jitters shook through him in waves, and still he stared, until he was convinced the killers truly had retreated for good.

Indeed, thank You, God.

He emerged from the greenery and blew out a long breath, grateful for life and air and hope. Searching the ground, he spied Mercy's trail, then began to follow it, thanking God all the more. At least there wouldn't be any tomahawks at their backs for the rest of the journey.

But a frown weighted his brow as he trekked along. No tomahawks, indeed, for the danger would be much closer.

He'd be transporting a deadly poisonous weapon on his body.

Far off in the distance, a stick cracked, and Mercy held her breath. Her horse shied sideways a step, and she narrowed her eyes, studying the greens and browns and . . . there. A single figure sprinted toward them, hardly more than a smear of a dirtied linen hunting frock and the bobbing of a dark-haired head. Relief sagged her shoulders. Elias. And by the looks of it, no angry warriors trailed him.

Nudging the horse with her heels, she trotted ahead, closing the distance between them.

He stopped as she pulled up in front of him. Dampened hair curled fierce against his temples and sweat dripped in rivulets down his forehead.

While he caught his breath, she slid down from her mount. "They are gone?"

"They are," he huffed out.

She tossed a smile over her shoulder to where Livvy landed on the ground behind her. "You were right. God *is* watching over us."

The girl's grin beamed brilliant in the gray afternoon.

Mercy turned back to Elias, this time searching for any sign of injury. "Are you well?"

"Just winded." He winced, belying his brave words. "I am getting too old for this."

"You sound like Matthew." The bittersweet truth struck her hard. While she yet missed her dear friend, the man in front of her, the one who'd just risked his life once again for her sake, was already filling spaces inside her that Matthew's friendship had never touched.

As if her mount agreed with Elias's words, the horse blew out a snort. Elias reached up and patted the mare's nose. "The horses need a break as well as I. Not much day left anyway. We will camp here."

Her gaze drifted from trunk to trunk, rock to rock. Each one familiar. So many memories. Oh, the dreams she would have tonight should she close her eyes on this patch of land. But in some small way, this might be her best chance to say goodbye to her people, to her father . . . to her mother. To lay to rest all the things she'd never spoken aloud, by chance or by choice.

"I . . ." She swallowed. How to say all that?

Elias cut her a glance.

She straightened her shoulders. The best way to fight an enemy was to run at it headlong. Had her father not taught her that well?

"My village — the one destroyed — is not far. I will take a horse and return. There are some things . . . I must . . . let go of." She stuttered to a halt.

Elias stepped toward her, reaching out as if he'd pull her into his arms, but a whisper away, he stopped. Concern ran deep and blue in his eyes. For a moment, he worked his jaw, seeming to fight his own battle of words. "Are you sure about this?"

"No." She reached to finger the locket at her throat, the smooth stone a reminder of the strength of her mother. "But it is something I must do."

He nodded slowly. "All right. Then we will come along." He turned to the girl. "Livvy, mount —"

"I go alone," Mercy blurted. As much

comfort as his presence would bring, this was something personal, something sacrosanct . . . something her very being knew that only God should witness.

He shook his head. "You know that is not safe, even with those men turning back."

She rested her hand on his sleeve, and the muscles beneath tensed at her touch. "Please, Elias," she whispered.

His gaze slid from her hold to her face, softening momentarily. "Fine." And then stern furrows lined his brow. "But if you are not back before dark, I am coming after you."

Elias kneaded a muscle in his neck as he watched Mercy ride off into the maze of trees and continued to stare long after she disappeared. He understood her need to slay whatever demons from her past tormented her. He'd had to slay his own a few years back when he'd first bent a knee toward God. He just didn't like it. Not out here. Not alone. He half-hoped she'd turn around and come back.

Feet shuffled behind him, reminding him Mercy wasn't his only concern. He pivoted, and pale blue eyes blinked up into his.

"Are you all right, Mr. Elias?"

"I am well, Livvy." He smiled down at her.

"And you? This has been quite the trek. How are you faring?"

"Well . . ." Her gaze lowered, and she toed the dirt. "I am rather hungry."

"My stomach is pinched a bit tight too." Taking care not to strain the wound still healing on his chest, he slung off the shoulder bag carrying what remained of their provisions. "How about we remedy that?"

He led the girl off the trail to a patch of maidenhair ferns growing amidst random boulders. He sank onto one, she onto another, and he fished out a piece of jerky for each of them.

"Thank you." Livvy bowed her head a moment before taking a bite.

He tore off a chunk of his own meat, marveling. Lord, but this girl was made of strong grace. How many other young ones would not only take such hardships in stride, but remember to thank God for them as well?

After swallowing, she lowered her piece of venison to her lap. A small frown followed the lines of a dirt smudge on her brow. "Mr. Elias?"

"Aye?"

"Are you going to marry Miss Mercy?"

His mouthful of meat went down sideways, lodging as crooked in his throat as the girl's question. He jerked a fist to his mouth and coughed into it. Very funny. Was this God's idea of retribution for all the times as a child he'd flung awkwardly candid queries at his grandfather? Clearing his throat, he lowered his hand. "Well now, that is a big question."

"My papa always says forthright speech is the godliest."

"Your father is a wise man." He dared another bite of jerky. Hopefully he'd dodged the girl's curiosity by getting her to think on her father. Whoever the man was, he surely must be desperate to get her back, for she was unlike any child he'd ever known.

"So are you?" Livvy's blue gaze pinned him in place. "Going to marry Miss Mercy, that is."

He shoved the whole chunk of jerky into his mouth, stalling for time. Despite his hesitation, Livvy's stare did not waver.

The lump of meat traveled down to his stomach like a rock. No. There was no way by heaven or sea he'd give this girl an answer when he did not even want to consider the question. He scrubbed his hand across his mouth. "You think I should?"

"Without a doubt." Gravity sobered her tone.

He hid a smile. Was this what Mercy had been like as a young girl? "What makes you think Miss Mercy would want to marry me?"

Livvy bent forward, leaning close, her long blond hair hanging like a windblown curtain. "I think she needs you."

His brows shot high. "She is a self-reliant woman. What makes you think she has need of anyone?"

"Well, she has not told me, not outright, but . . ." Livvy straightened, craning her neck to look past him toward the path where Mercy had disappeared. Apparently satisfied, she faced him again. "I think she is hiding a whole lot of hurt. Something to do with her mother."

Elias rubbed his hands along his thighs, thinking back on the many conversations he'd had with her. Had she ever mentioned her mother? Try as he might to remember, nothing came to mind. Shoot, he hadn't even known the woman was kin to a mighty Mohawk sachem. He shook his head. "Even if that is true, Livvy, only God can heal hurts down deep."

"Oh, I know, but I think you help her forget. Miss Mercy smiles more when she is with you. My papa says love is that which makes you smile, even when you're tired." She leaned forward again, this time a queer gleam lighting her eyes. "I think she loves you, Mr. Elias."

The girl's words hit him broadside. Not that he hadn't tasted Mercy's need in the kiss they had shared, but love? The thought was too big to wrap his arms around. And even if she did, would she truly give up her life of far-flung freedom to settle down with the likes of him?

Whatever the answer, this was not the time or place to even consider it. He shot to his feet and stalked past Livvy. "I will get some water. After that jerky, you will soon thirst."

"Mr. Elias?"

Ah, no. He'd not be pulled back into that bees' hive of a conversation. He glanced over his shoulder, saying nothing.

She smiled. "Don't worry. I won't breathe a word of this to Miss Mercy. Your secret is safe with me."

"What secret?"

Her pert little nose scrunched up. "That you love her too."

He turned and stalked off. Livvy had far too many years inside her to be stuck inside a little girl's body.

CHAPTER 32

Destruction was the great leveler. It didn't matter what kind of blood ran through one's veins when faced with singed timbers and charred dreams. Wyandot. Mohawk. White. Black. Mercy sank to the dirt, facedown, at the outskirts of what had been her childhood home. She grabbed handfuls of earth, trying to find something to cling to amid such devastation. There was no shame in it. No weakness. Were her worst enemy facing such loss, even he'd drop to the ground and weep.

She closed her eyes — but no good. The macabre skeletons of ruined longhouses had already seared forever into her mind. And though she tried to forget the image, she knew it would never leave. The awful picture of the flattened village was there to stay, like an unwelcome guest who'd slipped in through a half-open door.

Behind her, the horse snorted and pawed

the ground. Not that she blamed the beast. Her feet itched to jump up and tear back into Elias's arms.

But instead she sucked in a breath and stood. This was her chance — albeit a late one — to say goodbye to her father . . . and, yes, it was beyond time to bid farewell to Mother.

She padded down what used to be the path between two longhouses. How many times had she skipped here as a child? Followed after her brother in crooked leggings she'd sewn to her mother's dismay, hoping to join him and his friends as they set out on a hunt? Tears burned her eyes. She blinked them away. Tried to, anyway.

She glanced up at a sky as brooding as her heart. *God, why? You protected me. Why did You not protect these people? Why not Matthew? Why not my mother?*

No answers came, but she did not expect any. Her father had required complete obedience from her and her mother even when they did not understand his ways . . . and it was *always* for their good. Though it was impossible to believe anything good could come from the death of those she loved, she must trust that God was sovereign — or that He was not. Yet had He not proven in the past several weeks that He did reign supreme? Not in ways she'd choose, but in ways of His choosing.

Her feet slowed as she neared the blackened ribs of what had been the council lodge. War and peace collided here. The many decisions of when to fight, when to hold off. Had her father sat cross-legged, passing a pipe, when the attack came? Had he been smiling or reverent? Deep in conversation or alone?

She lifted her hand, holding it out as if she might take hold of his and feel the strength of his calloused fingers pressing into hers. She stood still for a long time, listening hard, straining to hear one last time the affection in his voice even as he rebuked her for being so strong-willed.

"Goodbye, Rake'niha," she whispered. *"Skén:nen tsi satonríshen."*

A raven swooped low in a graceful arc, then soared up into the sky and disappeared into the trees. Those more superstitious than she would take it as a sign. She merely lowered her hand. Sign or not, a tentative calm seeped into the thin spaces between flesh and bone. The empty hollow was still there in her chest, right next to the space left behind after Matthew's passing. But just seeing where her father may have spent his last minutes lay to rest a small portion of her grief.

Turning, she picked her way onward to the second longhouse past the council lodge . . . the one she'd shared with her mother.

Countless times she'd walked this way. This time though, when she stopped and imagined the bark-and-frame structure that had housed them, she imagined it with new eyes — and a new heart. Here, in the remnants of violence and death, a quiet appreciation blossomed, replacing her old scorn. Now that she'd tasted of captivity and knew firsthand such terror, she finally understood. How frightened her mother must've been, dragged into this village, not knowing the language or what would become of her. Yet despite the harsh treatment she'd suffered because of her abiding and outspoken faith in Iesos, her mother had survived . . . and never once stopped loving. Not the people. Not her father.

Not her.

She bowed her head with the knowledge. For so long, she'd believed one of the best reasons to be alive was never knowing what would happen next. But maybe an even better reason was to learn from the past to correct a future course.

Kneeling, she reached behind her neck

and unclasped the necklace. Tears fell, baptizing the ruby-red heart, puddling in the lines of her open palm.

"I apologize, Mother. Please" — a shaky breath tore through her — "forgive me." Why hadn't she said this when her mother was still alive?

Dampness leaked down her cheeks, chilly in the early evening air, and she shivered. "I did not see your strength because I did not look for it."

She swiped at her nose with her sleeve. "But you'd be happy for me, I think, for I–I've finally learned to trust. Just like you wanted me to."

Her voice broke, and she swallowed, saltiness tangy on her lips. "I believe what you told me, that God will dry each of my tears one day, like He has surely dried all of yours."

The necklace weighed heavy in her hand, and her whole arm shook like an old grandmother's. "I lay to rest my childish contempt. It will ever be dead to me. I only hope that you can forgive me for flaunting it all these years."

She lifted her face to the darkening sky. "Forgive me, oh Father, for leaving undone that which I should have mended."

Setting the locket down, she grabbed a

nearby rock and dug with determination. Each gouge reminded her of the grooves she'd surely worn deep into her mother's heart. Regret drove her to a frenzy of flung dirt and ragged cries.

Spent, she pitched the rock aside, then picked up the locket. Pressing the cool stone to her lips, she whispered against it, "I love you, Mother. Let us forever be at peace. Goodbye."

She set the necklace into the ground and covered it up, handful by handful, tear by tear. Pressing the loose dirt into a mound, she laid her hands atop it, finally still. Finally done.

Final.

In the growing darkness, she stood on legs still tingling from her cramped position. Early night air breathed on her like an animal on the prowl, tempting her to return to the same old torment of her darkest memories.

But a newly forged freedom burned like a brilliant light inside her. The memories remained, and always would — but the sharp-edged pain was gone, leaving behind a hard-won tranquility.

Insects began to scratch and whirr. Earthy moisture, pregnant with a damp chill, smelled musty, and the last bit of apathetic daylight melded into shadows. Night would fall hard soon — a darkness so complete, given aid by an overcast sky, that even if Mercy did know this stretch of land, she'd be hard-pressed to find her way back to camp. Elias glanced over to where Livvy curled up near a small fire. He loathed to leave her untended — but he hated even more the fact that Mercy was out there somewhere. Unguarded. Unbidden, his hands curled into fists. What to do? Leave the young girl to go after the woman? Or remain here and leave Mercy in God's hands alone?

Staring harder into the darkness, he ground his teeth, willing Mercy's horse to appear with her atop it. If this was the love Livvy had spoken of, this anguish, this awful burning skittishness to run into the fires of hell if need be just to pull Mercy out, well then . . . he wasn't sure he wanted it. The weighty responsibility of it pushed the air from his lungs.

A shrill cry rent the air, raising gooseflesh on his neck. Just a screech owl. Nothing more. But all the same, he retreated to go grab a horse.

But then turned back around.

Far off, leftover autumn leaves crushed

beneath a *thud-thud, thud-thud.* He yanked off his hat and raked his fingers through his hair, relief shaking through him. No doubt about it. This woman would be his death.

Slowly, far too slowly to his liking, a black silhouette approached. Mercy reined in her horse in front of him and slid from her mount, a quirk to one brow. "Why do you stand here? Is all aright?"

"No!" The word flew out like a bat from a cave, but it couldn't be helped. Lord, but he was tired. "Everything is not 'aright.' Not with you traipsing about alone in a dark wood."

Anger shook his voice, and he instantly repented. But it was too late. Her head dipped, her loose hair falling to the curve of her waist. "I apologize for having caused such worry."

Both his brows shot up. What was this? No defiance? No you-don't-need-to-fret-on-my-account, I-can-take-care-of-myself rebuttal? Alarmed, he studied the woman. There was no change in her broad stance, so unladylike yet strangely alluring. Her same slim shoulders held straight and ready to take on the world. Near as he could tell, not one thing was different in her appearance — but something was . . . what?

He softened his tone. "Well, no harm

done, thank God. I made a small fire sheltered from sight, and the smoke is minimal. I did not want to take any chances on those warriors in case they had second thoughts. Go warm yourself. I will see to your horse."

Working quickly, he led the animal to where he'd hobbled his mount, then relieved the horse of its bridle. "Easy, girl," he crooned while he patted her neck. Then he set about looping a rope around one hoof and, with plenty of slack, connecting it to another, keeping the beast from roaming off. After a quick rubdown, he returned to Mercy. By now, naught but coals glowed below her outstretched hands. Next to where she sat, Livvy slept soundly.

Mercy looked up at his approach, her pert chin hiding a smile. "You call this a fire?"

That bit of spunk, little as it was, eased the worry churning the bellyful of dried berries he'd eaten. Maybe she was fine after all. He sank to the ground at her side, opposite Livvy, and handed over the pouch of pemmican. "Did you find the peace you were after?"

A smile split white and broad. "I did."

While she ate, he watched, admiring the soft planes of her face, the curve of her cheeks, the lips that he'd kissed. His gaze sank lower, to her bare neck, the hollow between her collarbone — then stopped. The skin there was naked. No gold chain. No locket.

He jerked his gaze back to hers. "Seems you lost something."

"Hmm?" She chewed a moment more before swallowing. "Oh . . . ." Her fingers fluttered to her chest, resting right where the locket should've been. "No, not lost. Given."

He leaned back, eyeing her. "I thought that locket was important to you."

"It . . ." Her lips pressed together, and her hand fell to her lap. "It was time to let it go."

His throat tightened. Ah, that he might remove the unyielding griefs this woman had suffered. "Mercy." Her name came out jagged, and he cleared his throat. "I sorrow for your loss. I know it hurts —"

"No." She snapped her face toward his, eyes burning with the intensity of one of the coals. "Do not pity me. You should know what manner of woman you travel with."

"You owe me no explanations. I am content with who you are —"

"But I am not." She pushed the pouch back into his hands, cutting him off. "Years ago, that necklace was taken in a raid on some whites, led by my father. I was a young girl when the war party returned. My father awarded me with the trinket, for though he could be a harsh man, he was ever soft toward me."

He shook his head. If the thing were that important to her, why had she gotten rid of such a token? "I should think you would want to keep it then, being he is gone."

"You don't understand. This isn't about my father."

Once again her fingers rose, and she absently stroked the side of her neck where the chain had rested since her girlhood. Some kind of memories played across her face as she stared into the glowing coals, twitching her lips, bending her brow.

He waited, giving her the time she needed, wishing he could give her more than that, could comfort, could heal.

Her voice started low and so quiet he leaned in closer to catch her words.

"When my mother saw the stolen locket bouncing against my chest, it was a vivid reminder that she'd been taken in a raid. She asked me to take it off. I refused. She never asked me again, but I persisted in wearing that necklace, drawing a perverse strength from thinking it somehow made me stronger than her."

Her shoulders sagged for a moment; then

she straightened them, a new strength rising like an eagle. "But I was wrong, Elias — about so many things . . . and far too quick to judge others when it was my own heart that needed tending."

He grunted. "A lesson for us all, I think."

Her gaze met his — maybe. Hard to tell now, for he could barely distinguish her shape though she sat within reach.

"You're a good man, Elias Dubois."

Mercy's admiration crawled in and made a home deep inside. He'd been called many things by many people, but not good. Not for years . . . not since his own mother had died when he was a lad about Livvy's age. His lips pulled into a smirk. "There are plenty who would say otherwise."

"Well then, they are wrong."

There was no stopping the grin that stretched his mouth — or the chains that dropped from his heart. She could have no idea the healing her admiration brought. He could barely trust himself to speak, so he cleared his throat first. "Bed yourself down. I will take first watch."

He stood, aiming to give her space, but his name on her lips anchored his feet.

"Elias?"

"Aye?"

"Thank you."

He cocked his head. "For what?"

"Not many men besides my brother and Matthew ever look past my independent streak to see me . . . the real me."

He strode to the other side of the coals and sank down, hunkering in for a long watch. "Their loss," he breathed out.

And hopefully his gain — if she'd give up that independence to have him.

CHAPTER 33

Despite stiff joints and a tender bottom, gifts of a long day's ride, Mercy's spirits rose so high, she gripped the reins tight lest she fly away. Last night she'd slept more soundly than a snuggled babe and this morn awakened with a fresh view of the world. She should've made things right with her mother — and God — long ago. And she would have, had she known how sweet that freedom tasted.

Behind her, Livvy shifted. "Miss Mercy, you think we'll be stopping soon? Because, well . . . I need to."

"Aye." The girl was right. She could use a break herself. Not many hours of daylight remained though, so this would have to be a quick reprieve.

She nudged the horse with her heels to catch up to Elias's side, when he suddenly pulled on his reins.

His gaze slid to hers, and he pointed to

his ear, then aimed his finger down the road.

She listened. A nearby kingfisher rattled a low call, and a few squirrels played tag off to the side of the woods, scratching their claws against bark. Nothing out of the ordinary. She angled her head. What had Elias heard?

Her lips parted to ask — then as quickly she pressed them together. The distinct jingle of harness and tackle traveled on the late afternoon air.

Elias turned his mount, backtracking a ways. She followed, admiring his scouting sense to move out of range. If they could hear someone else's horses, that someone else could hear theirs as well.

Elias swerved off the road past a stand of birch, then stopped several yards into the greenery.

Mercy waited for Livvy to crawl down before she dismounted. "Here's your chance. Go do what you must, but don't be gone long."

The girl nodded, then darted off.

Giving his horse leave to nibble at the spring shoots, Elias stepped close to her. "Did you hear that?"

"I did. You think . . . ?"

"If it is not Rufus, then we have come a long way for nothing. You stay here, and I will scout it out."

"But I —"

He laid his finger on her lips. "You are better equipped to deal with Livvy than I, should she have needs. I shall be back shortly."

The set of his jaw left no room for argument.

But as soon as Livvy returned, Mercy handed off the care of the horses. "Think you're able to wait here by yourself?"

Blue eyes blinked up into hers. "Yes, Miss Mercy. I'm not afraid."

"You're a brave girl, Livvy." She reached out and squeezed the girl's arm with a light touch. Truly the girl would make a fine scout herself. "Thank you."

Then she turned and followed Elias's trail. Ah, but he was good, even when he wasn't trying. It took all her powers of sight to follow his scant markings of a bent branch or flattened bit of weeds.

The farther she went, the louder the sounds of horses grew. She caught up to Elias on silent feet just behind a screen of elderberries near the side of the road. The scowl on his face as she scooted next to him could make a bear tuck tail and run.

Ahead, on the other side of the shrubs, a male voice tightened into a whine. She and

Elias crouched lower and moved in to peer through the branches.

A small clearing opened beside the road. At its center, a wagon — *their* wagon — sat with its back end toward the elderberries, maybe ten yards ahead. They couldn't see Rufus, for he was likely at the front side, but no need. His distinct voice, carping about a need for fresh venison to roast, churned Mercy's empty belly.

A deep voice answered Rufus's complaint. "If young buck wants meat, then he should hunt it himself."

The words twanged with a distinct accent, one that slapped her hard. *Wyandot.* Would they never be free of those villains?

"Yer the blazin' hunter, ain't ya? I oughta see that your pay is docked, you no-good piece of —"

Mercy turned away. She'd heard more than enough.

Elias followed her out, and together they backtracked far enough to confer in whispers. They stopped next to the gnarled roots of an old oak.

"What's the plan?" she asked.

"Nothing."

Her jaw dropped. Had she misplaced her trust? Matthew not only would've concocted their tactical offense but also would've been working out a sharp defense just in case.

Elias smirked. "Nothing until dusk, that is. Semi-darkness is our best asset."

She couldn't argue with that and would have suggested it herself. "Then what?"

"Seems pretty straightforward, unless Rufus and his, er, reluctant friend move the wagon. I will crawl in the rear opening of the canvas, dig out that weapon, then hie myself back to the cover of the elderberries. Assuming I make it that far undetected, I shall head back to you, Livvy, and the horses."

"Oh, no." She folded her arms. "I am not sitting back there waiting to find out what happens."

"Mercy, if I am discovered or that weapon scratches me while I am unloading it —"

"All the more reason for me to be here with you."

A sigh ripped out of him. "All right. But if I do not make it, promise me you will get yourself and Livvy to safety. As near as I can tell, we are not far from Schoharie."

"Agreed. I will go tell Livvy, then return."

He nodded.

But that small task took longer than she expected. A horse had wandered off, for Livvy hadn't properly hobbled the animal. Then the girl had wandered off, her tummy upset from their scant diet. And by the time she grabbed a chunk of jerky for herself and settled the horses for Livvy to await her and Elias's return, the sun lay low on the horizon, ready to dip down for a good night's slumber.

She hurried back to Elias's side in the long line of shrubs. He studied her face a moment, concern etched into the creases at the sides of his eyes. She smiled back assurance. A twinge of sorrow stabbed her. How often had she wordlessly communicated so with Matthew?

They hunkered down, waiting for more shadows to blanket the clearing. She still couldn't see Rufus or his companion, but she could hear Rufus's complaining. The other man's grunts. The crackle of a fire. And the ever-present jingling of bridle and harness . . . wait a minute.

She edged to the far side of the shrubbery, just before it tapered to nothing near the road, and ignored Elias's hand signals for her to return. From this angle, she glimpsed the horses — still attached to the wagon. What in the world? Surely they would not be traveling tonight in the dark . . . would they? But if so, why make a fire? For there, not far in front of the wagon, a fire blazed, outlining Rufus and a large, broad-shouldered man, both sitting in front of the flames.

Frowning, she turned back toward Elias when a new sound stopped her flat. Pounding hooves. Coming down the road, straight for Rufus's camp. She peered past the elderberries. A black horse turned off the rugged track as the last of day's light bled out. The rider was nothing but a shadow — a round, fat blob of a shadow.

"Blast it, boy!" The voice sounded of crushed gravel with a slight slur, giving the speaker away. "What's this?"

Mercy gaped at Elias. Though it was hard to read his face through the maze of dark branches, she could make out the whites of his eyes opened wide. What the devil was Brigadier General Bragg doing here?

The thud of the stout man's feet hit the ground, and she turned back to watch. Rufus sidled up next to him.

"What's what, Pa? I got the gold here, just like you said. Shoot, I got even more than what you expected. So what for do you got your britches all bunched up? Forget to pack an extra bottle, did ya?"

The general's arm shot out. The slap echoed sharply in the early evening air. Rufus staggered from the blow, a string of ugly expletives unraveling from his mouth.

"You're a wastrel and a stain. Were you not my son — and it pains me to call you such — I'd not have included you in on my scheme. By heavens, stand straight when I'm talking to you!"

The first real flicker of understanding and pity for Rufus kindled in Mercy's heart. No wonder he abhorred the world around him, for what a world to have grown up in. Perhaps the real villain here was — and always had been — the general.

Rufus managed to straighten, though he didn't pull his palm from his cheek. And she didn't blame him. It had been a good wallop. Mercy glanced to where the Indian had been sitting, but that side of the fire was now empty. Was he as disgusted by this wrangling as she?

"I'm not talking about the gold." General Bragg swung out his arm. "I can see the wagon's there, you dullard."

Rufus turned aside and spit. "Then what you all riled up about?"

"Tell me, boy, how far will we get when those horses won't pull tomorrow, all because of skin rubbed raw from a night in a harness?"

"Well, I thought —"

Crack! Another mighty slap split the air. This time Rufus dropped to one knee.

Near to her, a crouched shadow slipped out from the shrubbery line, darting toward the back of the wagon.

Elias.

Mercy sucked in a breath, then breathed out a prayer. *And so it begins, eh, Lord? Please, God. Keep him safe.*

Elias ran full-out for the wagon, rage lighting fire to his steps. The general had been the one behind this? That drunken lout of a scoundrel! What a plan. What a horribly devious plan, stealing the stolen gold . . . that the French had purloined from the English. He smirked as he pulled himself up over the backboard. Indeed, the greed of men knew no bounds.

He landed lightly, taking care to move without a sound as he worked his way toward the front of the wagon. Night hadn't fallen hard yet, making the shape of two crates easy to spy. He ran his fingers around the bottom edge of the first one, seeking the notch he'd cut into the box. Outside, the Braggs' voices continued to argue.

"Did you pay off the Indians for their trouble?" the general rasped.

"Yeah, about that . . ."

"Speak up!" The smack of palm against skin once again erupted.

Rufus swore. "If you'd quit hitting me long enough, I'd answer. Dash it!"

"Time's wasting, boy."

The pad of Elias's finger dipped into a notch. Victory. Pulling out his knife, he wedged the blade into the crack between lid and crate. Then slowly applied pressure, bit by bit, so as not to creak the wood. A precaution maybe not necessary what with the quarrel raging outside, but better to be safe.

"I got the wagons to the clearing like you said, Pa." Rufus's voice pinched tighter. "But a blasted band of Frenchies was nearby. The old man and the traitor got it into their heads to bury the gold and ride out past 'em, as if we were nothing but the travelers we were s'posed to be."

A huff rasped from the general. "And?"

Tucking his knife back into his belt, Elias lifted the lid and set it aside atop the rest of the loose cargo. The back of this wagon, filled with pouches of trade silver and bars of gold, surely was an eerie dragon's den. Since the crate in front of him had never been opened, household goods made up the top layer. He reached in and, as quickly as possible, began removing random blankets and other frontier necessities, working his way down to the gold.

"By the time we got back to the glade," Rufus continued, "them redskins were hornet mad for the delay. I lit out of there and waited till Running Wolf returned with the horses. Then we loaded the gold — *all* of it. Worked out better than what you planned. We did not have to pay Red Bear one coin for the use of his braves."

The general grunted. "So the others are dead, yes?"

"The old man and that half-breed woman were killed straight off. The traitor ain't nothing but bones and rope by now, having been tied up in the woods."

Rage shook through Elias. The general had knowingly sent them to their deaths? It took all his restraint to keep from running out and choking the life from both men. What a wicked, filthy scheme!

He shoved his hand into the bottom of the crate, then pulled back just inches from the small leather packet at the bottom. If he grabbed the thing willy-nilly and a sharp point of the metal cut through the casing into his skin, he would be the dead man the Braggs expected him to be. His fingers shook, and he drew a deep breath to steady them, then reached again.

"And where is Running Wolf now?" the general growled. "You were to wait until I arrived to pay him."

"Flit! I can't keep track o' no Indian. They wander like cats."

Elias pinched the edge of the packet and retrieved the deadly thing. It seemed forever ago when he'd first hidden the thin piece of buckskin, wishing beyond anything for a thicker chunk of hide to contain the bits of metal. But just as now, there'd not been a spare minute, with the other French soldiers working so closely to him. He'd been blessed to have slipped the packet from inside his waistcoat without being seen or getting cut.

Ah Lord, would that You might bless me now as well.

With his free hand, he opened the flap on the pouch slung over his shoulder, then eased the packet inside. The deadly bits of metal could weigh no more than ounces, but all the same, the danger pressed down on him. One mistake, one tiny prick, would mean a death like none other.

Trepidation quaked through him, his fingers trembling like a rheumy old man's as he tucked the packet farther into the pouch. The cries of the children, the women's ragged screams, even the pathetic whimperings of the men who'd succumbed to the poison haunted from their graves. He could hear the sounds now — would hear them to his dying day. And Lord willing, that wouldn't be today.

Withdrawing his hand, he closed the flap of the pouch and turned to go.

"As usual, a backwards job by you, boy." The general's voice carried a grudge, and Elias listened carefully to pick up further information as he edged his way to the back of the wagon. "But I suppose you did get the cargo here. The blame will still land hard on those fools I sent with you, should anyone care to look into it . . . but by then, we'll be long gone."

"So I done good, Pa?"

Just before Elias slung his leg over the backboard, he hesitated, then turned back. Bending, he swiped up a pouch of trade silver and tucked that into his bag as well. The money could come in handy for the last stretch of their journey.

"Quit your groveling," Bragg roared. "And for heaven's sake get those horses unhitched!"

Elias straightened.

The horses spooked — and the wagon lurched.

He plummeted backward, out the canvas opening.

■ ■ ■ ■

Mercy clapped a hand to her mouth to keep from crying out. Elias whumped to the ground, flat on his back, wind no doubt knocked from his lungs. Two heads turned his way from up near the horses. Two guns were immediately primed and cocked.

And two curses rang out in unison.

"Blast it, boy! If you riled up that Indian and he's stealing us blind, you will have the devil to pay."

She pressed her hand tighter against her mouth, smashing her lips, stopping a scream. *Run, Elias. Run!*

He rolled, then stood, staggering.

"We'll see about that." Rufus hacked up a wad and spit, then advanced.

So did the general.

She bit her tongue, trapping the warning scream about to launch from her mouth. Narrowing her eyes, she studied the angles of the dark shapes, from horses, to wagon, to shrubbery, and the position of each man. Elias could still make it to the safety of the elderberries unseen, but only if he sprinted now.

As if reading her mind, he crouched to take off —

Out of the shadows from the other side of the wagon, the tall shape of a broad-shouldered man shot out. The Wyandot.

His musket barrel trained on Elias.

Mercy felt her heart stop, knowing it may never beat again if the lifeblood of Elias drained onto the ground right in front of her eyes. Better that she die here and now.

She dove out of the elderberries toward the road and broke into a dead run. If she could draw their fire, Elias might live — and so would many other men.

If.

CHAPTER 34

Elias had a split-second glimpse of a musket barrel before he snapped his gaze upward and stared into cold black eyes. Violence lived there — but so did intelligence. Slowly, he lifted his hands.

"My brother, do not do this." Elias spoke in Wyandot. "I am unarmed. Come with me." He jerked his head toward the elderberries.

The Indian — Running Wolf? — stared back, impassive.

Rufus and the general's feet pounded the ground, growing closer.

"Why should I?" The man spoke in the people's language as well.

Elias gritted his teeth. Exactly. Why? He'd need a whopper of a reason, for clearly this man sold out to the highest bidder, to have aligned himself with the Braggs . . . and therein might lie the solution. He'd have to up the ante.

"I offer you something more honorable than the tainted trinkets of the English dogs. Hear me out."

Footsteps thudded impossibly loud. Rufus swore. The general wheezed. Any minute now they would be swinging around the back of the wagon.

Running Wolf was a rock-hard shadow, not speaking, not moving.

Sweat trickled between Elias's shoulder blades. Was this where he'd die? Shot down in front of Mercy?

God, please.

The gun barrel lowered — slightly — but it was all the affirmation Elias needed. He sprinted toward the safety of the hedge, the warrior behind. It was a compromising position, running with a loaded weapon at his back, but if the man were going to kill him, he'd have done it by now — and may still if Elias didn't come up with something better to offer him.

Think. Think!

They tore into the cover of shadows just as Rufus's voice rang out, "Ain't nothin' back here, Pa. Blasted Indian musta stumbled to the woods to take a —"

"Spare me the details," the general gruffed out.

Elias turned to Running Wolf and — heedless of his better judgment — offered the only bargain he could think of. "If you bring those two men in to Fort Edward, you will get more than gold. You will get a trade, for they are wanted by the English for murder, thievery, and abandonment. Is not the life of Six Fingers worth more than anything the whites can promise you?"

The duplicity of what he suggested tasted like ashes. Six Fingers was a scoundrel of an Indian, and he'd been glad when he heard the villain had been captured. But if freeing the one gained him his own freedom, the lives of so many more would be spared.

The man narrowed his eyes. "Six Fingers has been captured?"

"Why do you think I am here? I was sent to tell you this." Inwardly, he winced. That was a stretch.

"By who?"

"Red Bear."

And that was an outright lie — one that grieved him to his core. *Oh Lord, forgive me. Again and again and —*

An ululating screech ripped a hole in the quiet, coming from the direction of the road. The cry of a warrior . . . a woman warrior.

Mercy.

His own cry caught in his throat. What

the deuce was the woman doing? Why attract attention to herself?

The crack of a musket fired, and then he knew.

She was drawing fire away from him and doing a blasted good job of it.

Another shot split the night.

The sharp report reverberated in the air, shaking Elias to the marrow of his bones. Flay the woman for such courage!

He speared the warrior with a scowl. "Go, now! Before they reload. This is your chance to vanquish those men and free Six Fingers."

The warrior wheeled about.

So did he — but in the opposite direction. He raced to the road and crouch-ran across it, keeping below the line of sight should Running Wolf change his mind and once again join with the Braggs. Speeding along the side farthest from the wagon, he swept the road with a feverish gaze. God help him. If he saw a dark-haired waif spread out on that dirt, there'd be no holding him back.

Across the road, men's voices raged. Another shot rang out. Rufus screamed. Elias used the noise to his advantage, rustling faster along the underbrush. Maybe Running Wolf would have only one man to bring in.

No matter. The only thing of value now was finding Mercy — or not. The thought of seeing her body crumpled and lifeless stabbed him in the chest.

The pouch with the poisoned weapon bounced against his back, but he did not slow until he searched well beyond the makeshift camp. No body slumped in a black shadow on the road. No Mercy. Sucking in a deep breath, he pivoted to retrace his steps back to where they had left Livvy with the horses. If Mercy was there, safe and whole, he just might kill her himself for taking such a harebrained risk. But if she wasn't . . .

His breath stuck in his throat. If she'd been hit and was losing her life's blood, lying cold somewhere in the woods, he'd never forgive himself.

"Livvy? Elias?" Mercy barreled into the brush, feeling her way more than seeing. Good thing they had picked the stand of white birch to hunker down in, so starkly did the trunks contrast with the night shadows.

"Over here, Miss Mercy."

She worked her way toward the girl's voice, barely spying her before she tripped over Livvy's legs. "Is Elias here?"

The useless question flew from her lips before she could stop it. Nor could she keep from peering around the flattened area where Livvy had stamped about — but no dark-haired man graced the small clearing. Of course it would take Elias longer to get here than her. She knew it in her head — but her heart still hoped to find him safe.

"I thought he was with you." There was a shiver in Livvy's voice.

She sank next to the girl, drinking in a lungful of damp air, trying not to tremble herself. "He is not."

Curling up her knees, she wrapped her arms about them and dropped her head. Had Elias gotten away? Or had one of those shots punched the life clear out of his body? And if so, how would she ever breathe again? For that was what he was now. So much a part of her she could hardly distinguish where she ended and he began.

A warm hand patted her arm. "Don't fret, Miss Mercy. I've been praying the whole time. No matter what happens, God is still sovereign."

The girl's faith put her own to shame. If Elias didn't come back, would she even have a faith at all? Her shoulders slumped with the question. It was hard to believe in a God who took as frequently as He gave. Yet not impossible, for the fingers pressing on her sleeve declared such an unyielding trust a reality. Oh, to own such a childlike confidence.

Keep me tethered to You, Lord . . . no matter what.

Her throat closed with the immensity of such a request — but she did not take it back. Not one word.

Livvy pulled her hand away and settled down on the ground. Mercy wished for a blanket she might throw over the girl's small form. But all she could do was scoot closer to her, sharing some of her body heat.

She tuned her ears to listen for the slightest hint of Elias's return. Far off, the eerie howl of coyotes sounded. Nearby, the grass rustled. A field mouse or two, most likely. The skip of a small pebble came from near the road.

And she shot like a musket ball to her feet.

Five steps later, she launched into Elias's open arms and buried her face against his chest.

The scruff of his beard tickled her brow as he bent close and whispered, "Are you hurt?"

Unwilling to pull away, she shook her head, inhaling his scent of smoke and leather and heated flesh.

"And you?" she murmured.

"No."

Then he released her. Just like that. Taking his warmth and strength with him.

She staggered from the sudden loss and peered up into his face. The first pale light of a lethargic moon broke free of a cloud, brushing over the slope of his nose, the shape of his lips, and a glower that would make a grown man retreat.

"What kind of foolish deed was that? Purposely drawing fire." He yanked off his hat and raked his fingers through his hair, then slapped it back on before the growl of his voice had a chance to fade.

Suddenly she was a little girl again, facing her father's wrath for joining the men on a hunt. She swallowed, weak in the knees. Elias was right of course. It had been a dangerous idea.

"You might have been killed!" He grabbed her by the shoulders and shoved his face into hers. "You hear me? Those men were aiming for you. You, Mercy! You could have been shot."

"So could you, and I couldn't bear the thought of it." She still couldn't. A tremor jittered across her shoulders, and she breathed out low, "How am I to live in a world without you?"

458

Elias deflated, pressing his forehead against hers. "Woman, I swear you are going to be the death of me. Please, do not ever do that again."

She matched her breathing to his. A small thing, but one that linked her to him. "Will there be a need? Are we finished with the Braggs?"

"Aye." He pulled back his head, his teeth bright against his dark beard. "Justice will be served, and by the hand of a Wyandot no less."

Her jaw dropped. By all that was holy, how had he managed that? "What did you do?"

"Let's just say that it is a good thing I speak the language."

She couldn't help but smile back. "You never stop surprising me."

"I should hope not." His hands slid from her shoulders to her back, drawing her next to his body. His mouth came down sweet and slow, lingering on hers so long, a warm ache pulsed through her.

"Promise me one thing?" he whispered against her lips.

"Hmm?" she murmured.

"That you will never stop surprising me."

CHAPTER 35

Nine Days Later,
Early Evening, Boston

Elias stood at attention, every muscle squalling to have given in to Mercy's suggestion to board for the night and visit the major's office first thing in the morning. But the sooner this weapon was delivered, the sooner he'd breathe freely. Tonight might be the first time in a year he'd sleep with both eyes closed.

He slid a glance to the mantel clock. If he did not miss his mark, Major Clement would enter before the second hand swept a full circle. A blessing, the man's punctuality, for it would mean less time Mercy and Livvy would remain sequestered in the small foyer with the large private.

Just before the tick of another minute, a door on the other side of the room opened, and in stepped a sprite of a man. The dainty, slim-boned major was the stuff of fairy tales, hardly more than a puff of wind. Elfish ears stuck out from his head. Almond-shaped eyes, brown as a cup of coffee, sat deep above the curve of high cheekbones. His step was light, his complexion even lighter. Most people gave the man nary a second look, so innocuous his appearance . . . and therein lay the irony. There wasn't a more powerful man in all of Boston — not since Elias's grandfather had died several years ago.

The major stretched out a hand, clasping Elias's with a strong shake. "So, the prodigal has returned." Releasing him, the man clapped him on the shoulder. "Good to have you back."

Elias resumed his crisp stance. "It is good to be back, sir."

"By all means, at ease, man! Better yet, sit. You look as if you could use a stout chair and an even stouter drink."

Major Clement strode to a side table and reached for a green bottle.

"Thank you, but none for me, Major." He slung off his pack and set it on Clement's big desk, then sank into one of the leather chairs opposite it. After a month of sitting on naught but a wagon bench, a horse's back, felled trees, or rocks, the cushion beneath him was a cloud. He stifled a sigh. Barely.

"As you wish." The major crossed to his seat behind the desk, a single drink in hand. He tossed back a swallow, then set the glass down — yet did not release it. His finger ran the curve of the rim, round and round, while his gaze studied the sack Elias had placed on his desk. At length, he leaned back in his chair and laced his fingers behind his head. "Seems you have brought me a little gift. Care to tell me about it?"

Elias nodded. "As you know, I infiltrated with the Second Battalion of the Guyenne Regiment. A brutal lot, nearly as rough edged as my father's voyageur ilk."

"Uncivilized beasts, I imagine."

"Worse. Killers, all." His hands curled into fists. For a moment, he saw red — the lacerations of English prisoners hit full in the face by bits of sharpened metal. Then the blood they'd heaved up afterward, bodies convulsing in a torturous death. He drew in a steadying breath. "Brigadier Nicolette's plan is to march on Fort Stanwix, though I am afraid I arrived here too late for you to pull together an ambush. A failure I truly regret."

"Stanwix?" The major grunted, then unlaced his fingers. He pulled open a top

462

drawer, rummaged a bit, then retrieved a slip of paper. "Your apology may be a bit premature. Take a look at this."

Clement held out the scrap, and Elias took it. The edges were ripped and a reddish-brown stain marred one side. Whoever had carried this intelligence had surely paid a price. Charcoal lines scrawled across it, connecting to others. An *X* crossed through one of them. The rendering looked like nothing more than a child's squiggles.

"Turn it the other way," the major suggested.

He did. Still . . . nothing.

"Now imagine that scrap were bigger, with Fort Le Boeuf down in the left corner."

A smile slowly lifted his lips. Those squiggles were a network of rivers — the waterway leading to the fort slated for destruction.

"Let me guess." He handed back the paper. "That *X* indicates the bridge, or shall I say, what *was* the bridge over Mud Creek?"

"Thank God for a cursed damp spring, eh? That ought to keep your Brigadier Nicolette at bay for a while."

Elias grinned. "I never thought to be thankful for a swollen river."

The major shoved the paper back into the

drawer, lifting his glass for another drink on the upsweep. "How many are on the march?"

"Three squads, including the Seventy-Second."

Clement choked, setting the glass down with a clatter. "So little?"

"They won't need any more if they deploy this." Leaning forward once again, Elias pushed the pouch with one finger toward the major. "Take care. The contents are deadly."

The major quirked a brow. "Then by all means, I shall give you the honor of presenting them."

Elias rose from his seat and opened the sack's flap. He reached for the major's silver-handled letter opener, then, using the tip, fished out the thin leather packet. A single piece of twine yet remained knotted around the thing, and he carefully worked it loose. Using precise movements, he wedged out a single, pointed bit of jagged metal, not much bigger than a musket ball.

Major Clement bent, his eyes narrowing. "What is it?"

"That is what I am hoping your resources can find out. The metal is coated with some kind of poison. What, exactly, is beyond me. All I know is one scratch will bring down a man within hours."

A muscle stood out like a cord on the major's neck. Lantern light slid along his clenched jaw like a knife blade. And Elias did not blame him. He'd had the same knotted-up reaction when he first discovered the vile thing.

Clement's gaze lifted to his. "How is it deployed?"

"The pieces are loaded into a glass bombshell, and grenadiers shoot them from a mortar."

The major huffed out a breath. "Surely the glass breaks when the mortar goes off."

"No." Elias shook his head. Had he not seen the thing in action, he'd not have believed it either. "It does not, sir. I suspect it is more than simply glass, but I was not able to secret one of those shells away. By faith, I barely got out of there alive with those snippets of metal. Yet if we — if you and your resources — can figure out what the poison is, then perhaps an antidote could be stocked."

"That will take time, Dubois." The major slammed his fist onto the desk, rattling his glass and the metal. "Time we don't have!"

"True, not for the first test load that is even now on the way to Stanwix. May God have mercy." He coaxed the bit of metal back into the leather with the letter opener, adding at least a small measure of safety should the major buffet the desk once again. Then he pushed the whole thing back into the pouch and closed the flap.

"Your words to God's ears, Dubois."

He retraced his steps to his seat and sank into it. "But all is not lost, Major. If we take out the storehouse of both glass and poison, that should buy us the time we need."

Clement's ears twitched as a smile replaced his scowl. "Location?"

"Louisbourg."

A low whistle circled the room. "That will be a hair-raising mission." The major cocked his head. "I don't suppose you are volunteering?"

Years ago he'd have jumped at the offer of adventure and glory. But now? He shifted on the cushion, wincing from scars and aches and too many bad memories. "No, sir. When I said this would be my last operation, I meant it."

"Never hurts to ask, eh?" The major shoved back his chair, then stood and rounded the desk, once again offering his hand. "You have done a fine job, Elias."

He rose, meeting Clement's firm grip. "Thank you, sir."

"Your service has been exemplary." The

major's dark eyes twinkled with a hint of hidden knowledge. "You shall have your reward as promised . . . and then some."

"To be honest, sir, I did not do this alone. Would you like to meet my team?"

"Team?" Both the major's brows rose. "By all means."

Elias strode to the door, peeked out at Mercy with a nod, then held the door wide for her and Livvy to enter. He stood at attention as they passed. "Allow me to introduce —"

Before he could finish, the major rushed over to Livvy, grabbing the girl by the shoulders. "Deliverance Hunter? Is that you? I can hardly believe it!"

Mercy shot Elias a glance — one he returned with as much fervor. What on earth?

"It is, sir." Livvy smiled as if they were old friends. "Won't my papa be surprised?"

"He'll be more than that." Major Clement looked past the girl to Elias. "Well, well, Dubois. You shall be greatly rewarded indeed."

Wall sconces shed ample light on the frail-looking man who smiled down at Livvy, but even so Mercy blinked, unsure of what she saw.

Next to her, Elias pulled the door shut, then angled his head toward the man. "Sir?"

The confusion in his tone was a comfort. At least she wasn't the only one to wonder at the odd reunion.

"Ah, yes." The man released his grip of the girl and faced Elias. "You have been out in the field so long, I suppose you missed the arrival of the illustrious General George Hunter, recently in with reinforcements from Bristol. The man's been quite out of his mind with worry ever since the girl's abduction — and been sparing no expense to find her. How the deuce did you manage to locate her?"

"In all truth, sir, it was providence, for I was not in search of the girl." Elias's eyes sought Mercy's, and he stepped closer to her, the sweep of his fingers resting on the small of her back. A simple gesture, but one that flushed her cheeks. How could this rugged man make her feel so precious by such a mundane act of chivalry?

"Major, allow me to introduce Miss Mercy Lytton. She is the one who found Livvy." Elias turned his face to her — a face she'd never tire of gazing upon, despite the scruff of a beard and layer of travel grime. "Mercy, meet Major Nathaniel Clement."

Leaving Livvy behind, the major settled in

front of her and reached for her hand, then bowed over it. "My pleasure, Miss . . ."

Slowly, he released her fingers and straightened. His gaze roamed her face, an inscrutable flicker in his eyes. She stood still as a doe scenting danger. Oh, to own a beaver pelt for each time men measured her so, trying to add up the mixed heritage evident in her features. She'd be a wealthy, wealthy woman.

"Lytton?" The major, slight as he was, stood head to head with her, staring straight into her eyes. "Are you the famed woman scout working with Captain Matthew Prinn?"

Her heart twisted. The slow bleed of sorrow inside her yet continued to drip, and she was more grateful than ever for Elias's warm touch that steadied her.

She lifted her chin. "I am, sir . . . or, I was. I regret to inform you that Captain Prinn is no longer alive."

A groan rumbled in the major's throat. "A shame. The man was the brightest — and I daresay best — of what the rangers have to offer."

A heavy silence fell. The tick of the clock and crackle of the fire in the hearth descended on them all until the major cleared his throat. "But pardon my manners. Please, have a seat, ladies." His brown eyes pierced Elias with a stare. "Unless you have any more surprise guests up your sleeve, Dubois?"

"None, sir."

"Very good." The man pivoted and strode toward an enormous desk. Livvy followed, taking up a chair in front of the thing.

Mercy took the opportunity to lean sideways to whisper to Elias. "How does he know who I am?"

He leaned close, smelling of smoke and horses, a bittersweet reminder they were at their journey's end. "There is none better than the major when it comes to military intelligence."

She took the seat next to Livvy, and Elias remained standing directly behind them.

"I won't keep you long, for the three of you look travel worn and in need of a hearty meal. Now then, Miss Hunter." The major smiled at Livvy. "I shall send a runner straightaway to inform your father of your safe return. I will also arrange for your passage to Virginia as soon as possible, where he has been reassigned. How does that sound?"

The girl beamed. "I would like nothing more, sir."

"Very good." Then he swiveled his face

toward her. "Miss Lytton, fortuitous indeed to have you here. You work out of Fort Wilderness, do you not?"

Elias was right — the man was a master of information, especially to have taken notice of a backwoods, slipshod fort. "Yes, sir."

"Excellent." He leaned back in his chair, leather creaking an accompaniment to the movement. "There is a certain matter that has come to my attention recently that perhaps you can clear up."

She pressed her lips flat to keep from frowning. What could she possibly know that would aid a major in Boston, especially since she'd not been on a scout for over a month?

He chuckled. "Oh, don't look so worried, Miss Lytton. I have no doubt you are just the person to ask. Currently there's a load of gold and three men being held at Fort Edward pending investigation. A native, a private, and the missing commander from Fort Wilderness. None of their stories correlate, and in fact all point the finger at each other for all manner of wrongdoing. Do you know anything about this?"

So, Elias's Wyandot had gotten the scoundrels and the cargo all the way to the fort. Not that it would bring Matthew back, but at least the Braggs would pay for their treachery. It was a small consolation — but likely the only one she'd get.

"What I know, sir, is that Brigadier General Bragg and his son are scoundrels of the worst sort. Both deserve a court-martial and time in jail. Or worse."

The major's brows shot high. "That is a strong sentiment."

" 'Tis the truth. The general abandoned his post, conspired with his son to steal that load of gold, and plotted our deaths." She glanced over her shoulder at Elias.

"Miss Lytton speaks true, sir," he confirmed.

The major grunted. "As I said, fortuitous indeed that you are here. Will you write up a document swearing to all you know and have experienced, both of you?"

"We will, sir." Her voice joined with Elias's.

"Then they just might get the court-martial you so desire, Miss Lytton." Major Clement pushed back his chair and stood. "For now, however, the hour grows late. I imagine the three of you might welcome beds to sleep on instead of the ground, am I right?"

Livvy's blond head nodded. Mercy smiled.

No doubt even Elias was grinning behind her.

Bypassing the desk, the major strode toward the door. "Dubois, I leave these ladies in your charge until three days hence, when we'll reconvene here."

"Yes, sir."

Livvy shoved her hand into Mercy's, and they both joined Elias's side in crossing the room.

The major held open the door. "I shall see that your expenses for room and board are covered at the Stag's Head Inn. Oh, and Dubois, make it a priority to provision yourselves with new clothing. Pardon my bluntness, ladies" — the major tucked his chin in mock repentance — "but those gowns have seen better days. Good night."

A half smile tugged her lips. The man was judicious in his words. No wonder he held such a position of power.

They had hardly cleared the threshold and the door closed when behind her Elias muttered, "Blast!"

She turned, trying to read the frown on his face and falling far short of what it could mean. "How can you be anything but pleased? The Braggs will get what they deserve, and Livvy shall be returned to her father."

"Aye, all is well save for one thing."

"What's that?"

Elias quirked one eyebrow. "The provisioning . . . I'd rather run the gauntlet of a Wyandot initiation rite than go shopping."

"Ah, but I believe, Mr. Dubois, that you promised me a new petticoat, did you not?"

A sheepish smile lifted one side of his mouth. "From now on, remind me to be careful what I promise you."

Heat flushed her cheeks, and she turned her face from him. The only thing she really wanted him to promise was to spend the rest of his life at her side.

CHAPTER 36

Mercy worked a pale green ribbon into Livvy's blond hair, smiling with the memory of Elias in the dress shop. His face had matched the ribbon's color that entire day he'd attended them from seamstress to milliner to shoe shop. But he'd had his revenge. The next day he'd escorted them to an afternoon tea, followed by a dinner and then a small spring soiree. She knew enough etiquette to survive the meals — thanks to her mother — but dancing had tangled her feet more thoroughly than a barefoot sprint over moss-covered rocks. If she listened hard, she'd likely still hear remnants of Elias's laughter over her ridiculous attempts . . . until he'd taken her in hand and tutored her until her heart raced.

"Miss Mercy?" Livvy's voice cut into her thoughts.

"Hmm?" She tied off the ribbon, and the girl turned to face her.

"I am surely going to miss you." Livvy wrapped her arms around her waist.

Mercy hugged her back fiercely, certain she would always remember this brave young lady, so like herself and so not. "I shall miss you too, Livvy."

She set the girl from her and bent, eye to eye. "But we shall never forget each other, shall we?"

Huge drops shimmered in Livvy's eyes. "No, ma'am. Never."

Tears threatened to choke her as well, and she swallowed against the tightness in her throat. "There is a word my people use, not a forever kind of goodbye, but one that means farewell for now. Would you like to learn it?"

Biting her lip, the girl nodded.

"Ó:nen kiʾ wáhi." She drawled out the word.

"Oh-key . . . oh-no-key . . ." Livvy stuttered to a stop.

"Ó:nen kiʾ wáhi," Mercy tried again.

"Oh . . ." The girl sucked in a big breath. "Oh-nen key wah-he."

Mercy grinned. "Very good. You'd make a fine —"

A rap on the door cut off her praise.

"Are you ladies ready?" Elias's deep voice filtered through the wood.

Mercy held out her hand. Livvy entwined her fingers with hers — and squeezed. They had shared quite an adventure, from backwoods to Boston, and she'd be sad to see the girl leave today. Ó:nen ki› wáhi indeed. May they somehow meet again.

Together they crossed to the door, but when she swung it open, her hand fell limply away from Livvy's, and it was a struggle to keep from gaping.

The man in the corridor was surely not Elias. This was a king, one who weakened her knees by the merit of his stature alone. A deep blue greatcoat rode the crest of his shoulders, with a caramel-colored waistcoat fitted snugly across his chest. An ivory cravat was tied neatly at his throat, set just above a row of pewter buttons. Buff breeches ran the length of his long legs, ending just below the knee at his off-white stockings. Shiny buckles glinted up from his black shoes.

But it wasn't the clothes that stole her breath. Not the planes of his clean-shaven face, the full lips, or the brown hair combed back into a queue and secured by a plain black ribbon. It wasn't even his scent of sandalwood soap with a leftover hint of his trademark smoky smell.

It was his eyes. Only and entirely his stunning blue gaze. The look of unashamed wonder and awe as he studied her ignited a fire that simmered hot and low.

"Elias?"

"Mercy?"

Their whispers mingled in unison, making them one.

Livvy tugged her sleeve. "We'll be late."

Elias cleared his throat, giving his head a little shake. "Of course." Then he held out both his arms. "Ladies, shall we?"

Giggling, Livvy claimed one arm. Mercy rested her fingertips atop the other, memorizing the feel of Elias's strong muscle flexing beneath her touch. He guided them out through the public room and then into a waiting carriage, just as he had the past several days. But today, rather than gawk out the window at the passing buildings and so many people swarming like a kicked-over anthill, Mercy sat silently, staring at the man seated across from her. It was hard — nay, impossible — to reconcile such a powerful-looking gentleman with the scruffy-bearded, hunting-frocked woodsman she'd known for the past month. Neither of them spoke a word the entire ride to the major's office, and even then, he once again cleared his throat to converse with the private on guard.

The major's door swung open, and they

entered to not just Major Clement, but another two soldiers standing at attention.

"Well, well, what a difference three days can make. Ladies, you are absolutely ravishing." The major bowed over her hand and then Livvy's.

"Thank you, Major," she and Livvy both murmured.

The major angled his head toward Elias. "I suppose you are presentable as well, Dubois."

"I try, sir."

Lord, the man did not even need to try, for he'd captured her heart as thoroughly in buckskin breeches and with a smear of dirt on his brow as in a new suit. Mercy forced her hands to remain at her sides to keep from fanning her flushed cheeks.

"Now then, Miss Hunter." The major faced Livvy. "Are you ready to go to your father? You shall have two officers to accompany you . . . and this time, you shall travel by ship. No more Indian adventures for you, hmm?"

"I should like that very much, sir." Livvy bobbed a little curtsy. "Thank you."

"Briggs, Hawthorne." Major Clement turned to the soldiers. "Here is your charge. See that nothing — and I mean *nothing* — happens to the girl until she is safely handed into her father's care."

"Yes, sir!" Both saluted, then broke rank and strode to the door, the taller of the two striding through, the shorter holding it wide for Livvy. "After you, Miss Hunter."

Livvy took one step toward the door, then backtracked and plowed into Elias, surprising them all. "Thank you, Mr. Elias, for keeping me safe. Because of you, I am going to see my papa again."

Elias blinked, then slowly wrapped his arms around the girl and patted her back. "Thank God, Livvy, not me . . . as we all must."

He released her, and she beamed up at him, then stepped over to Mercy.

The girl lifted a quivering chin, and Mercy couldn't help but choke up herself. If Livvy started weeping now, there'd be no holding back her own tears.

But Livvy held firm, standing as bravely as one of the soldiers, save for the trembling ribbon in her hair — the only hint of failed courage. "Ó:nen ki› wáhi, Miss Mercy."

Stifling a sob, Mercy tried a smile, a bit wavery, but a smile nonetheless. "Ó:nen ki› wáhi, my friend."

The girl turned and marched out the door, taking a piece of Mercy's heart along with her.

"Miss Hunter is quite the little lady." The major's shoes shushed across the carpet to his desk, where he retrieved an envelope, then held it out to her. "But so are you, Miss Lytton. This is yours."

She exchanged a glance with Elias.

He merely held out his hand. "After you."

Trepidation slowed her gait. The only experience she had with official documents was in the form of translating treaties or passing along intelligence, none of which seemed to bring joy to any of the recipients.

Her lips parted as she grasped the envelope. The thing was thick and heavy. "What is this?"

"Payment for a job well done. You have served king and country without fault."

She looked from the envelope to the major's brown eyes. "But it was my duty, Major. Nothing more." She offered back the envelope. "I require no payment."

He raised his hands and retreated a step, as if she held out a snake. "Yet you shall have it. I insist."

Obstinate man . . . much like Elias. No wonder the two worked together so well. She lowered the packet. "I thank you, Major. You are more than generous."

The major cocked his head. "If I may be so bold, Miss Lytton, may I inquire as to what your plans are now?"

She stiffened. Exactly. What was she to do now with no more Matthew? No more home? No more anything, really. The envelope weighed heavy with possibility in her hand. She could settle, now that she had the means, but did she really belong here in a big city? Could she stand not to run free beneath a big sky and breathe air untainted by man?

She met the major's stare with a confidence she did not feel. "That remains to be seen, Major."

A "hmm" purred in the major's throat. "May I make a suggestion?"

"Of course."

"I happen to know of a certain position opening up." He slipped a glance at Elias, then focused back on her. "A position that might be to your liking. A bit of danger. Lots of intrigue. And you'd report to no one except me."

She snapped her gaze to Elias and searched his face. What did he think of the major offering her his job, right here in front of him?

But Elias — the real Elias — disappeared behind a polished mask of indifference.

"With your background and capabilities, you'd be a valuable asset. So, Miss Lytton"

— the major spread his hands — "what do you say?"

Gallows. Musket barrels. Tomahawks and war clubs. Elias had faced them all — yet none were as terrible as the question Major Clement hurled at Mercy. He rooted his feet to the carpet, fighting the urge to throw himself between the two and shield her from such a query. If she said yes, he'd lose her . . . maybe forever. She could have no idea of the dangers involved in becoming a spy. He hadn't when the major first propositioned him, sitting here in this very room, surrounded by the comfort of hearth and the promises of glory — when in reality it was mostly a life of deception, blood, and misery.

He held his breath until his lungs burned, waiting for her answer. The mantel clock ticked years off his life. The scrape of wagon wheels outside shaved off more. And still she did not answer. She just stood there blinking, looking so beautiful his throat ached for want of telling her again and again and again.

Ah, but she'd transformed over the past three days from woodland scamp to a lady of poise and wonder. Her new blue gown clung to her body in all the right places.

483

She'd replaced her ruby heart necklace with a simple ribbon choker. And how easily she moved from one station of life to another was yet one more surprise. The only thing he missed was her long braid, swinging over her shoulder and trailing to her hips, for now she pinned up her dark hair, hiding most of it beneath a beribboned bonnet.

Her lips parted, and he couldn't help but lean toward her. So did the major.

"I am not certain what the future holds." She slipped him a glance, so many questions swimming in her brown eyes it would take him a lifetime to figure them out.

Even so, he breathed in relief. Good girl. She'd not jumped at the offer. He should've known she'd employ her usual shrewdness.

She smiled back at the major. "But I shall consider it."

Blast! If the woman had that much adventure still blazing in her blood, she'd never consent to settling down with him on a farm smack in the middle of a normal life.

Clement pursed his lips. "I suppose that is better than a no."

"It is the best I can give you at present, sir."

"Fair enough." The major turned back to his desk, this time retrieving yet another envelope. Smaller. Thinner. And with *"Mr.*

Elias Dubois" penned on the front.

"At long last, Dubois, what you have been working for these past five years." Clement held out the envelope. "The deed to one hundred acres in prime Connecticut farmland, as promised."

He hesitated, palms suddenly moist. This was it. His future. Written on a frail piece of parchment. The thing he'd dreamed of while lying cold, hungry, and, more often than not, surrounded by the enemy.

He inched out his hand, then paused. The prospect of farming tasted like ashes in his mouth, for now that he'd met Mercy, his heart yearned for something more. Her. How could he possibly leave her behind?

The major shoved the envelope into his hand. "And for a job well done . . ." The man once again turned back to his desk and this time picked up a small leather box. He opened the lid, but his hand hid the contents. "Because of your exemplary work and for the many lives you have saved, on behalf of the crown, I present you with this commendation of honor."

The major pulled out a ribbon with a copper medal dangling at the end.

Without thinking, he shot out his hand, staying the major from handing it over. The land he could accept, work for work. It made sense. But this? A disappointment such as himself did not deserve such a merit. "I apologize, sir, but I cannot accept —"

"Elias." The rebuke in the major's voice pulled him up short, and he snapped his gaze back to the man's face.

"It is time you let go of your past, son. My only regret is that your grandfather is not the one to award this, for I have no doubt the general would have been pleased to see the man you have become."

He froze — but his thoughts took off at a gallop, especially as the major stepped up to him and pinned the award onto his lapel. Major Clement spoke more words of acclamation and Mercy murmured something beside him, but sound suddenly receded. How could he — sinner, wretch, prodigal — even consider wearing such a thing? Him . . . honorable? Oh, the laugh that surely would have guffawed out of his father's throat. The apoplexy his grandfather would've suffered.

But slowly the incriminations faded, and an intense gratitude toward God ignited — for truly, the award decorating his dress coat was purely by grace and grace alone. Perhaps the major was right and it was time to let go of the past. To stop striving to prove

486

himself to a dead grandfather and instead live to serve a loving God.

The major clapped him on the back, jarring him. "Your grandfather, God rest him, would be proud of you, Elias. As am I." He bowed before them both. "My thanks to the two of you. Miss Lytton, I look forward to hearing from you at your earliest convenience. Elias, Godspeed in your new life."

He drew to attention and snapped a salute while Mercy curtseyed beside him.

"Thank you, Major." His voice wavered, and he swallowed. "Good day." He held out his arm, and Mercy's light touch rested on his sleeve.

Striding toward the door, he couldn't help but wonder at the sudden freedom filling him at finally, fully feeling that he'd done enough. That he was enough, simply by merit of God's mercy.

Mercy.

He glanced at the woman beside him and silently pleaded that somehow his future would include not only the wonder of God's grace, but Mercy Lytton as well.

CHAPTER 37

The streets outside the major's office writhed with people. Mercy waited while Elias hailed a carriage, unsure if she should stop up her ears or plug her nose, so noisome and smelly was the crush of the crowds. What she wouldn't give for a pair of buckskin breeches and a stretch of land to run clear of this fray . . . but only if Elias were running next to her.

Her gaze lingered on the long lines of his body as he turned and backtracked to her.

"Ready to go?" He held out his hand.

She wrapped her fingers around his, cursing the silly, useless gloves for blocking the feel of his skin against hers. He led her to the coach and steadied her as she ascended. By the time he joined her inside, she longed to be back out on the street. The carriage reeked of fish and sweat and something so cloyingly sweet that the tea she'd taken for breakfast gurgled in her stomach.

Elias settled on the hard leather seat opposite her and rapped his knuckles against the wall. The carriage lurched into motion.

So did her thoughts. The meeting with the major had raised more questions than had been answered. She angled her head, searching Elias's face. "Who are you, Elias Dubois?"

A half smile lifted his lips. "By now you know all my secrets."

"Save one." She leaned forward. "The major mentioned your grandfather . . . a general? Though I suppose 'tis apparent in the way you take charge of things, why did you not tell me?"

His smile twisted into a smirk. "If you recall, you did not inform me your father was a sachem."

She huffed, but of course he was right. Only strutting roosters crowed about their families. She'd come to learn Elias Dubois was many things — obstinate, compassionate, too handsome for his own good — but more than anything, humbleness resided inside that big chest of his. Still, with so powerful a grandfather, how had he managed not to become a man accustomed to privilege and power?

"Your family" — the carriage juddered over a bump, and she grabbed the seat to keep from tumbling — "tell me of them."

"That is quite a tangled story." Shifting, he left his seat and resettled next to her, shoring her up between his body and the wall. "Is that better?"

Much better to keep her from jostling about — but certainly not any safer, judging by the crazed beat of her heart from his nearness. Did he know the effect he had on her?

Ah . . . perhaps he did and was trying to throw her off the trail she'd scented. She speared him with a piercing gaze. "Your family story cannot be more snarled than mine, what with a mother captured by Wyandots and later rescued by a Mohawk leader."

For a moment he met her gaze, then turned his face to look out the window.

She frowned. Apparently she'd pushed him too far. Folding her hands in her lap, she worried a loose thread on the hem of her glove with the pad of her finger — until Elias's low voice murmured against the grind of the wheels.

Instantly, she straightened and leaned toward him, listening hard, for he yet kept his face turned toward the glass.

"I grew up in my grandfather's home. By faith, but he was a strict English patriarch.

My mother and I bore the brunt of his wrath for our rebellious ways — her by marrying a rogue voyageur on leave without Grandfather's blessing, I by running wild on the streets . . . the very ones we now travel."

He fell silent, giving her time to wonder on all he'd said. She dared a glimpse out her own window, trying to imagine such a young rebel darting in and out among the crowds. That was easy enough. But Elias had been nothing but kind the whole time she'd known him — unlike anything he said about his grandfather.

She turned back to him. "You are much like your mother, I think. I should like to meet her someday."

He shook his head. "She died when I was ten."

Unbidden, she reached for his hand, and when they touched, he jerked his face back to hers, a question arching one of his dark brows.

She merely smiled.

The carriage listed to one side as they veered around a corner, and she couldn't help but slide up against him. She started to scoot away, but as he looked at the way her hand entwined with his, he whispered, "Stay."

They rode in silence for a stretch, until he finally lifted his face back to hers. "I suppose it must have been hard on Grandfather, losing his daughter and trying to rein in a hellion like me. He sent me packing to my father when I turned thirteen, where I served as a voyageur myself for ten years." A tempest broke in the blue of his eyes, dark and raging — then as suddenly cleared. "He was right to do so, for I learned what kind of man I would become if I continued with my wayward conduct." He shrugged. "The rest you know."

She smiled. "You came back here and became a spy . . . where you still roamed the wilds, looking for trouble. Doesn't seem very different to me."

"No." He grinned back. "I suppose it was not."

"Which is why it suited you so well." She nudged him with her shoulder. "Do you think it will suit me?"

All the playfulness drained from his face, and she shuddered at the stranger staring out at her through Elias's eyes.

"Mercy, I . . ." His words ground to a halt — as did the carriage wheels. Before the coachman opened the door, Elias lurched sideways and flung it open.

Blast! She'd done it again. Pushed him

further than she ought have. Foxes and wolves, deer and elk, these animals she knew how and when to approach. But Elias? How could she possibly share all that was in her heart without scaring him away?

She grabbed his hand and stepped out of the coach. With so many petticoats and the weight of her gown, she stumbled as her foot hit the ground, and he tightened his grip, righting her. Thankfully the street in front of the inn was far less crowded with people to witness her inelegant descent.

Dropping her hand, Elias turned to her, a faraway look in his eyes, as if he'd already packed up his gear and moved on.

She froze, terrified. "Elias?"

"I guess this is goodbye." His voice was a husk, an empty shell of what it had been.

Panic welled, and she couldn't contain it even if she tried. "Is it?"

"My service is done . . . but yours? Mercy, if you go back to the major's office, I have no doubt he shall make you an offer you cannot refuse."

"But I'm not interested in what the major might offer."

His brows shot high. "You are going to turn him down?"

Heedless of what the few pedestrians darting back and forth might think, she stepped close to him, as if by sheer nearness alone she could make him know the desire in her soul. "That depends."

"On what?"

"On what you have to offer."

A slow smile split across his face. Life and light and brilliance once again gleamed in his eyes. "I am land rich but cash poor, and the truth is I have nothing to offer you save for hard work and" — he dropped to one knee and gathered her hand — "my heart, if you will have it. Will you, Mercy? Will you give up a life of running free and settle down with the likes of me?"

Behind her, a few whispers swirled like autumn leaves skittering in a whirl, but she did not care. Not one bit. She dropped to her knees as well, right there in front of God and country. "I might, as long as it doesn't involve me giving up my buckskin breeches. But do you suppose 'tis legal for me to marry my husband?"

His shoulders shook with a low chuckle. "You know what I love about you, Mercy Lytton?"

She shook her head.

"Everything." Lifting her hand, he kissed her knuckles.

Blast those gloves! Even so, she couldn't help but grin. "Tsi Nen:we Enkonnoronhkhwake, Elias."

He cupped her cheek with his fingers. "I have no idea what that means, but promise me you shall say it every day for the rest of my life."

"I promise, my love." She beamed. "I promise."

HISTORICAL NOTES

The Lost Gold of Minerva, Ohio

The idea for this story came from a legend that sprang up during the years of the French and Indian War and was first printed in an 1875 Ohio newspaper. Apparently a shipment of French gold was being moved from Fort Duquesne to Fort Detroit. En route, the French soldiers were afraid of an impending attack, either by Indians or by British soldiers — it's unclear which. They decided to bury the gold and then hide until the threat passed. When they went back to retrieve their cargo, it was gone. Where did it go? To this day, no one knows.

Fort Wilderness / Fort Stanwix

There really wasn't a Fort Wilderness, but I did base this fictional outpost on a real location: Fort Stanwix, which I also mention in the story. Fort Stanwix was never under a threat of attack by the French, but it was a key location during the war. It was originally built to guard a portage known as the Oneida Carrying Place, an important thruway for the fur trade.

The Story of Mademoiselle and the Pig
The folktale Elias tells to the Shaw boys in chapter 17 is a story that has been passed down for generations. It can be found in written format in the book *Body, Boots and Britches* by Harold W. Thompson, published in 1940 by J. B. Lippincott Company.

The Klocks
This family truly did homestead in the Mohawk River Valley in upstate New York. Johannes Klock built a fortified house to use as a trading post for nearby natives. The "fort" is still there and open for tours.

Glass Grenades
Grenades bring up images of World War I or II, but really they've been around since the time of the Romans. Grenadiers were originally the soldiers who specialized in throwing grenades. Most grenades of the French and Indian War period were made by filling a hollow iron ball with gunpowder, then sealing it with a wooden plug that contained the fuse. But some were made of

other materials, such as ceramics and even glass. These were not common, but I saw one during a tour of Fort Niagara, and the idea for a deadly weapon took root. No poisonous glass grenades were used during this war — but that doesn't mean they couldn't have been.

Wyandot or Wendat or Huron?

The French sometimes called this tribe of Native Americans the *Huron,* meaning "bristly" or "savage haired" because the men wore their coarse black hair cut in a mane, from forehead to the nape of the neck, and decorated this hairdo with a stiff roach headdress. French sailors thought such a hairstyle resembled the bristles on a wild boar. The people called themselves the *Wendat,* meaning "People of the Peninsula" — which sounded a lot like *Wyandot* to non-native speakers.

Berleth, Richard. *Bloody Mohawk: The French and Indian War and American Revolution on New York's Frontier.* Delmar, NY: Black Dome Press, 2010.

Drimmer, Frederick. *Captured by the Indians: 15 Firsthand Accounts, 1750–1870.* Mineola, NY: Dover, 1961.

Hamilton, Milton W. *Sir William Johnson and the Indians of New York.* Albany, NY: Univ. of the State of New York, 1975.

Hibernicus. *Letters on the Natural History and Internal Resources of the State of New York.* London: Forgotten Books, 2015.

Huey, Lois M., and Bonnie Pulis. *Molly Brant: A Legacy of Her Own.* Youngstown, NY: Old Fort Niagara Assoc., 1997.

MacNab, David. *Ten Exciting Historic Sites to Visit in Upstate New York.* New York: Page Publishing, 2016.

Thompson, Harold W. *Body, Boots and*

Britches. Philadelphia: J. B. Lippincott, 1940.

Todish, Timothy J. *America's First World War: The French and Indian War, 1754–1763.* Fleischmanns, NY: Purple Mountain Press, 2002.

ABOUT THE AUTHOR

Michelle Griep has been writing since she first discovered blank wall space and Crayolas. She seeks to glorify God in all that she writes — except for that graffiti phase she went through as a teenager. She resides in the frozen tundra of Minnesota, where she teaches history and writing classes for a local high school co-op. An Anglophile at heart, she runs away to England every chance she gets, under the guise of research. Really though, she's eating excessive amounts of scones while rambling around a castle. Keep up with her adventures at michellegriep.com. She loves to hear from readers, so go ahead and rattle her cage.

The employees of Thorndike Press hope you have enjoyed this Large Print book. All our Thorndike, Wheeler, and Kennebec Large Print titles are designed for easy reading, and all our books are made to last. Other Thorndike Press Large Print books are available at your library, through selected bookstores, or directly from us.

For information about titles, please call:
  (800) 223-1244

or visit our website at:
  gale.com/thorndike

To share your comments, please write:
  Publisher
  Thorndike Press
  10 Water St., Suite 310
  Waterville, ME 04901